DON'T BELIEVE THE HYPE!

BY   JACQUELINE FALL   &   NICOLE MICHAEL

ACCESS
PUBLISHING

DON'T BELIEVE THE HYPE!

BY JACQUELINE FALL & NICOLE MICHAEL

This novel is a work of fiction. Any resemblance to real people, living or dead, actual events, establishments, organizations, and/ or locales are intended to give the fiction a sense of reality and authenticity. Other names, characters, places and incidents are either products of the authors' imagination or are used fictitiously, as are those fictionalized events & incidents that involve real persons and did not occur or are set in the future.

Published By: ACCESS PUBLISHING
2 Division Street, Suite 8, Somerville, New Jersey 08876
http://www.dbthbook.com

ISBN 978-0-615-42245-9
First printing, July 2010
Copyright © 2008
Library of Congress Control Number: 1-50958948
Copyright: TXu001628625

Printed in the U.S.A.

PRAISE FROM READERS OF *DON'T BELIEVE THE HYPE!*

"It was a lot of fun and I think you guys did well on making the reader care about the characters.

I finished the book last night. I loved it! I kept thinking of it like a movie. Well done!!"

Susanna A.

"Please thank the authors for me. They kept me up all dang night reading this book. OMG, it is wonderful..........So impressed by your book.............

But it was very well written and cannot wait for the next one."

Treena S.

"The ending was good......................"

Joyce W.

"BOOK IS OFF THE HOOK!!!! .... Well written and I can relate to the characters..."

Alesia R.

"This book was one of the best that I have read in a very long time. Once I started reading, I couldn't put it down. It took me about 3 days to finish it once I started reading it because I needed to find out what would happen next. I cannot wait for the next one. Good Job ladies."

Debbie W.

Acknowledgements

Jacqueline Fall

I would like to give a special thanks to Rashida Shaw for all her input and feedback. Shi Shi your advice was priceless. I would like to thank Eleanor Allen for her tireless help in editing; we appreciate your time and opinion. To all my former Hunton & Williams co-workers for urging me to finish this project, your enthusiasm was encouraging. A special thanks to Assane, and all my friends who believed in our talent and encouraged me to follow my dreams.

Nicole Michael

This book is a labor of love that has taken years to finish. As many of you readers can understand, there were bills to pay, drama to solve and family to care for, as my co-author and I endeavored to feed our love and passion for writing.

So many to thank but I must start with the one who holds my heart. Q James, a man fearless enough to ask again and again, "Babe, what's going on with book?" Sometimes after I had just finished working a 12-hour day, which takes guts. Thank you baby for always helping me grow and encouraging every dream I have. I know I'm blessed.

Next, our first audience, the ones that cared enough to give us valuable feedback. My beloved Julia "Gang Gang" Baskerville grandmother extraordinaire, I read her many passages while she was in the hospital and at times, she thought the story was real and wanted to know why people were so crazy nowadays. Eleanor Allen, Angela Madison, and Sandra Rice, thank you for giving us your edits and feedback. You cannot imagine how much your time and effort was needed and appreciated.

Finally, family and friends, Mom and Dad, what can I say? You're all the best. Now that I'm grown and met so many people, I realize how good I had it and still do. Eric - thanks for encouraging me to do all your work in high school! I'm sure it made me a better writer. Amé and Eileen, the two friends that would bail me out of jail, you know what I mean - you're my girls.

To my co-author, we did it, through all the challenges and life changes. We did it!

This book is dedicated to Gang Gang, Park Avenue Queen, she led with a left and finished yelling 38 for her favorite exit. You are so very missed. We love you and without doubt, your legendary ways will live on in infamy.

Prologue

HOMEGIRL ONE - Back In The Day

She turned up the music and rolled down the windows. She knew everyone on the block was jealous when she rode by in her fly ride, stolen or not. She was in a great mood, she had figured it all out, two more runs across state lines and she would have enough money to buy her homegirl a car just like the one that had been stolen. Then all would be forgiven and they could all go back to the way things used to be. She was going to make extra money this run. She would be carrying more weight than usual, so the big man was going to be at the meet.

She walked into the abandoned building and something felt a bit eerie, but she shook it off immediately and reminded herself that she was invincible. She walked through the second door on the right as instructed. As soon as she turned the corner she saw 10 runners from the crew and knew something was very wrong. She cleared her throat to speak but before any words came out, she felt something hard and cold hit her in the back of the head. She screamed in pain and fell to the floor. When she rolled over she saw a boy who looked no more than 15 years old standing there looking half scared and half deranged. Then she heard a voice from the other side of the room. A voice she recognized.

"What are you waiting for? Do it! If you want to be one of us do it. Trust me kid this scheming bitch doesn't deserve your sympathy."

She was listening to the voice but her eyes were fixated on the eyes of her attacker. She saw those eyes turn from human to little balls of ice. She closed her eyes and said a prayer. She asked God for two things: forgiveness and to watch out for her bona fide homegirls.

▼▼▼▼▼▼▼▼▼▼▼▼▼▼▼▼▼▼▼▼▼▼▼▼▼▼

HOMEGIRL TWO - Present Day

"Damn girl you look extra tight tonight," Tony the bartender was salivating.

"Whatever, I need some drinks," she complained.

"Whatever," he answered in a huff. "What's the matter, you only know how to accept compliments from the rich and famous."

"I'm sorry Tone. I was thinking of something else. I need you to do me a favor," she asked, as she leaned in to give him a better view of her assets.

"Yeah what favor?" He asked cautiously.

"I'm getting drinks for me and a customer and I need you to make his extra special."

"What do you mean extra special?"

"Come on Tony don't play games, one of the dancers told me what you did for her one time."

"I know what you mean, I'm just surprised. I thought you said no man could resist your sexy ass."

She chuckled, "No man can, but the guy in there is green in more than one way if you catch my meaning. A little dissolved pharmaceutical in his drink will just help loosen him up a bit. Trust me by the way he's looking at me he wants to anyway."

"OK girl but you owe me one."

She threw her hair and gave Tony a sly look, "If things go as planned I won't owe anyone anything."

▼▼▼▼▼▼▼▼▼▼▼▼▼▼▼▼▼▼▼▼▼▼▼▼

HOMEGIRL THREE - Present Day

She waited impatiently. It seemed like every nerve in her body was on fire.

"I have to tell you something very disappointing and surprising about your boyfriend." The sentence hung in the air like the smell of a skunk. She crossed her fingers and hoped and prayed it wouldn't be anything too bad. She had never been so in love in her life and now everything was about to come crashing in on her. "I've located one of his ex-girlfriends and it seems like your man has some real anger management issues."

She was truly surprised, "We've been going out for awhile now and he hasn't been even remotely violent."

8

"I know, but apparently this is his MO. After he has your complete trust, and you do something he doesn't approve of, well let's just say I hope your health insurance is paid in full."

She felt like someone had punched her in the stomach. She didn't want to believe it.

"It sounds like you're being a little over dramatic."

"You won't think that once you hear what he did to this ex-girlfriend."

"What did he do?"

"It's not pretty. She was all head over heels in love, just like you are and she made a mistake and got pregnant. When she told Mr. Wonderful about it, she says he turned into a different person and beat her half to death."

"WHAT?"

"She had to be rushed to the hospital and she lost the baby. The only reason she didn't press charges was he told her if she did he would kill her." She felt like she was going to throw up.

This was unbelievable. She didn't believe it. Her voice was barely a whisper, "I don't believe it."

"I thought you might say that so I've made arrangements for you to meet his ex. You'll meet her right?" Her head was pounding and her heart beat like thunder. It took all her energy to keep her eyes dry and her head up.

She looked her informant dead in the eye and said with confidence, "Yes I'll meet her."

▼▼▼▼▼▼▼▼▼▼▼▼▼▼▼▼▼▼▼▼▼▼▼▼

HOMEGIRL FOUR - Present Day

She lay there with him moving back and forth on top of her, trying to decide if she should tell him that she couldn't breathe. There was nothing romantic or exciting about his lovemaking and she didn't even pretend to be into it anymore, it didn't matter. He never noticed. As long as he got his rocks off, she could be comatose. He was beyond selfish when it came to sex; his pleasure was the only thing on the agenda. But she reasoned this was the price she paid to be with a nigga that was paid. He was twenty years her senior and did not believe in exercise. He would exercise his fork up and down during dinner business meetings but that was it. She tried to hold out but his weight had become too much for her.

"Baby could you lie to the side just a bit." He looked up suddenly as if he had forgotten she was there.

"What?"

"Could you move a bit, I think I'm getting a cramp from being in this position too long?"

"Sure, as a matter of fact, get up and get on your knees, doggy style you know how I like it."

Yeah, she thought, I know how you like it. You want to be in some other world. Not looking at me probably fantasizing about being with three women at once or some other shit that will never happen. This mothafucka, she thought, he better be happy he has loot. She would never have cracked her legs, let alone open them this wide if he didn't. The way this particular sex session was going she was sure she would have to pleasure herself later; she needed the release. But it wasn't hard to find a man who could fuck her right; she already had a couple of them on hold. She used to sneak off for booty calls, but she was now completely focused on the mission at hand. She had to possess this man totally. She had to step up her game, she wanted to be the queen, she wanted to spend his money whenever the mood hit. She wanted designer clothes and rings and houses. She didn't remember when, but at some point, for some reason she decided this man and his money were going to change her life. She was deep in thought when all of a sudden she heard him grunt louder and louder. He violently yanked himself out of her and swiftly moved toward her head and began to release himself all over the back of her head and neck. Oh hell no, she thought. He is really getting extra; it must be all those damn porn tapes he watches. She jumped up as if he had shot her in the back.

"What the fuck do you think you're doing?"

"I'm sorry baby, but I always wanted to do that, it just turns me on."

Her voice changed as quickly as her mind was turning this situation to her advantage.

"That's what I would classify as extra."

He looked at her confused. "Extra?"

"Yes extra special treatment. I'm willing to give you extra special treatment. Things you can't imagine." She said this slow and nasty.

He began to almost pant with excitement. "Yes," he said with anticipation.

"Yes, but first you have to get a divorce."

▼▼▼▼▼▼▼▼▼▼▼▼▼▼▼▼▼▼▼▼▼▼

HOMEGIRL FIVE - Present Day

This was supposed to be the happiest time of her life, and she was happy. She was an aspiring lawyer with great family and friends, who was about to marry the man of her dreams. But lately something had been gnawing at her, something felt wrong. There was no question in her mind that he was the man for her. They were college sweethearts and she loved him long before the big pro contract and all the endorsement deals. She knew the real man behind the manufactured media image.

Damn the NBA, Damn basketball! She had come to realize that any other sport would have been easier for them to deal with. In football the players are hidden behind helmets, shoulder pads and long sleeve shirts. In baseball they are in full uniform with long pants and caps. But in basketball, they wore tank top jerseys and shorts, with all those muscular bodies running up and down the court, sweating and performing amazing athletic moves. She had decided there was something more provocative more sexual about this sport and it seemed to drive the women crazy.

She thought it was bad in college when girls would send him naked pictures. But after her man went into the NBA she soon realized these college girls were amateurs. She grew up loving sports. Her father took her to all the games. Basketball was always her favorite. But all she could think about a few days before her wedding was that basketball was her enemy. True there was the money and the fame and the perks. But there was also a price. The vultures - they all wanted a piece of him. The travel and the time apart, and last but certainly not least, the women, the women, the women! They knew where the ball players stayed, they knew their favorite drinks and they knew their weaknesses. It was so bad

11

that she had seen three women with her man's face and jersey number tattooed on their breast. It made her sick. After that they both decided it was best if she stayed away from certain events and situations.

She loved him so much but she just couldn't shake this feeling... She chalked it up to wedding jitters and decided to have a glass of wine and relax. She turned on the news and low and behold they were rehashing the Kobe Bryant scandal. She turned off the TV and turned on some music. She sipped her wine and took off the necklace she always wore. He had given it to her back in college when they were poor. It was a gold chain with a flat heart charm. On the back was the engraving "I'll never break your heart" with his initials. He had offered many times to replace it with something more expensive like platinum, but she refused. She loved her charm necklace; it held great symbolism for her. She held it as tight as she could, closed her eyes and prayed for God to guide her way. When she finished she opened her eyes and slowly looked down. She opened her hand and saw the heart had cracked into two pieces. She began to weep.

Chapter 1   LET'S GET PHYSICAL

Present Day

I wonder if this one is gonna last, I mean we've been going out for almost two whole weeks and Kyle hasn't got on my nerves once yet.

This was very unusual for Renee even with the guys she liked. Men would always have to do something ignorant, like start talkin about how they wanted a woman that was going to take care of them, cook their food, wash their clothes, and a whole lotta other outdated shit; not that Renee wouldn't do things for a man but there's a limit. Now Kyle - there was a tough one to figure out. When they met he certainly had a reputation with the ladies. According to him, it was overexag...

"Comin to you, Short!" Renee snapped out of it, she was so wrapped up in thought she almost forgot where she was. Great, she said to herself, all I need is to get hit upside my head with a softball, because I'm daydreaming about some man that probably won't last through the holiday. Which was alright with Renee because she had resigned herself to the fact that she would probably never marry. If her past relationships or the relationships of her friends were any indication, thanks but no thanks was her attitude. Crack! Renee was startled and looked around in confusion; she had no idea where the ball was. Foul ball, thank goodness she thought. Renee's shortstop position required her to pay more attention than most. Maybe if she were out in right field she could tie her hair up and blow kisses at some pretend boyfriend, the way she had seen so many of these careless players do, but not Renee. It was time to get serious, her team was 3 runs down but she wasn't about to give up without a fight.

So she started yelling, "Come on Tara, right down the middle, she won't swing, she's looking for the walk." This must have encouraged Tara, because she threw the ball right down the center of the plate. Whack! The ball was coming in Renee's direction, but it was toward the hole and moving fast. Renee twisted her body as hard as she could, ran a few steps and dove in the direction of the ball; just as she fell in a big heap on the hard sand, the ball whizzed past the tip of her glove. "Damn!" Renee yelled. It always annoyed her to exert so much effort and not come up with the ball. Her teammates were busy shouting, "Nice try, nice try," but Renee was disappointed, she could remember a day not so far past when that play would have been easy for her. But that was back in high school. She was in better shape then and more dedicated. Now Renee was 24 years old and on an intramural team where you were lucky if the women showed up, let alone took it seriously. ….

Renee looked in the mirror with her pants off and shirt tucked underneath her chin and tried to survey the damage. Yep, just as she suspected her leg was swelling and turning black and blue. She did not bruise easily, but she had hit the ground very hard, and since her arm was reaching out for the ball nothing cushioned her blow.

Just what I need, Renee thought. She was going out with Kyle tonight and even though they hadn't got completely intimate yet, they were at the point of long passionate kisses and Kyle's hands did tend to become very active. She would just have to tell him the story over dinner. Renee looked at the clock and it was 6 pm. That would give her exactly 2 hours to get ready, and judging by the way she looked now, Renee would need every bit of it.

"Girl, it's 7:45 and Kyle will be here in 15 minutes. You know how prompt he is, and I still have to finish my hair and put on some makeup."

"Alright, but call me as soon as you get home cause I still got some crazy mess to tell you."

"Ok, if I'm able to I'll call."

"Renee, what do you mean if you're able? I've known you a long time and my money says you'll be back on the phone with me at about 1:30 and Kyle will be home takin' a cold ass shower."

"Shut up Britney, you don't know what you're talkin' about. Just cause I don't spread my legs for every nigger with a smooth line and phony ass promises doesn't mean I ain't down for some lovin' when the time is right."

"Girl, relax I told you I know your ass, and if the last 14 years is a gauge you're not going to think the time is right tonight. Besides I thought you were in some sort of super rush, now you want to harass me about something I said that you know is true, please."

"Bye, Brittany."

Renee put the phone down and made a B-line for the bathroom. She loved her small but well decorated apartment. There was a beautiful painting on the wall directly across from the door, an abstract picture of 5 men in a jazz band playing their hearts out. Renee loved this painting, and the fact that she constantly received compliments on it, made up for spending more than she could afford to buy it.

Finally ready she looked in the mirror. Renee stood 5 ' 7 with the two inch heals she was wearing. She smoothed the gold and black dress down over her curvy athletic body. A slim waist with a rounded booty and hips let every man know this was a woman. The finishing touch was a purpled hued lip-gloss that complimented her caramel skin and long black hair   Renee looked at the clock, 8:15, late, late, late, she thought. Renee figured this could mean one of two things. A - Kyle is trying to play it cool and show her he's relaxed about the relationship; which is an ancient game men played to try and establish control. Or B - He ain't comin' at all.

Since Renee preferred to think the worse when it came to men, (it was less disappointing this way) she figured he wasn't coming. Fifteen minutes wasn't a lot of time, but up to this point Kyle had been punctual to a fault, which Renee found odd, but very refreshing. She thought, this brotha is really anxious to see me; every other date Kyle was on time, dressed nice, lookin' good and smellin' good. As a matter of fact, it had taken all the self-control she could muster not to throw him on the bed and rip his clothes off at the end of their last date.

But from the beginning Renee had gotten the feeling that a woman being attracted to Kyle was something he was used to, and the last thing Renee wanted to be was typical or predictable. She knew deep down men are primal creatures that enjoy the hunt. A tiger doesn't want the rabbit to sit still and get caught. It enjoys the chase - so do MEN! So she had positioned herself as casual about the whole relationship. A free spirited attitude concocted to make Kyle work at winning her attention and affection.

15

Keeping all this in mind, Renee knew that as badly as she wanted to see Kyle, if she did not receive a phone call, or he did not show up by 8:45, she'd have to leave. Kyle had to learn that her world did not revolve around him. Renee always worked hard to keep balance in her life - romance, career, friends and family, the full circle. She had seen people who lead lives controlled by only one factor and they always seemed on edge. If that one thing stopped working, their lives stopped working. All Renee could think was – "not me". She never wanted to give any external force that much control over her life.

At times it became difficult to maintain this balance. This was the case with Kyle. As much as she tried to play it cool, she found herself thinking about him more and more. She wondered if she was playing too hard to get and Kyle was getting frustrated, because she had not given him the bedroom invitation he was looking for. Maybe last time they went out she was too... STOP IT! Stop blaming yourself, and making excuses for some good for nothing nigga, who don't know how to show up for a date. If he's somewhere with someone else, its his loss, fuck hi . . .

Knock! Knock!

Just as Renee was putting the finishing touches on her 'Men ain't no good speech', there was Kyle at the door. A smile crept across Renee's face as she started hurriedly for the door. Half way there she took a deep breath and began to walk slower. Let him wonder for a minute if I'm still here, she thought with a devilish grin.

Look at those eyes and that smile, girl, don't let that man buy another drink, or that will be it. You'll wake up in the arms of that beautiful black man sitting across the table. She didn't want him to think his little late ploy worked. But Renee had to admit maybe it did because every part of her wanted to let loose . . . buy me three more drinks, tear my clothes off and keep me up all night, it said. And Renee was starting to listen.

Just as she finished that thought, she heard Kyle say, "I can't believe how close I feel to you, it's like we've known each other forever. You look so good tonight. Damn! I could just jump right across this table." It was like that with Kyle. They almost seemed connected. She would be thinking something and bam Kyle would say it.

Connection or no connection, 3 drinks and a whole lotta sweet-talkin' later, Renee found herself in the arms of the man she had spent the last week, day dreaming about. And as much as she hated to admit it, she felt safe, satisfied and secure in those arms. It had been a wonderful night. Kyle had been deliberate in his lovemaking with Renee. He took time to satisfy her. Come to think of it, this seemed to be his priority. Just as with every other part of their relationship, up to this point, Kyle was trying to put himself in a different category than other men.

Just as Renee began to enjoy this sublime feeling, her built in protection shield pulled her back to reality. Here you go, she thought, startin' to think like every other confused sister. This was SEX and as I try to turn it into a romantic plot from a screen play, he's probably laying over there thinking about how good it felt, and how in the world he could escape gracefully from my bed.

She wondered how sex would change their relationship. There was no doubt in Renee's mind that things would be different. They always were; the worse case scenario - no call. In these instances, Renee would add up the money the man had spent on dates to decide whether she was a cheap hooker or a classy call girl. Either way she was a victim of the booty call. Then there was the wait a few days and call men. They spent the rest of the relationship trying their hardest not to spend any more money on you, sleep in your bed as often as possible and convince you they let you know from the start they were looking for something casual, and finally the third type of man - the one who turns into your man, partner or boyfriend. The one who seems like the answer to all your dreams, until about six months later. At least this had been Renee's experience up to this point.

She thought back on past relationships to try to remember what made her so bitter toward men. It was actually contrary to Renee's personality to be so negative. With everything else in life she was positive and upbeat, a true optimist.

Renee's induction into the world of dating was vicious at best. The first serious boyfriend she had was truly a "boy." She was a senior in high school and he was a college athlete. A great catch to the naked eye. But Renee soon found out that wearing someone's team jacket, talking to them every night on the phone, and having their mother cut out newspaper articles about you and put them on the refrigerator, all meant nothing. All these years later and she could still remember the feeling in the pit of her stomach, when a so called high school friend informed her he was actually engaged to her cousin. (A fact "the friend" waited 8 months to tell Renee). She had never felt so betrayed in her life. But as she gathered up his things to return them, she decided to be as calm and cold as possible to "the joke" as she now refers to him, and to ask him for advice on her next relationship. When she showed up at his house after all the predictable stuff happened, Renee kept her promise to herself and asked advice for the future. After a long pause "the joke" looked at her and said, "You're too nice. Don't be so nice." And Renee never was again. From that point on she had a bulletproof shield around her heart. At times Renee was sure it cost her getting to know a potentially good man. But that was the price she was willing to pay to protect her self esteem.

Now here she was, trying to pretend she wasn't completely swept away by Kyle in an attempt to keep some form of control. But as hard as Renee tried to come up with an acceptable plan of attack, for the post sexual relationship, she knew this dilemma required some soul searching with the cheapest psychologists in the business ...... her friends.

Chapter 2   DRINK NIGHT

Present Day

"OK Simone, I've looked in five different cabinets and still no blender."

"Keep looking, I know it's there somewhere," Simone told Renee. This girl must have invented the word bachelorette.   Liquor and cigarettes were the only two things you were sure to find at Simone's apartment. Simone had recently saved enough for the security deposit on a two bedroom apartment and as quickly as she could sign the papers, it had replaced Friday's and Bennigans as the spot on "Drink Night" as they liked to call it.   Simone's place wasn't as nice as Brittany or Renee's, but she was centrally located for all three, and her ghetto surroundings insured that no neighbors would ever complain about the noise. They could blast the radio or laugh like hyenas and no one cared.

On Friday or Saturday depending on what was going on in each one of their lives Simone, Brittany and Renee would get together for therapy and liquor - a soothing combination.   Not that any of them were alcoholics, but between work, bills and men, it was a pleasant escape to hang with the girls. The three of them had known each other for what seemed like forever. You know the type of friends who saw you get embarrassed at corny high school parties by your overprotective father; or whose shoulder you cried on when you and your boyfriend broke up right before the prom. In other words, friends that know things about your past even you want to forget. So when they got together the conversations were up close, personal and raw.   Simone was thin, attractive, demanding and interracial. Her father was a white man that she had never laid eyes on. The slightest of the three, so it was hard to believe she was the one with the 3-year-old son.   She worked as a receptionist in a doctor's office, and a few drinks always encourage her to share her office annoyances.

"First of all going to medical school all those years and being that disorganized just don't make no sense." Simone was referring to Dr.

19

Fields who routinely would need Simone to find a chart she had given him 6 hours earlier, 10 minutes before an operation.

"He wants to wait until something is life or death to tell me he lost the chart. I suppose if I didn't find it in time it would be my fault. I'm telling y'all in two weeks I'm getting my review and it's raise or raise up. I've earned that raise. They always think they can nickel and dime a sister. If I were some blond headed white girl I'd be making $5,000 more a year easy." Simone continued to rant as Brittany lit a cigarette and Renee continued to look for the blender.

"Simone," Renee piped up "help me find this damn blender. I don't mean to stop your story, but something tells me it would sound better with a Mudslide in my hand." Simone went over and opened a pantry door that she hadn't even told Renee about and pulled out the blender.

"It's right here, I told you keep looking."

"Sorry Simone but I refuse to ransack your kitchen looking for a blender when you obviously knew where it was."

"Whatever girl," Simone said, "less talkin and more blendin please. Because before you disturbed me, I was making an important point about my career." Brittany was sitting across the room on the couch. Renee looked over as Brittany blow out a long stream of smoke.

"If you ask me, you're both bull shittin. Renee you must have really been drunk the last time we were here, because you put the blender away yourself. So know your limit. And you Simone telling us some story about Dr. Fields, when you know we want to hear about Dr. Feel good," Brittany smirked.

She was referring to Simone's current entanglement with a rich, handsome, older and, oh yeah, married doctor. Simone exhaled. She knew the question was coming and she felt obligated to share with her friends. But the truth was Simone was unsure of her own feelings. The whole encounter had started off as a rich nigga buying her all sorts of things she never asked for, which made Simone think why not, I deserve to be spoiled by a man, and if I don't get my feelings involved, no big deal. Convincing argument, but this man was no rookie; his words and promises were smoother around the edges than Simone counted on. And the longer she messed with him the tighter she became tangled in his web.

Gurggal vroom, the blender screamed as Renee pushed the highest setting. She was designated drink master and took pride in her concoctions. Tonight's selection was mudslide mix, vanilla yogurt; ice cubes and whip cream – a crowd favorite. Earlier when Renee was putting the ingredients in the blender, she lifted the yogurt carton to show Brittany – Brittany winked in appreciation. Brittany and Renee were both avid fans of any food that would be kind enough not to show up later on their thighs. Not that either was fat but both came from families where food was given a priority. Brittany was very voluptuous, so she had to be careful not to go from curvy to cow. The two were workout partners and both had a membership at "Shake It" the well known, over popular, national health club in Manhattan where they both worked. Although they enjoyed going to exercise after work together, both often complained about how completely over crowded it was. Brittany was in law school at Brooklyn Law while interning at a large firm. Renee was the only black executive at the well-known Q & A advertising agency.

Brittany quickly realized that Simone did not want to give too much detail about her unconventional relationship. So she turned her attention to Renee. "So Rae, what's your story? Last I heard you were about to go out on yet another hot date with Kyle?" Brittany smiled as she egged Renee on. She could tell by the big Kool Aid smile constantly on Renee's face whenever she talked about Kyle – that she was crazy about him.

"We'll since you asked, he took me to that new soul food restaurant in the Village and we were supposed to check out this jazz club he'd been telling me about after dinner. But, truth be told we never made it there."

"Why not?" Brittany probed.

"Well girl I don't know if it was the liquor, the conversation or the sweet potato pie – but I had to have that man sooner than later".

"I vote for the liquor," Simone commented sarcastically.

Renee ignored Simone and continued her story. "When he realized I was down, Kyle practically broke every moving violation getting us back to my place."

"I bet you two broke some more once you got there." Brittany laughed. "Well girl, was it worth the wait?"

"Was it? A perfect blend of sweet and nasty. He made sure I was satisfied and then held me all night long."

"Sounds like someone's got a Love Jones." Brittany remarked. She was happy for her friend. Brittany always knew Renee would need a very special man and she hoped Kyle was it. Brittany was a bit concerned about Simone's silence, but figured that, with her relationship being a bunch of twisted up lies, hearing about Renee and Kyle's sexual bliss was not exactly first on her agenda. "Well I, for one, think that's great," Brittany said staring at Simone to show her disapproval for her lack of comment.

"You think so? I mean I thought it was romantic and special, but I just don't want him to change. You know how some men can be after sex." Renee admitted.

"Yeah I know", Simone, said, "they can start showin their ass."

"Yeah". Renee sulked.

"Listen Renee. Things WILL change, but that does not mean they will change for the worse. They may change for the better. Besides you have to take chances in life. Just think of it this way. The worse case scenario, you were in the mood and had some great sex. The best case scenario you may have met your soul mate." Renee smiled and let out a slight sigh of relief. Brittany always made her feel better by dispensing simple but meaningful words of wisdom. Renee also noticed Simone's silence, but had long since decided she would bring this up with Brittany during one of their gym visits.

Just then Simone spoke up, "No offense Brit but it's easy to be so optimistic about men when you're lucky enough to be with a cute, rich soon to be top star in the NBA." Here it comes Brittany thought with a smile to herself, the jealousy. Brittany and her all-star boyfriend Tyson were the resident dream couple of the crew. Of course back when both Brittany and Tyson were sacrificing to get where they were now, Simone was out on the town having fun. But Simone conveniently forgot the hard work or all the times Brittany was alone because Tyson was away on road trips with his college team. To hear Simone tell it, Brittany was sitting at home one day and her fairy Godmother appeared and said, " Here Brittany I'm giving you this perfect man that every women wants;

and by the way I figured I'd throw in a college diploma and admission to a great law school just to make your life a little easier."

Simone continued, "If you want some advice from a sistah that lives in the real world, don't get sprung over this fool. It sounds like he's really good in bed and hey don't think I'm selling that short because not every man is. I'm just saying be careful because he sounds real smooth." Simone continued to speak almost in one run-on sentence because she intentionally did not want either of her friends to make a comment.

"Anyway, you two, I'm pretty tired. It's been a really long week – what do you say we call it a night?" Brittany and Renee both looked at each other in shock. It was not like Simone to ask them to leave.

Renee laughed out loud, "So let me see if I have this straight. Brittany is living in a pretend dream world, and I'm delusional if I think Kyle wants anything more than sex. Oh, and by the way, you two can get out now."

"Don't be so dramatic Renee," Simone huffed. "I'm just tired, we can pick this conversation up next time."

Simone was about to comment but Brittany spoke over her, "Come on Rae it's obvious Simone is tired or in the mood to be alone, either way it's time for us to go." They both got their purses and keys and headed for the door. "We love you anyway Miss Moody girl," Brittany yelled over her shoulder on the way out.

"Stank, moody girl," Renee chimed in.

Simone felt bad asking her friends to leave and could tell by the looks on their faces that they thought the request was strange. But after Renee's little Cinderella story, she didn't want to admit that Joe might be coming over. He was supposed to get there at 1:00am if he managed to make some lame excuse and sneak away from his wife. Yeah right! She thought. She could just hear herself. "Congratulations Renee on finding Mr. Perfect but excuse me while I kick you two out so I can fuck my married old ass boyfriend." Thanks but no thanks. The worst part was Simone was not even sure if he would be able to get away but just the possibility was enough to send her friends packing. Simone took the last sip from her drink and lay back. She wondered what events in her life had led her to this point. When they were young she and Carmen could have any guy they wanted. Carmen was the missing fourth to Brittany,

Renee and Simone's threesome. She had just disappeared off the planet. When Carmen was still around, she and Simone were definitely the Divas of the bunch. If a cute guy came around they would both turn on the charm and see who could get him first. Simone loved this competitive relationship and missed Carmen immensely. Neither Brittany nor Renee had this competitive nature for men; it would be completely unacceptable to them if their man made a pass. But Carmen would take this as a challenge, prop her boobs up throw her hair in his face and hope for the best.

Simone missed the good old days. All she could think was now she lay here a single mother having an affair with a married 45-year-old man. In a way she was glad Carmen wasn't around to see this. Brittany and Renee were a lot less judgmental than she would be. Life is so odd, Simone thought. Renee never put a high priority on men. Renee liked men but she didn't go out of her way to flirt or show interest, yet she finds this great guy. Life's weird. Then there was Brittany, who was leading this perfect little charmed life. Simone could still remember when Carmen first disappeared; they had all been shocked and concerned. They would get together and talk about trying to find her, but all that ended when Brittany met Tyson, Mr. Everything. Simone couldn't help but roll her eyes as she realized that if they hadn't been friends since grade school, Brittany was the type of woman she would despise. Things came a little too easy for Brittany in Simone's opinion. But the truth was Brittany was sweet, kind and non-judgmental. Simone poured another drink and told herself to stop thinking like a jealous bitch. She looked at the clock 2:00am. Still no Joe. "Great" Simone thought, I get to go to sleep depressed and horny.

Chapter 3   NIKES FLAT

Present Day

On the ride home from Simone's house, Brittany was reflecting on Simone's comments. Even her own friends didn't really know what it was like to know a superstar, before there was anything SUPER about him. Tyson was her college sweetheart, and she would have loved him no matter what profession he chose. She loved him for the man he was, but because he was such a huge hoops star now people lost sight of their humble beginnings. Brittany thought back to when they first met at Jersey University in her sophomore year:

Back In The Day

"Ty, stop playin! You have to memorize these formulas or else you'll fail the test. I'm telling you Chemistry is all memorization. Now what's the formula for water?"

"Ohhhhh that's an easy one. Give me something to challenge my brain."

"OK - what's the formula for sodium?"

".... Mmmmm, I know it. Its on the tip of my tongue, uuuhhhhhh." Tyson started lifting up his notebook to look for the answer.

"You're cheating!!!" Brittany screamed at him. People looked up from their study sessions, and gave her the evil eye. *"Damn library is about to close anyway, I don't know why yall trippin'. If you don't know it by now, you're screwed,"* Brittany said as she rolled her eyes.

Tyson laughed at her. *"You don't miss anything Britty."*

"Ty you know if you don't pass this midterm, you will be in jeopardy of losing your spot on the team. You know that Jersey U. has a strict policy on athletes maintaining a 2.0 G.P.A, and coach already warned you. Babe you're in your sophomore year. Next year the pros are going

to start coming out to look at you. You grew 3 inches this year alone. Don't blow it."

"I know babe, I know. You see that's why a brother needs a strong sister like you by his side to make sure he stays in line. I don't know where I'd be without you."

"Yeah, well, remember that next time ho-bag comes up to you shaking her tail at you in the student lounge, laughing at all your jokes."

Tyson chuckled. He loved when Britt showed jealously towards the other girls at school. She really hated Jennifer Stewart though. She was a cheerleader, who had been trying to get at him since his freshman year. She wasn't his type though. She was gorgeous and all, and her body was real tight, but Tyson hated aggressive women, especially ones with no brains. A lot of the guys on the team used to tease him about her. They would say man; "if I had pretty ass like that being thrown in my face all the time, I would hit and run man". He would laugh with them but he knew he never would. His mother always told him – "get you a woman with beauty and brains, and not one of these fast chicks that's just looking to latch on to a rising star. Bring me home an honorable woman." Tyson was very close to his Moms, since she single-handedly raised him and his 4 sisters. His father was a no-good faggot, who took the back door on them when he was just 5. He didn't really remember him, but he always admired his mother for being such a strong woman. Therefore, he looked for that same quality in his females. He could have any girl he wanted in high school; being the star basketball player who took his team to the national championship 2 years in a row. And it seemed like when he got to Jersey U. the girls were lined up waiting for him. However it was Brittany who first took his breath away. She was fine, with the cutest brown dreadlocks that had just a hint of blonde on the ends -

He first met her in the spring semester of his sophomore year. They were in the same African-American history class. She sat in the front of the class, and Tyson sat in the back. Of course he always came in late because it was an early morning class. He first noticed her because she used to always ask lots of questions and the professor would always comment on how insightful her questions were. The day that she really caught his attention was when she got into a heated debate with Herbert

26

Alexander IV, the class nerd, who was sure to graduate magna cum laude. The class was discussing whether or not black people had the right to call themselves "African-Americans" or were they simply "Black Americans." Well, apparently Ms. Martin had to get the last word, and it turned into a heated debate between the two. From that moment on Tyson knew he had to get with her. She was pretty and smart, and his mother would love her. Another thing about her, she didn't seem to notice him like all the other girls on campus. She was a definite challenge. And there was nothing more appealing to Tyson Myers than a challenge.

It was spring semester of Tyson's sophomore year at Jersey U. He was sitting on the 2nd level of the library by the windows, the area that Brittany Martin always studied in. He was looking out the window at all the students gathered on the campus lawn. A lot of students opted to sit outside when the weather began to change, as opposed to being cooped up in the library. But Tyson noticed Brittany never changed her pattern when it came to studying. He thought of approaching her in the student union, but she only went there with her girls, and he did not want to approach her in front of her friends. Tyson didn't notice her come in while he was daydreaming. When he turned back to his books, she had just sat down at a table. He put a lot of thought into his approach, Brittany Martin gave you the impression that you better step correctly when dealing with her, or don't bother stepping at all.

Tyson had decided he wasn't going to use any corny lines with her, cause he knew he would be playing himself. He decided to be casual.

"Excuse me Brittany." She looked up from her books at him.

"Hi, I'm Tyson Myers. We're in the same Black History class with Professor Johnson."

"Yeah, I know who you are, you always come in late."

Tyson laughed at her honesty. "Well, I can't help but notice how on top of your studies you are and I need a good study partner. I need to keep my grades up in order to stay on the team. Jersey U doesn't let athletes slide like most schools."

"So you chose me?" she said, sounding amused.

"Why you say it like that, you are an intelligent sistah aren't you? I ain't tryna study with no C student. I can do average by myself."

She looked at him for a second before she answered. *"Well, I respect the fact that you're an athlete who takes his schoolwork seriously, especially considering that you will probably go to the pros after this school year is over."*

"Oh yeah, you think so." Tyson was tickled by her prediction.

"I'm a die-hard basketball fan, and I follow college ball pretty closely. You'll probably be one of the best shooting guards in the conference this year, and I'm sure the scouts will be after you for an early draft."

"Well, I can't argue with those facts, can I?" Tyson said, with the biggest Kool-Aid smile he had shown in a while.

"I'm here Monday and Wednesday nights from 6 to 9, same place" Brittany said.

"Well I'll see you Wednesday then Brittany."

Ever since that first session, Tyson and Brittany were inseparable.

Chapter 4   Diamonds Are A Girl's Best Friend

Present Day

Joe cruised down the expressway in his Jaguar down to the *Diamonds are Love* store. He knew the saying "diamonds are a girls best friend." And he wanted to be his girl's best friend, so he would be the giver of this beautiful gift. That girl had really stuck by him through all the drama. He had been seeing her for a while now and she was very faithful to their arrangement. He figured 'arrangement' was the more appropriate word over relationship. In a relationship people spent quality time together and took trips, etc. Simone accepted whatever time he gave her, as long as he took care of her. That had been the deal from the moment they met. She knew he was married, but in order to pull a dime like her at his age, he had to lie a little bit. What was a brother to do, he couldn't very well tell her - sistah, you look damn good and all, but I have no intention on leaving my wife for you. He had way too much to lose under those circumstances. Lorraine would destroy him if she found out he was having an extra-marital affair. Although the love and romance had left their relationship a long time ago, he still had 3 beautiful kids with this woman, whose lives would be destroyed if he were exposed. Besides, he loved being seen with a woman half his age. All his buddies would drool over Simone wishing they had a young chic on the side like him, who did not interfere with their marriage. But those guys were old fogies, unlike him. In Joe's mind he didn't look anywhere near his 45 years, and he knew how to handle a woman. His wife no longer fit the standards to be seen with him when he was macking. Lorraine was fine for the company Christmas party and picnics, but not for the nightlife he enjoyed. He sometimes wondered if he would tire of Simone once she was out of her prime. He had grown to really care for her, but he knew it was purely physical. She didn't have half the brains of his wife, who held a masters degree in business administration, nor could he hold a decent conversation with her about the stock market, but boy did she keep his Jimmie hard, and that was all that mattered to Joe, after all she was not his wife, she was his mistress.

He closed the moon roof to his car as he pulled into the mall parking lot. As soon as he entered the jewelry store a young girl greeted him with a cheery, "Can I help you sir?"

"Yes, I'm looking for a diamond clustered ring in pink or opal, something unique."

"Is this for an engagement sir?"

"No!" he snapped. "Why do you women always think because a man wants to buy a woman diamonds, they have to marry her. Why can't I just be buying my lady a nice gift!" he responded in a hostile tone.

The saleswoman was taken aback at his angry tone. A few of the customers looked up from their browsing to get a load of this pompous jerk.

"I'm sorry sir. I just wanted to offer you the right selection. We have engagement diamonds and regular diamond rings. Please step over here."

That's more like it he thought to himself. He had no time for other people's insinuations. People were always trying to pass judgment without knowing the circumstances surrounding a situation. Cocksuckers. This salesgirl was about to make a helluva commission, so she better kiss his ass.

"I want your highest quality diamond cut, set in a cluster, in an opal color."

"Well let me show you this set sir, its very unique." He looked at the opal clustered diamond ring, and he had to admit even he was impressed; and he'd seen many diamonds. He knew immediately this was the ring for his Simmy.

"I'll take it!" he responded, without even asking the price. "Wrap it up in a beautiful box with a little gift bow on it, with a message that reads - you are my world."

"Yes sir". He threw his credit card on the counter.

As Joe exited the mall, he thought about how he would present the ring to her on their next date. He would place the ring on her finger of the right hand, because she would never wear a diamond he gave her on her left that was only for his wife. The more Joe thought about it the more excited he became. Lorraine would always be his wife and have his devotion, but Simmy would always be his Bitch, and she better never leave him. He smiled at the thought as he stepped on the gas. He had to hurry home for dinner.

Chapter 5   The Apple Doesn't Fall Far

Present Day

Simone held the phone from her ear and rolled her eyes as her mother, Liz, chastised her. "I just wanted you to know I saw that car pull up in front of your apartment at five in the morning and worse yet I saw it leave at six.

"So," Simone said matter-of-factly.

"So!" Liz gasped, "I didn't raise no daughter of mine to let a man come in her house 5 in the morning, run up inside her real quick and leave at six, like he's late for an appointment. I don't care what kind of car he drives."

Simone couldn't believe what she was hearing, this was the same woman that let herself get pregnant by a white man because she thought it would be like hitting the lottery. Of course Simone's mother didn't know that she knew that story. But when Simone was about 10 years old one of her more ghetto aunts told her the whole drama. She could still hear the words like it was yesterday. "Why do you think you got that good hair and your skin so light?" Her aunt had asked. The whole conversation had scarred her deeper than her aunt would ever know. Apparently Liz had tried to be slick. This white boy was curious and had a little jungle fever. So she indulged him inside his expensive car, bought for him by mommy and daddy. Liz told him she was on the pill and he wouldn't know how good black pussy could feel with a condom on. Well sure enough four months later Liz went to tell the white boy she was pregnant and it was too late for an abortion. He was horrified and went running home for daddy's help. His father told Liz he would give her eight thousand dollars if she would sign a document. The boy would have no responsibility to the child, and a non-disclosure document that she would never divulge the identity of Simone's father.

Liz had tried to be smart. She refused, and said she would take him to court for child support. The father just laughed and told her they would move out of state and she would get nothing. She called his bluff and the family moved. Liz had no idea how to find them. She was ignorant in the ways of the law and had no money to pay for someone else's expertise. So until Simone was 3 no word from her father's family and no money. Then one day Liz received a phone call putting the original offer back on the table $8000 hush money. This time Simone's mother accepted. She signed the papers and used the $8,000 to buy a new car. Eventually insurance payments and gas were too expensive and Liz ended up selling the car for $3000 dollars, Simone's aunt said she was telling her the story because Liz could not, by law tell her. Simone's aunt said that Liz was always threatening to take them to court but she still didn't know where they were. Liz had never told Simone this story, but she did tell her the only gift her father ever gave her was her looks, and she should use them to get a man with money so the family could be comfortable. But ever since Simone had given birth to little KJ by a man her mother considered a bum – their relationship had been strained. Little did her mom know, Simone was going to do it right. The way she saw it - that man broke his neck to get to her house at 5 in the morning because he needed her coochie, the way a crack head needs crack and she planned on exploiting that need for all it was worth.

Besides, Simone knew this phone conversation was her mother's shallow attempt to get information on Simone's moneyman. But Simone refused to divulge anything about her scheme. She knew her mother would overreact about the married thing. But in Simone's mind this was a minor obstacle. Let my mother wonder, Simone thought. Soon I'll be inviting her to my mansion and her mouth will be open so wide she'll look like she saw a ghost. Yeah just give me a few more months of working these hips right, and I'll get from my "soon to be divorced black man" what my mother never could get from her white boy.

33

Chapter 6   GIRL BE CAREFUL

Present Day

Beep, Beep. Renee hit the horn as hard as she could. "Damn," she yelled aloud. An obviously sleepy tractor-trailer driver had just tried to single handedly end her life and Renee was pissed. This guy interrupted her vibe. A clear night, nice music and thoughts of Kyle had put her in a magical mood. But when this truck almost crashed into her, Renee's heart skipped a beat and her internal music was momentarily paused. Luckily, Renee was in too good a mood to stay mad. She was on her way to meet Brit at the gym and for now, all was right in her world.

As she pulled into the crowded parking lot she scanned for Brittany's car. Renee turned down the second row of vehicles and there it was, Brit's Jeep Cherokee.

"Hey girl," Brittany smiled as she gave Renee a hug.

"What's first?" Renee questioned "the elliptical or weights?"

"Let's get on the machines while we can get two together." Brittany answered.

After programming her machine and getting into rhythm Brit asked Renee, "So what's up? You look extra happy today."

"I don't know. But I think the combination of spring fever and Kyle has put me in some sort of goofy trance."

Brittany laughed out loud at Renee's comment. "Damn girl, I don't think I've ever seen you so sprung over anyone."

"I know, but as happy as I am I'm starting to get a little scared." Renee admitted.

"Scared of what? I thought you said he treats you like gold."

"He does. But we are both experienced enough to know that you can't get too comfortable. Because as soon as you do; that's when they pull the rug out from under you."

"You're right girl so tell me what scares you."

"Well the first thing is, as crazy as I am over Kyle, he is moving a little fast. The other day he asked me to move in with him."

"WHAT?" Brittany gulped, "When did you two get THAT serious – seems like you just met him."

"Exactly," Renee responded. "I'm not ready to move in with anyone. Although I must admit when he asked me it didn't seem impossible. But I did tell him that when I was a little girl my dream was not to shack up with some guy I just met a month ago."

"You said that." Brittany asked stunned.

"Yes I did and I regretted saying it about two seconds after. Kyle backed away from me and said so I'm just some guy well thanks for letting me know. I realized immediately that my word choice was horrible. So I spent half the night apologizing to him and the other half making love to him. You know with men sex makes everything better. So I put out that fire, but we never really discussed the cohabitation thing again."

"Are you thinking about it?" Brittany asked.

"To be honest my mind doesn't want to, but my heart has been considering it."

"WOW." Brittany was obviously surprised and starting to get concerned. Between sisterly love for her friend and her attorney instincts, her protectiveness took over.

"O.K. Renee this relationship is on a whole different level than I thought. So I want you to think about a couple of things. Don't get me wrong Kyle seems like a nice guy, but how well do you really know him? Do you know about his family, his past, other women, what he aspires to?"

"Wow that's a lot of questions Brit?"

"Yeah it is and you need to know the answer to all of them before you even think about moving in with a brotha. I'm just saying Renee; interning at the firm I see crazy stuff everyday. People who were head over heels in love and now the only thing they are concerned about is who gets what. It would be nice if life was a fairytale, but it's not. And I would not be a very good friend if I didn't help you protect yourself." Brittany didn't want to ruin Renee's bliss but it was time to get serious.

"I'm aware of all the things you're saying and this is what scares me, but what can I really do, relationships are a risk." Renee responded.

Brittany took a moment to process what her friend had said; she knew she needed to choose her words carefully. "O.K. Renee here it is. You are a successful free spirited sistah and I don't want to see anyone take advantage of you. If you're really really into this brotha, you may want to consider checking him out."

"What do you mean, check him out?"

"Well, I know this guy, his name is Sean. Cool dude. I was going to hook you two up before you met Kyle. Anyway he's a private investigator and the firm hires him to help with cases sometimes. Leave it to me. I'll set the whole thing up, but for now," Brittany sang in her most convincing club it up voice, "Work that body. Move that body."

Two hours later, and they were both thoroughly tired and sweaty. When they were in the locker room Renee questioned Brittany again. She was still not convinced a private investigator was a good idea.

"Hey Brit," Renee started, "I'm just curious - when you and Tyson started dating did you have him checked out?"

Brittany laughed out loud at this question. "First of all we met when we were in school and neither of us had anything. I was so young and goofy I probably didn't know you could have people checked out." Brittany continued, "I understand why you're a little reluctant but let's be real Renee we're not silly school girls anymore and we're both driven career woman and could be taken advantage of. Hell if memory serves me correctly we were taken advantage of in college."

"Don't bring that up," Renee tensed. "You must really be trying to ruin my good mood."

Brittany was referring to Raysheeda, their friend and surrogate sister from their college days at Jersey University. Raysheeda was from a troubled home with troubled circumstances; but her luck started to change when she was fortunate enough to become Brittany's roommate. Renee was at Jersey U. also and by the time second semester started they had found a way to all share a place just off campus. Renee remembered those were great times with great memories until Raysheeda managed to destroy it all - the friendship and the memories. Brittany had just managed to remind Renee that people weren't always what they seemed.

"Yeah you're right Brit. Set up a meeting between me and this Sean guy, but I still feel like I'm being a little silly." Renee admitted.

"Better to be silly then to be suckered." Brittany concluded.

Chapter 7 JACKED

Back In The Day

"Oh man Brit that was some party", Carmen said. "I got mad numbers! There were mad cuties in the house. I met me a Lexus, a Beamer and a Benz! We'll see which one of these ballers is a shot caller. May the best man win."

"You crazy girl! But I ain't mad at you! Sheeeeeeeeeet". I love Brooklyn parties. "Ain't no party like a Brooklyn party" they sang as they cruised down the Turnpike back to Jersey.

"I hope that chick is up when we get there," said Carmen. I got to use the *bano*. She should be, as much as she wanted us to spend the night. Raysheeda knew they were coming back to Jersey to Carmen's house, so she offered her place for them to crash when they got back, since she lived closer to the city. Knowing how tired and drunk they would be, the girls readily accepted. Brit knew the main reason Sheeda had offered was because she knew they would all go to breakfast in the morning; and she loved riding in Brit's car with the top down. She was like a little kid in the back seat constantly saying "Brit pump up the music," wanting to be seen by all her people riding around in a fly car with the music blasting. She was simple like that.

"We're almost there, its all these damn lights in Newark that make it seem so long."

Brittany turned the corner by Raysheeda's house, and proceeded to pull up on the curb. She really didn't like the idea of parking her brand new car on the street, but Sheeda's aunt was always bugging about people parking in her driveway.

As soon as Brit turned the ignition off, she noticed bright headlights appear right behind her. The next thing she knew 3 men with ski masks jumped out of the car and ran up to them, shotguns in hand.

"Get out of the car, get out," one of the gunmen screamed at Brit. Her life flashed in front of her. She was terrified. The thug looked like he would not hesitate to use his piece on her. She ran from the car in a panic, Carmen was hot on her trail. She turned back in time to see the thugs peel out in her brand new drop-top Beamer, which still had the temporary tags on it. Carmen and Brit were crying when they reached Ra on the back steps.

"Call 911; call 911" they screamed at her! Those motherfuckers stole my car and I want it back!"

Raysheeda picked up the phone and got an operator on the line, "is this 911? I need to report a carjacking. I said I need to report a carjacking!" The next thing Brit and Carmen knew Raysheeda was hanging up on the operator.

"What the hell did you do that for?" Brit screamed at her.

"The Bitch wasn't understanding what I was saying. She was acting retarded."

"I don't give a damn about that. Get the operator back on the line." Every minute we waste these bitches are getting off." Brittany was livid! How the hell could Raysheeda hang up on the fucking operator trying to get the information? That shit rubbed her the wrong way and bad!

"Call the Mothafuckers back! Matter fact, give me the damn phone." She looked at Carmen and rolled her eyes.

"Yes, I'd like to report a car jacking…"

Brittany hoped that when she woke up it would all be a bad nightmare - the jacking, the guns, and the ski masks. It seemed surreal. How could something so gangsta and thuggish happen to her. She had just finished her first year at Jersey University. That car was a present from her parents. Brittany had graduated at the top of her class in high school and done exceptionally well her first year in college. To think that someone could take something away from her, in just seconds, that she worked so hard to achieve. The way she was feeling right now, she could pump bullets in them, if she came face to face with her attackers. Bastards! As the sun came through the window, Brit looked over at Carmen who was also lying with her eyes open and she realized it was not a nightmare but an ugly reality of the mean streets of Newark.

"Did I get jacked last night?" Brittany said to Carmen.

Carmen was teary-eyed, "girl I'm ready to move to Idaho and marry a rich man! I'm so tired of this ghetto shit!! "

"I know what you mean girl." They both sort of cried together.

Raysheeda must have woken up early, because she was already downstairs on the telephone.

"Yall want some breakfast?" She asked cheerfully.

"I can't think of food at a time like this! I'm ready to go home." Brit was still mad about the antics Raysheeda pulled with 911. "Carmen call Simone and see if she can come pick us up." Brit was furious that she couldn't call Rasan, her current boyfriend - he was locked up again, and useless! Carmen picked up her cell and tried to reach Simone at work. She heard her say 'girl, you will never believe what the hell happened to us last night.' Brit had to leave the room, she wasn't ready to hear an instant replay, it would just bring tears to her eyes and all the emotions back. She went to the bathroom to wash her face.

When she came out of the bathroom, Raysheeda was sitting on her bed looking at her.

"Girl, don't worry, you'll be alright. It's just a car. You'll get another one just like you got that one. That's what you pay insurance for isn't it?"

Brittany just looked at her and didn't respond.

"Carmen did you get in touch with Sim?"

"Yeah she said she'd be here right after her shift."

"I need some fresh air." Brit went out to the front porch to have a cigarette, she suddenly couldn't breathe in that house.

Chapter 8   PRETTY BROWN EYES

Present Day

Lola looked around and surveyed the competition.   These Southern girls had a whole different style from Northern chicks. She was not worried at all about her audition. If these chicken heads that were sitting around her were supposed to be competition, she had it in the bag. She pulled out her compact and began checking her makeup and hair. Her make-up was flawless. She woke up early to make sure it looked professional. She liked to choose colors that accentuated her hazel eyes and caramel skin. Lola was a product of Dominican and black parents. She felt she had the best of both features -naturally curly hair, that could be blown slick and straight, and cascaded down her shoulders or natural curly, when she wanted the wet and wild look. Today she had opted for the wet and wavy look, since she was going to be dancing seductively. She figured it went with the image. She picked out a low cut halter top, which brought out her double D's, and a thong bikini bottom to go under her micro-mini, complimented with a pair of spikes to show off her long legs. Lola thought back to how she got this audition:

Bruce Jacobson, the guy she was currently dating (or so he thought) had hooked her up with this audition. Pumps In the Bump was the most popular and exclusive strip club in Hotlanta, it was frequented by professional athletes, entertainers and hordes of successful businessmen. In other words the kind of place Lola could make a serious living. She met Bruce while she was waiting tables at one of Atlanta's hottest sports bars, Slam Drunk. She took the job in hopes of meeting some ballers, because it was located in the lobby of Atlanta's poshest hotel, The Regis Inn. She was new to Atlanta, but her roommate had put her down with the job when she first moved to town. She just needed something to pay the bills, but Lola always had dreams of bigger and better things. One night she was closing, and working the bar. Bruce had come in with a couple of his buddies, but had remained after his friends left. She noticed that he kept staring at her while she was working. She then put a little twist in her hips, and stuck out her chest. She noticed the Rolex watch he was wearing, the Armani suit and Ferragamo shoes. He had to be some kind of baller, sure enough when she switched passed him again, he spoke.

"Bedroom eyes, you working too hard. Why don't you sit your pretty self down here and let me buy you a drink." Lola flashed her golden smile.

"Man, I can't take a break now, my boss will kill me. We're short-staffed tonight, and I have to help close the kitchen."

"Girl, you too pretty to be working hard like that. A woman like you should have people waiting on her."

Lola liked that compliment. She fed off of attention. "Well a girls gotta make a livin', its not like I have someone taking care of me." She knew that would get his attention.

"I'll tell you what," Bruce responded. "Here's my business card. Why don't you give me a call tomorrow, and we'll discuss how a sexy sistah like you can make some real money."

Lola smiled and took the card. "Thank you. I'll give you a call." She read the business card that read BRUCE JACOBSON - SPORTS AGENT AND ATTORNEY AT LAW. " Jackpot" Lola thought to herself.

Lola smiled and walked away, shaking that ass like never before. Bruce was not really her type, but she knew he was the type of man that could help her out.

While Lola was checking herself out in the compact she caught some of the girls looking at her. She was used to that. Her looks tended to intimidate women all the time. She couldn't help it if she was drop-dead gorgeous. Just then she heard her name being called over the loud speaker, she was next.

"Lola you're up next". The girls were required to perform a sexy number in front of the clubs management and staff. If the management loved you, you were in. Bruce had told her all about what to expect during the audition. He said, "I got you in, but its up to you to sell your body. They will only hire you if you are a very good dancer, and exude lots of sex appeal." He told her she must always appear natural and as if she is enjoying herself. The clientele at *Pumps in the Bump* was exclusive and rich and they would not pay to see anyone fat, out of shape, or boring on the stage. Lola had practiced her sexy dance routine for hours in her living room. She looked so sexy in the mirror that she even got herself excited.

The reggae song by Shabba Ranks - "Punani" began booming from the system. She had chosen this song, because she knew none of the other girls would choose reggae music to dance to. Most of them danced to the country rap that was popular in that part of the country. And she was right. She noticed the crowd was a little surprised when they heard the song come on.

Lola proceeded onto the stage in a seductive saunter and made eye contact with every gentleman in the room. She then began her sexy wining dance with all her clothes on. Little by little she systematically took off her clothes to the music, while maintaining her sexy dance routine. No one would have ever known, that she had never done this before, because she was so confident. She actually fed off the crowd. When Lola saw the men salivating, it made her want to do more. Lola was very flexible from her years of gymnastics as a child, and that's what set her apart from the other girls. She ended her routine with a dramatic Russian split that brought all the men to their feet. She noticed the scowls on some of the other girl's faces, but that just made her smile more. Needless to say, she got the position and became the number one dancer at Pumps in the Bump.

Chapter 9   SOMETHING JUST AIN'T RIGHT

Back In The Day

Brittany stared at the trees as they rode down the Parkway. Simone was rambling on about how Toby was getting on her last nerve, and she was ready to kick him out. Carmen was carrying on a polite conversation with her, but Brit couldn't think about men and their bullshit at a time like this. Britt just couldn't shake the eerie feelings she was having right now towards Raysheeda. She kept replaying in her mind all the weird coincidences that had taken place over the past 24 hours, and how they just didn't sit right with her. How about the fact that Ra had asked her and Carmen – "Yall didn't get your purses?"   Bitch, we just told you these thugs had guns to our heads, why the hell would be so worried about something as petty as our pocketbooks, when they had just stolen a $20,000.00 dollar car from us at gunpoint. Then there was the weird scene with the 911 operator. How the hell could someone hang up on a 911 operator, when her friends had just been carjacked! Any fool knows that time is of the essence when recovering a stolen car. Then there was the fact that she had slammed the front door closed after she had just witnessed what happened first-hand. How weird was that! It was much faster to run up the front stairs, than to have to run to the back of the house and then up the stairs. Shouldn't she have been more concerned about their safety? And why weren't they allowed to park in the driveway? It was 4:00 in the morning. Brit knew Ra's aunt acted funny about people parking in her driveway, but this would have only been for a few hours, and they would have obviously moved the car when she needed to get out in the morning.

Somethin', somethin', just ain't right Brit thought. She would share her suspicions with Carmen later. She wanted to see how she felt about this whole shady situation. But Brittany definitely smelled a rat.

Chapter 10   LOADED GUN

Back In The Day

"Bullets or no bullets?" Loco asked in almost demonic fashion. He was gleaming at his sawed off shotgun like the proud father of a new baby boy.

"Bullets, what the fuck, yall motherfuckas better not load them guns!" Sheeda answered pissed off. "Yall some ignant thug niggas."

At this comment Born C jumped up and yelled with a real rah rah attitude, "What you say bitch?" Sheeda could feel her blood get instantly hot. She instinctively balled up her fist. Sheeda was no small girl and all the brothas from the way knew she would bitch a nigga up in a minute. But this was Born C and she knew better.

Born C stood for Born Crazy. He got that name at nine years old when he shot and killed his mothers no good drug dealin' boyfriend. He had come home from hangin at the basketball courts, and as usual his mother was getting beatin' and screamed on. This particular altercation stemmed from Born's mother stealing some drug money to help pay the rent.

As a rule Born and Petey (his mother's boyfriend) would stay out of each other's way. But on this day Born decided to give this nigga a gut check. "Yo Pete," Born yelled "Why don't your punk ass leave my moms alone." Petey stopped as if frozen and turned with a look of disbelief.

"What'd you say little nigga," Petey asked in a threatening way.

"You heard me mothafucka!" Born stood his ground.

At this point Petey cocked back and hit Born in the face as hard as he could. Born fell on the floor and blood rushed from his mouth and nose. Satisfied that he had taught Born a lesson – Petey turned his attention back to Born's mom and didn't even notice when Born left to get Petey's 9mm from the stash spot. When Petey turned and saw Born with the gun – he just smiled and said, "I know your little ass ain't that crazy."

It was then that Born blasted Petey with the final comment, "Mothafucka I was Born Crazy!"

This story was legendary and so was Born. Everyone from around the way knew not to fuck with Born. He would shoot a mothafucka cause he was in a bad mood. So Sheeda decided it was best to use her brain not brawn this time. Sheeda changed her tune to low and relaxed, "Chill Born. I'm just sayin' we got a bonafide plan. We're dealing with two harmless girls and a situation I will control."

"Oh, Are we?" Born said still obviously pissed. "Check this Sheeda your master plot sounds good but I been in the game long enough to know things don't always go as planned. So these are your girls right?"

"Right", Sheeda said proudly.

Born shook his head and said, "Damn you a scandalous Ho!"

"It's not even like that Born. This is just a car, and I know she has insurance. If they wasn't my girls I wouldn't give a fuck if you used bullets."

"Her shit is brand new right?" Baldy yelled from the couch.

It was Loco, Baldy, Born and Sheeda in her aunt's house.

"Nigga yes, I told you this shit 50 times, fuckin' ink ain't dry!"

Baldy twisted his mouth up a little annoyed, but he knew better then to fuck with Raysheeda. He wasn't Born and Sheeda's respect for Baldy and Loco was non-existent.

"If they was really your girls you should have a picture right?" Born asked

"I have lots of pictures," Sheeda beamed.

"Let me see one," Born demanded.

Raysheeda looked through her top drawer until she found a real cute one of her, Brit and Carmen. She was proud of her rich friends and wanted to pick a flattering photo.

These fools would never understand, but she loved her friends. She just couldn't have them bling blingin' while she was catchin' the bus. Sheeda had even convinced herself that this would bring them closer together. She would comfort them and cook them breakfast in the morning. They wouldn't be able to drive away and the three of them would spend the day together. The car would be gone but they would still have their pocketbooks. Raysheeda was very specific with her thug friends; they were to take only the car. Brittany and Carmen always had money and they would treat Sheeda to things she could never afford. Yes, even with the initial trauma, Sheeda was confident her girls would have a fun visit.

She handed Born the picture, she could tell by his expression he thought they were fly. As Sheeda watched him Born slowly began to smile and then started laughing out loud as hard as he could. After grabbing his gut and losing his breath he looked over at Loco and Baldy and said, "Y'all mothafuckas load them gats full and cock that shit."

"WHAT?" Sheeda yelled at Born mystified.

"WHAT Bitch WHAT? Them two harmless honeys are fine as hell, and you told me they're coming here after a party in the city."

"Yeah, so," Sheeda commented.

"So!" Born huffed "Every nigga with a dick from Manhattan to Brooklyn will be tryin' to push his way up in that brand new whip with the fly honeys. That's the jackpot! And if they decide to let one of these niggas ride, he might try and be Rambo out this bitch. And if he does I'm going to twist his cap back for him."

"But one of them could get hurt," Sheeda pleaded.

"Bitch please – you concentrate on trying to win the Academy Award for concerned friend and I'll deal with the real shit." Born warned "Now shut the fuck up and start dialin'!"

Chapter 11   SHE'S OUT

Back In The Day

Carmen, Renee and Simone were over Britt's house, crankin' up the blender. She had invited them over for drinks and movies. She had declined Renee's offer to go out for drinks. Since the whole car-jacking incident Carmen and Brit, hadn't felt much like hanging out on the town. They were both super paranoid and suspicious of EVERYONE. When they were in the car together lately the sight of headlights behind them made them jittery. Just the idea of going out at night made Brittany very nervous. She was fine in the daylight hours, but as soon as the sunset, she became ultra paranoid. She realized these thugs had her frickin' drivers license and knew where she lived. What was to stop them from coming and robbing her home? They would be some bold MF's if they did but she didn't even want to think about that possibility right now. The thought sickened her. Once again she was in the middle of some real live gangsta shit. Her father was always preachin' to her that if she stopped hanging with "sewer rats" these things wouldn't happen to her. At first she was offended by his comments, but now she was beginning to understand how hanging with the wrong people could really affect your life in a bad way. She just wondered how she would cut ties with the latest wanna be gangsta without a lot of drama.

"Hey Carm, do you find anything fishy about us getting jacked so smooth like that?" They all turned in astonishment to look at Brit.

"I'm serious yall, I smell a rat. That shit just went down too smooth. I feel like they knew we were going to be coming home at 4:20 am, and they were so sure we were women, who were defenseless. I have been replaying this shit over and over in my mind and I can't remember seeing someone tailing us when we got off the Parkway. I feel like that car pulled up behind us, after we turned the corner to Raysheeda's house."

"You don't think ...." Simone started

"You damn right I think that Bitch had something to do with this Simone! Think about it, all her broke ass ever talked about was - Oh I'm

48

going to get my jeep, my Landcruiser, BLAH, BLAH, BLAH!! How the hell was she going to do all that being a dishwasher at a take out barbeque! You tell me," Brit yelled.

"You know I have been thinking the same thing, but I just hadn't said anything. You weren't there Sim so you don't get the same vibe we do. Something is shady", Carmen agreed.

"Are you serious!" Renee interjected. "If you really feel this way, someone give a recap for the sisters who weren't there." At this point anxious to get her suspicious off her mind. Brittany proceeded to tell Renee and Simone all the details of the terrifying experience. When she finished they were both speechless.

"Well what do you think? I am paranoid or do things not add up?" Brittany asked with anticipation. Renee was rubbing her chin and staring directly at the floor.

"What's on your mind Rae?" Carmen asked.

"I'm telling yall now I'm ready to go psycho on that bitch. She set my girls up, after all we did for that broke ho. Brit you know we really looked out for her in school and this is the thanks you get!"

"Straight up, that story I just heard was not about Raysheeda. Sheeda the hardest girl from the hood is so frightened she slams the front door shut. The Raysheeda I know would have been yelling curses and threats about how there's nowhere they could hide your car up in her neighborhood. She slams down the phone on the 911 operator and matter of factly says "why didn't yall get your purses." Yeah right. Lest I remind you Brit this is the same bitch that was so pissed when they stole my rims at Jersey U she was ready to shank mothafuckas. Let's be honest we always knew she was shady. She was clepto like a mug in school. But I guess I always thought we were FAM and her dirt was for strangers. Straight up this is some next level shit. She must really think people are stupid." Renee was furious.

"Calm down Rae" Simone pleaded. "I didn't know her from school like yall but this seems impossible. Friends just don't do this. Carmen you haven't said much what's up?"

Carmen looked Simone dead in the eyes and said, "Sim that Bitch set us up!" That was enough for Simone – Simone felt a special bond with Carmen and always trusted her instincts.

"Damn" so what now?

"What Now, What Now, I want my ride back and the way I feel right now I could slam Sheeda's face into a brick wall." Brittany was on the edge of tears. And Renee's blood was on fire. Rae and Brit were like sisters and she knew how much Brittany loved that car. It had symbolized two things, how hard she studied in high school to graduate at the top of the class and more importantly how proud her parents were of her achievement.

Out of the four Renee was always the most ready for action and vengeance. She was raised in a family where an eye for an eye was preached often. It was a joke amongst the crew that her father was "Shaft". Rae's parents had moved out of the hood so she and her brother could go to better schools and have a chance at success. Renee had gone to college and made good on all her parents hopes for her, but she still had family members that stayed in the ghetto and would probably never leave. From a young age Rae's father, Stan taught her to shoot a gun, never take no shit, only respect those who respect you, protect your family and above all loyalty. Renee's father never hesitated to tell her if anyone ever did anything to his baby girl while he was alive they would die at his hands. To Rae, her girls were family and this was a violation.

She thought back to when her brother's friend had stolen a car from her family. She was only 10 but she remembered her father bringing her along to see how he dealt with the matter. Rae was amazed; he went to the house of this kid and pulled him out right in front of his mother and father. He was a white boy and Rae guessed they wanted no part of her hardcore black father. Within two hours Stan found the car and had given "The bitch ass" white boy an ultimatum. Stan put his 44 magnum to the boy's gut and told him he could confess to the cops and deal with their justice or lie and deal with his. The next day the police called to say a young man had confessed to stealing the car. When they asked Rae's father if he wanted to press charges he declined. Renee was confused and asked her father why he didn't press charges? Stan explained that cops were ignorant, corrupt egomaniacs and in his lifetime he would never do anything to help them. Besides he added he wanted the terrified white boy to let all his little hoodlum friends know that their house wasn't the place to fuck around. They were never robbed again and Rae learned how her family dealt with disrespect.

"This bitch needs to pay!" Renee yelled, "Fuckin guns to your head this ain't no let it slide shit. That crazy bitch must think she's the only one that knows niggas with guns."

"Chill," Simone countered, "This ain't your call Rae. Brit and Carmen need to tell us what they want to do." It was hard but Renee decided to bite her tongue and listen to Brittany and Carmen.

Brit couldn't believe it - but hearing Renee go off actually made her feel better. She knew Rae had her back and it made Brit feel more powerful. Brittany wondered for a minute if Sheeda would have done this if Rae were there, when they were on the phone, Raysheeda kept asking if it were just her and Carmen. As angry as she had been Brittany was still the most level headed of the crew and decided to calm the situation down. Unlike Renee, Brittany was raised more religious and knew she would have to step back and pray about the whole thing.

"Check it yall," Brittany started slow and steady, "I am majorly pissed off but I don't want us to do something we will regret later. I appreciate your concern Rae but I am not sure if we should sink to this bitch's level. Do you think her simple ass would have done this if she'd grown up like we did? She's always been jealous and now she's gone over the edge." Renee knew Brittany was making sense but she still wanted to avenge her friend.

Carmen chimed in to let everyone know after staring down the barrel of a gun if she never saw one again it would be too soon.

"I hear you girl, "Brittany agreed. "You know what" Brittany concluded, "The more I think about it, if she's that off the chain now let's just let the streets take care of her ass. But from now on she gets nothing and I mean NOTHING from the Bonafide Homegirls."

Bonafide Homegirls had been their mantra for years. They all knew what Brittany meant. Raysheeda could be starving on the street and no matter how much she begged, she would never get the help they had generously offered as friends – Sheeda was out for life. Renee thought Sheeda's offense should have been met with stiffer punishment but she

had to respect her friend's choice. Still Rae made a promise to herself –
she would keep tabs on this scandalous bitch and if the opportunity arose
Sheeda would regret turning her good friends into bitter enemies.

Chapter 12   THE ART OF DECEPTION

Present Day

Renee

"Ah heaven", Renee thought as she lay back in the bubble filled piping hot bath. Sade's mellow voice sang to her soul as Renee closed her eyes and pretended she was on the most gorgeous beach in the world. Her partner of choice in this daydream was Kyle. This was a first, Renee usually dreamt of someone unattainable like Denzel or Morris Chestnut. But not this time, the prospect of Kyle, the beach and time off was sublime. Renee opened her eyes long enough to find her glass of wine sitting neatly on the bathroom floor, she sipped and smiled as Sade sang. The song was about love sneaking up like a silent but deadly weapon. That's how she felt about Kyle's love. She was going about her life trying to have as much fun as possible and protect her heart; then Kyle came along and broke down her barriers. Kyle was not perfect, but in so many ways he was perfect for Renee. Still the combination of a James Bond spirit and an overprotective friend was causing Renee to do something that in her heart she knew was wrong. But as long as all went smoothly no one would get hurt and Renee's peace of mind would be helped. She glimpsed at the clock and sighed in disappointment as she realized it was time to leave her comfortable bath and get dressed for her covert meeting…

"Brown skinned, tall and cute with a charming smile", this was how Brit had described Sean. Renee giggled to herself as she thought about Brittany's description. It sounded more like the dating game than anything. Frankly Renee thought, *"I would prefer he was a pudgy white guy"* that way she could keep her mind on the task at hand.

The coffee shop they were meeting at was full of yuppies so Renee felt confident Sean would be easy to spot. The girl at the counter was sassy, young and bordering on hoochie. She had too much make up, too much jewelry and too much attitude. Renee thought to herself class and sophistication is becoming a lost art. "Can I help you"? The girl asked as if she were annoyed and unhappy to be there.

"Yes, could I please have a tall frappacino", Renee responded. All of a sudden the girl began to smile and Renee was about to engage her in conversation until she realized it wasn't her the girl was smiling at. Renee turned around and behind her stood the most beautifully tall and delicious man she had ever seen. No wonder Miss attitude behind the counter was turning on the charm.

Before she could speak, the tall stranger said, "Renee"? Like a question.

Renee responded, "Sean". The word had barely slipped through her lips when a big boyish grin crept across his face. Then he began to look Renee up and down to let her know he liked what he saw.

"Why don't you grab a table and I'll take care of this." Renee liked him instantly not only was he gorgeous but he talked like a man. There was one word in the back of her mind TROUBLE. She picked a quiet table in the back, and justified this by telling herself she didn't want anyone that her and Kyle knew to see them.

Before she could gather her thoughts Sean was at the table with two drinks. "So you're Renee. Brittany has been telling me about you for almost a year now. "I've been wanting to meet you but you're a busy woman."

Renee smiled, "I've heard a lot about you too" – Sean gave her a curious look.

She answered his look with – "Don't worry all good."

"If it was so good, how come we haven't met until now?" She pondered his question for a moment and finally commented, "Bad timing." It seemed as if Sean could sense Renee was a bit uncomfortable so he got down to the business at hand. Well, maybe at some point time will be on my side. "Anyway tell me about Mr. Wonderful." Renee didn't appreciate the sarcasm in Sean's voice and decided it was important he understood her intentions.

"Listen Sean, I don't know what Brittany has told you, but I really care about this guy and he hasn't done anything to me. I'm not a suspicious wife or a vindictive lover. I'm just being cautious. This whole thing was more Brit's idea than mine, I really"….."

"Hey, Hey Sean interrupted calm down I was just kidding, I am completely aware of the situation. I know you're just being careful. It's understandable; things are crazy out there nowadays. Let me go over how things work. I've brought some paperwork." At this point Sean opened a black briefcase that had been closed on his lap. He pulled out four sheets of paper and began to explain them to Renee. "This first sheet is simply a brief description of Kyle, right that's his name?"

"Yes" Renee answered almost ashamed.

"Well, I will need his first and last name, his approximate height and weight, where he lives etc". This next sheet is where you lay out his schedule. It doesn't have to be exact, it can be loose -like where and when he goes to work, does he go somewhere to workout regularly etc." The next sheet is his background - anything he has told you like how many brothers and sisters he has, where his father and mother live, friends etc. This last sheet is info about his past relationships- names and places, if he's told you about them."

"WOW" Renee was speechless. "This is way more involved than I thought, honestly, Sean, I'm kinda feeling a little sleazy doing this."

"Well let's talk about that. Are you scared of what you might find out?"

"No, believe it or not that's not what's bothering me, I've always been able to handle the truth. I guess I feel like I'm betraying him."

"In what way" Sean asked.

"Having someone check into his past is like a complete lack of trust."

"That's one way to look at, but you could also say that doing this now will make you trust him that much more later. That is if he IS trustworthy, and believe me if he's not I will definitely find out. Brittany is a good friend of mine and I won't let her best friend be taken advantage of."

"You seem to be sure you will find some dirt."

"No I'm just saying an attractive, intelligent woman like you could have lots of men. I wouldn't want to see you settle for someone dishonest. I know Brittany feels the same way. That's why she suggested you use my services."

"OK" Renee said, "but I want to make sure that no one sets him up, I just want him checked out."

"No problem" Sean answered, "I will simply observe and report."

It took Renee about 45 minutes to finish filling out the paperwork, and the whole time there was subtle flirtation between her and Sean. As she got up to leave, Sean stood up and Renee extended her hand. Sean took it but then pulled her in for a hug. She didn't want to admit it but his embrace felt nice. As she walked away from Sean, Renee closed her eyes and hoped he would not find anything on Kyle. At the same time Sean closed his eyes and hoped he did.

Sean

Sean sat at the table of the coffee shop with a satisfied smile on his face. He looked at his watch. Twenty minutes had elapsed since Renee left. Sean looked up just in time to see the final piece to his plan walking toward him.

"Dwight, what's up?" Sean stood up and slapped his friend's hand, pulled him in for a half hug and pounded him on the back.

"Did I wait long enough man"? Dwight asked a bit nervous.

"Perfect - 20 minutes just like we said, you watched her drive off right?" Sean questioned

"Of course! You know I'm a pro," Dwight beamed.

"Cool, Cool." Sean seemed to relax. "Let me see it." Dwight pulled out his high-tech digital camera and showed Sean the picture. He watched Sean's face for signs of satisfaction. Dwight was a bit scared of Sean and was worried about disappointing him. To the outside world, Sean seemed like the greatest guy on the planet, but Dwight knew better. He saw the corners of Sean's mouth begin to curve upward and sighed in relief.

"Yeah, yeah that's the shit right there." Sean said with satisfaction. "She's wrapped in my arms like she's been my lady for years. Check it man, this picture of her is only for insurance. So you have some time to work on it. What could you do to make a nigga really flip when he sees it?"

56

"I already got you covered. I figured you might want to add a little drama." Dwight continued, "you see your right hand that's at the small of her back, well I have this phat editing package and with a little work, that hand could be on her ass!"

"Sold"! Sean laughed.

"Go back to your lab, put my hand on her ass and deliver it to me in 3 days, and you got 3 bills."

"No problem", Dwight promised as he made his exit.

Sean decided to stay and plot a bit longer. He thought about his friend Brittany for a moment. He wished he could share this with her, but she would never understand. In fact, she would probably want to kill him if she knew, which was funny because unknowingly she had started all of this. For months Sean had listened to Brittany talk about her best friend Renee. Renee sounded interesting to Sean and one day when he had some free time he decided to put a face with a name, and that's how it all began. Whenever he had some free time he would check up on Renee. Sean knew he was no stalker. He looked at it as doing Brit a favor. He was looking out for her best friend. But as the weeks passed it grew into more for Sean, until one day he realized he was watching his wife. Renee just didn't know it yet. He had already bought the ring that would one day be worn proudly on her finger. In Sean's mind everything had been going fine. He knew everything about Renee - down to her favorite restaurant and perfume. Soon Brittany would introduce them and they would live happily ever after. Then this Kyle mothafucka came along and threw a monkey wrench in his plans. If Kyle were just another guy everything would have been fine, but Kyle was crazy about Renee and he treated her better than the typical brother, else Renee would have dumped his ass long ago. She had self-respect - Sean loved that. So Sean figured he had a choice. Let the woman he had grown to love go, or devise a plan. Sean chose the latter.

At the beginning of his plan he was casual and it cost him. Sean had calculated when Kyle and Renee might begin to get sexual. He had delayed Kyle that night by letting the air out of one of his tires. But it wasn't enough. Sean never blamed Renee for this. He blamed himself and swore he would be meticulous from now on. He even set things up so Brittany would think it was her idea to get Kyle checked out. Every time Brit would talk about Kyle and Renee. Sean would make comments like: "If it looks too good to be true." "Why wonder when you can always find out."

Sean was careful to never actually come out and offer, until one day Brittany says, "I think I should talk to Renee about having this guy checked out," to which Sean calmly replied, "Smart move." But inside he was celebrating. Obviously he had already checked Kyle out and to his displeasure there was nothing to find. Lucky for Sean he was the only one with this information. But more importantly he now had free reign to manipulate the situation. Sean figured he had 3 things in his favor: time, technology and Brittany's friendship. Sean knew Brittany and Renee were like sisters and if Brit thought he was trustworthy it would go a long way with Renee. So Sean would take a slow and methodical approach in triggering the demise of Renee and Kyle's relationship.

Chapter 13   DRAFT NIGHT

Back In The Day

The big night had finally arrived. Tyson's family gathered in the players lounge in Madison Square Garden. Everyone was so excited. His mother Francine was there and his four sisters- Donna, Jeanine, Chanel, and Neece, along with Brittany, Millie, Lamont and Renee. This was the night they had all been waiting for.

Tyson was excited and nervous. The whole thing seemed like a fantasy that someone was about to wake him up from. He had worked his entire life for this moment and now his biggest dream in life was becoming a reality. He was about to be drafted into the NBA!! Only the greatest players in the world made it into the NBA and he was one of them.

Brittany and Tyson had spent the past several weeks looking for the perfect suit for this night. They had just picked it up from the tailor this morning. Tyson settled on a charcoal grey Armani suit. Brittany had picked out a bad Versace dress that was conservative yet celebratory, and she wore some Manolo Blanik sling backs.

"My baby's lookin like a real stud tonight. Do your stud walk for me boo." Tyson walked by like a model and stopped to put his hand under his chin, like he was on stage.

"Ahh shucks", Brit responded.

Renee came over, "Awwww…. Yall stand together so I can take a picture of the two of you. This is definitely one for the photo album." Brit and Ty kissed as the camera flashed.

"Come on yall," Ms. Myers said, "lets get together for a family prayer. This is my baby's big night and we need God's blessings."

Everyone said "Amen" after Ms. Myers finished praying then they turned their attention to Jim Stern, the NBA commissioner, as he began the draft selection. Tyson held Brittany's hand really tight as he looked on stage.

"It's you baby, it's you." Brit said, as she squeezed his hand tighter.

Tyson looked at her with nervous eyes then looked down on the floor. His heart was beating 100 mile per hour.

"And for the #1 draft pick in the 2004 NBA draft......................

....

The New Jersey Slammers select...

....

Tyson Myers from Jersey State University!

The room erupted into cheer and applause. It all felt so surreal to Brittany. She knew it would happen one day, but she never knew it would feel like this, with the whole world watching. Tyson hugged and kissed his Mom and sisters, then he gave Brittany the biggest kiss before he lifted her in the air and swung her around. He then proceeded to go up to the podium to get his NJ Slammers cap and shake the commissioner's hand.

Everyone in the crowd was congratulating him and giving him pounds on the way up. Tyson couldn't believe this was real – he was the number one draft pick in the country!! He tried to pull his cap over his eyes to conceal the tears of joy that had formed after he heard his name called. Tyson couldn't remember the last time he cried. When Tyson got back to the table where his family was, his mother greeted him with wide-open arms and tears in her eyes. "My baby did it, you did it against all odds Tyson. I am so proud of you." They hugged for several minutes sharing a moment where no words were needed.

Renee and Brittany hugged, and then they all had a group hug. Everyone had tears in their eyes. This was the beginning of a new life for all of them. Finally their dreams were becoming a reality – and life as they knew it would never be the same.

Present Day

Tyson walked out of the gym carrying about 5 of his teammates' gym bags to the bus as he reminisced about that night. He was at his first training camp with the Slammers and he was exhausted. Rookies were treated like gophers their entire first year and the guys had started on him from the first day of training camp. They told him – don't take it personal Rookie – it's a rite of passage. Tyson had to suck it up. After he took the gym bags to the bus he had to pick up Chinese food for all his teammates for dinner and bring it back to the hotel. He knew this was just the beginning, but he definitely felt blessed to be so rich now, and able to take care of his family and give them what they never had.

"Yo rookie – make sure that food is hot when you bring it back." Michael Greene the veteran on the team yelled after him as he dragged the heavy bags to the bus. Some of his other teammates laughed at him.

Tyson just shook his head – this definitely felt real now.

Chapter 14   DEATH CERTIFICATE

Back In The Day

Renee could feel the wind on her shoulders and the sun on her face. She loved when the weather was perfect - like a friend you knew would make you laugh and enjoy life. Nothing could compare to a pleasant day. If Renee could choose, she'd spend the day at the beach. She would get a big blanket, some wine, make some sandwiches, and invite Brittany, Carmen and Simone to enjoy the sun and waves. But this was all just a fantasy - in reality Renee was on her way to the Jones annual family reunion or what Renee and her cousins liked to call the Jones Jump off. At the beginning of each summer, Memorial Day weekend, the Jones family would show the world you don't need money to know how to party. Renee was not exactly excited about this shindig. This event, though joyous, reminded her of hard times. But throughout the years whenever Renee tried to talk her way out of going, her mother or father would call and threaten -"Don't forget where you come from. This event and these people are your family." In her heart Renee knew they were right, so she always went.

The only problem this year was that usually Brittany went with her, and they would crack jokes on her crazy aunts and uncles, and the whole thing would be great. Renee loved that Brittany never judged her ghetto family, and they all loved Brittany like she was part of the clan. But this year Brittany was fresh off a car jacking, and in no mood for any type of ghetto interaction. She could have asked Simone but Simone was way too judgmental for Renee's taste. She would have spent the whole day scared to sit on the dirty chairs --making comments like, 'I can't believe you're related to these people'. Of course Simone herself lived in the hood, but she considered herself ghetto fabulous and relished the opportunity to feel like she was better than someone. Renee had wanted to invite Carmen but she had burnt one of Renee's cousins for $300 and he was still pissed about it. Renee had tried to warn him that Carmen liked his wallet better than him but he wouldn't listen, and Renee needed to give the situation the proper healing time before bringing Carmen back around.

So Renee would go it alone. She'd meet her parents there and try and catch up with some of her wild cousins. As Renee exited the Parkway and headed toward Newark she locked the doors and began to scan her surroundings. She hadn't lost the survival instincts instilled in her by the streets. Red light - don't get too close to the car in front of you. People start Rollin up on you too fast; fuck it - run the light. That's what her father had taught her. If need be take the ticket but save your life. She looked at the vacant lots and burnt down buildings and actually began to giggle, not because it wasn't sad, but she knew if Brittany were there she would be singing the theme from the old TV show Good Times.

When she pulled into GranGran's driveway the party was in full effect. GranGran was Renee's grandmother - heck it seemed like GranGran was everyone's grandmother. Renee was crazy about her Gran and it went both ways. GranGran was so proud of her grandbaby the college girl. She would tell anybody that would listen; my baby got herself an education. To Gran, an uneducated, but very loving woman, Renee might as well have been president. That's why no matter how late Renee showed up there was always a space for her in the driveway. Renee could smell the food and liquor, and passed some relatives that were already drunk on her way to greet Gran. She walked in the kitchen and Gran was sitting down looking tired and annoyed.

As soon as she saw Renee her face brightened up, "My baby come give GranGran a hug."

"Hey Gran, it so good to see you. You look as feisty as ever."

"Chile these boys done got me upset up in here, you know that crazy cousin of yours Reggie, well he's drunk or high or whatever these kids do nowadays. Anyway he had the nerve to try and park some stolen car with the wires still hangin out the dashboard in your spot. I was outside so I told him to take that car out a here, but he had his friends in the car so he ignored me tryin to be cute. His friends were already out the car fixin plates. I had to come inside and get your father. When Stan went out they practically broke they necks jumpin back in that car to drive away. They probably didn't know he was here cause him and your mom got a nice new car that no one recognizes."

"I know Gran it's real nice, it's a Toyota Camry with leather interior. Mom finally talked dad into buying it."

"They should have got a nice big Cadillac or Lincoln, something comfortable for me to ride in."

"Don't worry Gran it's comfortable, you'll like it after you take a ride." Renee promised.

"Where's my other granddaughter at?" Gran was trying to look around Renee to find Brittany.

But before she could finish Renee spoke up "Gran Brittany's not with me today."

"But she always comes."

"I know but Brittany had some bad luck. She and Carmen were car jacked about a month ago. It was only a few streets from here so she felt kind of funny coming back to the area so soon."

"Chile no", GranGran clutched her chest, "Is she alright? They didn't hurt her none did they?"

"No Gran she's alright."

"Well if it was just a couple streets from here you better go outside and ask some of your fake gangsta cousins bout it. I hate to say it but you know they probably got some type of idea what happened."

"OK Gran, I'll make sure I come back in and talk to you before I leave." Renee went outside and was again brushed by the friendly air. She went to the table and started fixing herself a plate but before she could finish; someone bumped into her hard and took her plate. She was about to yell when she turned to see her brother Jacob. He was cracking up like he had pulled the best prank ever.

"Damn it J, you had me ready to stomp someone."

"Yeah, come on show me what you got," J was poking Renee in the sides they way he used to when they were little. "Come on tuff girl show me your skills."

"Leave me alone J I'm not in the mood for your foolishness." Renee said annoyed.

"I don't know little sister all that education's making you soft." The smell of liquor on J's breath was strong.

Renee waved her hand over her nose. "J what time did you start drinking?"

Jacob laughed at the question. "Officer I plead the fifth - or is it I drank a fifth. I know there's a fifth in there somewhere" Jacob was cracking himself up.

Renee was unimpressed, "Anyway give me back my plate".

"Nope this plate is payment."

"Payment for what?" Renee huffed.

Jacob started slow like he was trying hard to be coherent "Well in the middle of my sinful drinking I was doing some investigating about what the hell happened to my other little sis". Jacob was referring to Brittany, Renee had told him about the jacking right after it happened. "Apparently you haven't told any of our shady cousins your suspicions or conclusions about your homeboy Raysheeda." J was trying to be funny. He always thought Raysheeda dressed and acted like a dude. "Anyway Craig, excuse me Cmoney has a current business relationship with your girl."

"What!" Renee was fuming. "No one in this family helps that bitch, you hear me," Renee was almost shouting.

"Hey Hey" J whispered, "Don't tell me - go talk to your cousin, he'll give you the low down."

Renee went over to talk to Cmoney and J yelled, "Thanks for the plate."

"Hey C," Renee greeted.

"Well if it's not my beautiful cousin, how you doin?"

"I'm OK C, how are you?"

"You know doin' what a brother needs to do to be a man."

Renee smiled "I here you, but listen C I need you to tell me what's up with you and Raysheeda."

"Yeah your girl right."

"Wrong! She did some foul shit."

"What?" Cmoney looked genuinely surprised. "What did she do?"

"I'll tell you in a minute, but first tell me what kind of business you two have together."

"OK cuz - I'm a break it down for you, but before I start I don't need none of your judgmental shit. We ain't all got college diploma's up in this piece."

"C straight up - I know shit's a struggle, I'm not even coming at you like that right now." Renee could jump in and out of street slang with the ease of a magician making a card disappear, besides the way she felt right now she was more street than suburbs.

"Cool, Cool yeah well about three weeks ago this bitch comes up to me. You know every one out here on the block knows I'm the one making shit move. Anyway she tells me she's looking to make some paper and she heard I need someone to take that risk - you know the short haul runner across NJ/NY lines. Don't no one want that job cause it's mad risk, all that quantity in one car, we're talking a major bid, and to find a girl willing, that's all good, you know Five 0 don't sweat no girl like they sweatin the niggas. Anyway you know me, I'm mad cautious so I'm still not sure, but then she reminds me she's your homegirl from school, so I don't have to worry that she's some undercover or something and that sealed it. She's been runnin for me for three weeks."

Renee could almost feel smoke coming out of her ears. "C why didn't you call me to check? She could have been a Narco, one of my old friends is a cop now, you never know."

"I know cuz. I was planning on calling but time can get away from a brother."

"Well if you get locked up time will really have meaning then."

"Damn Renee! Why you gotta be like that."

"I'm sorry C I'm just pissed. OK check it, she cannot be trusted. You know me and Brit practically gave her the shirts off our backs in college, well anyway...." Renee proceeded to tell Cmoney the whole sordid story. When she was done everything was clear to him.

"So when we gonna roll on this bitch?" C Money questioned.

"No we can't" Renee responded.

"Can't, what do you mean can't??? Cuz you getting soft."

Renee kinda laughed. "Yeah J said the same thing earlier. Believe me C - I wanted to - Brittany's like my sister, but she didn't want it and I wasn't there when it happened, so it was her call."

"So what do you want me to do?" C asked

"I just want you to fire her or whatever you call it in your business. I don't want her to make money off anyone in this family."

66

"You know anything for you cuz." Cmoney was extremely loyal to Renee. When he got arrested one time Renee was the only one that would bail him out. His girl at the time and his number two man both had money he had given them for this reason, and neither came through. They had each spent it on something else. After Renee bailed Cmoney out, his number two man ended up dead. Somehow no one knows the details, and his girl went from glamour girl to crack ho and everyone on the streets knew not to fuck with Cmoney. And now Renee was telling him Raysheeda was shady and she wanted him to fire her. He told Renee what she wanted to hear. He would fire Raysheeda. But C Money knew in his world it wasn't that simple, the streets aren't Madison Avenue, and Raysheeda knew too much about Cmoney's business for him to say you're fired, have a nice day. But C would not let his cousin down. Renee didn't know it but she had just signed Raysheeda's death certificate.

Chapter 15 FUN IN THE SUN

Present Day

Tyson called Brittany early in the morning Saturday to make sure she would be awake when the limousine got there to pick them up.

"Baby you up, the stretch is going to be there within the hour. They will pick you up, and then come get me. I don't want us to miss the plane because you know when we arrive in Miami there will be another stretch waiting for us."

"Yes baby I set my alarm clock, I am about to get in the shower now and my bags are waiting by the door."

"Ok Boo – I'll see you in a little bit."

"K- bye."

Brittany rolled over and looked at the ceiling. Wow, Tyson is really in the big league now she thought to herself. Just yesterday we were counting quarters in college trying to buy something from the dollar menu, now we have stretch limos coming to pick us up from the airport. This is just the beginning. Brittany thought about how Tyson entered the draft after his junior year in college. He had contemplated entering after his sophomore year, but his Coach and Brit convinced him that he should spend one more year developing his game. He was reluctant with all the pressure from his family and friends to enter early, but he knew she had his best interest at heart. A lot of guys, who were superstars in college, entered the draft and never saw playing time in the NBA, and eventually wound up back in the CBA. Tyson did not want to be one of those guys, especially since he wasn't extremely big. He was only 6'3, which was like minimum height in the NBA.

Now they were headed down to Miami to meet with some advertising execs from Nike, who wanted to shoot a promo with the new poster boy of the NBA. Ever since draft night, when Tyson was drafted number one with the New Jersey Slammers their lives had been one big whirlwind. It seemed that every time she was out with Tyson their picture was being snapped and people were *always* seeking her man's autograph. Before it was just the avid basketball fan that knew Tyson

Myers, now it had spread, and the endorsement deals just kept pouring in. Brit told Tyson that once she graduated from law school, she would love to be his agent, and would work with one of his sisters to be his manager. He had smiled, and told her they would be the only people he'd trust. Brittany secretly wondered how much the fame would change Tyson.

Ty had insisted that she come because he said he could not make any decisions without her. Brittany was about to enter law school, so she really had to focus on maintaining her G.P.A this semester. Tyson convinced her it would be a good time to take a vacation before her schoolwork got really heavy and she got bogged down with her studies. Brittany agreed and was looking forward to spending time in South Beach.

"Once the pilot takes off the fasten seat belt sign, you will be free to move about the cabin."

"Good because I'm ready to get up," Brittany said.

Tyson was still snoring when the flight attendant spoke.

"Ty baby wake up, we're in Miami." He rubbed his eyes and looked up.

"Oh, we need to get on our connecting flight."

"What are you talking about Boo?"

"Our connecting flight to the Bahamas."

"The Bahamas!!!!!!" Brittany screamed out in shock, causing a few of the passengers to look at her. She shook Tyson, "you didn't tell me we were going to the Bahamas. What about Nike? They will be expecting you at the airport."

"Yeah on Tuesday when we come back from the Bahamas." Brittany had never looked at the tickets because the company had paid them for and Tyson handled all of the arrangements.

"What!!!! How did you sneak that by me?"

"It's called a surprise Brit. I know you've never been to the Caribbean before. I figured this would be a good time for us to spend time alone before things start getting crazy."

"But wait, I don't have my passport."

"Don't worry your pretty self about that. Millie had me covered," he said with a smile, as he pulled out her passport.

She just looked at him smiling. "I love you Tyson!" she said as she gave him a big hug and wet kiss on the lips.

"I love you too Boo."

Once they arrived in Paradise Island, Bahamas Brittany thought she was in paradise. It was so beautiful! Nothing in Brooklyn could compare to the beauty before her eyes. The crystal blue water and the white sand were enough to make her think she had died and gone to heaven.

"I need my camcorder babe. This is beautiful."

"I got you covered." Tyson pulled a small camcorder out of his carry on bag and handed it to Britt.

Brit looked at him and smiled, "you always think of everything". Brittany kissed him on the cheek and held his hand as they rode to the hotel in the taxi. Once they got to the hotel Brit was in for another surprise. They were staying at the famous *Atlantis* hotel.

Tyson commented, "I'm taking you to the telly where all the ballers ball and the playas play. They got everything you want up in here. This is a five star hotel."

"Oh yeah."

Brittany felt like someone needed to pinch her quick because this felt like a dream. Everything was so extravagant in this hotel. The bellhop interrupted her thoughts telling her, "I'll take your bags up Mam." They got on the private elevator together, and Tyson told the bellhop, "Penthouse please."

Brittany looked wide-eyed at Tyson, "mmmmmmmmmmmm Penthouse."

Chapter 16   ANIMAL ATTRACTION

Present Day

Renee walked into the elevator and relaxed. All day long she was in charge of an 8-person sales team that had to overachieve for Renee to stay comfortable in her position at Q & A advertising. She was the only black Area Coordinator in the whole company, and she knew the only reason they gave her the title and position was the company's greed. Renee was a cash cow for them. She was hard working, diligent and had an uncanny knack for reading people, which allowed her to keep clients and superiors happy.

But lately Renee was unfocused at work. Her mind was preoccupied with thoughts of Kyle. She would think about what sexy outfit she was going to put on that weekend and how Kyle would touch her, or what he would whisper in her ear as they caressed each other. Renee closed her eyes for a moment as she allowed her thoughts to take over. She could feel her breathing get a bit heavier and there was actually a gnawing pain in her stomach.

Renee snapped back into reality when she heard someone say louder "Renee do you hear me?" She opened her eyes and realized it was someone from her sales team, her top producer as it happened. "Are you going home or are you going to ride back up with me?"

"Very funny John", Renee replied.

"You know I'm just playing with you," he said. "It's already late and you seem tired, so go home. I promise I'll go back up and work hard enough for both of us."

"That's a deal," Renee said smiling. "But don't burn yourself out - you know you're invaluable to me."

"Yeah tell me anything," John said as the elevator door closed.

Renee took a deep breath and told herself to keep it together. She could not believe she was actually having some type of wet dream in the elevator at work. Renee had never felt this way before in her life. She actually craved this man. It was Tuesday and it would take all her self-control not to drive to Kyle's place and attack him. But she had

71

promised herself she would make Kyle pursue her. She definitely did not want him to know she was trippin like this over him.

Renee found her keys and began walking toward the parking deck, with a cold shower on her mind – she preferred to drive into the city when she worked late. As she got closer and closer she realized there were flowers on the windshield.

She picked them up and put them to her nose, and a voice behind her said, "You like them?" She turned and it was Kyle standing there with a big smile, looking like the sexiest creature on earth.

"They're gorgeous! You remembered pink roses are my favorite." Renee exclaimed. She went over to give him a hug and he put his hands up. "What's wrong?" she asked.

"Nothing really but I've been waiting here to surprise you for over an hour. I know you said you work late sometimes but seven o'clock, there's no little office romance going on with someone is there?" Kyle asked sort of sheepishly.

Renee smiled and touched his face, "The only thing I've been thinking about all day is you."

Kyle grinned and rubbed his nose playfully against hers. "Good" he said, "because we haven't talked about this yet but I consider you to be my woman." He lifted Renee's chin and looked directly in her eyes "Exclusively my woman."

Renee stared back and said, "I am."

With that, Kyle kissed her hard, his tongue darted in her mouth and mixed with hers in perfect motion, they both could feel themselves losing control, finally Renee pushed him away. She looked in his eyes and they were hungry and wanting. She whispered in his ear, "Baby I want you too but I can't have sex up against my car in the parking lot of work."

Kyle kind of chuckled but still seemed focused on what his body needed. "Forget that car," he picked her up in his arms and twirled her around to his truck. He opened the door and placed her in the passenger seat. Before he closed the door he kissed her neck and bit her nipple through her blouse.

As he started to drive, Renee slid over kissed his neck and worked her hand up his leg until she reached his manhood, which was throbbing in need. She massaged him and kissed his neck until Kyle couldn't take it anymore. He pulled over onto a side street and in one motion yanked himself and Renee into the back seat. They grabbed at each other desperately; no piece of clothing could come off fast enough. Kyle pulled Renee's skirt up and pushed her panties and stockings down. When he put his hand between her legs and found that she was wet it nearly drove him crazy. She was tugging at his jeans and his hand ripped her blouse off. He was hungrily licking and sucking her breast and nipples. Kyle finally took a hand away from Renee long enough to pull his pants down.

"Wait," Renee grabbed his chest, "Protection." Kyle pulled a condom out of his pocket and put it on at the speed of light. Then at once he was inside her pumping and grunting as she panted, "Oh yeah's" in his ear and clawed at his back.

It was so good Renee felt like she was going to faint, her whole body was on fire. They began rocking in a perfect motion, their muscles tensed and their bodies finally exploded together. As they both relaxed Kyle fell in a big heap on top of Renee. He stayed inside her not wanting to leave.

"You realize" Renee said playfully "that if we stay here like this we're going to get arrested for indecent exposure."

Kyle laughed, "I know, but you feel so good right now."

"You feel good too," Renee replied. Then she tensed for a minute and said, "We haven't talked about this yet, but I need you to know I consider you my man." Then Renee grabbed his chin and pulled his head up to look him in the eyes and said, "Exclusively my man."

"I am", Kyle replied and gave her a long passionate kiss.

Chapter 17   IT'S BETTER IN THE BAHAMAS

Present Day

"Wo babe check out this hammock on the terrace. We can nap in it together." Brit looked over the ledge and took in the people sunbathing on the beach, and all the young people doing water sports in the ocean, and the sailboats that went back and forth in the distance. She could sit out here for hours.

Tyson stood in the room looking at his baby, like a father looks at a child when they discover something new and exciting for the first time. He was smiling from ear to ear. He loved making her happy. Brittany had loved him when she had no idea he would be going to the Pros, and that meant more to him than some sexy groupie, who just wanted to be seen with a professional basketball player, and the minute you had nothing to offer them was the minute they were not interested. He made a promise to God and his mother that he would do right by her, because outside of his family she had been his biggest supporter and source of inspiration.

"Tyson come out here and look at this!" Brittany yelled, interrupting his thoughts.

Tyson walked out onto the terrace to join Brit. "Now this is what I'm talking about! Tomorrow we're going to have to check out the water sports. I want you to ride with me on the back of a jet ski while I make you scream when we hit those waves."

"You can't scare me. I'm a better swimmer than you."

"Alright – we'll see how adventurous you are."

"Baby, how about we change out of these hot clothes, put on our bathing suits and go chill out on the beach with a Pina Colada or Bahama Mama or something like that."

"Oooooh I would love it! I'm going to put on my new 2-piece string bikini that I bought especially for you." She walked seductively past him caressing his *bolas*. "You're not going to be able to keep your hands off of me – big boy."

Tyson's jimmy got hard just at the thought of seeing Brit's curvy body in a bikini.

"Mmmmm these Bahama Mamas are gooooooooood!" Brittany said, sipping on her third one. "You really can't taste the liquor at first."

"Be careful lightweight, you know what happened the last time you didn't 'taste the liquor'." Brittney threw an ice chip at him.

"Very funny, wiseass." Tyson was referring to the open bar at his college teammate's wedding, when Brit sipped on Cosmos all night, and Tyson had to carry her out of the reception.

"Last one in the water has to sit in the aisle seat", Tyson yelled as he ran down the sand towards the beach. Brittany put down her drink and ran to catch him. Tyson was already at the sand when she got to him so she jumped on his back as they fell into the water, laughing hysterically. The two of them spent the afternoon swimming and doing all the water sports there were; the banana boat, parasailing, and Tyson managed to scare the hell out of Brit when he drove the Jet Ski through the ocean. She held on for dear life as he rode the waves fast and furious. It was her first time on the wave runner, but she knew she was in good hands with Tyson, not to mention the lifejacket she wore.

After the sun began to go down they were exhausted. They collapsed onto the sand in front of their private beach. The beach was just steps away from their hotel, and it also gave them privacy from the main part of the beach. As they lay there watching the sunset, and as the cool ocean breeze swept over her, Brit was getting horny. She looked over at her handsome man, who had started to doze off. Tyson's rich mocha skin was even more gorgeous after being kissed by the sun, and it seemed like his body was developing muscles where he never had them, and it was turning her on. She leaned into him and lowered herself down on his body. She took his manhood out of his trunks and began to give him the best head he ever had. Tyson became aroused and started playing with her locks while she satisfied him.

"Dayam baby I got to bring you to the Caribbean more often."

Brit continued and when he was ready she mounted him right on the blanket. She whispered in his ear, "I always wanted to have sex on the beach but not in Coney Island." They both laughed. They rolled around in the sand making passionate love to each other. It seemed that they could not get enough of each other on this vacation. When they woke up from their lovemaking they went back in to eat and make love again.

The next afternoon Brittany sat out on the balcony in her thong filming the ocean on her new camcorder. She never got sick of sitting outside looking at the beautiful scenery. She found it to be therapeutic, with the warm island breeze caressing her skin.

Tyson came to the terrace where he found his woman recording half naked.

"My my my, that camcorder should be facing the other direction sexy."

Brittany blushed. "You look sexy too with just your trunks on."

"Hey Baby we got plenty of wine in here, want me to bring you out a glass?"

"Yes, that would be nice. And bring my cover-up out too."

"I don't know why, I'm just gonna take it off in a minute."

Tyson joined Britt back on the terrace; "you look sexy too with your birthday suit on." He chuckled as he pulled her into him to sit on his lap.

"Last night was really good babe. Was it as good to you as it was to me? I can't remember the last time you gave it to me like that. Got a brotha all whipped and shit."

Brittany smiled, "I can't help the way you make me feel Ty. You bring me to this romantic island, in this beautiful hotel and then you drop your drawers, and 'big poppa' is staring at me, what's a girl supposed to do…"

"How many kids do you want to have one day baby?"

Brittany looked lovingly at Ty; he didn't talk much about kids, especially with all the basketball issues going on around him. She sometimes wondered if he still wanted kids. Brit knew they had a lot of time because both of them were still in their early twenties – but a woman likes to hear her man's desires. "I would say I want 2 boys and a girl, so I can spoil my little girl rotten, and if anyone tries to pick on her, her brothers can beat them silly."

"How about you babe, how many kids do you want?"

"At least 5, I came from a big family so I want one. I believe children benefit from having other siblings to share with and play with."

"Easy for you to say pahtna, cause you ain't pushing them out."

"I know I'm pushing them in! But seriously babe, you know you're the best thing to ever happen to me, and I mean the best - before basketball and everything."

Brittany arched her eyebrows at that one, because most of the time she felt like a close second, but she did not comment, she let him continue to speak.

"Britti you believed in me when no one else did. Remember when I was trying to fit in with the big boys, and you used to pump me up before the games, remember that babe? Remember when we used to be in the library together until closing, because I had to maintain a 2.0 G.P.A. to play on the team, and you used to drill me until I had those formulas memorized – remember? Remember all the fights I had to pull you out of cause hoochies was always trying to holler, and my baby wasn't tryna hear that – remember? Remember when you and my Moms looked beyond the dough and convinced me to stay another year in college to develop my game, so I would be drafted higher – remember that? Well babe I will never forget those things cause they made me who I am today."

Tyson got on his knees and took her hand in his, "Britt this ring represents all of the special things about you that I will *never* forget, the things that only me and you can share, and the reason I love you with all of my heart. Baby will you be my wife, cause I can't breathe without you?"

Brittany's eyes filled with tears, she couldn't have fantasized about a more romantic proposal.

Tyson pulled out the prettiest platinum engagement ring she had ever laid eyes on. He slid it on her ring finger and it fit like a glove – just like their love. Brittany threw herself on him right on the balcony and smothered him with wet kisses, "Yes baby! Of course I'll marry you! You're the only man I'll ever love."

"You've just made me the happiest man in the world."

Chapter 18 INTIMATE STRANGERS

Present Day

Sean

"Stop Stop," Renee giggled as Kyle tickled her. "You're cheating you have an unfair advantage because you're not ticklish," she complained.

"Hey baby all's fair in love and war," he countered. As Kyle and Renee playfully fought and romped in the comfort of her candle lit bedroom, outside in a cold lonely van Sean seethed in anger. He disliked Kyle from the start, but ever since Sean had decided to bug Renee's apartment, his dislike had turned into a blinding hatred.

Sean began fidgeting with nervous energy as the laughter and giggles turned into pants and moans. Sean listened hoping to hear Renee's sultry voice moan some sexy remark that he could pretend was meant for him. But it was Kyle's voice that came through his headphones first in a lusty growl.

"Oh Yeah, Yeah baby like that. Whose pussy is this? Come on baby I want to hear you Who's (grunt) Pussy (grunt) is this?"

Sean violently pulled the headphones from his ears and threw them to the floor of the van. He could not bear to listen to Renee's reply. Sean was recording this as he recorded every time Kyle and Renee were in her apartment together. The worst part of their lovemaking for Sean was that Kyle was extremely jealous and possessive and the things he said and did during sex made it obvious to anyone listening that he wanted complete ownership of Renee. The best part of their recorded sex was Sean would take the tapes and have them edited to only Renee's voice. Sean would listen to these tapes and dream and fantasize, while he pleasured himself, that it was him Renee was making love to. He wanted to get the vision of Kyle touching Renee out of his mind as quickly as possible, so he grabbed his files and lay back on the mattress.

Sean had bought the same type of white van used by PSE&G and Verizon. He purchased 5 different magnetic signs so he could change the appearance of the van often. He would vary the signs and change parking positions to avoid looking suspicious. Inside the van was surveillance equipment straight out of an FBI movie. Sean kept several disguises in the back just in case. One side of the van had a window for Sean to take pictures. On the outside of the van the window was a mirror so no one could look in. On the other side of the van were pictures of Renee. Sean would stare at these pictures for hours and dream about the life they would have together.

The files Sean grabbed were the extensive background checks he had done on both Kyle and Renee. Sean had discovered that Renee came from a no-nonsense family from the streets. Her parents struggled to give her and her brother Jacob the opportunities they didn't have. Renee made the most of every opportunity and now enjoyed an executive position at a major ad agency in the city, and a comfortable life style. Her past relationships showed Renee to be self confident and proud. She demanded to be treated with respect. Sean loved that about Renee. Sean also discovered through surveillance that once Renee loved and trusted someone she would surrender herself completely. Renee loved with loyalty and passion. And Sean was determined to do whatever it took to be the benefactor of this love.

A single mother and two older sisters raised Kyle. His surroundings were lower middle class but his education was superior to other kids in his neighborhood because his mother was a teacher. Kyle was crazy about his mother and sisters, and this love for women had carried into his adult years. Unlike Renee who had a few very meaningful relationships Kyle had left a truckload of women behind when he met Renee. Kyle worked at UPS but aspired to be an artist. Sean's problem was despite Kyle's adoration for women he was completely faithful and satisfied with Renee. So Sean had decided he would have to concoct a story guaranteed to make Renee distance herself from Kyle.

Sean had to approach Renee with a story because he had decided long ago not to confront Kyle. Sean had convinced himself that he wasn't scared of anyone. So instead he reasoned that Kyle was naturally paranoid. Kyle always sat with his back to the wall and his eyes on the door. Even when he took Renee to the movies Kyle always wanted to sit in the back row so he could see everyone. Sean figured this was a natural byproduct of Kyle being the only man in his immediate family, and the need he felt to protect his mother and sisters. Plus Sean was tall and slender, while Kyle was slightly shorter than Sean; he had an athletic build. Kyle played football and basketball with his buddies, and deep in his heart Sean realized that face-to-face and hand-to-hand he didn't stand a chance against Kyle, so if it came down to it Sean would have to shoot Kyle.

Sean slowly flipped through Kyle's file. He narrowed Kyle's ex girlfriends down to 8 potential ones. Sean would need the cooperation of one of these women for his plan to work. Sean had separate pictures of each woman with their history on the back. One woman stood out - she was different from the rest, she was younger and less educated than the rest. Her name was Tamyka; Sean had followed her one day and listened in as she and her friends talked about how men are only good for sex and what you can get from them. Sean looked over a couple more photos but kept coming back to the same one. Yeah Sean thought, for enough money this one would say anything. Sean grabbed a red magic marker. He drew a circle around Tamyka's face and wrote the word SIMPLE across the photo. Sean had found his accomplice.

Chapter 19   PART OF THE FAMILY

Back In The Day

A Ford Explorer, rims and the right song on the radio, Raysheeda had arrived and she did it all by herself. The whole car-jacking scheme had gone horribly wrong. Born C had cheated Raysheeda out of most of her cut, and worse yet Sheeda's friends whom she considered family were suspicious and consequently cut her off. Nobody, even friends who weren't there that night would take her calls or even acknowledge her existence.

One day Raysheeda called Renee and blocked the caller ID. As soon as she heard Sheeda's voice, Renee said in a tone Raysheeda had never heard before, "Stop talking bitch, if I had been in the car that night your ass would have already been handled. You must have forgotten who my family is. Before you go to sleep tonight say a silent thank you to Brittany, because of her I didn't tell my family. Lose my number or I might remember to tell some of my gangsta cousins about your simple ass." With this Renee hung up and Sheeda's life changed.

The truth was Raysheeda knew to make sure Renee was not in the car that night. Everyone knew her cousin C Money ran the block and was ruthless. For the most part Renee was nothing like the criminal side of her family. But the Jones family was close, and Renee's loyalty had forced her to bail some of her cousins out of trouble more than once. So Sheeda knew Renee was not barking idle threats. She had family that would do anything she asked them to!

This conversation told Raysheeda several things: first, all her friends had judged her guilty, what had gone wrong - did Loco or Born C or somebody rat her out, second she had to find a way to get her friends back. Brit and Renee had really looked out in college. There were many nights Sheeda could not afford to eat and they always got enough for her too! Every once in awhile she would make it up to them by shoplifting some steaks or fish. But they both encouraged Raysheeda not to do that because they did not want her to have a record and ruin her chance at making a life. Sheeda knew they really cared. They would all sit down for dinner together like a little college family. Those dinners were the closest thing Raysheeda ever had to a normal family life. But time passed and she failed out of school and ran out of money. Brit and Renee stayed in touch though and encouraged her to go to trade school and to try and get grants. But Raysheeda was surrounded by too much crime and fast money. She had lost her will to struggle and do things the right way. And now that her friends had written her off it was the perfect time to take things to the next level.

Since Renee had done her the favor of telling her that C Money did not know about their falling out, she had approached him to ask if he had any work. She reminded him she was Renee's homegirl and could be trusted. She told him the whole college thing hadn't worked out and she needed money, and was willing to take chances to get it. He had asked her if Renee was cool with it and Sheeda told him Renee wouldn't want her friend to starve. C wanted to give her a small safe gig. But Raysheeda told him she wasn't interested in no short money. She wanted to start mackin. C Money told her, "You know more money means more risk." She convinced him she knew the deal and a female would get hassled less by Five – O. C was sold, so he gave her a car and she started running large quantities of weed and cocaine across the New York/New Jersey border. Raysheeda couldn't be happier. The money was coming fast and Sheeda finally had enough money to plan for the future. She had devised a plan to win her friends back. She would save enough money to buy Brittany a nicer car than the one that was stolen. She had come up with this whole convoluted story of how Born C and Loco had threatened to kill her aunt if she didn't agree to help. She was sure it would work. Raysheeda was finding out fast that money made everything in life a lot better.

So when C Money called to tell her he had a run that was extremely dangerous because of the massive weight, and the Jamaicans she would have to deal with in Harlem -she jumped at the opportunity. C was talking major money, $10,000 to be exact! Raysheeda knew people that didn't make that in a year. Hell she used to be one of them. And she didn't care about no shady Harlem Jamaicans. Shit Sheeda had a heater, a glock 9 to be exact and she knew how to use it.

She had changed since her girls abandoned her. Her new motto was -whatever it takes, and she knew if you could pull the trigger you could make more paper, and this was her ultimate goal. C Money had told Raysheeda to meet him in this vacant building in Newark. This was unusual; C never came to meets. He liked to insulate himself against any charges. But he said with this amount of money at stake he didn't want anyone else giving Sheeda the dough or the instructions.

She got to the building and proceeded to the room he said he would be in. When she turned the corner she saw 10 runners from his crew and knew something was very wrong. She was knocked to the floor and heard C Money's voice on the other side of the room. "Sheeda you stupid ho, you didn't think Renee and I would ever see each other or talk. You're a scandalous bitch! I thought you all were girls, you let a mental patient like Born C put a loaded sawed off shot gun in your girl's faces over some money."

Sheeda's voice was tight and scared, "No one got hurt, I swear C Renee wasn't in the car. I would never disrespect you by..." before she could finish C Money had walked over to her and kicked her in the face.

"Shut the fuck up." Pain shot up to Sheeda's brain. "Don't you think I know that? If she had been there, I would have made you watch me torture Born C and Loco and then I would have killed you slow and painful. Everyone knows not to fuck with my family!" C Money yelled. "Right?" and the whole Crew yelled "Right!" back at him.

Raysheeda knew she was being made an example. She was hoping and praying he would just give her a bad beating, Sheeda was strong, she could live through that.

"However, you and I still have a problem if you would have your girls set up, how am I supposed to trust you. Renee told me yawl were like family, that's how you treat family Bitch! Shit I guess you'd slice my throat for a Big Mac." Sheeda heard members of the crew laughing. C Money barked, "Yo Little Tim, come over here and show me you're a man."

Raysheeda opened her eyes and saw a little boy with a big gun staring down at her. C Money had walked back across the room. He was still giving orders, "this crew is a family, but this family looks out for each other. You must be willing to die for this family."

"Little Tim you want to be part of this family?"

"Yes." Little Tim yelled back.

C Money continued, "Then show us your loyalty. Show us you can do what it takes to be respected."

"No, PLEASE!" Raysheeda pleaded.

C Money yelled, "IF YOU WANT TO BE ONE OF US DO IT!"

Raysheeda closed her eyes and prayed. She heard the gun cock.

It would be the last sound she ever heard. Little Tim ended Raysheeda's life and became part of the family.

.

Chapter 20   HAPPY DAYS

Present Day

"OK", Renee began, "now I've mixed the drinks Brit, but I must tell you - since we all know I'm a true artist when it comes to liquid concoctions, that *Sex on the Beach* is not one of my specialties."

Brittany laughed out loud and said in a sassy voice, "Well I suggest you add it to your repertoire because girl it's amazing."

Brittany smacked a high five with Simone as Renee raised an eyebrow; "Sounds to me like someone did more than swim in the ocean and tan on the beach during their little surprise trip to the Bahamas."

"Trust me Rae there was nothing little about this trip, we're talking penthouse, balconies, hammocks, the best food, the best lovin."

"Stop, stop already." Simone put her hand up, "if you're trying to make us jealous you've succeeded. Damn girl that sounds like the type of trip a sister like me should be taking."

Brittany just giggled at the comment and continued. "Anyway the reason I wanted Rae to make us special drinks tonight is I have a toast and an announcement to make, but first I need you two to stand up and turn around." Renee turned around immediately anxious to hear what her friend had to say. Predictably Simone resisted,

"Just tell us Brit I'm comfortable I don't feel like standing up."

Brittany was about to respond but before she could Renee grabbed Simone's arm yanked her up and spun her around. "Damn Rae you didn't have to grab me so hard," Simone complained.

"You didn't have to be so lazy, besides I wanna know what's going on don't' you?"

Brittany listened to Renee and Simone squabble as usual. These two were always going at each other. Brit just smiled to herself and took the opportunity to slip the ring out of her pocketbook and back on her finger. Then she put her left hand behind her back and picked up her drink with the right hand. "OK" she announced, "You can turn around now." They both did and saw that nothing had changed.

"What the fuck Brit," Simone said annoyed, "I expected to see some cool shot glasses or maybe a keychain or Bahamas t-shirt."

Simone was about to continue but Renee cut her off. "Sim can you stop thinking about yourself for one second so we can listen to Brit."

Simone began again, "Rae don't try and play it off like you're not disappointed. You know we were both trying to guess what Brittany would bring us."

"Would you both stop," Brittany was fed up. Brittany used her best lawyer voice and told them both to pick up their glasses for a toast. They did and she began, "we have all been friends for as long as I can remember. We've been through some real shit together and my girls have always had my back. I'm afraid I'm going to need you both now more then ever, because Tyson is no longer my boyfriend."

"What?!!" Renee yelled and Simone's mouth was open. Neither thought that Tyson and Brittany would ever break up.

"Nope," Brittany continued no longer able to contain her smile, "now he's my fiancé", and with the last word she pulled her left hand from behind her back and said, "BAM!" while showing them the massive rock on her ring finger. There was a momentary pause and then all three women screamed at once. Renee grabbed Brit in a hug knocking some of the liquid from her drink as Simone clutched her hand to get a better look at the ring. Then they both began throwing questions at Brittany quicker than she could respond. Brittany was on cloud nine and anxious to answer any and all the questions they had. She told them exactly how he proposed, the romantic setting, the heartfelt words - all of it. Renee was so elated she made Brit tell them the story twice. Renee was such a romantic, and she loved Tyson like a brother. In her mind it was only a matter of time for Brit and Tyson - Rae knew they were made for each other.

After hearing it the second time Rae sighed and said, "If I'm ever lucky enough to be proposed to I hope it's romantic like that."

Simone looked at Rae and shook her head and began, "Don't rely on luck Rae or it will never happen. Let me school you on how to work it. You find the man that can give you what you need and you systematically make him yours. Say what he wants to hear, stroke his ego a little, keep your body tight, and work it right in the bedroom and you can have whatever man you choose." Simone finished with cocky confidence.

"If that's the case", Renee began "then why are you with someone who's married to someone else?"

Simone was not even bothered by the off-hand comment, "Don't get it twisted Rae, Joe is not in love with his wife. They are on the verge of a separation, and I'm with him because, how many black men do you know that are doctors, and can give a woman whatever she wants. I get all types of luxury shit I don't even ask for. You want to know why? Because he'll do any thing I want not to lose me. No one can satisfy him the way I can. And guess what - little by little he's spending more and more time with me, until one day he will be spending all his time with me. Whatever I ask for I'll get." Renee was itching to comment but didn't want to ruin Brittany's good mood with an argument. Simone knew Renee well enough to know the reason she was behaving, but took advantage of it anyway. She put her glass down and went to her bedroom and came back with a box. They were both sipping their drinks planning out the wedding.

Brit looked over at Simone, "I'm glad you're back. We're trying to decide the colors for the bridesmaid dresses."

Simone just looked at the two of them like they were crazy, "You two need to slow down. The wedding is not tomorrow is it?" Simone asked getting a little nervous.

"No," Brittany answered, "we haven't set an exact date yet but we will. We both decided it's not going to be a long engagement."

Simone jumped in "Well don't rush it, with him traveling all the time and you busy with school and work it will probably take time to pick out a house and stuff."

Renee couldn't hold her tongue, "Rush it! They've been together for a long while now Sim, they couldn't rush it if they tried, too late."

"You're right about that," Brittany laughed out loud. Renee finished, "I can't see any reason they should wait."

I can Simone was thinking. She was secretly hoping she would get her own mansion and sugar daddy first. But she reasoned there was still time, maybe she would.

Simone interrupted, "Can you guys put the dresses on hold for just a minute because I have something to share too. Simone picked up the ring box as Brit and Renee looked on in amazement. Renee could feel her temper start to rise. She really didn't want Simone stealing Brit's moment.

Then Brit said, "That's not what I think it is, is it?"

Simone paused for a moment enjoying their shocked looks. "Well yes and no," Simone answered as she opened the box. Brit and Renee looked and waited for an explanation. "Joe told me it was a symbol of our relationship," she said. "When he gave it to me he kissed my right hand and put it on my finger."

"Right hand," Renee said out loud the relief obvious in her voice. "So it's just a present."

"No", Simone said angry now. "It's not just a present Rae, it's a diamond fuckin' ring. How many men have bought you a diamond ring Rae."

"None" she admitted sorry for her comment.

"Look Sim I didn't mean it like that. It's a beautiful ring. It's just this guy is married already and you know that doesn't sit right with me. And I would have been upset if he had the nerve to propose to you while still married to someone else, it's just not right."

Simone was livid, "Don't give me no judgmental bullshit, you're just mad cause Brit and I both got diamonds and you don't."

Renee's temper was beginning to flare, calm down, calm down she told herself.

Brittany had been silent but she could see Renee was about to blow her top. So she cleared her throat and said real loud, "Excuse me but whether you two like it or not I just got engaged, and we are going to have a fun and crazy night. This is a celebration bitches. Then she stood up and put her left hand out again. After about ten seconds of Simone and Renee staring at each other they all bust out laughing and started screaming again.

"You're really getting married," Renee said with a tear in her eye.

"I am" Brittany assured her, then she put her other hand on Simone and said, "That ring is gorgeous."

Simone beamed, "thanks Brit."

Then after a couple more seconds Renee looked at Simone knowingly, "It is an incredible ring Sim," and then couldn't help but add, "Did you get it appraised yet?"

Simone clenched her chest in mock horror. "How dare you ask me such a question?" She said in her best prim and proper voice, which let Brit and Renee know she was teasing. Renee just waited for the real answer. She knew what made Simone tick. Finally she answered, "Hell yeah and it's worth a bundle." Simone gave her a satisfied grin.

"Well good for you girl," Renee raised her glass in congratulations and took a sip of her drink. Brit was amazed and happy that Renee was holding her temper in check. But this wasn't good enough she wanted everyone to feel really good tonight and Simone's ring comment was hurtful. Brittany closed her eyes and prayed 'Come on Kyle I need you to come through for me I don't know you yet but give me this one and I'll be the coolest when we meet'.

Then she spoke up "So to recap - I'm engaged, Simone is pimpin' a big rock, so that leaves you Renee - no Kyle news?"

Renee's face lit up immediately. Thank God Brittany thought. "Well," Renee began "it's not as exciting as diamond rings and all that, but something did happen that made me feel pretty special." She proceeded to tell them both about the parking lot rendezvous and the flowers but she conveniently left out wild sex in Kyle's truck. By the time she was done they both knew Renee was falling hard for her new boyfriend.

"Wow," Brittany said, "so now you two are exclusive, congrats Rae I know you're crazy about him."

"I am" Renee smiled. After hearing Brittany's beach story and Renee's romantic adventure Simone knew she needed to give one of her maintenance men a call - sex with Joe just didn't compare.

Brittany was satisfied everyone was again in good spirits. Brit put her glass down and grabbed her car keys from her pocketbook. "All right you two put on your shoes and come help me with these bags."

"What bags?" Simone asked.

Brittany looked over her shoulder and smiled "Your souvenirs of course." Renee and Simone smiled happily. Brittany was the best.

Chapter 21   DEAL WITH THE DEVIL

Present Day

Sean

Sean had just turned the corner into Paterson, New Jersey and almost immediately he saw the sign "East Side High School Home of the Ghosts." All Sean could think was he wished Kyle were a ghost or a memory. These streets in Paterson weren't easy to grow up on. Kyle could have fallen the way so many young black men had on the pavement of these unforgiving streets. But he hadn't fallen and was proving to be a thorn in Sean's side, a worthy opponent. Sean decided to stop in at the high school to see if there was any additional information about Kyle that could help him. Sean looked in the proud athletic display case that every high school seemed to have and there he was, pictures of Kyle, school star. Kyle was a football and track star, he had a promising future, it seemed every college wanted to offer him a scholarship, and then during the state championship game while Kyle was going for the all time high school football record for most rushing yards in a season, two lineman on the opposing team tackled him so hard his left ankle was cracked apart in five places. He had to undergo three separate and painful operations, and since he had not yet signed with any school his scholarship offers were rescinded. Sean still couldn't believe that this testosterone filled jock had resisted the two women that he had thrown at him. It would have made everything so much simpler for Sean, just take a few photos of Kyle sexing up some hoochie and Renee would have run for the hills. But Sean wasn't going to let a little extra work deter him from his goal. This whole mission had become Sean's main purpose in life and he refused to lose.

"Damn it where is this road," Sean complained under his breath. There it is, Remsen Ave. He was looking for the Hook It Up hair salon, Kyle's ex-girlfriend Tamyka worked there and her shift was about to end. Sean would meet her outside and make her an offer she couldn't refuse. He had rented a Benz because he knew that's how you get the attention of this type of woman. Sean had done plenty of research on Tamyka and she was perfect for his plan. She and Kyle had actually gone out for about 8 months, which back then as Sean had found was a long time for Kyle. After some deeper digging he discovered she had treated Kyle like a king until of course he got injured. At first she stuck by his side but as soon as it became obvious his sports career was over, she dropped Kyle and began flirting with one of his less talented but uninjured teammates. After that everyone in the school knew what she was about and Sean was hoping her personality hadn't changed.

Several women stepped out of the salon and stopped right in front of the glass picture window to light their cigarettes. One's hair was done in an extravagant style and the other two had short but neatly cropped hair. Hairdressers are notorious for keeping their hair simple. Sean recognized Tamyka right away. She was slightly bigger than her high school picture but still in good shape, and her face hadn't changed at all. She was cute but in that homegirl from the block kind of way. Nobody Sean would be attracted to, and in his opinion not in the same league with Renee.

Sean turned on an Usher song that he wasn't crazy about but he knew the ladies loved it. He began creeping slowly down the street in his rented silver Mercedes CLK. As he rolled up on the three ladies he rolled down his passenger window.

"Do any of you ladies know how to get to MLK Blvd?" The customer with the fresh new do piped up first, but it was obvious she was horrible at giving directions.

Then Tamyka chimed in, "Yeah cutie just go to the end of this block make a right, and then the next make a left, after that."

"Hold up, hold up shortie," Sean cut her off "that sounds kind of complicated why don't you get in and show me, then I'll bring you back and I'll know how to go."

Sean could see she wanted to, but she was trying to play it cool in front of her friends. But he knew how to deal with women like her, she was an easy puzzle to solve.

"Look if you're scared it's cool, I mean I really liked your directions," with this Sean looked her up and down so she would know what he meant, "but if you're too busy maybe your friend here with the nice do will show me." He could barely finish his sentence before Tamyka's friend was reaching for the door. But Tamyka stopped her.

"Darshell you don't even drive. Don't worry honey I'll show you."
And with a big smile Tamyka jumped in the Benz. It didn't take Sean
long to talk her into having dinner with him. During dinner he convinced
her to help him set Kyle up. At first she was a bit hesitant, but Sean told
her as a businesswoman she should look at this as a past investment
paying off. He only offered her a thousand dollars but it came wrapped
in slick talk and compliments. Sean made Tamyka feel good about
herself and she ate it up. By the time they finished their meal he had laid
out the whole sick story and she was down. What a simple bitch, Sean
thought to himself. He would let her tell her lie and give her the
thousand dollars. But he also knew he would pay her one more visit
when everything was done. Because when he was successful in winning
Renee's affection, Sean could not afford or allow this simple bitch to be
traced back to him and ruin everything. No way, he thought. He smiled
at Tamyka and put his hand out.

"It's a deal then, right partner."

Tamyka extended her hand and made a deal with the devil.

Chapter 22   LAST SECOND SHOT

Present Day

"It looks like this one is going to go down to the wire. There have been 22 lead changes in the game and the Slammers are now up by 2 with 34 seconds left in the game. The Pirates have just called a time out, and the noise in the arena is deafening. Clyde, you could barely hear the ref blow his whistle when Coach Thomas signaled for time."

"I know Jack, the Pirate arena is known for its loud fans. Tyson Myers will have to make a pressure free throw to put his team up by 3. But this is still a 2 possession game, so even if the Pirates come down the floor and make a 3point play, there is still plenty of time on the clock for the Slammers to tie it."

Tyson took a deep breath as he walked toward the free throw line. He was an 85% percent free throw shooter and he told himself, you have made plenty of these shots, there's nothing different. He dribbled the ball in his customary fashion at the line, to the front, to the side, and back to the front. Normally he would look up into the stands at Brit, his good luck charm, and she would put up the peace symbol - meaning no pressure. But since they were on the road, he just had to picture her face. Swish the ball went through the net and all his teammates gave him the pound. This time the Slammers called for time. Tyson walked to the bench and took pounds from the rest of his teammates on the bench. Twenty seconds later the Slammers were setting up the zone defense as coach had outlined in the timeout. The fans were going crazy. It was always tough playing on the road in tight games, because you always felt like the home team got the benefit of the calls when the clock was under 2 minutes. This was a huge game for the Slammers, because a win would signify a playoff birth for them, and guarantee the team home court advantage throughout the playoffs.

Tyson got down low and was guarding Malik Johnson close. He knew Johnson always went to his left with the crossover, so he stuck to him like glue. As soon as Johnson crossed the ball over, Tyson swatted the ball away and ran down the court for the fast break dunk!!!!!

Johnson never had a chance to catch him. Game over!!! With a 5-point lead and 15 seconds left there was not much hope for the home team. Tyson's teammates ran up to him and chest bumped him one by one. He lived for these moments. The home fans began filing out of the arena, succumbing to their team's loss. Coach Harris hit em on the butt, saying "Good game kid". A reporter from TNT was waiting to get an after-game interview. Tyson did the interview and ended it with his customary 'Hi Ma'. He knew she was watching from home and it made her night when he gave her a shout out.

As he exited the gym, there were kids holding their hands out for high fives and he always tagged a few on his way out. And of course the proverbial groupies were hanging by the tunnel door with all their assets hanging out, screaming his name. One blonde woman yelled, "Tyson can you autograph my shirt right here?" As she pointed to her bosom. He just looked down and chuckled as he made his way to the locker room. He just wanted to take a hot shower and call his baby.

Tyson was elated as he walked through the tunnel to the locker room. This had undoubtedly been his best game of the season. It was the first triple double of his career and he was feeling it, especially with the W.

When he entered the locker room, his teammates all started clapping for him. "Lets hear it for the Rookie yall!!" They all gave him high fives and props for his first triple double and game.

Rasheed came up to him and said "Yo Rookie, a couple of us fellows are heading over to Hot Willies for some drinks and food, why don't you come? I heard the wings ain't the only thing that's hot up in that piece man," Rasheed added with a chuckle.

Tyson thought for about 2 seconds because he was feeling celebratory, but not in that way. If Brittany was here he would have preferred to have a private party with her, but she was back home studying.

"Nah man, I'm gonna pass tonight, I just want to order up some room service.

Rasheed looked at him sideways for a second like he was trying to figure out if he was serious, and then decided to drop it. "Aight man, do you."

"Later Man."

Tyson couldn't wait to get back to his room to call Brit. He was truly savoring this moment in his career. A triple double!! Wow. He couldn't wait to watch the tape. His body was really tired after the long game, and he was glad he had decided to chill in his room. When the concierge alerted him to his floor, he got off the elevator. The team usually reserved a whole floor for themselves. He loved his fans and stuff, and he never liked to come across as arrogant, but there were times when he just was not in the mood for autographs; and a lot of times the fans didn't understand that. So he really appreciated having the private elevator and floor on nights like this.

Tyson searched in his wallet for his card key, he was looking forward to watching ESPN. When he opened the door to his hotel room he damn near had a heart attack!

Chapter 23   OH NO SHE DIDN'T

Present Day

"Wow Dion, you have a really nice house! Did you decorate it or did your woman?"

"We both did," he responded.

They had just entered the townhouse, after a long night of clubbin' in the city. Simone had no idea his house was so immaculate. There was wall-to-wall carpeting in soft pale colors, skylights, and very tall ceilings. The furniture was ultra modern and the kitchen was gorgeous with all modern appliances. The living room was decked in beautiful Italian leather. Even the African artwork that hung from the walls looked like something from a high-end gallery. I bet they're originals Simone thought to herself unlike the prints she bought off the street. Then she looked at the mantle over the fireplace and noticed the family pictures. There were several of them with the children, and the children by themselves. Then she came across a picture of him and Tammy. They looked to be newlyweds in this picture, because they were both much younger. It was taken in a park at a family barbeque, but they looked to be the perfect happy couple. Both of them smiling like they didn't have a care in the world. Simone wondered when things had changed so much between them. Simone just sat there in amazement.

"Do you want something to drink?" Dion asked her interrupting her thoughts.

"Yeah, what do you have?" Simone replied.

"We keep a full bar, you name it."

Wow Simone thought to herself, honey had it going on. "In that case a vodka Martini please."

"You got it Babe."

Simone was already very tipsy from the 4 Martinis she had at the club, but she wanted to stay that way. After Dion gave her her drink, he left the room and came back with a joint. He lit it up as he walked over to her. It always surprised her that he smoked so much being a prosecutor. He said it took the edge off and kept the pressure down. She imagined he had his share of stress with all the crime in this city. He passed it to her after he hit it.

"Where are your kids tonight?" Simone asked as she took a pull.

"They're with their grandmother. She loves watching the triplets."

"Where is your wife?"

"Don't you worry your pretty little head about her she's doing a double shift at the hospital, and she won't be home until tomorrow. Listen, all that clubbin got me a little salty, how about we take a nice shower before we get comfortable." Dion gave her that sly smile that made her melt. He got up to lead her to the master bathroom.

"Hold on one minute, I want to refill my martini and I will meet you up there."

"Aight, I'll get the water warmed up," he said as he winked at her.

Simone made her way into the kitchen, and she heard Dion turn the shower on in the upstairs bathroom. Suddenly the phone in the kitchen began to ring. She looked at the caller ID box and noticed it was East Orange General Hospital. After the second ring she figured Dion couldn't hear the phone over the music and the shower so she picked it up.

"Hello", Simone answered the phone feeling like the queen of the house.

"Hello, who is this?" Tammy asked.

"Who's calling?" Simone giggled.

"Dion's wife!" Tammy was getting tight. "Is that music I hear in the background? Is there a party going on, who is this?"

"Yeah there's a party, a private party with me and D. He's waiting for me in the shower – I gotta go." She giggled to herself and hung up the phone. As she walked up the spiral staircase she yelled to Dion, "Your sex goddess is on her way up."

Simone undressed and joined Dion in the shower. Dion eased closer to her as he started feeling himself. "You know you're beautiful right," he said as he kissed on her neck. Simone smiled, as she ate up his compliments. He began to wash her from head to toe, starting on her back, he lingered between her legs with the washcloth, trying to tantalize her, she felt herself getting really weak in the knees. Then he worked his way all the way down to her toes. She had never had a man bathe her and with so much passion. Simone made sure she returned the favor, dropping to her knees in the shower and went to work on his big d, she sucked him until he couldn't take it anymore. She knew his wife never took care of him like this, she was too busy working. "Come on let's get out of the shower, I need you in the bedroom", Dion said with his eyes closed.

Simone couldn't believe she was in their room. "Woo, I like this waterbed, come over here and swim with me" she said, as she fell on the bed and threw her legs up. Dion joined her in the king size bed, which had gold satin sheets on it. "Very sexy" she commented. Then he slid his tongue into her ear as he began caressing her. He was such a good lover, the best she'd ever had. He began fondling her breasts while he smothered her with kisses. Then he put his lips on her nipples and began sucking them very tenderly. He dropped to the floor and opened up her legs, and began eatin' her cat like a vulture. She came on his face. She was putty in his hands at that point. Simone was thinking he's going to make love to me right in his wife's bedroom! The thought excited her. He wanted her so bad, that he would fuck her in the same place he made his babies. Good Lord.

He stood in front of her with his Jimmy sticking straight out. He entered her raw and penetrated very slowly.

"You feel so good" he said.

"You do too, nobody makes me feel the way you do." The two of them were so caught up in the moment that they didn't hear the front door open.

"You skank heffer! Get the hell out of my bed. Where the fuck do you get off tramping around in my bed, with my husband!"

Dion jumped up and threw the sheet around him – looking like he saw a ghost. "Tammy its not what you think!"

"I don't know where you came from but get the hell out of my house, before I start throwing your shit out the window! It's tired heifers like you that cause black men to lose respect for the beds and their bedrooms, by disrespecting another sister, to please your weak ego!"

"Who the hell do you think you are calling me a skank – if he's your husband why is he all up in me?" Tammy lunged at Simone ready to beat her down.

Dion jumped in the middle naked trying to break it up. "Get the hell off of me nigga" after I beat her ass, then I'm going to deal with you." Dion was overpowering her as they rolled around the floor, her kicking and screaming and him trying to calm her down.

As mad as Simone was she knew she ought to get her stuff and get out of there before this sister started hurling shit! The look in her eyes was that of a crazed devil and she was the target, the hell with that, this brother ain't got enough money anyway for me to be bothered. Simone quickly ran into the bathroom and gathered her clothes off the floor. She was getting the hell out of there.

"Don't touch me Motherfucker, because I got a right mind to start throwing your shit out the window too – so back the hell up!" She heard Tammy screaming at Dion as she ran out the door. She had a hair appointment in the morning. Simone had accomplished what she came for anyway.

Chapter 24 AFTER PARTY

Present Day

Laid out on his bed like a harem, were three naked women - one Black, one Asian and one White.

"Hi Tyson" they all said in unison. "We came here to congratulate you on a job well done. Why don't you come over here and party with us? We promise we won't hurt you." They all giggled.

"How the hell did you get into my room?" He demanded, still in shock.

The Asian one responded, "Well lets just say we are part of the welcoming committee and we spend a lot of time in this hotel," she said this as she started walking towards him. Tyson couldn't believe what was happening. He ran out the door and down the hall to his teammate's room. He found himself sweating as he looked for Mike's room. He kept looking behind him to make sure none of those hookers were following him. The last thing he needed was some type of scandal that he wanted no part of. When he got to Mike's room he began to bang fast and hard. He knew Mike didn't really hang out after the games with the fellows. He always said he was too old for that now, and he had 'been there done that' kind of thing. He heard the TV so he knew Mike was in there, "Yo Mike open up its me Ty!"

"Aight man, hold on, I'm coming. Man you banging on the door like the cops is after you."

As soon as Mike opened up his door Tyson ran in and closed the door.

"Yo, Mike, you'll never believe what was waiting for me when I got back to room tonight!"

Mike took a look at Tyson, and knowing the type of brotha he was, not as thirsty as the others, he said, "I'll bet I can guess".

"Nah man, you ain't gonna believe this," Tyson said shaking his head.

"Well, did it have something to do with women, looking like hookas?"

100

"Tyson looked at Mike incredulously, "did you send them to my room man?!!!"

"Hell no nigga! We're in LA, and these things happen all the time to athletes and entertainers. These women are par for the course man, and you ain't seen nothing yet. It's like a business over here dude. They hang around these fancy hotels, make friends with the staff, some of them even work here. Man in my rookie year I had so many chics meeting me after games, everywhere I went, and I wasn't even up for rookie of the year. You are a target man. But you're different than most Youngblood, cause when I was your age it was hard for a brotha to turn away from all that pussy being thrown in his face man. And we're talking beautiful exotic women, looking like Playboy centerfolds, just throwing themselves at you, with no strings attached really. A lot of them just want to say they been with Tyson Myers from the NBA. And some of them want a lot more and you gotta be careful cause they'll have you in court. So man you got to get used to this. A lot of these guys, especially in their rookie season man, will jump at the bait, they love the attention, but you I sense are a little different. I mean you ran down here like the Feds was waiting for you man," Mike started laughing. "A lot of these guys married or otherwise feel, 'what happens on the road, stays on the road.' I guess your fiancé really got you whipped huh?"

"It ain't even about being whipped man, I'm just not interested. I know most brothas egos get going when women of all races start dropping their panties for them, but I'm not feeling it. I'm saying Britty was with me before I had all this fame and money and she loved me just the same. These gold diggers don't give a damn about me, they just want to be with *Tyson Myers,* and I can't risk messing up what we have for five minutes of fun. Besides my Moms would beat my ass cause she loves Brittany, and threatens me all the time about doing her wrong."

"You one in a million man. I hope that stays with you. Tell them hos your wife is coming over and to get out your room. Call housekeeping and tell them to change your sheets."

"Aight, thanks man."

Tyson walked back down the hall to handle his business. He put his shoulders back and opened the door real hard. When he opened the door the women were still there.

"Ty Ty, we've been getting lonesome waiting for you."

"Listen hookas, I don't know how you got in my room but you got get the hell out!! I ain't interested in what you selling."

The black one responded, "Tyson we're not selling anything to you baby, it's on the house."

Tyson put his hand up, "like I said get to steppin, my wifey is on her way over here and if she comes here, and sees you all – you will get a Brooklyn beat down."

At that they jumped up and started putting on their clothes.

Tyson left the room and waited outside for them to leave. He made sure they didn't leave with anything they didn't come with.

As Tyson lay in his bed that night trying to fall asleep, he was no longer thinking about his triple double. He couldn't get over what had taken place that night. He'd heard stories about groupies but never to this extent. I mean these ho's were bold. Mike had said that this was just the beginning. Tyson just hoped that he would be able to handle himself the same the next time it happened.

Chapter 25 THE REVENGE

Present Day

Tammy sat in her car contemplating the unthinkable. How could Dion do this to her after all they had been through, especially in their own home. She hadn't spoken to him in 3 weeks, since she caught him with that heifer in her bed. He tried to talk to her, but she only spoke to him regarding their children. She had been sleeping in the guest bedroom since she caught him. She couldn't stand the thought of sleeping with him in the same bed he was doing the nasty in with his mistress. The thought made her sick to her stomach. In her heart she knew she would eventually forgive him, after all they had the triplets to consider. The last thing she wanted was for her children to grow up like she did. After her mission was complete she would feel better. Sometimes a woman had to do what a woman had to do.

As Tammy approached the apartment complex she surveyed the neighborhood. Boy, Dion sure knew how to pick his hos from the worst neighborhoods. She made sure the doors were locked on her E-class Benz. God knows the last thing she needed was to be carjacked out here.

For the life of her she could not understand why her husband felt a need to cheat on her. For a while she thought it was just a stage he was going through, they say couples experience a 7-year itch after being married that long. She had a lot of patience with Dion though because he had supported her while she was in medical school. They always had a dream of being like the Huxtables. He was older than her, and since he was in law school, and law school was only 3 years, he finished up and then she started medical school. Tammy swore she would never leave him after the undaunting support he showed her, because if it hadn't been for him, she would have never done it. Her family never had the means to help her.

This is why she refused to let some no-good ghetto B, mess up her marriage. Tammy thought the arrival of the triplets would change his attitude - but it seemed to push him away. That was ok though because Simone Johnson was going to pay for her actions. Tammy Lewis was nobody's fool. This would be the last time she entered another woman's bed.

Tammy slowly drove past the projects while looking for the address on the license. There were a lot of brothers hanging out on the street, drinking beer and smoking weed. The music was playing loud as if it were broad daylight and not 11:30 at night. She felt very conspicuous in her shiny silver E-class Benz; driving slowly she didn't want any of these gangsters to think she was doing a drive-by.

Finally she came to Building 3. She wondered how often Dion came to visit her here. They both grew up in the projects, but Tammy liked to put the past behind her. She never went there to visit her family. She always insisted they come to her house. Tammy could not take the horrible memories of pissy staircases, dirty hallways and all the thug luvin' that went on. She guessed Dion got a rush by returning to his past. Tammy circled the building a few times, looking for an inconspicuous place to park. She wanted to be able to get away quickly after she returned the driver license to this Bitch. She got out of the car and slowly approached the apartment. She tried to crouch down as to not be seen by anyone before she wanted to be. Tammy felt a sudden pang of guilt for carrying on like this. Here she was a 35-year-old physician, running through the projects like a gangster with her .38 in tact.

There was something about her love for Dion that made her delirious. She just couldn't control herself, when bitches tried to get between a good thing. She had worked long and hard at her marriage, and she would be damned if some tramp was going to take her man. Tammy placed the gun in the inside of her trench coat, and slid on her gloves, not wanting to leave any fingerprints behind.

After she got off the elevator, she tiptoed up to #27 and heard music playing from inside the apartment. Tammy tapped lightly on the door, as she did not want to alarm Simone at this late hour to anything suspicious. Tammy stood waiting for her to ask who it was. She knew Simone would look through the peephole so she put a picture of her driver's license over the peephole. Tammy spoke, "this is security - you must have dropped your license in the lobby." With that Simone took her chain off the door. Tammy pushed her way through, gun in tow and slammed the door behind her.

"I don't think we formally met Simone. You left your license at my house bitch, when you came to fuck my husband in my bed!" Simone started backing up, looking like she had just seen a ghost. She was moving towards the cordless phone that was sitting on the living room couch.

"Don't even think about it ho!" Tammy brandished the gun to let this bitch know she meant business. Simone stopped dead in her tracks and fell to the ground.

"Please don't kill me, please don't kill me! I promise I'll never speak to Dion again!" She had the look of terror in her eyes that Tammy longed to see.

"Shut-up!" Tammy screamed. She cut her off. She had no time for a soap opera. She knew her time was limited, so she had to make it quick.

"Lets get one thing straight," she held the gun to her side. "Dion is my husband and he is not leaving me, for no one, especially no trifling ho that lives in the projects! I'm sure you sleep around for money and a good time. I never want to see your skank ass anywhere near my husband, or my home, or I swear to God I will come back here blasting, because I know where you live! Do you understand me?" She screamed.

By now Simone was trembling with tears rolling down her face. This was a far cry from the cocky ho that was in her house weeks ago with that smug look on her face, like yeah B I slept with your man in your bed, Tammy thought! The thought made Tammy's blood curdle.

"Do you understand me?" She slapped her in the face with the gun to let her know she was serious.

Simone fell down with blood drooling from her mouth saying - "I'm sorry, I'm sorry."

"No, you will really be sorry if I ever catch you within 10 feet of my husband." Simone held her mouth and nodded her head really fast.

Tammy knew she had to go before someone heard their screams. With that she dropped Simone's license on the floor and walked out. She was smiling as she ran towards her car, that'll teach a bitch!

Chapter 26   BE CAREFUL WHO YOU TRUST

Present Day

"Man yall better not come in here past curfew tonight. You know coach don't play that. I know you're in the middle of Hotlanta, and you rookies done heard all kinds of things about the club *Pumps in the Bump*. But if you go to that club, I guarantee you, you will not get back to this hotel before 12:30. Take it from a veteran, yall will be turned inside out. You think you've seen a lot of groupies and hos so far, you ain't seen nothin' yet son," said Michael Greene, a veteran for the *New Jersey Slammers*.

Tyson and Jake, the two rookies on the team just rolled their eyes.

"Man you always preaching," Jake, said. "We've heard all the warnings before man. We're grown ass men and we know how to handle our *bizniss*. Hey we just going for a little eye candy and fun, man we ain't going to be wilin' out." The two rookies gave each other a high five.

"Later G." With that Jake picked up his keys and told Ty, "Come on man lets roll."

Tyson didn't know why, but something in his gut told him that he was going to regret going out with Jake. Jake was a hothead and could be a showboat at times. Tyson preferred to stay low-key. As far as he was concerned, being a rookie brought enough attention to you without having to seek it. But there were a lot of guys in the league who were in love with being famous. Tyson's mother always taught him if you hear that little voice in your head telling you something's wrong, you ought to follow it. That's God trying to tell you something.

"Yo man slow down. I know this is a rental and all but you need not attract any attention by the cops. I don't want to end up on the front page of the paper."

Jake laughed at him. "Man you need to relax a little, we're going to have the time of our lives tonight."

Jake and Tyson pulled into the parking lot of *Pumps in the Bump,* Atlanta's famous strip club. Jake was all excited, "Man I'm telling you this is the best strip club you have ever been to. You ain't never seen no broads like this before man. These are the best of the best! Ain't gonna be no fat girls, or ugly girls on stage."

Tyson responded, "As far as I'm concerned man - you been to one strip club you been to them all. I don't know what the hell you getting so excited for. You're a professional basketball player, you're surrounded by beautiful, sexy women all the time."

They entered the club through the V.I.P. entrance, which was located in the back of the building. The owner Sal greeted them personally. "How you doing fellas? Welcome to *Pumps in the Bump.* Can I get you fellas some drinks?"

Jake responded, "yeah man get us two Tanqueray and tonics."

"Coming right up," Sal said.

Tyson took in the VIP room, it was pretty nice. It was decorated with leather furniture, a big flat screen TV that gave you a view of the main stage dancers, and a stereo system that was piped into the room. There was a refrigerator in the corner, which was stocked with water, wine and beer. One side of the room was all mirrors and the other side of the room had a door, which look like it led to another room.

Ty and Jake were taking off their coats getting comfortable when the prettiest woman Tyson ever laid eyes on walked in with their drinks.

"Hello gentleman, my name is Lola. I will be your hostess for tonight, so whatever you need or want", her eyebrow raised when she said this, "just buzz me."

Was she looking dead at Tyson when she said that or was it his imagination? He looked over at Jake and saw the same reaction from him. His mouth was wide open. But then again Jake's mouth was always wide open.

"Well we certainly will pretty brown eyes. MMM mmmm hmmmph you fine woman." Jake said to Lola as he eyed her up and down. "Have a seat and join us with your fine self."

Tyson just stared at this woman; she was so breathtaking to him. She was shaped like an hourglass, and had a very exotic look about her. The outfit she wore complimented her in all the right places.

As if she noticed him staring at her - she said, "Well I told you guys my name, you haven't told me yours." She seemed to be staring at Tyson specifically. However that didn't stop Jake from answering first.

"My teammates call me 'Jake the Snake', because I sneak up behind niggas on the court without them even knowing it. Yeah!"

Tyson was always curious about women who did not recognize them immediately as professional ball players. He never knew if they were trying to be coy and act like they were not groupies, and didn't follow sports, or if it was part of their game to lure the men in.

So Tyson spoke up, "I see you're not much of a basketball fan huh? We play for one of the best teams in the East, the *New Jersey Slammers*."

"I'm sorry, I really don't follow sports. Sports tend to follow me," she added with a smile.

Jake became very excited - "Oh yeah, what you mean by that honey-dip?"

Just at that moment another scantily clad dancer entered the room, and walked right up to Jake. "Hey big boy. My name is Peaches and I'm here to do a private dance just for you."

"Well Peaches you sure are juicy-fruit." Jake responded, forgetting all about Lola.

Tyson thought to himself Jake is so thirsty. Any pretty woman with a nice body would get him going. He was secretly happy for the distraction though because Lola had piqued his curiosity from the moment he laid eyes on her.

Tyson was starting to feel the Tanqueray and Tonic. Lola instinctively took a seat next to him, and gazed at him with her pretty hazel eyes. Tyson thought how he had never seen eyes this beautiful on a woman. They were captivating.

She crossed her legs in front of him as she sat down to face him on the loveseat he was sitting on, showing off her long, toned legs. Tyson couldn't help but look at her breasts, they seemed to be barely covered by the halter-top she was wearing. He wondered to himself if they were real - they looked so perfect.

"So Mr. ballplayer, is this your first time at P&B?"

"Yeah, can't you tell?" Tyson was actually nervous talking to this woman. He couldn't believe it. He was never nervous talking to chicks.

Women from all walks of life approached him all the time. They waited for you after games, whether you were married or not. They booked rooms in your hotel when your team was on the road, and spent a lot of time in the hotel bar. They hung out at professional sports events, and places where ball players hung out. They were often beautiful women, but Tyson never got caught up in that scene. This is why he couldn't understand why he was so taken with this woman.

"Yeah, I could tell from the look in your eyes when I first came in, that this was a new experience for you. But your pahtna over there, seems like he is a regular." They both cracked up laughing at that, because Jake was overly eager to be pleased.

"But seriously though, athletes and entertainers love coming to a place like this. They can unwind and be entertained by some of the most beautiful girls in the world. They are treated like royalty the moment they walk in the door, because as far as Sal is concerned you all are his bread and butter. They are very selective as far as who they let in the club, because most of the girls are very sensitive about being groped, and then followed after work. When the women take jobs here they are assured that they will be among the best company. If you are not among the Who's Who in America, you will have a hard time getting in."

"Is that right" Tyson said, finishing up the last of his drink. "Hey Lola would you mind getting a brother another T&T on the rocks."

"Sure thing handsome, anything you want." Again it looked like her eyebrow went up when she said that. Was that an invitation?

She got up from the seat and Tyson couldn't take his eyes off of her body. She sauntered out of the room giving him something to look at.

Lola could feel his eyes on her ass as she left the room. She lived for these moments.

Tyson looked over at his friend who was oblivious to everything in the room. He was tuned in to his private dancer. Peaches had just turned up the music and dimmed the lights. Beyonce's, *"Naughty Girl"* was pumping through the speakers. All Tyson could do was chuckle at his friend, who lived for things like this. This was new territory for Ty.

Lola returned to the room with his T&T, and she had brought herself another refill.

"So," she said as she sat even closer to him on the loveseat this time. "What is it that you enjoy doing in your spare time when you're not playing ball? Or playing women?"

"Oh you got jokes I see. I told you I'm not that type of guy. Women come at me all the time but I'm just not interested. If I'm not working out, I'm spending time with my family or overseeing one of my business ventures. I don't have time to play baby."

"So are you a dancer here at the club?" A stripper was really not Tyson's kind. He couldn't believe he was even having this conversation with her.

"I used to be for a minute, but I worked my way up. Now I'm a hostess, and my primary purpose is to make people like you happy. One day I want to own my own though."

Tyson was afraid to ask what a stripper had to do to "work her way up" but he figured she definitely did it by her good looks.

"Oh so you got a little entrepreneur in you huh?"

"Got to," she responded. "The only way to make any real money is by being the boss, not doing the boss. You know what I'm sayin'." She said as she laughed at herself.

"True, True." Tyson responded.

At that moment Lola noticed that the liquor was really starting to go to Tyson's head. She had told the bartender to *hook it up* for her.

"Well Mr. Myers", she said as she leaned into him and put her hand between his legs. "Why don't you and I go into the private VIP room so I can put a smile on that face."

Tyson didn't resist as she led the way.

Chapter 27 HELP ME PLEASE

Present Day

Two hours had passed but Simone could still feel the imprint of the gun on her temple. It must have taken all of Dion's wife's self control to not pull the trigger. The whole incident seemed like a scene from a movie. She went to the bathroom and looked in the mirror. "Oh my God", she yelled aloud. She looked like death. Simone's face was pale, the type of pale people have after suffering a long illness. The side of her head was swelling and turning black and blue. She began to sob uncontrollably. All this over some dick, Simone thought. That nigga will never see her face again. She didn't want to tell anybody. She was embarrassed and just wanted the whole thing to go away like a bad dream. But this wasn't a dream and Simone needed help. So she decided, even though she really didn't want them to know, to call Brittany and Renee. Besides, she thought, who knows when psycho wife will show up again. She may need back up. Telling her mom was not an option...

Brittany showed up first, and Simone was so relieved that she started crying and actually let Brittany give her a hug. At some point in her life, Simone could not remember when, she became uncomfortable giving and receiving hugs. The only time an embrace felt natural was after she had finished having sex. But after having a gun put to her head and working herself into a panic about Renee showing up first, Simone even held the embrace for a couple of seconds. Renee, though Simone loved her, was definitely the most emotional of the bunch. She would fly off the handle when she saw Simone's face. And if Simone confessed to her crime, Renee's anger would redirect itself at Simone. Yup, Simone thought, the man that winds up with Renee will be loved stronger and harder than he ever thought possible. But Simone would not take a million dollars to be in his shoes if he messed up.

"My God", Brittany gasped. "What happened?"

"It's a long story," Simone exhaled. "If you don't mind Brit, Renee should be here any minute, could we wait until she comes, cause I definitely don't want to tell this story more than once." Just as Simone was finishing her request there was a knock on the door. It was Renee. Simone let Brittany answer so she could turn her face away. Renee came through the door in obvious high spirits.

"What's up homies? I'm not even mad that Simone's crazy ass got us out here in the middle of the night, cause I have something to tell you two also."

"Re," Brittany cut off Renee. "This is serious look at Simone."

Brit turned and saw that Simone had her back to them. "Simone," Brittany said softly, "please turn around." Simone turned slowly with tears in her eyes. Renee's mouth fell open.

"What the fuck?" Renee said stunned. "Who did this shit?" Was it that married, fake wanna be a mack nigga? What's that mothafucka's name, Joe?"

Simone just started crying harder as Renee continued to rant. Brittany was getting upset too. "Damn, Renee just stop please."

Renee was surprised by Brittany's tone, "Well excuse me for caring!"

"It's not that. I don't even know the story yet, could we please let Simone tells us what happened so we know who to be mad at?" Renee knew Brittany had a point, but her temper made it hard for her to bite her tongue.

"You're right Brit," Renee agreed, "but before you tell us what happened do you need to go to the hospital, or could I at least get some ice for your head?" Renee questioned.

"No and No," were Simone's answers. "Stop worrying Re it looks a lot worse than it is."

"Well now I'm relieved," Renee said sarcastically.

Brittany gave Renee a look and Renee decided to keep quiet. "Just tell us what happened," Brit said with reassurance.

"Well, it's not what you think. A woman did this." Over the next hour Simone told her story, leaving out and putting in key elements in order to show herself in a more favorable light. But the way she told her story didn't make sense to either of her friends.

The lawyer in Brittany was beginning to show. "Ok Simone so you're going out with this other married guy, Dion," Brittany questioned.

"Well I wouldn't say going out. He's more of just like you know a jump off," Simone interjected.

"A friend with benefits," Renee snickered.

"Whatever," Brittany continued. "You two have sex on occasion. You saw him a couple of weeks ago, you two had dinner and went to a hotel. But you two had done this before? Was he feeling guilty? Did he say he was going to tell his wife? I mean how did she find out about you and how did she get your address?"

As Brittany questioned Simone a light bulb went off in Renee's head, "Maybe she hired a private investigator." Renee's guilty conscious was showing. Brittany looked at Renee unconvinced.

"I don't think so but if she did I could look into it. I know a lot of PI's in this state and some owe me favors."

Simone didn't want anyone looking into anything so she spoke up, "I think you're right Brit. I mean private investigator that's white people shit."

"Is it?" Renee asked, "Then how do you think Mrs. disgruntled wife found your ass?"

Both Brittany and Renee were staring and eagerly awaiting Simone's answer. She tried her hardest to come up with something that sounded believable but nothing came. The truth would have to be told.

"OK look there's one small detail I left out." Both of Simone's friends just continued to stare. "Well Dion kept telling me that his wife was working a triple shift, and ever since I met him, he's been bragging about his house and the bar and the fly artwork. So he was going to just swing me by there to see it real quick. But when we got there he offered me a drink and one thing led to another and we sort of ended up in his bed."

"Oh shit," Renee yelled, "Do you even know what kind of line you crossed?"

"Wait," Simone exclaimed, "it gets worse. So in the middle of you know, his wife comes home. We didn't even hear her come through the door and she caught us in the middle."

"What did she say?" Brittany asked

"Well she didn't ask me if I wanted a cup of coffee. She started screaming and losing her mind, what do you think?"

113

"Ok," Renee added, "Maybe the better question is what did you say?"

"Look Renee before you start judging me I was drunk and high, you know how it is."

"No the fuck I don't know how it is. Your ass must have been crack high. Do you know how lucky you are? Do they have kids?"

"Damn Re one question at a time," Simone answered. "And I don't feel so lucky, all pale and bruised up."

Renee wasn't finished. "Well let me break it down for you my ignant friend - you're lucky to be alive. I can tell you if it were me you'd be dead. You've known me a long time Simone, and I always blame the man for cheating. He's the one with the commitment. However, if a bitch is disrespectful enough to come up in my house and look at pictures of me and my kids, then has the nerve to go with my husband to our marital bed and open her legs - she must want to get shot. I don't know one woman in my family that wouldn't come out blastin or stabbin or something."

"Well your family is far from typical Renee." Simone huffed.

Brittany interrupted, "I'm still waiting to hear how she found your address."

"When I grabbed my stuff to leave I was in a panic and my pocketbook fell over, I picked everything up quick and must have left my license."

Renee started laughing out loud, "Poetic justice."

"Thanks a lot," Simone growled. "Anyway," she put her hand up at Renee. "What do you think Brit? You've been pretty quiet."

Brittany just gave Simone a sad look and said, "I'm disappointed in you."

"What?" Simone was taken aback; Brittany always tried to be understanding.

"What," Renee huffed. "What the fuck did you expect her to say? Her and Tyson are practically married. What do you think she would do if she caught Tyson in her bed with one of those scandalous groupies? Even more accurate and you know this is true Simone, what would the 3 of us do to that ho?" Renee finished.

"I'm afraid Re is right on this one Simone, do I have to remind you that people have died for less." With that Brittany tapped her side and all three of them understood. Underneath Brittany's blouse were scars from bullets that ripped through her one sunny afternoon. The incident with Carmen that lead to this was forever etched on Brittany's body and soul.

"I know you two are right," Simone conceded, "but don't worry I plan to never see him again, I promise."

Brittany commended her, "that's good, but you might want to plan on never sleeping in a married man's bed again."

"I won't, I've learned my lesson," Simone answered. "But what if Dion's wife comes back?" Simone pleaded and stole a glance at Renee.

"Don't worry," Renee responded. "Even though you can be a scandalous ho, you're still my girl. We got your back."

Simone smiled to herself and remembered why these were her best friends in the world.

Chapter 28   RESULTS OF THE INVESTIGATION

Present Day

Renee nervously tapped her left leg up and down as she waited for Sean to show up with the results of his investigation. Kyle she thought, my sweet tender lover. In the time between hiring Sean to check him out and now, Renee and Kyle had gotten much closer. They had proclaimed their commitment to each other and Renee was completely head over heels for him. She had regretted the whole private investigator thing from the start but whenever she tried to call Sean and have him stop the investigation, he would say things to convince her it was in her best interest to let him continue. And for Renee, old self-preservation habits died hard. A few times she had come close to telling Kyle about the whole situation but every time she chickened out.

Sean walked through the door of Evelyn's restaurant looking sharp. Renee saw a few of the women at the bar give him a double take. Yeah Sean was a looker Renee thought, he was a little too pretty for her taste, but she was sure he had plenty of women to choose from. When he saw Renee, Sean smiled broadly, came over and gave Renee a big hug and held on a little too long. Renee was in sales so she always noticed the little things - like a hug that was too tight or too long, or a fresh haircut, or a little too much cologne. These things helped Renee in her line of work; she had closed many advertising deals by flirting with some good ole boy that obviously wanted more than just a good ad slogan from her. Renee never cared; she would use her advantages to a point. The good old boys never got to brag about sleeping with the cute black ad exec, but by the time they figured out she wasn't going to sleep with them, they had also figured out she was the best.

Yup Renee's instincts had made her a lot of money. Now all of Renee's instincts were telling her Sean was going on a date.

"Don't you look nice," Renee commented. "You must be meeting your girl or going on a hot date after this." Sean sort of drew back and made a funny face. She immediately apologized, "Hey, I'm sorry, too personal? You probably have a hard time keeping clients out of your business with the nature of what you do. I didn't mean to take any liberties."

Sean's face softened immediately, "Nonsense – too personal. Renee I want you to know I'm your friend and protector, you can ask me anything, and to answer your question, no I don't have a date. I haven't been lucky enough to meet a quality woman like you - beautiful, successful, independent."

Putting her hand up Renee blushed, "Stop Sean you're going to give me a big head. You're very charming. It's hard to believe there's no special someone in your life."

"Well," Sean answered. "I'm in the process of working on that right now."

"Good luck," Renee encouraged. "She's a lucky girl."

"Thank you," Sean beamed. "Would you like another drink?"

"No thanks," Renee declined. "If you don't mind I'd like to get down to business. Kyle and I are supposed to meet for dinner and he'll get worried if I'm too late."

Sean could feel his jaw tense at Renee's request. Fuck that shit he thought, this is my time with Renee. Sean had every intention of buying Renee at least two more drinks, having her cry on his shoulder and if he played his cards just right getting a kiss tonight.

"I'm sorry to break this to you Renee but I have something pretty serious to tell you and it would be completely unprofessional of me to just blurt it out, and then let you go spend time with the individual under investigation."

"Something serious?" Renee questioned.

"Yes," Sean said firmly. "And since you're the client and I'm the trained professional, I suggest you cancel your dinner with Kyle so we can take our time, and you can digest all that I'm telling you."

Renee began to feel her stomach churn and her muscles tense. Stay calm Renee, she told herself. Renee had worked hard in her adult years to learn to control her temper. A quick temper and vengeful spirit were attributes in Renee's old neighborhood, but in her new life they clouded Renee's judgment.

"I'd prefer not to lie to Kyle," Renee said in a laid back tone.

Composed and calm, Sean noted to himself, he was impressed.

Sean countered, "Why don't you tell him one of your business deals took an unexpected turn and it requires your immediate attention. Then you won't be lying just bending the truth slightly."

"OK," Renee agreed. "Excuse me for a moment."

"No problem," Sean stood out of courtesy as Renee left the bar. Several minutes later Renee returned and there was a drink waiting for her.

Sean smiled, "I took the liberty of ordering you a Cosmo with grey goose."

Renee looked puzzled, "How did you know that was my drink?"

Sean paused for a moment and then answered, "The bartender remembered."

Renee looked around at the crowd and said impressed, "Good bartender."

Sean ignored her comment, "I reserved a table in back so we can talk in private."

Once at the table Renee wasted no time, "So what's going on, what's the big news about my man?"

Sean noticed that Kyle had graduated to my man, Renee was being protective. They had gotten even closer than Sean realized.

"Look Renee don't shoot the messenger," Sean protested.

Renee calmed, "No offense Sean I'm just really anxious to hear the news, so I can begin dealing with it." With this Renee took a big swallow and drained her Cosmo. Sean put his hand up and quickly told the waitress to bring another drink.

"OK, Renee here's the situation. I'm sure you're aware that Kyle has dated and slept with a lot of women. But what you're probably not aware of is his anger management issues."

"What exactly does that mean?" asked Renee.

For the next hour and a half Sean told Renee an incredible story about Kyle beating his ex-girlfriend Tamyka half way to the grave. According to Sean her only crime was getting pregnant and wanting to keep the baby because they were so in love. "Tamyka almost died. The doctors said it was a miracle she lived, but they couldn't save the baby." Sean put his hand on top of Renee's, "Yes you heard me right Renee,

118

Kyle is a murderer. The only reason he's not in jail now is Tamyka was too scared of him to press charges."

Renee's head was spinning, too many cosmos and too much information. This person Sean was talking about couldn't be her Kyle, this guy sounded like a stranger. After staring for a long time at her fifth drink of the night, Renee blurted out, "I don't believe it."

Sean seemed ready for this, "I know it's an amazing story and I thought it might be hard for you to believe coming from a third party. So I've taken it upon myself to arrange a meeting between you and Tamyka. You'll meet her right?"

Renee straightened her shoulders and took a deep breath, "Yes I'll meet her."

"That's why you impress me so much Renee. You're a strong woman, now let's get you home," Sean finished.

"I can get myself home," Renee snapped.

"Don't be that way," Sean soothed. "I know you're probably angry and confused about the information I just told you, it's a lot to absorb. But don't lash out at me; I'm only doing the job you hired me to do. You've had a bunch of drinks tonight and I wouldn't be much of a gentleman if I let you drive in this condition. I'll take you home and you can get a friend, or a cab, or me to bring you back tomorrow. It's the weekend so you don't need your car in the morning."

In her heart Renee knew he was right. The last thing she needed on top of everything else was to crash or get caught driving drunk. "OK", she answered. Sean paid the bill and grabbed his keys.

When he pulled up in front of Renee's building the car stopping jerked her back into consciousness. She was so drunk she didn't even remember giving Sean directions to her home. But she reasoned she must of because here they were. Renee told him thank you and tried to open the door but it wouldn't budge.

"Let me help you," Sean smiled. "That door gets stuck all the time. He got out walked around to Renee's door unlocked it with his key and let her out. Sean grabbed her hand to help her out and it seemed like he yanked her so hard she had to stumble. But Renee was so drunk she couldn't be sure.

Sean caught her in both arms and said, "easy there I got you," as he pulled Renee in so tight she could feel her chest pressed against his. "Let me help you to the door," he continued. Once there he asked for Renee's keys and opened the door.

"Let me just help you to the couch here." Sean laid Renee down looked at her and smiled. She was even cute drunk. He kneeled down next to her and began to caress her cheek. Sean was aroused and could feel his penis getting hard. He wanted desperately to touch Renee's lips and feel her tongue but she wasn't an incoherent drunk; and Sean had put in too much work to ruin his chances by rushing things. Instead he brushed his hand across her chest as if by accident, leaned in and whispered in her ear, "Renee you know I'm attracted to you." Renee was only semi coherent. But she knew someone smelled good and was talking sweet in her ear. She hoped it was Kyle. She hoped this whole thing had been a horrible nightmare. But when she opened her eyes it was Sean.

She grabbed his arm and asked, "Are you sure it's true?"

"Yes Renee it's true." Sean said annoyed.

"Thanks for everything," she replied. "But I want to be alone right now."

Sean left and Renee cried herself into a drunken coma.

Chapter 29 BLASTIN!

Brittany drove home exhausted. She and Renee had stayed at Simone's long enough to calm her down and let her fall asleep. She was stopped at a red light so she closed her eyes and said a quick thank you to God for keeping her trifling friend alive. Gun to the head Brittany shivered at the thought and rubbed her side. For someone so non-violent Brittany had been the victim of too many guns in her life. But all that was before Carmen disappeared. She and Carmen were hardcore runnin buddies back in the day, but as much as Brittany missed her AWOL friend she had to admit to herself that intentionally or unintentionally, Carmen was bad for her health. She thought back to the summer before she went to college.

Back In The Day
Brittany and Carmen

"Could you put some designs on my toes please."
"That $5.00 dolla."
"I know that's for both toes." Brittany looked at Carmen, *"everything is $5.00."* Carmen laughed at her.
"Well you know I got to keep my feet right for my honey Rasan. He loves for my toes to be done – that's why he's always giving me the money to get them done."
"Speaking of money, I need to stop by Jamal's house and pick up some cash for the tolls on the way home."
Jamal Carter was Carmen's latest conquest. She was always on the prowl for the biggest ballers in Brooklyn. Carmen set the mold for the term gold-digger, but she always got what she wanted with her hazel eyes, Indian type hair and voluptuous shape. All she had to do was give a man the look and they seemed to be putty in her hands. When Brit watched her in action she always marveled at how simple men were.
Brit didn't say anything to Carmen, but she was thinking - didn't you just sleep with that cat last night, and if so, shouldn't you have gotten all

121

the loot before he dropped you off at my house this morning. But Brittany knew better. That was just Carmen's excuse for seeing Jamal one more time before she hit the road. She could never seem to get enough of her big-time drug dealin' ballers.

"I need to get home by 9:00 Carmen. I start my new job tomorrow."

"Don't worry it will only take a minute, I'm going to call him now to let him know we're on our way." She pulled out her cell phone to call him. Carmen was the only person Brit knew who could afford a cell phone in the early 90s. After Carmen hung up she said, "Jamal said we can come in and have dinner, his mom cooked on the grill and wants us to come over."

Brittany didn't know why she always let Carmen talk her into things against her will, but she was so smooth at it that sometimes Brit didn't even know she was being suckered.

"Well let's go" Brit responded. "My toenails can dry in the car, I have my flip-flops."

They jumped in the jeep Wrangler and headed to Jamal's house in East New York.

When they pulled onto Jamal's block, there was a big block party going on at the house across the street from Jamal, and there must have been hundreds of people on the block. "I hope we can find a place to park," Brittany said, cause I ain't gonna be here all night." They found a park a few houses down.

When they got to the house, Jamal answered the door, and Carmen was all smiles – chest was out, voice changed, and she was working it. Carmen proceeded to introduce Brit to Jamal's mother and siblings. Brit put on a polite smile, and said hello.

"Yall come on in the kitchen and have a seat. You want something to drink?" She asked in a heavy southern accent. Brit had to admit she didn't expect Jamal's mom to look so Southernly. She was a big woman, who was at least in her late fifties, and very homely. Jamal was the sole breadwinner in the house, and played the role of father and brother to his five siblings. The home was beautifully decorated with expensive Italian furniture, a large screen TV in the living room, and brand new appliances in the kitchen. You would think a woman like Ms. Carter would not tolerate a drug-dealing son in her home, but it just goes to show that some people don't care where the money comes from, as long as it comes. I suppose she would be living in the projects somewhere, with her five kids, had it not been for Jamal and his fast money.

Brittany had to admit the food looked good - fried chicken, barbeque chicken from the grill, red beans and rice, plantains, collard greens, cornbread and plenty of liquor. Brittany started with a couple of glasses of wine, to calm down. If she wasn't a little tipsy, this night would seem endless with Carmen constantly flirting with Jamal and momma feeding them like it was Thanksgiving.

After they finished eating Brit looked at Carmen and pointed to her watch, like what's up.

"Oh Brit, Jamal stepped out to the store he'll be right back, then we can leave."

Brittany couldn't help but wonder why Carmen didn't just get the money from him before he went to the store, after all that was the main reason she came over here. Nonetheless Brit stayed mum.

"Wanna go outside and have a cigarette?"

"Yeah the air will do me good." It was getting real warm in the house from all the cooking that was going on, and Brit was starting to feel the effects of the liquor.

When they went outside the music was pumping from the block party across the street. They were playing all the latest reggae hits, and Brit and Carmen loved their reggae music. When Murder She Wrote by Shabba Ranks came on Brit and Carmen started doing the Bogle dance on the porch bugging out. The sun was starting to go down, and Jamal came down the block, back from his apparent errand. Brittany was leaning up against the wall on the porch watching the people across the street at the block party. There must have been about 300 people outside.

Jamal walked up to them and said, "I saw yall dancing when I was walking down the block, why you stop?" They both laughed.

"You know how we get Jamal when we hear our reggae music." Then Butterfly came on and they both simultaneously broke into the butterfly dance.

"Damn, what are yall twins, when you hear a song you break out into the same dance", Jamal chuckled.

"You got jokes," Britt responded.

Then Jamal came over to Brit and said, "what's up with you and my boy Everton?"

Britt rolled her eyes. Everton was one of Jamal's drug dealin' homies who Brit had met the last time her and Carmen came out to Brooklyn. They had gone out for drinks and dancing with the two of them. However, Brit was never really into the drug dealing men. She didn't mind hanging out occasionally, but she could never take them seriously, based on their lifestyle. It was ironic, because although Carmen and her were best friends, their values were opposite. Carmen would make a living out of dating dealers if she could.

"Jamal, I told you I'm seeing somebody in Jersey. I can't play him like that."

"I know you ain't talkin' about Rasan", Carmen retorted. Carmen hated Rasan. Brittany thought it was because he never found her as attractive as most of Carmen's friends' boyfriends did. And Rasan's money came from working hard at a good job and not hustlin' on the street.

"Yes I am talking about Rasan", Brittany responded defensively.

Jamal leaned over her, and said "girl you need to drop that zero and get with this hero", referring to his friend Everton.

"For real" Carmen added.

Brittany just rolled her eyes.

"I'm telling you girl, you don't know what you're missing unless ....

Suddenly Brit heard something that sounded like firecrackers. Buck buck, buck, buck, buck, buck, buck, buck,!! Then suddenly screams- lots of them. The next thing she knew Jamal was on top of her shielding her from his attacker. Then he was on the floor. The two thugs who had been standing on the sidewalk shooting at him ran down the block.

Carmen began screaming at the top of her lungs and then crying hysterically." Brittany you're bleeding!!" Brittany looked down at her shirt, and to her horror there was blood coming out of her waist. "Oh my God, I've been shot, Carmen, I've been shot!!" She hadn't even felt the bullet go through her. Then she looked down at her legs and saw that they were bleeding. This was all Brittany could bear at that point. She fell down crying hysterically. What would her parents think? "Somebody call 911!" Carmen screamed. It seemed the whole family was motionless, wondering if they had lost their breadwinner to a senseless crime.

The whole family gathered in the living room waiting for the ambulance to arrive. It seemed like hours before the ambulance arrived.

She screamed in agony, "Where the hell is the ambulance!" She felt like she was going to bleed to death. The whole family, including Carmen was gathered around Jamal, making sure he was ok, and she suddenly wished her mother was there to comfort her.

After what seemed like an eternity the ambulance arrived. They cut off Britney's shoes and any clothes that were around the gunshots. They were careful not to move any body parts, as they loaded her onto the stretcher and into the ambulance. She noticed a crowd had gathered around her and Jamal. Brittany would not forget the face of a man she saw before she got on the ambulance. He was smiling.

That night Britt remembered praying to God that she would be able walk again because she had been shot 5 times. And she promised herself that was all the gangsta shit she would ever experience.

Chapter 30   A FAIR TRIAL

Present Day

Kyle

"Damn Man!" Brandon complained as he spit blood from his mouth. "Watch them elbows."

"Stop bitchin and check ball nigga," Kyle huffed in annoyance.

"Fine," Brandon caught the basketball in obvious anger.

Good Kyle thought. Get mad. Bring it - bring me your A game. Kyle tensed all his muscles as Brandon began to back him down to the basket. Brandon was throwing elbows as hard as he could. Kyle absorbed the blows with a small grunt but stood his ground. The shot went up and Kyle blocked it hard.

"Get that shit outta here," Kyle taunted as he ran to get the ball. Ball in hand Kyle rushed the basket crossed over and hit a jumper.

"Game!" he exclaimed as the ball went through the net. "You wanna run it back?" Kyle asked.

"Hell no," answered Brandon quickly, "I've taken enough abuse for one day.

"What's the matter?" Kyle asked.

"What's the matter?" Brandon repeated as he held a towel to his bloody mouth. "Man you been playing me today like I stole something from your Moms. You didn't even calm down when I elbowed the shit out of you. Sometimes I think your crazy ass likes pain."

Kyle couldn't help but chuckle at his last comment. "I'm sorry man, I've just had a lot on my mind lately."

"Well don't take it out on me," Brandon responded still nursing his wounds.

"Come on man chill, you know you're my boy," With that they gave each other pound and all was forgiven.

The truth was Kyle needed that game of basketball more than Brandon could know. The past five days Renee was not returning his calls and Kyle was losing it. The worse part was Kyle couldn't figure out why - everything had been going so well. He had never treated any women the way he treated Renee - gifts, meals, concerts, nothing was too good for her. Kyle thought for a moment, was he just so open, he was getting played? No, Kyle concluded it was a two way street. It was all-good until that night she needed to cancel cause of work. No more dates, no more sweet calls, nothing. Renee would call Kyle using different names and voices. She would talk all sexy and low and they would have phone sex. That shit would turn Kyle on and he would be feigning by the time they saw each other again. Damn he was getting worked up just thinking about it. Fuck this, he finally decided, that's my woman, and it's time to see what's up. In the back of Kyle's mind he wanted to play it cool, like he had with other women in his life, but it was too late, Renee was like the best drug in the world, and Kyle needed a fix.

Kyle sat on the steps of Renee's building waiting with anticipation. He finally saw her coming out of the parking lot. She had on a cute business suit, matching heels and an attaché case. She was walking with purpose like she could change the world. Look at my baby, he thought, she's adorable.

Renee

Renee pulled into the parking lot of her complex exhausted and relieved to be home. She had turned herself back into a workaholic in hopes of getting Kyle off her mind, but it hadn't worked. Twelve hours a day and she still had Kyle on the brain, Kyle biting her ear, Kyle licking her neck. What's wrong with me? Renee thought. This guy is some type of psychotic abuser. According to Tamyka their relationship was something right off the Lifetime channel, but somehow Renee still found herself fantasizing about Kyle. This was confusing to Renee, for the first time in her life the information didn't match Renee's gut instinct. The instinct she always trusted, the instinct she thought would never fail her. Get it together she told herself. It's over, no more Kyle, because if he hits me I'll have to kill him and I care about him too much to hurt him.

I can do this, Renee decided, As long as I don't have to see him in person. I'll take cold showers, work and hang out with my friends until I forget all about him. Renee was proud of her new resolution and began to walk with a renewed strength toward her door. Just then she looked up to see Kyle sitting on the steps. Renee could feel all the strength leave her body as she looked at his face. She began to walk slower and hoped he didn't notice. What am I going to tell him, she thought. She had promised Tamyka she would not tell Kyle. Tamyka explained that she was still terrified of Kyle and was convinced he would find her and kill her if Renee told. It was too late. There was no time to think of a plan. When she reached him Kyle stood up and gave her a hug. Renee tried to tense but he smelled so good, and he felt like happiness. When he let go he gave her a serious look.

"So what's up why haven't you returned my calls," he demanded.

"I'm sorry Kyle but I've been real busy at work," Renee responded.

"Come on Renee don't give me some bullshit answer like I'm some client you haven't been able to get back to. I'm your man! You never had problems calling me before. As a matter of fact before that night you used to call me more than I called you."

"What night?" She asked confused.

"The night we were supposed to have dinner, and you called me sounding all strange and on edge talking about an emergency at work. Well you don't work in a hospital or fire station so what the fuck?" Kyle seethed.

"Kyle you need to chill," Renee could feel her anger rise. "Important things do come up at work, things that need my immediate attention."

"OK fine, is that what happened that night?" Kyle waited.

Renee contemplated for a moment and then decided against lying. "No that's not what happened." Renee answered defiantly.

"I knew that shit went down shady," Kyle hissed. "Then what? Tell me now Renee, you seeing someone else?"

Renee looked in Kyle's eyes and they were on fire. She wondered for a moment if she should say yes, just to see if he would get violent. No bad idea she thought.

"Because if I remember correctly, I specifically asked you if you were my woman and you specifically said yes. So if you're seeing someone why didn't you just…."

Renee put her hand over his mouth. "Kyle," she yelled. "I'm not seeing anyone else, no one, there's been no one but you."

Kyle kissed her hand and grabbed her neck. He pulled Renee in so hard she couldn't stop him. He used his lips to open hers. His tongue savagely darted into her mouth and she could feel the desire and emotion in his kiss. Renee felt her knees buckle and her defenses fade. Just one last time she told herself then I'll break up with him forever.

Chapter 31   LIKE A THIEF IN THE NIGHT

Present Day

Tyson slowly opened his eyes. His head felt like there was a ton of rocks in it. He screamed in agony from the pain. He thought to himself, I ain't never had no damn hangover like this. What the fuck? Somebody please kill me, and take me out of my misery.

He looked at the clock on the wall; it read 10:30 a.m. "Where the hell am I?" Tyson spoke out loud, even though there was no one else in the room. He did not recognize his surroundings. He sat up in the bed and at that moment he realized that he only had his boxers on.

"What the fuck happened here!" he said when he realized the ramifications of the situation. He got up and walked around the room. He did not recognize his surroundings. He stumbled into the bathroom to take a look at himself in the mirror. He thought maybe he was in the middle of a bad dream and that he would wake up soon. Tyson turned on the bathroom light and noticed that there were pictures of dancers hanging up on the wall in the bathroom. They had on skimpy outfits and very large assets. Tyson suddenly had a memory jolt - assets, outfits. He started remembering his teammate Jake and the 2 strippers that were entertaining them the night before. Then he had visions of a woman with hazel eyes and a seductive voice. But he couldn't remember what happened after that. The last thing he recalled was chilling in a private room with these 2 women.

Tyson proceeded to get dressed. He walked out of the room and into another room and realized he wasn't in New Jersey. He was on the road with his team and at this very moment he was missing the morning shoot around.

"Oh Shit!" Tyson said out loud. I missed my damn curfew and that snake Jake didn't even bother to see about me. Wait until I get a hold of his ass.

Tyson ran into the main area of the club and noticed an older gentleman sweeping the floor whistling.

"Hello Sir, could you tell me where Sal the owner is?"

The man looked up from his work and his eyes got big. "Tyson Myers! If it ain't one of the best shooting guards in the NBA. It's a pleasure to meet you son. You know I've been following your career since you was at Jersey University. I told my grandson, that boy going to go pro one day - mark my words. Boy you break down *dem* defenses like nobody else can! I like to call you Shake n' Bake. Cause you shake 'em and bake 'em every time!" The old man doubled over laughing at himself.

"Thank you sir. I appreciate the compliment. But have you seen Sal?" Tyson went to hold his head because suddenly it began pounding again.

"Call me Leroy. Sir makes me feel like a senior citizen, and old Leroy can still roll with the best of em' you know what I mean. He began to chuckle at himself again. Sal don't never come in before 12:00. What ya need son? I've been working here for 7 years."

"Leroy right now I have the worst hangover of my life and I need to get back to my hotel fast. I have to change and get over to the practice facility."

"Relax son I'll call up one of our car services and have them pick you up in ten minutes. But can I ask you a small favor before you go *Shake*."

"What is it Mr. Leroy?" Tyson was never rude to older folks because his mother didn't raise him that way, but right now he could barely think let alone talk.

"Could you give me an autograph for my grandson, he loves you more than me?"

"Sure Leroy give me a piece of paper" Tyson said as he sat down at the nearest table. He felt like his head was too heavy to support his body.

As Tyson wrote out the autograph Leroy went to call him a car.

As Tyson sat in the car he just kept thinking about how he could not wait to get his hands on his so-called friend Jake. How he gonna just leave me to miss curfew and the morning practice. He would surely be benched now for the big game tonight. He thought back to last night and the gut feeling he had. What was it that momma used to say? If you get a bad feeling about something – it's God trying to tell you something.

Tyson had ignored his intuition yesterday, and now he was paying the price.

Lola

Mission fucking accomplished - Lola thought to herself as she lay in her bed looking up at the ceiling. She didn't think it was going to be this easy. Shakira had boasted to her about how Tone the bartender had hooked her up before, but Lola had been hesitant. Tone was greedy for money so if you slipped him a big enough bill he would do just about anything *fo' ya*. The dancers sometimes referred to him as Mr. Mickey, because he didn't have a problem slipping a Mickey in someone's drink.

Tyson Myers had been putty in Lola's hands. She recognized that she had his undivided attention from the moment he saw her. She could always tell when a man would be a challenge and when he would be her slave from the way he looked at her. There was always a weakness for beauty that she could see right through - after all she was the master of manipulation. She'd had that power all of her life. It was a survivor skill for her.

Last night she didn't know how long it would take for the drug to take effect but she knew she was going to get Mr. Myers by any means necessary. After that second drink he didn't know what the hell was happening to him. His friend Jake was so pre-occupied with Peaches, her homegirl, who was one of the most popular dancers at the club that he didn't notice Tyson and her slipping into the private room. Lola had told Peaches to tell Jake that she would have the car service drop him off at the hotel. Tyson was so erect by the time she laid him on the bed that she didn't have to do much work. She didn't even have to slob on the knob. He didn't even know he wasn't wearing a condom because the Mickey had dulled his awareness. Once he came, Lola did not want to hang around and answer any questions when he woke up. She figured she and Tyson would have plenty of time to talk once she conceived his child. She had left him sleeping in the bed like a baby. When he came to she knew his memory would be foggy, and he would assume that one thing had let to another or he had taken advantage of her drunken state after they were intoxicated, and that was the story she was sticking to.

Mr. Myers get ready to be a daddy, because I'm going to be your first baby momma, and we expect to live in style!

Chapter 32 HARD TO SAY GOODBYE

Present Day

Renee woke up to the wonderful smells of food and flowers. She looked at the clock and it was 10:20 am. She couldn't believe she had slept so late. The past week had been so stressful; she was barely able to sleep a couple of hours each night. She looked at her dresser and there was a big beautiful bouquet of flowers catching the Saturday sunlight, which was shining, through her bedroom window. What is Kyle doing she thought. The flowers were one thing but cooking breakfast, this was new. Renee was definitely the cook in the relationship. Besides she remembered, shouldn't he be at work? Kyle worked Saturdays for the delivery service and he was very conscientious about his work. Renee had counted on this. She would spend all day composing a long letter breaking up with Kyle. Then she would go put it on the windshield of his truck while he was working. Renee knew it was corny to break up in a letter, but she couldn't help it, she was too weak around Kyle. In fact the more she thought about it, the more she was starting to think ending their relationship was for the best. Renee needed to be strong so she could overcome anything. She could not allow this man so much power over her. Suddenly Renee was feeling her old self coming back. It was time to wake up from the fantasy. This was never real in the first place, she convinced herself. It was only a matter of time before he would start to change, it's better she found out early. A nice, simple, safe guy that I'm not obsessing over all day – that's what she needed she reasoned. Renee put on shorts and a form fitting white t-shirt. OK she thought time to face the music.

She walked in the kitchen and Kyle was over by the stove burning some eggs. He had on his jeans and no shirt. God he's sexy, Renee thought but then she caught herself. FOCUS, she yelled at herself.

"Kyle turn off the flame it's burning," she scolded.

"I know," he looked at her and smiled. "I'm sorry baby. I was trying to do everything at once like a short order cook, that way I could of brought you breakfast in bed," Kyle said proud of himself.

"Is that why you didn't wake me up?" Renee asked.

"Yeah, plus you really looked like you needed the rest, you never sleep so hard. I went to the store and got you flowers. Did you see them?"

Renee knew the reason he was asking. She loved flowers and would usually make a huge deal over them. She liked rearranging them and bringing them into any room they went into. She always thought beautiful flowers should be appreciated and not sit in a room where no one could see them.

"Yes, they're gorgeous, thank you," she responded.

"Why didn't you bring them in the kitchen with you?" Kyle puzzled.

Damn Renee thought, he can feel I'm not my usual self. "I guess I was just rushing to see what you were cooking," Renee answered.

"It's OK I'll get them," Kyle decided. When he passed her in the doorway he grabbed her in typical Kyle fashion.

"Damn baby you lookin' sexy in that tight shirt and them shorts. I think I should make up for my bad cooking and show you something I'm good at." With that Kyle lifted her shirt and licked her belly button.

But Renee grabbed his head firmly "Kyle stop I'm hungry."

Kyle held on and groaned, "Me too baby" as he kissed her stomach.

"I mean it," Renee warned.

"OK, take it easy I'm getting the flowers," he surrendered.

This guy is unbelievable Renee thought, you would think he had been away at war for a year as horny as he was. She had specifically not put on her silk robe because she knew she would be naked in about 5 seconds with Kyle around. Kyle was like a magician when it came to getting her clothes off. When Kyle returned to the kitchen Renee was at the stove finishing up breakfast. Kyle came up behind her and licked her ear whispering, "You want to take a shower together after breakfast?"

"Kyle stop, you want me to burn the rest of the food we have left? Just go sit down and behave yourself."

"Fine," Kyle said in a hurt voice. "Well excuse me for missing you Ms. I'm so busy at work."

Renee decided to let the comment slide. "Speaking of work," she said. "Aren't you late for work?"

"You know I wouldn't go into work this late. I got one of my co-workers to cover my shift. There's a bunch of them that owe me favors - especially after last week. See, I have this crazy girlfriend who doesn't want to return my calls, so I pulled a lot of overtime and extra shifts to get my mind off of her." Kyle said with a sly grin.

"So today I'm commencing with my new mission, which I'm calling By Any Means Necessary, it's a tribute to my boy Malcolm."

"What does that mean - by any means necessary?" Renee questioned.

"I'm glad you asked," Kyle continued. "After last nights reunion or reunions," he chuckled, "I'm pretty sure you're not sleeping with anyone else, because I could tell your body missed mine. This is why you can probably tell I'm in a very good mood this morning. I'm positive anything else we can work out. But I can tell you're trying to hide something from me. So we are going to stay together all day, and by any means necessary get to the bottom of whatever bullshit is going down." Kyle finished.

Wow - Renee was speechless. Kyle was not going to make this easy.

"Listen Kyle," Renee began but he cut her off.

"Nope, I'm not finished," Kyle, continued. "I need to tell you how I feel about you. You may think I'm just some type of smooth operator that buys flowers and talks sweet to every chick but I don't. You might think everything I've said to you was just a ploy to get between your legs. But it wasn't. Don't get me wrong I love it between your legs, when I'm there it's like the best vacation I've ever taken. Anyway staying on point, as much as my body craves yours, it's not just about that. It's deeper. I've never cared for any woman the way I care for you. I think everything about you is adorable. The way you're all head strong and proud let me know from the start you wouldn't be taking no shit from me. I think that's sexy as hell. I have a strong personality and I need a woman that can hang with me - mentally, emotionally and yes sexually. I feel we're compatible in every way, and and ah fuck it, I actually hurt when things feel wrong between us. I guess what I'm trying to say is that I lo…"

"Wait," Renee interrupted Kyle in a panic. Her head was spinning. All she could think was don't let those words leave his lips. It would be more than she could handle. The word sounded like a slap and she could see by the look on Kyle's face he felt it.

"Wait, did you just say wait?" Kyle's voice was no longer proud and confident. It was unsure and confused. Kyle's whole demeanor changed, "What's the problem Renee, you know you're being a real bitch right now. You think this shit has been easy to say. Maybe I got the whole thing wrong. Maybe you're the one playing games. Maybe you just like the flowers, and the dinners, and the dick and you're not really checkin' for me."

His words stabbed Renee like a knife. She could tell she had hurt Kyle and now he wanted to hurt her back.

"Please wait Kyle," Renee pleaded. "I gave you a chance to speak, now please give me a chance."

"Fine," Kyle said shortly.

"I know you're saying ugly things to me because I haven't been so nice lately. The truth is - that night I cancelled our date it was because I had found out something about you. Something about the type of man you are."

"What the hell are you talking about?" Kyle huffed.

"What the hell am I talking about? You want to know what I'm talking about. Kyle do you have a temper?"

"Yeah, so what? So do you, your temper is probably worse than mine."

Renee ignored his comment and continued. "Do you like to hit women Kyle?"

"Are you serious?" Kyle started laughing. "Are you asking me this cause I smacked your ass last night during sex, because you seemed to like it. I know I did," he reminisced.

"Trust me Kyle, this is no time for one of your sarcastic little comments," Renee warned.

136

"You're seriously asking me if I like to hit women?" Kyle puzzled. "You actually think I would hit or abuse a woman. I spent my life protecting my mother and sisters and you would ask me this. It really hurts that you would think I could do this."

"I wouldn't think you could, I wouldn't imagine you could!" Renee was screaming now. "But someone told me you did and when they told me, it was like getting punched in the gut," Renee admitted.

"But you believed them, some stranger. You didn't even ask me, you believed them. Fuck this shit!" Kyle growled.

He was putting on his shirt and getting his wallet. "I guess you don't know me at all." With that comment he walked over to Renee, grabbed her shoulders and looked in her eyes. "We wrestle and play all the time and I've never abused your silly ass. If I wanted to I could lay you out with one punch and you know it's true. But I won't, because the truth is I have never hit a woman in my life, even the bitches that deserved it, and now I'm going to leave and once again not hit a woman. See Renee, when I get mad or someone falsely accuses me, or things go to far, I LEAVE!" He screamed right in her face. "I don't HIT and if you never want me to come back just say so," Kyle demanded.

But Renee was speechless. Kyle turned, left the apartment and slammed the door so hard she felt her body shake. Renee fell back against the stove stunned. In the course of three minutes, Kyle went from almost saying I love you to never coming back. Renee felt dizzy and she slid down to the floor confused. She thought this was what she wanted – to break up and get him out of her system. But now that it had happened, everything felt wrong. Everything felt really wrong. Renee knew one thing for sure. Kyle did have a temper and he didn't hit her.

Chapter 33   SON OF A …

Present Day

Tyson could only see red as he got out of the taxi and headed into the practice facility. Wait until I get my hands on that snake Jake. Not only had he left me in the strip club but he also had the nerve to be at practice on time without me. I didn't even want to go to the damn club and he gone leave me up in there to sleep while I'm f-d up!

As Tyson entered the gym most of the guys were just warming up because Coach hadn't started the official practice yet. Tyson headed to the locker room to change his clothes. When he came out of the locker room, Jake spotted him and shouted, "What's up playa," as he began jogging towards him.

As soon as Jake was within arms reach Tyson reached out as if he was about to give him a pound, but instead he flipped Jake on the floor, causing him to hit the ground pretty hard.

"What's up playa? What the hell is wrong with you Jake?! You drag me to this fucking club that I don't want to go to in the first place, and then you leave me there to fend for myself with them freaks, when you knew I was messed up man! Fuck you nigga!!!"

Jake was just staring at him like he was crazy. Ty knew he never saw him loose his cool, but last night was too much.

A couple of the guys from the team were laughing at Jake as he got up holding his back.

"Come on Ladies - break it up", Raheem, one of their teammates yelled to them.

"Yo man - why you bugging out?" Jake yelled. "You were in the room with that fly honey, when I was ready to go. Peaches wasn't nothing but a tease so I decided to bounce. I saw how you was looking at honey dude, so I figured I would let you do your thing. How was I supposed to know you would sleep in there all night nigga? You need to calm the hell down!"

"Man you knew if I was late from curfew I wouldn't be able to play in the game tonight!"

"Man well the way you was lookin' at that hottie, I wouldn't put it past you. Ty I never seen you salivatin' over a woman before, you always so 'loyal' to Brit."

"Keep your fuckin' voice down man. I don't need the whole team in my business. You know I got a woman back at home, and it only takes one of their wives to find out, and Brittany will know the whole damn story!"

"True dat, true dat", Jake responded, not wanting his own business in the street either. His girlfriend Cynthia would not hesitate to show out if she ever got a whiff of his infidelities, and although Jake was probably the biggest playboy on the team since he was still single, he did plan on marrying Cynthia one day.

Tyson and Jake began walking towards the locker room to discuss last night, this way they wouldn't be in earshot of the other guys.

"Yo man, I'm sorry about that. I just never saw you so open over another woman in my life man. The whole time I've known you - you've had eyes only for Brit. I thought maybe her punani was made of gold, cause you know how the honeys be throwing it at you, and you never even sniff dog!! Last night it's like you forgot I was even in the room, your eyes never left shorty's body. Did you hit it man?!"

"You know Jake, I don't even know what happened last night," Tyson said as he held his head in his hands and slouched down on the bench in the locker room.

Jake just looked at Tyson suspiciously with one eyebrow up, he didn't know what his friend meant by that, but he wasn't going to pry.

Chapter 34 HATERS

Present Day

Brittany was home studying and looking forward to Tyson's return from his current road trip. It saddened her to think the better Ty did in the NBA the crazier their lives had become. She thought back to the last home game she went to after a road trip........

Brit told Renee, "let me go powder my nose real quick so I can look good for my man when he comes out the locker room. You know he's been on the road for a while, so I haven't seen him since he left."

"Go head gurl, get dolled up fo yo man!"

"You so silly," Brittany laughed at Renee's silly self.

Brittany walked down the hall to the closest restroom. She went inside to use the bathroom. As soon as she closed the door to the stall, some girls came in giggling with one another. The two had obviously been drinking because of the way they were laughing and carrying on.

"Guuuurl did you see that fine-azz Tyson Myers do his thing. He is so fiiiiine, he don't even have to dribble the ball, he could just go out there and profile as far as I'm concerned."

"I don't think he made it to the Pros based on his good looks Shelly", the other girl said to her friend giggling.

"I know but the things that I would do to him if I could just get close enough to him. I mean really now, what can a girl like – what's her face Brittany Martin; do for a fine-ass specimen like Mr. Myers! Huh you tell me. I mean homegirl with the 'Natty Dreads' might be a good match for Buju Banton or somebody."

Her friend busts out laughing in hysterics at her friend's comment.

Brittany hovered in the stall longer because this was getting interesting. These little chicken heads were always hatin'.

"But a look at this here '38-24-37' ok – Real hair, naturally straight – thank you very much, and caramel skin, who could ask for more."

"One night with Mr. Myers and I'll have him speaking in tongues – ya better recognize!"

At her little speech the chicken heads high-fived each other.

It was at this moment that Brit busted open the door to the stall. The 2 chicken heads almost fell over each other. Brittany washed her hands and turned to face the Black Barbie.

"I'll tell you what you don't have besides fake breasts! Brittany sneered. "Ya need a brain to get my man's attention, and a life! And my beauty might not be the same as yours, but you better believe my man luvs running his hands through me 'Natty Dreads' ya Bombaclot!!"

And with that she strutted out of the bathroom leaving Tweedle Dee and Tweedle Dumb with their mouths wide open.

Brittany chuckled to herself as she headed towards the locker room. This wasn't the first time she had dealt with competition from females but the thing that really scared her was that the games had just begun… Lord help her.

Brittany pulled her Jeep Cherokee up in front of the building, happy to have a close spot. She did not hang out in the lounge after the game, like she usually did. After she congratulated Tyson on a good game, she faked a headache and left on her own. She didn't even share the latest incident with Renee, because she didn't want to get Renee upset, and herself more upset.

After Brittany got inside her apartment, she poured herself a glass of wine. She turned the TV on and then off again, after the news media was rehashing a basketball scandal of all things. She decided to head for her bedroom. She did not feel good, but not in the way she had told her man. She thought it might be wedding jitters, but she knew it was deeper than that. For the first time in her life she felt insecure. She was definitely used to the groupies and the hoochies throwing themselves at her man, and all the players for that matter, but the constant competition and scrutiny from these hos was starting to wear on her. She knew that she was more of a woman than them and they were all plastic chics with no soul, but she didn't know how Tyson was really feeling throughout the changes in their lives. He always told her how much he loved her, but he was surrounded by different people in the pros. In college he didn't have people living this glamorous lifestyle around him so there were not as many temptations and negative influences, because he was still on the come-up. She was worried that now he would have to remind himself why he was with her – instead of knowing.

141

She looked at her reflection in the mirror and stared at the precious charm Tyson had given her in college. The original 10k gold heart charm that she refused to let him 'trade up' as he always wanted to do. The charm as it was, held so many memories to her, and symbolized that their relationship was not built on diamonds and pearls, but love and honesty. She closed her eyes and prayed to God that this is how it would stay.

When she opened her eyes, the heart was cracked into two pieces. Brittany cried herself to sleep.

Chapter 35 ILLUSIONS OF GRANDUER

Present Day

Lola had read in a magazine that Tyson Myers was engaged. But it didn't matter, whatever woman Tyson Myers was going to marry was not going to stop Lola's show. She hadn't seen a picture of the chic, but she was sure that she wasn't as fine as her. Lola was 24 and it was time for her to get what was hers before it was too late.

Lola had been ovulating during her intercourse with Tyson, so she was almost positive she would get pregnant. She'd had a number of abortions so she knew that she was fertile. But all of her previous conceptions had been by bums. She would never allow herself to be pregnant by some no-good, broke-ass negro. That would make her like her mother, and that's the one person in the world who she did not want to be like!! Her mother, Isabella was a Dominican immigrant who had struggled her entire life cleaning houses, trying to make a way for her kids, and Lola never understood why. If she had married into money, Lola would not have had the miserable childhood she did. Being teased by kids in school because she had to wear hand-me down clothes. She didn't have her first new pants until she got her own job. She never had the same privileges that most of her friends had growing up, and she was always jealous of them because of how close they were with their families, and were able to go to college. What the hell did she have?? A dollar and a dream?? Huhhhh!

That's why Lola was going to be smart. She had been following Tyson Myers since he was in college. He was from the same state as her so she was familiar with his background. He was fine, as he wanted to be just like Lola. She knew from interviews she had read and seen him in that he was a family-oriented guy and did not believe in having children out of wedlock. Tyson was one of the few NBA stars she knew that had not fathered any kids, and she wanted to be the first; working at P&B you found out a lot of gossip about the rich and famous. It was Lola's manipulation and good looks that got her where she was today and she was not finished.

Lola continued daydreaming in her bedroom. She had just finished watching the Slammers play, and her future husband, Tyson Myers run the point. Dayam he was fine! She could never get too much of him, and soon he would be hers.

Lola could not get the image of how Tyson was looking at her the first time he saw her out of her head. She knew when she had successfully seduced a man, and she had done so with Tyson, by getting him into the VIP room for the 'Red Light Special'. Lola knew from his friend Jake that it was his first time at P&B, so her plan worked to perfection. Mrs. Lola Elsa Myers, mmm that had a nice ring to it, Lola thought to herself. She couldn't wait for them to purchase a nice home, probably somewhere in Englewood Cliffs, New Jersey, where all the ballers lived. Lola would never work another day in her life! This strip club shit was played out. She was tired of dealing with these catty women – who were all jealous of her, and men thinking she was interested in them because they flashed a $100 bill at her, huuuh Lola only dealt in the big league.

Mrs. Lola Myers, mmmmmm. I'm coming for you baby – as soon as I have my test results. It's all about you, and me and no one will come between us.

Chapter 36   LOSING IT

Present Day

Sean watched as Kyle slammed his truck door shut. He studied Kyle as he sat there for a long moment thinking.

"Just leave." Sean growled to himself.

Then as if he could hear him, Kyle sped off with a screech. Sean sat in the van and looked at the picture of him and Renee hugging. He reminisced often about meeting her in that coffee shop. The way she smelled, the way she felt, her lips, her eyes. He needed Renee - needed to be with her, needed to feel her wrap those legs around him. He couldn't take it much longer. Sean never really thought he'd have to use the picture, he always thought the abuse story would be enough and after hearing the argument in her kitchen this morning, he figured he was finally successful in ending their relationship. But that pause, that fucking pause before Kyle left.

Sean rewound the tape to right before the argument started - there it was Kyle's voice, "Pretty sure you're not sleeping with someone else…. and I'm positive anything else we can work out." 'Anything else', Sean thought meaning that that was a deal breaker for Kyle. If he thought Renee was sleeping with someone else, he would stop fighting so hard to keep her. Yeah Sean reasoned, he would have to use the picture. As he looked at it now he could truly appreciate what a magnificent job his friend had done editing the original. In the picture he was turned so no one could make out his face, but you could definitely see Renee, and the way she was wrapped in his one arm while the other grabbed her ass, definitely made them look like lovers.

Now all Sean had to do was figure out when to get Kyle the picture and the note he would include. Regardless Sean had decided this would be the last effort to do this thing clean. Sean wanted to make the transition smooth. Renee would be sad for a couple of weeks but Sean would be there as a friend for her to talk to and then eventually he would make his move. Then they would be together always - her the successful advertising exec, and him the owner of his own private investigation firm. Renee would help him with the marketing and paperwork and he could expand. With her by his side he knew life would be perfect. They would buy a big house and have some kids. They'd be the textbook attractive, happy and successful couple that everyone else aspired to be like. Sean could see it all clearly, that was why he didn't mind the sacrifices he was making now - sleeping in an uncomfortable van, having to listen to Renee and Kyle make love and what he had to do to Tamyka. But he reasoned she was trash that no one would miss. Besides, he justified, he made it quick and painless; most people aren't lucky enough to die so peacefully. Most suffer long illnesses in hospitals and waste away to almost nothing.

That's how his mother had died Sean remembered. The only one that came to see her every day was Sean. His father just left, ran away one day; couldn't take the responsibility of a young son and a dying wife. He remembered his mother used to drill into his head that most men are no good and he should be the exception, and that if he found the right woman to never let her go and to stick with her through everything. He stuck with his mom even when all the doctors said she was starting to get brain damage from the tumor. They told him she wasn't in her right mind and the things she said might be warped. But Sean never listened to them. He only listened to his mom. She would tell him to kill for love if he had to. She told him if she knew where his father was or the name of the woman he was with, she would have Sean go kill them. She died soon after that and Sean's life was never the same. He was shuffled from relative to relative, none of which really wanted him there. But Sean didn't mind. He focused on school, overachieved and vowed to avenge his mother's death, the only person that ever really loved him. After he was grown and became a PI, his first investigation was to find his father. Sean did so with minimal effort. His father was living a new life, with a new wife and new kids, like Sean and his mother never existed. Sean knew at that moment that his mother was right, his father had to pay. When Sean was through with his mission, he took the wedding ring off his father's hand and the other wife's. He was so proud of himself; he visited his mother's grave and laid the rings down. Now you can rest in peace mom, he had told her. Sean remembered feeling surprisingly empty afterward. He hadn't truly felt fulfilled again until this new mission for Renee. She would be the second and the last woman to love him.

Now the time had come for Sean to go get that love. Sean closed his eyes and it hit him. He probably knew Kyle better than a lot of people just from listening to his conversations with Renee. He knew how to punch Kyle below the belt. Sean composed the note:

KYLE,

RENEE IS MY WOMAN. STAY AWAY. YOU SEE HER WRAPPED IN MY ARMS. SHE TOLD ME YOU BEAT WOMEN AND THREATENED TO KNOCK HER OUT WITH ONE PUNCH IF SHE WOULDN'T DATE YOU. WE'VE BEEN TOGETHER FOR TWO YEARS AND WERE GETTING MARRIED. IF YOU CALL OR BOTHER HER AGAIN I'LL KILL YOU. DON'T TEST ME!

FROM A REAL MAN

Sean smiled. This will make him flip. Time to cut your loses Kyle, find another woman and move on, Sean thought. Sean knew the letter would destroy Kyle's ego. But if by some miracle Kyle came back for more it would be the biggest mistake of his life.

Chapter 37   BE A MAN

Present Day

Kyle jumped into his truck and slammed the door. He was truly furious. What the fuck was Renee talking about? Was she trying to make him crazy? First she's all sweet and perfect and now she's some type of paranoid psycho. The Renee Kyle thought he had fallen in love with was turning out to be crazier than most chicks. After Kyle calmed down he thought about everything she had said with a clearer head. Was she lying or telling the truth? Kyle decided it was time to get away and go see two of his favorite girls.

Two hours later he was in Hershey, Pennsylvania at his sister Audrey's house. When she opened the door a huge smile came over her face and she gave him a big hug. "Come in baby brother, what a surprise!"

Before Kyle could get all the way through the door Audrey's daughter Autumn jumped up in Kyle's arms screaming, "Uncle Kyle, Uncle Kyle." He threw her in the air and spun her around like an airplane. "Again Uncle Kyle again!" she begged. He did it one more time and put her down. "Do you want to come play with me?" little Autumn asked as she tugged his arm.

"That's enough now Autumn," Audrey warned. "Mommy hasn't seen Uncle Kyle in a long time and we need to talk about grown up things so go upstairs and play with your dolls or videos. I'll call you in about an hour to come get some lunch."

Autumn looked upset and in a sad tone replied, "Yes mommy." But before she could leave Kyle promised he would play with her later. Autumn then smiled and ran up the stairs cheerfully.

When she was out of earshot Audrey looked at Kyle and said "So what's wrong?"

What makes you think something's wrong" Kyle replied.

"Well, let's see - besides the fact that I've only known you your whole nappy life, you don't exactly drive out here on a whim every

Saturday morning, and you especially would not drive out here without calling. It's Saturday, we could have been out doing anything. And you always tell me what a long drive it is that's why I don't see you more. But today you just pop up on my doorstep."

"So once again what's wrong?"

"You really do know me," Kyle admitted. "I've missed you it's really good to see you sis."

Audrey moved to Hershey with her daughter Autumn about 2 years ago, before she left New Jersey, her and Kyle were definitely the closest of all the siblings. He didn't want her to leave but her husband Tim had been hit and killed by some thugs that were trying to outrun the cops. Kyle knew she needed to get away, too many memories. Besides, their daughter Autumn was 4 years old at the time and Audrey had vowed to find a better school system and safer streets for her baby girl. She was hoping for southern Jersey, but the job she found was in Pennsylvania and Audrey was willing to make the sacrifice for Autumn.

"If you miss me you should come out more often. Leaving me out here in the sticks with all these white folks." She mused.

"I'm sorry. I know I should come more often but life just gets busy," Kyle answered.

"So are you going to tell me what's wrong?"

"OK," Kyle surrendered, "So I met this girl"

"There's a shock," Audrey cut him off sarcastically.

"No not like that Audrey. This one is different," Kyle explained.

"Really," Audrey listened more intently now.

"Well we've been going out for awhile now and she's my lady you know, we're exclusive. She's just amazing, she's pretty, and funny and strong willed. You would love her Audrey you two would really get along!" Kyle praised.

"So bring her out here to meet me. I don't see what the problem is", Audrey puzzled.

"That brings me to the problem. We had a huge fight this morning and I'm confused and don't know how to handle it." Kyle admitted.

"Let's start with this. What did you do to her?" Audrey huffed.

"What makes you think it was me?"

149

"First off you're a man, second off you're a black man with a job, and last but not least you're a man that loves women." Audrey surmised. Kyle could feel himself getting annoyed. He didn't leave one fight just to come out here to another. His sister was always like this - she kept it real. She was not the type to let any man take advantage of her and she hated it when she saw her sisters letting men treat them bad. Audrey had some bad experiences, and had seen some of her friends go through horror stories. Because of this her first instinct was always to side with the woman.

"Damn Audrey, could you please just give a brother a break for a change? I guarantee when you hear what happened you'll change your tune." Kyle assured. Over the next hour Kyle proceeded to tell Audrey everything. He explained how they met at her office when he was on a delivery. He told Audrey that even though Renee was a top executive and successful she never acted sadity and always made him feel like a man.

"But then she just flips on me. Asking me if I like to hit women? Telling me someone told her I've abused women in the past. Can you believe this shit?" Kyle huffed. Kyle looked over at Audrey impatiently, he was expecting her to be pissed off the way he was but she remained calm. Finally he couldn't wait any longer.

"Audrey what the fuck! Are you going to say anything or just stare off into space," he barked.

"Keep your voice down, I don't want Autumn to hear you down here cursing and yelling," she warned.

"I'm sorry, I just want to know what you're thinking."

"First off," Audrey started in a semi-whisper, "I know you would not hit a woman - so that's a given. But I'm not so quick to think your friend is crazy either."

"Girlfriend," Kyle corrected.

"Boy you got it bad for this one don't you baby brother," Audrey chuckled "If that's the case we really need to figure this out." Audrey began slow and steady, "First off let's assume she didn't just wake up this morning and go crazy. Did she get a phone call or something before the argument?"

"No," Kyle answered. "I think someone told her this before last night. She had been acting funny all week. She wasn't returning my calls and I couldn't take it any more so I kinda waited at her place for her to get home. We had a quick argument because I thought she was seeing someone else. When she guaranteed that there was no one else, well you know one thing lead to another."

"She didn't ask you about this last night?" Audrey said puzzled.

"I didn't really give her a chance, I was all over her and even if she didn't want to admit it she missed me. There's a lot of heat between us and we both lose ourselves in it sometimes. You know what I mean?" Kyle asked.

"Yes unfortunately I do. There was lots of heat between me and Tim."

At this comment Kyle put his hands up, "Spare me the details."

Audrey looked at him in annoyance, "Oh you can tell me about tossin your little girlfriend around, but I can't reminisce about my husband. We're both grown now Kyle you can stop protecting me from all the boys you think have bad intentions. It's time to give that up, you did a good job. I was never a ho, I had and still have self-respect and I was married before I was pregnant. I would say your battin a thousand in the 'I have to make sure my sister is a respectable challenge', that you've taken on."

Kyle put his hands up in surrender, "Sorry Audrey, but no guy wants to hear about his sisters sex life."

"Well you don't have to worry about that because mine is non-existent, even if I wasn't too proud to have a man come up in here just to satisfy my needs, I have Autumn to think about, and I won't have her around a bunch of losers just cause I'm horny," Audrey assured.

"But let's get back to the point at hand. Here are the questions you need to ask yourself. One, who told her this and why? Two, do any of your old girlfriends or sex partners have a vendetta against you? Cause let's face it baby bro you were not nearly as picky as you wanted me to be, and last but not least - is she seeing someone else that maybe wants you out of the picture?"

Kyle looked at Audrey thoughtfully. "I was so mad I didn't even ask her who told her but I got the feeling she wasn't trying to give me that information even if I had asked. As far as my ex's, I don't think any of them are pissed at me but I should probably make a list and really think about it. And No she's not seeing someone else." Kyle said this last sentence with an edge to his voice and Audrey picked up on it.

"I can see you still have a temper Kyle but you need to stay calm so you can really assess the situation. What makes you so sure she's not?" Audrey asked.

"First off she's a workaholic. She barely has time to see me. And before you even ask I've popped up unannounced at her work several times and she was always there and always happy to see me. Second I had to work really hard to get her into bed, like she really valued herself and didn't just want to be another sexual conquest for me. It's hard to explain, we just share something deeper and I can't imagine her in bed with someone else. The thought of it make me want to punch something or someone." Kyle huffed.

"OK ease back little brother. If it makes you feel better it sounds to me like she's got it bad for you too." Audrey smiled to herself.

"What makes you say that?" Kyle inquired.

"Well she obviously already knew you had supposedly beaten some woman like a savage, but she still couldn't stop herself from letting you stay last night. Which probably means two things, somewhere in her heart or mind she doesn't believe you did it, and she didn't have enough strength to push you away. Probably because she had been struggling with the decision and missing you all week."

Kyle sat for a long moment thinking about what Audrey said. Then a big smile crept across his face. "You're right, she doesn't really believe this. I should drive right back to her place and we can settle this thing."

"Slow down Kyle," Audrey warned. "You also told me she has certain morals and standards, and a proud black woman would never let herself be with a man that abuses women."

"I'm not a man that abuses women, what the fuck Audrey!"

"I didn't say you are but someone obviously did a pretty good job convincing your girlfriend." Audrey reminded.

"My advice would be don't rush to any conclusions. Do your research, there are a lot of haters out there. Renee sounds attractive and successful - something women are jealous of and men want. You're no dummy Kyle you know what I mean. If you really care about this girl don't just give up, be a man fight a little. If you find out you were wrong about her at least you'll know for sure." Audrey surmised.

"You're right sis I can find out a lot of shit if I put my mind to it."

"I know I'm right. Now go play with my daughter, I don't let any man lie to her not even her uncle," Audrey said.

"I was going to play with her even before you asked. And sis, I'll never stop protecting you." Kyle gave Audrey a kiss and ran up the stairs.

Chapter 38   SO MUCH DRAMA

Present Day

Brittany was at Simone's counter attempting to mix the drinks. She looked over at her two friends and all she could think was - this sucks. Usually it would be Renee mixing the drinks. Brittany would happily be having her occasional cigarette with Simone. The music would be louder and Renee would be taking request for drinks like Isaac from The Love boat.

Brittany never felt like it was unfair of her and Simone to sit back while Renee mixed, because she could tell Renee really enjoyed making the drinks, while she shook her hips to the beat. Besides Renee didn't smoke, and Brittany and Simone loved their weekend drink and cigarette combo. But tonight was not the typical drink night. Renee was in such bad spirits, she was almost comatose, and Simone was still recovering from her bout with the crazed wife. Brittany looked at Simone and giggled to herself for a moment. There Simone sat at night in her apartment with her makeup and sunglasses on. Brittany couldn't help but think how completely vain her friend was, she didn't want anyone to see her black eyes, so she went out and bought the biggest darkest sunglasses she could find, and had yet to take them off. Brittany finished the drinks and passed them to her friends.

"Here you two," she said. "I put extra alcohol tonight because everyone obviously needs to loosen up."

Simone immediately began to sip in compliance. Brittany suspected the liquor helped numb her face pain. But Renee looked at her drink and then put it down on the table. "On no sister," Brittany scolded as she picked her drink back up and gave it to her, "you don't have to drink it fast just keep it in your hands and sip from time to time."

Renee was unconvinced, "Look Brit," she stated rather sharply, "after my nightmare last weekend I swore off liquor, and after my prize fight this morning I swore off men. And I fully intend to keep both those promises to myself."

At these comments Simone's ears perked up, "What are you talking about Re?" Simone asked. Brittany and Renee had yet to tell Simone all the drama with Kyle and Sean, and the beatings and old girlfriends. Brittany could tell by the look of exhaustion on Renee's face that she didn't have the energy to go into it.

Finally after a long silence Renee said, "Let Brit tell you, all I want to do is stare into space and be left alone."

Now Simone was really intrigued. With what she had recently been through she didn't think anyone's life was as fucked up as hers. Now she was energized by the prospect of some dirt in Renee's life. Little Miss morals, Miss judgmental, Simone couldn't wait to hear what was going on.

"Well Brittany are you going to tell me or what?" Simone asked impatiently.

"In a minute Sim," Brit said with a bit of annoyance.

Brittany then changed her voice to soothing and turned to address Renee again, "Look Re I understand you're upset. The truth is I've never seen you like this and I'm worried. You know I know you, and I can see you're too tense. You're thinking too hard. You need to relax your mind a little bit and loosen up. So please, for me just one drink. Think of it like your medicine, if nothing else it will help you sleep tonight."

Renee thought about this for a minute, thinking about all the sleep she had missed last week. The only good sleep she had was last night after Kyle had made love to her again and again. With that thought her mind was made up. "Alright," Renee huffed as she picked up the drink and took a big gulp. Thank goodness Brittany thought. She wasn't one to push liquor on people but Renee needed to escape, and a few drinks never hurt anyone. It was better than all these crazy prescription drugs people were on with all their side effects Brittany reasoned. She was confident Renee would have more than one drink because she put enough alcohol in the first to break down Renee's resistance. With Renee safely on her way to a much-needed buzz Brit turned her attention to Simone who was waiting with a quizzical look on her face.

"Well", she said in annoyance.

But Brittany wasn't ready to tell Simone about Renee's heartbreak, especially with the satisfied look Simone had on her face. Brittany wasn't stupid. She knew Simone and Renee had a somewhat adversarial relationship at times. Renee had really laid into Simone about sleeping in a married man's bed, and Brit suspected that Simone couldn't wait to hear something bad about Renee.

"Well what?" Brittany acted confused.

"Are you going to tell me?" Simone said agitated. "Re said you could," Simone reminded Brit.

"I know," Brit responded," "but I need another drink first." She went back to the counter to mix more drinks. When she caught Simone looking at her Brittany motioned silently for Simone to come into the kitchen.

Once Simone was by her side Brit whispered, "I'm going to tell you but give it a minute for Renee to have another drink or so. She needs to talk to us to get it out. I don't even know everything yet, so just chill for a minute." Simone agreed and they went back to the couch. Once there, Brit took Renee's empty glass and replaced it with a full one. They didn't speak but Renee took the glass and drank.

Sensing that the mood was changing slightly Brit piped up, "Simone I'm dying to know - can you see us right now in your dark shades or do you go by sound like Stevie Wonder?"

Renee chuckled and Simone sneered, "Very funny, I can see you ho's." Renee had finished her second drink and was obviously feeling a little better. "I been meaning to ask you Sim what story have you been giving people, you know what I mean the one for public broadcast?" Renee asked in a sincere tone.

Simone did know what she meant. "I've been telling my co-workers that I got into a car accident with one of you clowns and I've been telling family and friends that I got into a car accident with a co-worker. I never mention anyone's specific name. When the people at work say which friend, I say you wouldn't know her. And when family asks about the person at work I say the same thing. That way I don't have to remember which name I'm using, and if they meet one of you they won't say -oh I heard about the accident are you OK. So no one but me has to lie. Pretty smart right?" Simone was obviously pleased with herself.

Renee just chuckled and said, "Pretty smart."

Brittany and Simone both waited a moment for Renee to make a snide comment about the incident but it never came. Simone was relieved but Brittany was a bit disappointed. She had been counting on a comment from Renee to be her opening so she could share with her friends, but Renee was not herself, so Brittany would have to charge ahead alone.

"Since you two brought up the subject of women in other women's beds," Brittany began slowly, "you two won't believe what happened to Tyson on the road the other day. It was after a big game. You remember the game Renee, you called me and told me to give Tyson your congratulations."

"Of course I remember, your man was the best player on the court that night. I really got into that game. It was a nice escape to watch my brother play and run them other chumps off the floor," Renee giggled obviously tipsy and happy for Tyson.

Brittany made a mental note to watch how much Renee was drinking; else her friend was going to be very sick in the morning.

"How about you Simone, did you see that game?" Brittany asked.

Simone just looked at her and rolled her eyes. Even if Simone were into basketball, which she wasn't, she wouldn't be watching Tyson's team. Why so she could be reminded of how successful and rich he was becoming and how happy the two of them were – Please. "Brit you know I'm not really into sports like that." Simone responded.

Brittany grinned inwardly. She knew Simone probably hadn't seen the game and it wasn't cause she didn't like sports. She knew rich basketball players were the exact type of men Simone would love to take advantage of. She had asked Brittany if she could hook her up with one of Tyson's teammates but Brittany had explained to Simone that she had a couple of bad experiences with the matchmaker thing in college. Plus she had told her that Tyson was the exception. Most of these ball players just used groupies and women, and threw them away after. Brittany had told Simone she would be happy to bring her to some B Ball functions, and if she met someone on her own so be it. But by this point in their conversation Simone had gotten indignant and trapped herself into a corner. She had told Brittany with an attitude, "Don't do me any favors I don't need help to get a man." Brittany took Simone at her word and never asked Simone to any NBA events; especially since Simone was always talking about how much she disliked basketball and never watched a game. Brittany suspected that Simone regretted the remark and wished she could go to some functions, but her pride would never allow her to ask.

"Well it's like Renee said, Tyson won the game for his team. I've seen him have better games in college but this was his best game so far in the NBA. Anyway he called and we celebrated over the phone, and of course he wished I could be there in person, all the usual. But then he got quiet for a minute and I asked him what was wrong. He told me that something strange had happened earlier and he wanted me to know so we could talk about how to deal with these things." Brittany took a deep breath, "Before I continue I think it's necessary to tell you two what it's like now. I know every woman probably thinks it's all cookies and cream, and a wonderful dream to be with an NBA player but it's not. There are a lot of challenges, especially if you actually love your man and you aren't just using him for what you can get. I know you remember all the crazy shit in college Re."

"Do I!" Renee responded. "Those bitches were scandalous. You're too nice Brit, you know there were at least four of them that we should have stomped."

Brittany smiled at her quick-tempered friend. "Re you know if we went around trying to beat up every chick that was after Tyson neither one of us would have graduated."

After a moment of thought Renee just chuckled and said, "True, true" as she gave Brittany a hi-five.

Simone just sat there looking at both of them annoyed. She hated when they reminisced about college in front of her. She thought it was rude. "I hate to break up your college reunion but could you finish the story." Simone huffed.

"Well things are about a thousand times worse in the NBA than college. I haven't told you two but there are a lot of things I don't go to because it's just too much. I have seen women with my Tyson's named tattooed on their chest and their ass, and they all want him to sign autographs on their bodies. I just don't want to see it, and Tyson wants to protect me from it. We have had long talks, and he let me know that he's not stupid and knows these women just want money and fame. Luckily our relationship is very strong, or we would not be able to overcome these challenges. I think you both know me well enough to know I'm no free spirit about love. What's mine is mine and Tyson belongs to me. Anyway after all the interviews and pats on the back, he went back to his room to call me. When he opened his door there were three naked women in his bed. They said they were there to help him celebrate his amazing game."

"Simple ho's!" Renee said with disgust "What did Tyson do?"

"He went to his older teammate's room because the rest of the team had gone out partying. He asked him how these things are usually handled, and after a few wise cracks he told him which team staff member handles these situations." Brittany concluded.

"Do you believe him?" Simone asked.

"Of course I believe him. If I didn't trust Ty our relationship wouldn't work. But I'm just getting frustrated and tired of all these women throwing themselves at him all the time. I mean relationships are hard enough without having to factor in this type of crap." Brittany finished.

"How did these women get in his room?" Simone asked suspiciously. "I'm sure you can't just go into a hotel and break into any room at will. I think that would discourage customers from staying there," Simone said in a wise guy voice.

"What are you trying to say Simone?" Renee said with anger in her voice. She was about to continue but Brittany stopped her.

"No it's alright Re. I want to hear what Simone has to say. I figured she might have a different perspective on this." Brittany explained

"Why? Because I've been with another women's man?" Simone said agitated.

"Don't put words in my mouth Simone," Brittany said with more attitude than Simone expected. "But since you brought it up - yeah. And I don't think you have the right to act pissed at me. You're my friend and I've always gone out of the way to be understanding and patient whenever you have gone through anything. Now I need your help, like it or not. You DO have a different perspective on this sort of thing. We are different people, but we're still friends, and it shouldn't be too much to ask for your input and help, now that I'm the one with the problem."

Simone looked at her friend for a long time as she felt the guilt rise up in her chest. "I'm sorry Brit it's just everything is so messed up right now. My life's been threatened and I have bruises all over my face. You've got three hookers just lying naked in your man's bed and I don't even know what's up with Renee. But if the way she's drinking is any indication it must be pretty bad. You're right I am your friend and I do want to help. The way I look at things Tyson is a man so he's weak. Any man's buttons can be pushed. You just need to know the buttons. I'm not saying he's cheating it's just with different women always trying different buttons I would be worried. I'm not in the NBA world, but I can tell you in the doctor world when women want to get into a convention hotel or function they flirt with a bouncer or hotel staff. They even have sex with them if they need to, just to get what they want." Brittany listened wondering if Simone was talking about herself or someone else but didn't dare ask. Simone continued, "I don't think I've ever had the type of relationship you and Tyson do, so I can't say what he would or wouldn't do. It's just I've seen some shit, so keep your eyes open Brit."

Brittany reached out and put her hand over Simone's. This was the Simone that Brittany loved. "Thank you for that." Brittany said softly.

"Anyway," Renee said obviously disgusted with this type of woman. "What did the staff member do?"

Brittany looked over at Renee as she began. "Well believe it or not they actually have a standard operating procedure. The staff member goes to the room and has the women sign a waiver that says the team won't press charges for breaking and entering, if the women consent to a gag order. They can't tell any reporters or rag magazines anything about Tyson, like what kind of cologne he wears or whether it's briefs or boxers. Then they get their asses thrown out, and that particular hotel bans them for life."

"Wow they're thoooroo. I wouldn't have even thought 'bout any of that stuff." Renee slurred obviously drunk.

"OK that's enough," Brittany scolded as she grabbed the fourth drink from Renee's hand.

"Hey I taut you wanna me da drink," Renee said like a bratty child.

"I wanted you to sip," Brittany smiled, but Renee was already onto another thought.

"Hey Sim how did your ho ish buddies like it ven day got their ass thrown outta different places. I mean iss dat par a de citement." Renee was definitely drunk and starting to get on Simone's nerves. But instead of getting mad she seized the opportunity.

"Let's forget all that for a minute. I'm still waiting to hear what the hell is going on in your life. How's Mister dreamboat Kyle doing?" Simone said this last sentence slow like she was sticking a knife into Renee. That will teach her to make smart remarks Simone thought. Brittany could see things getting ugly quick but didn't have time to jump in.

"Fine," Renee half yelled with less fun in her voice. "I know you been dying to hear it Simone - he's no dreamboat. I was told he beat an ex- girlfriend. "He beat her he beat her..." Renee was having trouble saying it "He beat her till she losss deir baby." As she finished the sentence Brit could see tears welling up in Renee's eyes and her stomach retch. Renee jumped up and ran to Simone's bathroom, and started throwing up like crazy.

When she was gone Brittany looked at Simone with disdain, "Are you happy now?" she asked.

"Hey in my defense she provoked me," Simone alibied.

"She's drunk and obviously hurting, and she's pissed about what happened to me. You know how she gets Sim."

"I know, and if it makes you feel any better I'm not happy. That wasn't nearly as satisfying as I thought it would be. I'm actually a little stunned. I've never seen her like this over a guy, never."

"I know," Brittany whispered and hushed Simone as she heard Renee stumbling out of the bathroom. Brittany got up to go give Renee a hug, "Hey there you alright?" Brittany looked concerned.

"No," Renee said as she sat down, her mind a little clearer now. "Could someone put on some coffee I need a couple of cups before I can make the drive home."

Simone spoke up. "I'll make coffee, but I'm not letting you drive home tonight. You'll stay here." Simone demanded.

"Thanks anyway but I'm going home," Renee responded.

Simone just laughed, "That wasn't a request Renee. I already took your keys and hid them. Brit is going to sleep over too. We're going to have an old fashioned burn your boyfriend's team jacket slumber party." Even Renee had to laugh. Simone was making a high school reference to them all getting together and burning the team jacket Brittany's boyfriend had given her once she found out he was cheating. Everything was crazy and fun back then. It didn't seem like their lives they way it did now. It was just a moment in time and there was always something better coming over the horizon.

Renee looked at her two friends and smiled. "You know I love you nutty chicks. Anyway Simone you don't know this but a while back Brittany encouraged me to hire a PI to check out Kyle. He hadn't done anything. I just think Brit thought I was falling too hard and too fast. Kyle had been talking about us living together and Brit got worried."

"That would have been fast," Simone commented.

"I know but please Sim. Just let me finish or I don't know if I'll get it out. So in the process of an investigation that I thought was taking way too long Kyle and I became exclusive. He's very possessive, and made it abundantly clear he didn't want anyone else touching me. Which was fine with me because I didn't want anyone else touching him. It all seemed perfect until Sean called, he's the Private investigator, Brittany's friend. Anyway he called and told me he had disturbing news. We met for drinks and to get the report. I had a date with Kyle that night and Sean told me I should cancel it because there was a lot to tell me. Unfortunately Sean kept ordering drinks and I got drunk that night because it was hard for me to hear these things that didn't sound true. I know Kyle really well. He was the only boy in his family and grew up protecting his mother and sisters. He is a gentleman to a fault - always opens the door, pulls my chair out, flowers, pays the bills, etc. Now someone's telling me he beat someone almost to death and she lost their baby. Since it was so hard for me to believe, Sean arranged for me to meet this chick."

"You met with the girl," Brittany said surprised.

"Yeah I needed to hear it first hand. I don't like rumors or stories. I needed to know the truth. When we met she didn't seem like his type.

She was too hoochie. She felt the differences between us also, and explained that they went out back in high school. She seemed sincere enough, but it's still not sitting well with me. Regardless you both know I'm not going to be with an abusive man because I would end up killing him."

"Yeah you and your whole family," Simone reminded.

Renee continued, "So I decided to just end it. But the whole ending it thing has been a lot harder than I ever thought. I spent the week ignoring his calls and working ridiculous hours, but he was still on my mind. So I was walking to my building last night trying to figure if I should call or leave a letter to break up, when I see him sitting on the steps to my building. Anyway to try and shorten this saga we ended up in bed. I just need him."

"The flesh is weak isn't it Re?" Simone said knowingly.

"So is the heart," Renee answered. "Anyway I thought he'd be gone to work in the morning like usual but he had called out and wanted to spend the day getting to the bottom of the problem. So my temper got the best of me and I just told him outright I heard he beats women."

"What?" Brittany said shocked. "Weren't you scared he would hit you?"

"That's the thing Brit I provoked him pretty bad and he should of hit me, but he didn't. All he did was say he doesn't hit women and left so he wouldn't start today. Can you understand my confusion?"

"Yes and no," Brittany replied.

"I know when the hearts involved everything gets confused. But this was the whole idea behind you hiring Sean. This isn't a street rumor.

Sean's a professional. Abusive guys always start out as the most charming, and they are very possessive which you say Kyle is right." Brittany reasoned.

"Yeah Re beating a woman until she lost her baby, that's pretty bad," Simone chimed in.

"I know you two are right I just need a little time to get him out of my system. He really felt like the one."

"I'm sorry for you Re but you know what they say?" Simone hinted.

"What's that?" Renee asked.

"The best way to get over a man is to go out with another."

163

"Oh no! I told you guys at the beginning of the night I'm swearing off men and dating. I need a definite break."

"Don't be silly you're too young for a break. Anyway you also told us you were swearing off liquor and we all see how long that lasted," Simone reminded.

"Hey that was some serious peer pressure. Brittany practically poured the liquor down my throat." Renee whined.

"Well since you're giving into my peer pressure," Brittany started "you know Sean has a crush on you."

"What?" Renee said surprised.

"Yeah all he does is talk about you. Renee's so smart, Renee's so pretty, she successful and on and on," Brittany continued. "Sometimes I have to stop him and remind him that I know you better than he does and he just gives me this look like he knows something I don't. Have you felt anything between you two?" Brittany asked.

"Felt anything? I've been way to into Kyle to be thinking about Sean. He was all dressed up when he met me for drinks, and I thought it was my imagination but when he brought me home..." Simone gave Renee a look. "Not brought me home like that, brought me home because I had drank too much. I could of swore he snuck a feel of my chest."

"See what I mean. He really likes you Re you should go out with him. At least we know he's safe and it would help get your mind off Kyle," Brittany urged.

"I'll think about it, but could we please just pop some popcorn and watch a bad blacksploitation film for the rest of the night. If I think about this anymore I'll go crazy."

"Alright Foxy Brown it is," Simone said as she went to the TV.

Chapter 39   WHEN A MAN IS FED UP

Present Day

Simone looked in the mirror as she finished putting on her make up for work. She turned her head slowly from left to right as she felt the bruises to test for pain. "Damn" she said aloud. Things like this were not supposed to happen anymore, not to the new Simone, the smart Simone. The young stupid Simone who believed in love and romance was dumb enough to let things like this happen. This is what I get Simone thought for deviating from my plan. She tried to take a quick break from the ultimate goal and attain a little physical pleasure and look what it cost her. She stared at herself in the mirror and said aloud, "I need to stay focused and use my body to get what I want. My body is my greatest asset and I will use it to get Joe, and in the end get it all - the house, the car and the status. Simone took a deep breath and felt better. She put her sunglasses on and promised herself that if she were ever black and blue again, it would be by her husband. At least she would be getting paid for her misery.

Back In The Day
Brittany and Renee

As they walked in the door, they were not ready for what they were about to see. Broken glass everywhere a brother went crazy, like he just didn't care. The fish tank had been knocked off its stand and splattered into a thousand pieces, looking like it was never the home of beautiful tropical fish, and the coffee table, which used to sit so pretty in the middle of the living room was smashed in as if someone had dropped a ton of bricks on it. Pieces of the kitchen furniture were scattered about the house as if used for weapons during an all-out-brawl. There were bloodstains on the wall that got smeared in an apparent struggle. The once beige carpet was now splattered with red and black marks. It was a monstrosity to say the least. Re and Brit were speechless. They had not anticipated this in their worst nightmare. They were both at a loss for words as they assessed the damage. Brit gave Simone that - I'm so sorry girl look, before she began to speak. She chose her words carefully because she did not want to offend an already sensitive Simone. "Was KJ home when this happened?"

"Thank God I took him to his grandparents house before Toby came home."

"Girrrrrrrl, was the brother drunk? What got into him to make him do some shit like this!!???" Brittany quickly continued saying, "don't worry girl, we're here to help you, that's what friends are for."

Renee was less generous. "He better be glad he did this shit to you and not me. I would have shot his ass with my .38! Then I would have taken him outside and let the dog finish his sorry-ass off! . . .."

Brit interrupted Renee. She could see the direction of this conversation was hurting Simone. Brit gently offered their assistance.

"Where do you want us to start Sim? Do you have a vacuum cleaner so we can start by picking up these small pieces of broken glass, before I mess around and bleed to death?" She was really trying to lighten the mood, because it was getting more depressing by the moment. Simone looked terrible. She wore some old baggy sweatpants and a t-shirt that looked like the T-shirt she had on when she was defending herself. It had traces of blood on it. She had dark circles under her eyes as if she hadn't slept for days and a black and blue mark under her right eye (surely a result of their altercation). Her hair was matted up and wild as if she had been in a wild catfight, and hadn't recovered since. Simone, being the beauty queen that she was, made this a monumental incident. You could tell her spirit was down, because the usually vivacious Simone was very downbeat and looked extremely depressed. Renee took the hint and started looking through Simone's cleaning supplies (which wasn't much, because Simone and her mother were never the domestic types) to find something to wipe the walls down with before the stains set.

"Girl, you need some Clorox, to get these walls back to new. No he didn't break this beautiful coffee table that your aunt bought you guys. This table has to be worth at least $1,000.00. That would have been enough motivation alone to cut his damn balls off," Renee screamed! Brit gave her that look, like can't you see she's in enough pain. Re took heed and started scrubbing the walls. Brit proceeded to the closet to get the vacuum cleaner out and she started picking up the pieces of glass that were too big for the vacuum. They all were working in silence, when Simone just let out this loud wail and fell to her knees crying and sobbing, nose running. "I loved him, I took his broke ass in when nobody else would, including his sorry-ass family. I helped him through umpteen rehabs and this is the fucking thanks I get! So what if I was sleeping with another man! What else was I supposed to do while he was in and out of rehab! My vibrator can only do but so much. Dammit! I loved him through good and bad, but shit when his broke ass was out of work, that money Rob gave me helped all of us. Thank God my mom went down to Atlantic city with some friends this weekend because I couldn't deal with her 'I told you so's' right now!"

Renee asked, "Was he high when he went on this rampage?" while she wiped the walls down.

"Girl he was high, like I never seen him before. He must have been mixing drugs. He had this wild look in eyes, like an animal that had just got let out of a cage, and hadn't been fed for weeks. I was so scared yawl." Simone started crying again. Brittany went over and put her arm around Sim, while she sobbed. Renee gave Brittany a look, while Simone's head was down, that said - I told you she should have left his no-good ass alone a long time ago.

"Its gonna be alright girl. He's in jail now, so he can't hurt you," Brittany soothed.

"Yeah, but he's going to be out soon, and then what the hell do I do. I know he's going to come back after me, besides he still has some of his stuff in the room."

Renee jumped in. . . .. "Since you're too peaceful to handle things my way girl, you get a restraining order for that S.O.B. You have a child to think about. You can't afford to have him showing up at your door, high and crazy, ready to bug out on you again." This time Brit did not interrupt because this was advice that Simone needed to take.

"Do you hear what she's saying Simone?" Brit asked soothingly.

Simone shook her head up and down in agreement. "You're right Re, little KJ could be here next time. But he'll still has to come by to get his stuff."

"The hell he will." Renee snapped. "I have a better idea," with that, Renee walked into the kitchen and grabbed a huge hefty bag from under the sink. She looked at Brit and smiled "ghetto suitcase," she explained. "OK Simone where's asshole's stuff?" Renee inquired.

"In the room, but it's not all going to fit in that bag," she protested. Simone was unsure but Renee was determined, "Then we'll use two bags."

Simone was still a bit apprehensive and looked to Brit for guidance.

Brittany looked at her with soft understanding, "You heard her Sim, and you know once Re gets this way there's no changing her mind. So think about a friend or relative where we can drop the stuff so he can't claim you stole it." Simone decided on his cousin's house. They spent a long time cleaning up; in hopes that it would make the fight that Simone and her mother were going to have less intense. Then they piled into Brittany's car and drove his possessions to the cousin's house. Once there, Renee threw the three bags in front of the door and banged hard. When he opened the door Renee did not make any attempt to say hello or explain who she was. She looked him in the eye and said, "After you bail him out, keep him the fuck away from my friend. If he asks you who said it tell him Renee, he knows me." Then she turned and left.

As they drove back Brittany and Renee both told Simone she should find a nice guy with a good job that could treat her right and give her things. Simone listened to every word.

Chapter 40 DEADLINES

Present Day

Jonathan dropped a box of files on Brit's desk on his way out of the door. "Brit I need a memo on all of these cases by Monday morning. We have to submit a brief to the judge by next week."

Brittany looked up at her boss. Jonathan Khan was a big partner at Kravitz & Khan - his name was on the door. Brittany was interning at the firm while attending Brooklyn law. She enjoyed working at Kravitz, a full service law firm, and they wanted her to come back the following summer after seeing how ambitious she was. Brittany often stayed later than the other interns, and arrived early in the morning. She went out of her way not to let anyone know that she was Tyson Myer's fiancé because she did not want any preferential treatment; or the resentment that sometimes comes along with being engaged to such a superstar. It always amused her when people found out she was engaged to a superstar. People who disliked her, were suddenly her best friend, people she hardly knew would start giving her stuff and inviting 'them' to their parties and affairs. Brit hated the attention; she wasn't in it for that.

"Jonathan, you're giving me 2 days to finish this brief?"

"Three days if you count the holiday."

"I need more time than that. I was planning a weekend trip with Ty this weekend. He was taking me to Myrtle Beach. Our flight leaves tonight."

Jonathan paused and looked at her for a second. "Brit when you first started working here I told you this business was not for the faint of heart, and being a lawyer does not always agree with your schedule. I'm afraid I can't tell the client that my firm will not be able to help him because one of my brightest young stars has a weekend planned in sunny Myrtle Beach. Brittany if you are serious about becoming an attorney in a firm like this, making a 6-figure salary, you are going to have to accept that these things will happen from time to time. I need your memo in my office by Tuesday morning. Call the office manager to let her know if you need secretarial assistance this weekend. I'm counting on you Brit," and with that he grabbed his briefcase and left.

Brittany dropped her head on the desk, and asked herself, why did I choose this field, why am I doing this to myself? Once I marry Tyson, I won't need this kind of money anyway. She sat there motionless for about 10 minutes, thinking how she was going to tell Tyson that she couldn't go when her phone rang.

"Hey girl, you all ready for your trip to South Carolina? Wait til Ty sees that sexy bathing suit you bought last night. I'm so jealous girl I wish I was going down there. I hear it's really nice. I'll be stuck in Jersey City watching DVD's all weekend nursing a broken heart."

"Renee, I'm not going!!!"

"What! What happened?"

"Work is what happened. My boss just told me I have to have a brief on his desk by Tuesday morning, and I will be stuck researching and writing it this weekend."

"Damn that sucks!"

"Who you telling, and I haven't even told Tyson yet. As a matter of fact girl, let me get off this phone and call him now. He's going to flip."

"Good luck girl."

Brittany got up from her desk and looked out of her window on the 50th floor. She had a view of Rockefeller Center. She watched as people hurried about their business, shopping and picking up last minute things as they got ready for their fantastic weekends. Tyson had really been looking forward to them spending time together. She knew he would be disappointed.

"Hey Sexy," Tyson said.

"Hey baby, I have some bad news."

"What happened, you alright?"

"I just got dumped with a brief and Jonathan needs it by Tuesday morning. I haven't even begun to work on it, so that leaves no room for our weekend getaway to Myrtle Beach. I'm so sorry baby I know you already bought the tickets and made the reservations, but I had no control over this."

There was dead silence on the line. Brittany knew this meant Tyson was mad.

"Hello, Baby, don't hang up. I promise I'll make it up to you." More silence.

"Ty, don't be like that, I'm just as upset as you."

"Baby, I would be lying if I said I wasn't heated, and I don't like how ol boy just dropped this on you at the last minute. But, when I proposed to you, I knew I was marrying a woman with a career and a life of her own. That's always what attracted me to you over all the rest, so I guess a brotha got to deal with it............."

"Oh Tyson, I know it took a lot for you to say that as mad as you are. I promise I will make it up to you."

"Yeah you better woman, brother had a penthouse and everything ready for you. I'll see if Mom wants to go with one of her sisters, if not I'll ask one of the fellas."

"I tell you what, we might not have a ocean view in my Brooklyn apartment, but I'll give you something to dream about if you meet me at my house at 12:00 tonight. Bring some Chardonnay."

"You got it boo. One Love."

Brittany swung around in her chair, feeling revived, as she began her outline. She was so lucky to have Ty.

Brittany had been so engrossed in her work, that she'd lost track of time at the office. She knew that she wanted to get the majority of her research and outline done on Friday, so that on the weekend she would just have to proofread it, revise it, and double check some of the law to make sure all of her cases were on point. Everyone had left the office early so she was left to work with little distractions.

When the black car pulled onto her street, she told the driver to slow down, to drop her off in front of her building. She saw Tyson's Escalade parked on the street, and hoped that he hadn't been waiting long. She was hoping to beat him there so she could arrange the Red Light Special ahead of him, but it was too late now. Brittany loved being romantic with him because that really turned Tyson on more than anything. Most women did not know him as well as she did. Brittany knew all the right buttons to push.

She made her way past the young kids hanging out in front of her building and spoke to her neighbor Trevor as he went out the door.

171

"What a gwon sexy? Ya just now comin hom from work? Me Miss seein' ya round the neighborhood, ya working too much gal. If I was ya mon me wouldn't let ya work a bloody day."

Brittany giggled, "You know I love what I do Trevor. Its not about the money."

"Dats what you say."

"How you been Trevor, you takin' care of that handsome son of yours?"

"You know it baby doll, every ting is every ting."

"Later Trevor."

"Later baby gurl, and if you ever want to link up, you know where I am."

Brittany smiled as she walked to her mailbox. When she was in college she would have loved a sexy Jamaican guy like Trevor, she loved the way West Indian men catered to a woman. But Trevor was definitely a Rude Boy, and even if she wasn't with Ty she couldn't seriously date him. She heard some of the people in the building say he had killed a man before for stealing from him. Brittany had been shot at once and that was enough gangster to last her the rest of her life.

When Brittany got to the fourth floor she smelled a tantalizing aroma coming from her apartment. As she fumbled for her keys she wondered what Tyson was up to in there. Brittany opened the door and a big smile spread across her face. There were candles burning on the table, and there was a delicious seafood spread. She saw Ty had placed a big Rock lobster in the center of the table, salad with fresh pepper, jumbo shrimp on the side, and a bottle of Kendall Jackson to wash it down with. "Oh Tyson you didn't have to do this."

"I know but I wanted to."

Brittany opened the fridge to get some water and saw two slices of Juniors strawberry cheesecake in the fridge. Man her baby was good. "Oh Baby Juniors too!"

"That was supposed to be a surprise for later. I was planning on feeding it to you," he said with a wink.

"I am surprised! I thought you would still be mad at me for canceling the trip on you."

172

"Well, I can't say I wasn't pissed when I hung up the phone on you, but I chose to marry a beauty with brains and ambition, so I'll let you make a name for yourself for now."

Brittany walked over to Tyson and tongued him down. This man was too good to be true. After she came up for air she said, "Well let's eat, I'm starved." They broke open the wine, and talked over dinner. "Baby the food is delicious. I can't believe you cook so good, you gotta be the best cooking basketball player in the country boo. No lie."

"Only for you boo, only for you."

After, Brittany rubbed her belly she was full. "Baby I have been at the office for over 12 hours. I need to take a shower and put on something sexy. I'm not feeling this suit right now."

"Aight do your thing, I'm going to check out the game on tv."

Brittany showered with her favorite scent, *Mango Melange* from *Carol's Daughter*. Tyson loved that scent too, he said it made him want to eat her alive. Yummmmmmmmmmmmmmm.

When Brittany got out of the shower she lotioned down with the mango body butter and took one of their favorite CD's out of the disk holder. She slipped on her *Victoria Secrets* lingerie and high heel slip ons. She put TLC's *Red Light Special* on and came out to her baby.

"May I have this dance"? She said as she stood seductively against the wall. Tyson undressed her with his eyes. Brittany began a little strip tease for her baby, while he sat on the couch and watched her every move.

"Mm hmm mmm, of all the strips clubs I been dragged to I ain't never seen a sistah who can work it like you baby."

"I know and you never will. So dessert or me?"

"Baby you are the dessert." Tyson came over and picked her up, she throw her legs around his waist. He pulled her thong off and began to enter her.

"Oh Tyson baby, that feels good. I've been thinking about this all night. Mmmmhmmm this is my mandingo right. No body else can get it."

"Yeah baby its all yours."

They made love in the living room, the hallway and the bedroom.

They could never get enough of each other. They fell asleep in each other's arms in the bedroom, with the sounds of TLC still playing. As Brittany drifted off to sleep she couldn't stop hoping that things would always be this simple between them.

Chapter 41   AND THEN THERE WAS LIGHT

Present Day

Kyle

Kyle finished his shift exhausted but hopeful. He still felt an uneasiness knowing things were not right between him and Renee. But he was positive that once they spoke the situation would be rectified. Kyle decided he should go home take a shower and figure out how to deal with the Renee problem. As he walked toward his truck he saw a manila envelope under his windshield wiper. He began to smile as he sped up a bit.

He figured it had to be a note or letter from Renee. She must have realized how crazy it was to think Kyle would abuse any woman. 'Don't worry baby I'll let you make it up to me,' he was thinking as he reached for the envelope. He settled in behind the wheel and pulled out an 8 ½ by 11-inch photo of Renee hugging some guy. Kyle could feel the fire rise in his chest as he noticed the guy's right hand grabbing Renee's ass.

What the fuck is this he thought. His mind was racing and his heart felt like it would beat out of his chest. Kyle tried to relax and realized he had dropped the picture and both his fists were clenched. He told himself to calm down and began looking for a note or a clue to what this shit was all about. Kyle looked, nothing written on the front or back of the envelope, nothing inside but then he turned the picture over and there it was:

KYLE,

RENEE IS MY WOMAN. STAY AWAY. YOU SEE HER WRAPPED IN MY ARMS. SHE TOLD ME YOU BEAT WOMEN AND THREATENED TO KNOCK HER OUT WITH ONE PUNCH IF SHE WOULDN'T DATE YOU. WE'VE BEEN TOGETHER FOR TWO YEARS AND WERE GETTING MARRIED. IF YOU CALL OR BOTHER HER AGAIN I'LL KILL YOU. DON'T TEST ME!

FROM A REAL MAN

That was it, that was the last straw and Kyle lost it. Kyle yelled out loud "Really Really you little bitch you're a real man you're gonna kill me. Don't ever let me meet you face to face." Kyle drove wildly as he flipped open his cell phone and hit Renee on the speed dial. After two rings the mechanical voice informed him his party wasn't available. What the fuck! Kyle cursed. This wasn't how her phone worked either. She answered, or he would get her sweet little voicemail promising that she would call back as soon as she could. Something was wrong; Kyle could feel it in his bones. After settling down he decided that maybe it was best Renee didn't answer he had to work some things out for himself. Damn! Was Renee engaged to someone else? Did he allow himself to get played like that?

The gloves hit the heavy bag hard as Kyle's muscles tensed and the sweat poured off his body. His muscles were burning, hurting, exhausted, but it still wasn't enough. The anger was still there lingering like a bitter taste in his mouth. Just forget it he kept telling himself, forget her and all this bullshit. First I beat women and now she's engaged to some other dude. This is becoming way too complicated. His brain kept trying to convince the rest of him to let Renee go. But as Kyle continued to punch the bag it seemed like his brain was losing the argument.

He was deep in thought when his doorbell rang. Who the hell is this? He thought. No one was invited and Kyle definitely did not want company on this night. He tried to ignore the door but whoever it was would not stop ringing the bell. Finally Kyle stomped over and opened the door with a growl. "What!" he yelled in intimidating fashion.

"What!" Is that how you answer the door? Well I definitely thought I raised you better than that. I can't imagine how you would have any friends with that temperament. Now settle down and give your momma a proper hello."

Kyle's demeanor changed immediately as he smiled and swept his mother into his arms. "Hey mom what are you doing here?"

"Why do you think I'm here? To see my baby boy."

"Mom," Kyle said with a slight grin. "I haven't been a baby in a long time."

"Nonsense you'll always be my baby. Now invite me in so we can talk."

"Audrey tells me you have a problem and need a little motherly advice." Kyle looked at his mother in admiration as she gracefully sat down on the sofa. Evie as her friends liked to call her was an exceptional woman. She was only 5'4 but her character made her much taller. She raised three children in bad circumstances, but somehow managed to keep her sense of humor, and was able to pass her quiet dignity down to all three children.

"I appreciate the thought Mom but Audrey really should not have brought you into my mess," Kyle reasoned. "Come sit down son," Evie requested.

"OK Let me just go throw on a clean t-shirt." Kyle was back within seconds and went over to take a seat by his mom.

"Now I don't want you to be mad at your sister. She was just worried about you. She said that you never acted like this over a female before and she was so taken aback she thought it might be a good idea if we talked. Anyway Audrey sent a message. She wanted me to say that she didn't tell me everything and if you think there's anyway you might end up with this girl that you shouldn't tell me everything either. I guess you know what's she's talking about. I don't like being shut out but she made me promise, and I don't lie to my kids." Kyle laughed to himself. Audrey knew that their mother could not stand for anyone to challenge her children's character. He realized Audrey was right. He didn't want his mother thinking badly of Renee before they even met. "So baby why don't you tell mama about this girl." Kyle spent the next twenty minutes telling Evie about Renee and how close they had gotten. "So what happened?" she asked.

"We had a fight and some other crazy and weird stuff has happened and I'm seriously considering just moving on." Kyle admitted.

"I'm going to assume that you are not willing to tell me the crazy and weird stuff." She paused but there was only silence. She continued, "therefore I can only give you advice from the stuff I know. First off son - don't be so quick to let something special go. I know all you black men think there's another chick around the corner but I know you, you want a quality woman, and they my son are not around every corner. Second - until all this happened I liked this Renee without even knowing her. Whenever you've called me the past couple of months you've been real happy with a new kind of excitement in your voice. It's the excitement you used to have before your football injury. You stopped coming by as much for food. So I figured she must be cooking and taking care of you. Even though you say she's some big executive she still found time to make you feel like a man. She was making you happy and I like people that make my kids happy. Remember as I say all this I don't know what foolishness has transpired. But here's my last piece of advice. When I came here tonight you were mad and when you're mad you can't think straight. Even as a kid when you were mad you just reacted instead of thinking. You have to get past your anger. You are one of the most intelligent people I've ever known. When you're thinking right there's nothing you can't figure out. I remember all the coaches used to say you had such a high football IQ, that's why all them schools wanted you."

Kyle cut her off, "Mom I don't want to talk about that, that's ancient history."

Evie put her hands over his to still him. "Please son let it go, you had some bad luck. I've had plenty and there are lots of folks out there that have had a lot worse happen to them. You're young and intelligent with your whole life in front of you. There's nothing you can't do. Now get past the anger so you can think, and I'm sure you will figure this whole thing out on your own." With that Evie got up and went to the door. She gave Kyle a big hug and looked into his eyes. "When you two get this thing figured out you best be bringing her by the house so we can meet."

Kyle smiled at his mother's warning, "I love you mom let me walk you to your car."

"Still overprotective I see," Evie smiled. "Always mom always."

Once Kyle was back inside his apartment he thought about his mother's words - "Get past the anger and think." Kyle agreed it was time to get busy. Figure this thing out one way or another and move on in one direction or the other. He was not built for this in limbo shit. So Kyle went and pulled the photo off the punching bag, placed it in front of him on the kitchen table and began to think. He looked at the note again. "We've been together for two years." This was hard for Kyle to swallow. He had been with a lot of women and he knew how women acted when they had a man. You could feel the sneakiness and the apprehension that they might get caught. They didn't want to do things too close to home for fear that someone their man knew might see them.   Renee was nothing like this she was carefree.   She had stayed over at his place on occasion and Kyle had stayed over her place countless times, and she never rushed him out the door, or acted funny when she answered the phone. 'Of course not because she's my woman,' Kyle thought. He flipped the picture back over and looked at the guy.   So who are you - that's the question. How convenient Kyle thought, I can't see your face. So what can I see? That hand on Renee's ass was really distracting Kyle. Then he noticed it. Something on that hand on the right pinky finger, what is that a birth mark, no a small tattoo of some letters interwoven. Now that he was thinking Kyle could see so much more.   He had a general description - light skin black male, approximately 6'2 with short hair and a tattoo on his right pinky finger.   The thing about the picture that was absolute is that the woman was definitely Renee. Since his countless phone calls were met with a mechanical voice, Kyle decided to stake out Renee's and wait to catch her going to the car. Kyle got his friend Harold to cover his shift the next day. He also asked Harold to switch cars with him because he didn't want Renee to bolt if she saw his truck. Harold had an old Corolla so he was more than happy to profile in Kyle's Dodge Ram for the day.

Kyle decided to go and wait two hours early because Renee could be a workaholic, and he wanted to make sure he caught her even if she left early for work. He was sitting back in the drivers seat lounging with a Yankee cap pulled low on his eyes when he began to notice some strange activity. The first odd thing was a Con Ed van out on the streets way to early. One of Kyle's homeboys worked for the power company and he knew they never started this time of morning. Just as he was thinking this the side door of the van opened and a tall black dude got out. He looked around nervously; Kyle saw this and ducked down a bit further. He walked quickly over to the parking lot and stopped at Renee's car. After looking around for any onlookers he bent down and started letting the air out of one of her tires.

What are you doing Kyle thought? He considered jumping out of the car and confronting him but something told him it was better to let this play out.

The stranger got back up and jogged to a different vehicle. It looked to Kyle like an Infinity QX4. After about two minutes he left the Infinity and ran back to the van. What are you up to? Kyle wondered.

Twenty minutes later the same guy jumped out of the van dressed nicely in slacks and a button down shirt with a briefcase. He walked briskly back to the Infinity, got in and backed up out of view from the building. He stopped the vehicle and waited looking at the door to Renee's building. At this point Kyle was watching intently, he was still perplexed as to what exactly was going on but he was sure that coming to Renee's this morning was proving to be an excellent idea.

Sean

Sean barely slept an hour all night. He was too excited by the day he had planned. It seemed like Kyle had given up and Sean was thrilled. He had placed the photo on Kyle's truck during work. Sean had figured Kyle would react one of two ways - either he would rush over to Renee's and confront her about the picture or he would go home think about it and realize it was better to move on. Sean had taken precautions to make sure things went his way. He had placed a block on both their phones. Renee's phone would not accept calls from Kyle, and Kyle's phone would not accept calls from Renee. It was easy to do. He had both their social security numbers and knew everything about them, so he simply called the phone company and requested the blocks. He didn't want them communicating with each other and figuring anything out. Sean also placed tracking devices on both their cars. That way if Kyle had sped over to Renee's he would have been ready. He had stayed in the van all night waiting, and had Kyle shown up, Sean was prepared to make good on his threat to Kyle's life. But as it turned out things were going very smooth according to his tracker. Kyle was at work apparently having given up, and Sean was free to manipulate the situation with Renee. He had left a message on Renee's machine that he would be dropping off the final paperwork from the investigation this morning. The message implied he would simply leave it by her door. But Sean had a different plan. He would just by coincidence be coming by with the paperwork as she was leaving for work, then they would both notice her flat tire and he would offer to drive her to work. Renee might put up a slight protest but Sean could be convincing when he wanted. He would then drive her back home from work explaining that it would be his pleasure to help fix her tire. She would invite him in to clean up after and then he would make his move. The beginning of a lifelong love affair, Sean smiled. He could actually feel goose bumps on his arms as he waited for Renee to emerge from the building's front door. Sean hadn't felt this alive in a long time.

Kyle

Kyle could feel the nerve in his temple throbbing as he watched Renee exit her building. He had already decided to let this thing play out. He had to know what was going on, but part of him wanted to jump out of the car and protect Renee. As he suspected as soon as Renee began walking down the steps the mysterious stranger in the Infinity began driving slowly up the street. Renee was walking hurriedly toward the parking lot obviously rushing to work. Just as she reached the car and noticed the tire, she couldn't miss it, it was on the front driver side. Mr. Con Ed/Infinity man beeped his horn rolled down the window and shouted some corny line, like funny running into you here. Yeah I bet you're real surprised Kyle seethed. You've only spent the last two hours setting this whole thing up. Who are you? You devious bastard! But then Renee smiled, waved and walked over to the window. So Renee knows this asshole, he's not a stranger. This gets more interesting by the moment Kyle thought. Next Kyle watched the mystery man hop out of his vehicle, go over to Renee's car and manage to look truly perplexed and sorry for Renee's misfortune. Then the two became involved in a conversation. Renee was shaking her head with a look on her face that said I appreciate the offer but no thanks. But the sneaky man persisted, and finally after glancing at her watch several times she seemed to be giving a thank you and polite smile as he opened the passenger door and she climbed in. As the trickster walked around the car to the driver side Kyle saw the satisfied grin on his face, and when his right hand went to open the door there it was, clear as day a tattoo on his pinky finger. Well, well, well Kyle thought looks like we're going to get to meet after all. He didn't want Renee in the car with this stalker but he would follow them and protect her. He had already deduced that this guy was probably giving her a ride to work. No one worked this hard to rob or rape someone. This guy obviously had a different agenda and Kyle was determined to find out what it was. After only 10 minutes it was clear

Kyle was right they were definitely headed to Renee's job. Once there she stayed in the SUV for a few minutes. Then Mr. Happy jumped out of the truck and ran around to open the passenger door for her. She looked at her watch again and placed a hand on his arm and squeezed it in appreciation. Renee turned to walk away but dude grabbed her. Kyle was about to jump from the car and stopped when he noticed it was just a hug that the loser wanted. As he got back in the truck Kyle noticed a look of pure satisfaction on his face. Yeah enjoy it now buddy cause I can promise that you'll be paying for every touch Kyle thought to himself as his hands gripped the steering wheel a bit tighter.

Renee

Renee looked over her left shoulder as Sean drove away. Sean, the safe guy that her girlfriend's thought she should date to get over the whole Kyle debacle. But for some reason Renee got a weird eerie feeling whenever she was around him. Sean was always dressed perfectly, wore her favorite cologne, opened her car door and was polite and attentive, but she just felt like something was amiss. He was coming back to pick her up from work and then fix her tire. He had been her savior this morning after seeing the flat tire. She figured she would have to reschedule the big sales meeting she had planned but Sean was more than happy to take her to work. By all accounts Sean was perfect. But no matter how hard she tried it was Kyle that occupied her thoughts. She had even broke down and tried to call him a few times but his phone was always unavailable. Renee checked her voicemail often with secret hopes that Kyle would leave a message but it was not to be. He had probably moved on. Kyle wasn't the type of guy that had trouble attracting women. Why she wanted some abusive guy in her life was beyond Renee. But she couldn't deny the empty feeling she felt since their argument. Argument is how Renee had been thinking of it, but now it was time to admit that they were broken up. Renee wanted to cry at the thought. Instead she straightened her shoulders, put her head up and walked into the one thing she could depend on - her career.

Kyle

Kyle had to make a quick decision. He really wanted to speak with Renee but something told him he would get more answers by following Mr. Tricky. He knew Renee was safe. She would be at work for at least 8 hours. Deciding it was the logical move, Kyle began to follow the Infinity with hopes of solving this mystery. First he stopped and got a bagel and some coffee, which served to remind Kyle of how hungry he was. Then he stopped by Pep Boys and bought a bag of items. Next he drove to a small house and was there long enough for Kyle to decide this was his home. Kyle grabbed some paper and a pen and jotted down the address. After an hour the guy emerged from the door in a different outfit. He probably took a shower.Kyle guessed it was a safe bet that the van didn't have running water.

His next stop surprised Kyle, The law firm of Kravitz & Kahn. That was where Renee's best friend Brittany worked. What's he doing here Kyle thought? He stayed put in the Corolla as he watched the stranger enter the building. Ten minutes later he was back out the door with Brittany by his side. Kyle had never met Brittany but he had seen enough pictures to know it was her. Brittany knows this guy too. What the Hell. Was she behind this? Renee always talked about Brittany like they were sisters. Could she be behind this? Whatever this was? Kyle was getting more confused by the minute. After following the two to a working lunch, there was lots of paperwork and things did not seem intimate. Kyle was debating whether or not he should confront Brittany. She obviously knew who the mystery man was and he could get a name from her. Then Kyle could ask her about the picture. Kyle was suspicious by nature but it was hard even for him to fathom Brittany hurting Renee. They were grade school friends - they went way back. What could be her reason? Kyle decided to stop guessing. When Brittany's mysterious friend dropped her off Kyle would go into the law firm and ask her point blank. It was past time for answers.

Chapter 42 THE PAYBACK

Present Day

Dion pulled up in front of the Brooklyn Motor Lodge. This had been his new home for the past 3 weeks, and it sucked. He hated every aspect of it – the smelly bed covers, the old stinking carpet that hadn't been cleaned in years, the closet size bathroom and the constant bangin of the walls with pimps and hos getting their groove on for the 4-hour stay. This was the type of place that you would only want to stay for 4 hours, but since Dion could not afford the Hilton and child support payments, he was stuck with this dump.

Tammy hadn't been trying to hear nothing he had to say when he came home. He found his bags on the front lawn. Their relationship had been pretty strained since she caught him in their bed with Simone. But it went from bad to worse when she found out that it was not a one-night stand, but an affair that he had been carrying on for a long time. Dion knew that the main reason Tammy was making this so hard on him was because Simone was much younger than her, and she always felt like he had a weakness for young girls. Simone was also very attractive. The affair devastated Tammy and she could not believe that he was not in love with Simone.   words kept going through Dion's head - "If you didn't love her, then why did you bring her in our house, and screw her in our bed, and disrespect your family like that!"

This was a question Dion still could not answer to this day. Why did he play himself like that? He started thinking back to when he'd first met Shorty at his doctor's office:

Simone was the receptionist, and a fine one at that. She gave him the biggest smile when he'd walked in for his appointment, and honey was throwing it on hard, smacking her gum and flirting with him shamelessly. She didn't seem to care that he had a wedding ban on, and that made her all the more tantalizing.

When she got up from her desk, she made a point to pass in front of him and switch that tail. When he saw the banging body on Simone, he knew he had to have her. Dion loved his wife but ever since the triplets,

184

she had kind of let herself go, and her sex drive had gone from 100 to Zero. At the time Simone seemed to be just what a brother needed to lift his spirits. He could tell by her designer clothes, fancy hairstyle and manicured nails that she wasn't phuckin with no broke nigga, so on his way out he dropped her his card and said call me sometime as he smiled down at her and licked his lips. The prosecutor title and the sexy lips always got them hyped. He walked to the parking lot, and got in his Lexus, thinking about how he couldn't wait to dig that young chick's back out, and hoped she would call.

As he was driving out he looked through his rearview mirror, and like a typical gold digger, she was standing in the door of the office, looking to see what kind of car he was driving. Dion couldn't help but laugh.

The next day Simone called him. They spent the entire summer fucking all over Brooklyn - his car, her house, hotels, his office. She loved to be spontaneous and wild. That was last summer.

Now this bitch had cost him his family and his life and she was going to pay for it.

It was all Simone's fault. She had put on that sexy ass voice and convinced him that it would be fun, and they would never get caught. Meanwhile, that tramp had told his wife that he and Simone were having a sex party when she called the house that night. After he found out what she did, he went ballistic. Oooh, just the thought of it got his blood boiling. He loved his sons more than life itself. He might have been a cheater, but when his wife told him that she was fighting for sole custody of the triplets, he felt like he had just been stabbed in the heart. He wanted to be there full-time for his boys, and having them on weekends and holidays was not going to cut it. Unfortunately he knew the courts would probably side with Tammy because she made a lot more money, she hadn't had an extra-marital affair, and she was a damn good mother. "WHY GOD WHY MEEEEEE WHY GOD WHY MEEEEEE WHYYYY," he screamed. Then someone on the other side of the wall banged on the wall.

"Would you keep it down buddy. Some of us are trying to sleep."

"Fuck you and everybody in this dump!" he screamed back.

Dion walked over to the closet and looked at the 9mm Skeeter had hooked him up with. He then took the silencer out of the closet. He was not playing with this Bitch. She had systematically ruined his life and his future, and she would pay!

It was raining pretty hard outside when Dion came out of his room at 11:00 pm. He thought the element of surprise was always the best attack. He was too angry to feel any remorse in the matter. Simone had ruined his life and caused him to lose the only thing that mattered to him. No woman was allowed to do that to Dion Williams. No one. He was so angry tears were developing in his eyes and his hands were trembling on the steering wheel. No good tramp, home wrecker! I bet she won't do this to anyone else again.

Dion reached the Pennsylvania Avenue exit and made the turn into the housing project. He turned off his lights, as he did not want to draw attention to himself. He did not plan on having any witnesses. Since it was raining, there wasn't the normal crowd of brothas hanging in front of the building, just a few crackheads and small time dealers. Dion parked his car alongside the curb to ensure a quick getaway. He walked quickly into the building and took the stairs up to her apartment. As he ran through the pissy staircase, he started thinking about how Simone wished she could get her broke ass out of these projects and into his luxury townhouse. He would never marry a skank like her whose punani goes to the highest bidder and nothing else matters. He ran faster thinking about the back stabbing ho.

"Yo Justice" - he hadn't heard that name since he graduated high school. And he slowed down – cursing to himself. He knew he should have worn the ski mask, but he didn't want to look like OJ running through the staircase.

"What up dogg!" It was Paul they used to call him P-dog back in the day. Back when Paul was runnin' wild on the streets.

"What you doin' slummin in this neighborhood man, so late at night? What you doing some investigative work or something," Paul joked. Paul had given him the out he needed.

"Exactly man why the hell else would I be here? I'm checking up on some witnesses in a case."

Paul looked at him sideways, "damn man you sure do take your job seriously. The state got you working like that?!"

"Tryin to move up to head prosecutor man. Gotta go above and beyond. Later man."

Dion was happy to escape out of there, and he ran up the final flight. He made a note to himself to take the other staircase down on his way out. He didn't need any more witnesses.

When he got to Simone's door he felt his adrenaline pumping so hard he thought his heart would jump out of his chest.

Simone looked around the apartment for a match. She usually ended up hiding them because she didn't want KJ to get to them. He had a fetish for playing with matches that was liable to kill both of them. She had picked up her favorite candle, Vanilla Sugar from Bath N' Body Rub. She enjoyed burning the sexy scent while she took a bubble bath. KJ was at his nana's house so she could really enjoy a nice bath without him calling her name every 5 minutes. Joe was supposed to bring his stank butt over later to try to make up for standing her up for dinner the other night. She was really getting tired of him and his old wife. I mean, his wife Lorraine was probably pushing 50, and her punani was probably all dried up and wrinkled, not to mention her flabby body. She had seen pictures of her in Joe's office and all she could do was scoff at them. She remembered saying to him, "does this old biddy still get your Jimmy hard baby? Don't tell me, she used to be a knockout when you met her back in the 1920s," laughing at her own joke. Joe didn't find it amusing. He said, "you'll see your day will come – age and wrinkles will catch up to you too, Ms. Vanity." She hated it when he defended Lorraine. Huhhh, Simone knew she would never let herself go. When old age took over, she would be the first one at the plastic surgeon, tightening and tucking every step of the way. Whatever man she was with, would definitely have to have enough money to pay for it. I mean there was just no other way.

Ahhhhh, Simone said as she lowered herself into the tub. One day she would have one of those Jacuzzi tubs that Dion had in his house. Then she would really be living in the lap of luxury. These project tubs wasn't hittin' on nothing, and it didn't help that she had to kill 3 roaches before she could get comfortable in there. Nothing destroys the mood more than a big cockroach crawling around the wall when you're trying to unwind in the tub. She listened to the smooth sounds of Jill Scott floating from the living room, as she closed her eyes.

Chapter 43   ALL THE ANSWERS

Present Day

Kyle

Kyle watched as Sean drove away. Time for some answers he thought. He looked over at the passengers seat, there sat a bouquet of flowers he was hoping to give to Renee as a sort of peace offering. But this was not to be instead Kyle had decided to use it as a decoy to gain access in Brittany's office.

He walked into the building and told security he had a flower delivery for a Brittany (since Kyle couldn't remember her last name he paused and acted as if he was searching for the card that accompanied the flowers) but before he could finish his pretend search the guard had answered the question for him.

"Its Brittany Martin. I'll call her office and let them know you're on your way up. I'm sure Ms. Martin will be excited to get such beautiful flowers," said the female security guard with a bit of envy in her voice.

Once upstairs, Kyle was met by Brittany's secretary, who tried to take the flowers from him but Kyle told her that these were direct delivery and they came with a message. The secretary looked at him a bit leery and unconvinced.

Kyle just looked at her un-phased and gave her his best smile, "I'm sorry I should have explained it better you've heard of singing telegrams well this is sort of like singing flowers."

Her eyes brightened up after he said this, "Do you think I could come in her office and listen in, it sounds so romantic?"

Kyle responded with an apologetic look, "I'm sorry but the instructions on this one says her ears only." As he said the word instructions he gestured toward the manila envelope under his right arm which of course contained the picture of Mystery man with his hand on Renee's ass.

"Oh well," the secretary conceded, "let me tell Brittany you're on the way in.

On his way into her office Kyle lifted the flowers to cover his face he figured Brittany may have seen his picture. He closed the door and lowered the flowers, Brittany had a big someone sent me flowers smile on her face that quickly faded.

"Wait a minute I know you you're Renee's boyf…", she stopped and corrected herself "ex-boyfriend."

Kyle could feel the heat in his body rise, "Really," he responded "am I the ex because Renee never told me that."

"Well if she was able to get in touch with you, she would have," Brittany said with attitude.

"What do you mean, she's been the one avoiding and blocking out my calls," Kyle said confused.

"Typical," Brittany began in a disgusted tone "first she finds out from another woman that you're some type of abusive jerk, then you're not man enough to face the music and now you lie and say she's the one avoiding you. I can't tell you how glad I am you're out of my friends life." The last sentenced stabbed Kyle like a knife. But Brittany wasn't finished "What are you doing here anyway and make it good or I'm going to have security throw you out on your ass."

Kyle had to laugh at this last remark and replied, "who the little 5 foot 3 security guard at the front desk. He put his hand up before Brittany could respond, "look truce OK, here's the deal almost everything you've said since I've walked through that door is incorrect and I'm getting the idea that you have been as misled as me and Renee." Brittany went to speak but Kyle stopped her again. "Look Brittany you're a lawyer right so if anyone can appreciate looking at all the evidence before coming to a conclusion it should be you." As Kyle continued to speak Brittany became more intrigued he definitely was not what Brittany had envisioned when Sean told her about this ignorant, drunken asshole he had helped Renee get out of her life.

Kyle stopped talking for a moment and Brittany piped up "What evidence?" Kyle blew out in relief. Brittany was willing to listen. He handed her the envelope with the picture in it. She opened it pulled out the picture and was shocked she recognized Renee immediately and after studying the picture for a few more seconds she recognized Sean. After the initial shock Brittany thought what's the big deal so Renee and Sean went out and during a hug he grabbed her ass. Renee wasn't some cowering little schoolgirl, if Sean did something she didn't like he probably got an ear full and maybe even worse. Plus this is what Sean and Brittany wanted, to set him and Renee up. The more Brittany thought about it she was happy the two were hitting it off.

Finally Brittany spoke up, "So what Kyle now you're a women beater and a stalker, maybe Renee's trying to move on. You have no idea how much you hurt her." Once again Brittany's words dug deep into his heart but he kept his composure. He responded in a calm voice, "I'm not the stalker Brittany turn the picture over." She did and there it was:

KYLE,

RENEE IS MY WOMAN. STAY AWAY. YOU SEE HER WRAPPED IN MY ARMS. SHE TOLD ME YOU BEAT WOMEN AND THREATENED TO KNOCK HER OUT WITH ONE PUNCH IF SHE WOULDN'T DATE YOU. WE'VE BEEN TOGETHER FOR TWO YEARS AND WE'RE GETTING MARRIED. IF YOU CALL OR BOTHER HER AGAIN I'LL KILL YOU. DON'T TEST ME!

FROM A REAL MAN

Brittany just stared at the words for a long time. Finally it was Kyle that spoke, "I didn't take this picture it was left on the steering wheel of my truck at work. I know you don't know me that well but you can believe I was beyond angry. I don't like thinking something's mine and it isn't. So tell me Brittany because I know you're her best friend, was Renee playing me this whole time? Is she engaged to someone else? Or is this guy playing games?" Brittany simply remained silent and Kyle could see her lawyer mind trying to work it's way through the puzzle so he decided to give her more information.

"So lawyer Brittany that brings me to why I'm here. I followed the asshole in that picture to you. I watched the two of you have a friendly working lunch. And I honestly wondered if the two of you were working together to try and deceive my girl. But then I thought of all the times Renee talked about you about how far you two went back and how you were like sisters. So I decided to take a chance and hoped you were the true friend Renee obviously trusts so much." Kyle finished.

Brittany finally spoke up, "No Kyle she's not engaged and never has been, Renee doesn't play games she's not that type of woman," Brittany continued as she looked Kyle dead in the eyes, "And she certainly was not playing games with you. I am very disturbed by the note on the back of this picture. The person I went to lunch with and this note don't match. I'm confused but something tells me you have more information and I will draw my conclusions once I here it. So please Kyle sit down and tell me everything you know. Oh Kyle one last thing before you begin. You never have to question my loyalty to Renee she is my best and dearest friend and if I find out someone has been fucking with her life you'll see what anger is." Kyle spent the next 20 minutes rehashing the morning's events to Brittany. He was telling her that it probably sounded crazy but she had to believe him.

Brittany just smiled and said, "No I don't have to believe you, but if you give me five minutes I'll tell you if I do." Brittany proceeded to pick up her phone and dial quickly then she said "Renee Jones please. After a few seconds Kyle heard Brittany's speech pattern change "Hey girl what up? How'd the big meet go today? What do mean you were almost late? He did, just a coincidence, Wow Yeah that is sweet. I gotta go girl you know the life of a soon to be lawyer I gotta go prove another asshole is a liar."

Brittany hung up the phone looked at Kyle and said, "Yeah I believe you. And there's a lot I have to tell you." Kyle and Brittany formed a plan, Brittany cancelled the rest of her day and her and Kyle drove back to Renee's apartment. Kyle pointed out the white van. By this time Brittany had told Kyle who Sean was and how she had encouraged Renee to check Kyle out. Kyle had given her a mean look but Brittany just shrugged her shoulders and said "hey sue me OK but things were happening way fast with you two and Renee is never that trusting or reckless so I felt I had to look out for her." Kyle decided to let it go at the moment. He was angrier with Renee for her lack of trust beside they had bigger problems at the moment.

"What Now," Brittany said.

Kyle responded, "Now we take a look inside that van." Out of instinct Brittany protested, "We can't legally search that van."

Kyle growled back at her, "You think I give a shit about legally anything. I want to see how sick this guy is. You think I want some type of mental patient around my girl."

Brittany was still struggling with the situation, "I've known Sean for awhile and I don't think he would be capable of hurting anybody."

Kyle was frustrated, "You don't know this guy at all, you only know what he wants you to see. I'm from the streets and I've seen people flip. The same guy that rocks his baby to sleep and kisses his girls hand two hours later is shooting some crack head in the chest for fun. Didn't you tell me he seems so perfect, do you really think any ones that perfect?" For some reason when Kyle said this Brittany had a fleeting thought of Tyson.

"Well," Brittany finally gave in "I guess there's only one way to find out lets see what's in the van."

It turned out the van contained a nightmare. First the walls were full of different pictures of Renee a sick, psychotic sort of mural, which instantly made Brittany feel sick to her stomach. There were monitors and stacks of mini-cassettes and VCR tapes. The monitors were labeled, 'front of Renee's building, Renee's parking lot, GPS Renee's car, and GPS Kyle's truck'.

"Check this out Brittany," he said pointing to the monitor that tracked his truck.

"We got lucky I borrowed my friends car today because I thought maybe Renee would bolt if she saw my truck. If I came in my truck he would have known the bastard thinks I'm at work right now."

Brittany just listened growing angrier by the second. Kyle then noticed the earphones and different switches on a device that looked like a home stereo they were also labeled - Renee's kitchen, Renee's living room, Renee's bathroom and Renee's bedroom. After seeing this Kyle grabbed some of the mini cassettes to see if they were labeled. To his horror they were, Renee and Kyle sex raw, Renee edited no Kyle and Renee's sex talk my favorite. All these tapes were dated and Kyle was furious. All of sudden he needed to get out of the van, he jumped out and Brittany was right behind him, she could no longer breath in the van.

She looked at Kyle and he was tense and breathing hard, his fists were clenched like he wanted to hit something.

He turned and looked at Brittany and said, "I'm going to fucking kill him." She looked in his eyes and could tell he meant it.

"Kyle please you've got to calm down, you going to jail is not going to help Renee. I'm the one at fault here and I intend to make it right. I feel like shit. I can't believe I turned this psycho loose on my best friend. He seemed like such a nice guy but he's obviously very sick, he needs professional help." Brittany explained.

Kyle raged on, "I really could give two shits about what he needs, what he wants is my woman and he can't have her. He's already been more intimate with her then is allowed and he's going to pay. What kind of sick fuck tapes the girl he's supposedly infatuated with have sex with someone else. That shit is private between us."

Kyle was yelling now, "How would you feel Brittany? I know you got a man, you two make love have sex, I'm sure you say things and I'm sure he says things. How would you feel knowing your little fucked up friend Sean who needs professional help was jerking off to you?" Kyle had gone too far and Brittany finally lost it she bend over the sidewalk and throw up in disgust. This seemed to bring Kyle back to his senses.

"Jesus' I'm sorry," he was rubbing Brittany's back, "I was just so mad I needed to lash out. It's not your fault. I know you love Renee. I just need to get my hands on Sean." Brittany was recovering, she got a tissue out of her pocketbook to wipe her mouth.

"It's OK Kyle I can only imagine how you feel but we don't have time for this we need to come up with a plan. Sean's picking Renee up from work," Brittany began.

Kyle snapped again, "No fucking way, call her now." Brittany looked at her watch it's too late. Kyle growled, "What do you mean too late it's only 6:10, Renee always works to at least 6:30pm."

"Yeah but her tire had a flat remember and she didn't want to be rude and have Sean out half the night just to pick her up. Here's my suggestion," Brittany continued "I don't think I should call her cell because if she starts acting funny Sean might sense it and hurt her or try to take her away. Right now he thinks he has all the cards and everyone is fooled so he's free to manipulate everyone, this gives us the advantage.

194

We'll close up the van like nothing happened, I'll call in some favors to get the cops out here and well make sure he never gets close to Renee again. Deal?" Brittany let the question hang in the air.

"On one condition", Kyle answered. "You don't call your cops until I get to talk to him."

"Talk Kyle," Brittany asked suspiciously.

Kyle answered her patiently, "Brittany you're not a man there are things that go on between men that you could never understand. Between the picture, the note and all the shit in that van over there he has spit in my face. I'm not the type of man that cowers behind the police. If another man was trying to rape my woman in an alley I wouldn't call 911 and hope they got there in time, I would protect her no matter what it cost me. You do understand once all this is explained to Renee she will feel emotionally violated. So once again I need to deal with him one on one before you call the cops. Deal."

Brittany gave in, "Deal, but we need a plan because if you go to jail she would never forgive me."

Renee

She waited by the front entrance patiently she didn't want Sean to have to wait after all he was the one doing her a favor. He pulled up in the Infinity Jeep. She walked over to jump in but before she could get to close he had run around the front and told her to wait while he opened her door. Of course perfect gentlemen she thought somewhat sarcastically. But then she chastised herself - us women are always complaining about guys not treating us right and when one does we're suspicious. She decided then and there to give Sean a chance. She needed to stop obsessing over Kyle and move on.

Just as she was finishing the thought Sean said, "Can I buy you dinner?"

Renee smiled and said sure, "But can we stop by my place first so I can change?"

"Absolutely," Sean answered feeling like he was finally going to get his girl. He took the car ride as an opportunity to flirt shamelessly, telling Renee what an amazing woman she was and how the right man would treat her like a precious gem. By the time they had arrived at her apartment he had decided to make his first move before dinner. He wanted to taste her sweet lips. Once again he told her to wait while he opened her door. He grabbed her hand as she got out but she reflexively pulled it away. Sean ignored this and simply put his hand at the small of her back as they walked through her front door. Once inside her place Renee offered to make Sean a drink and he responded with the suggestion that she make a drink for them both and sit and talk for a minute. Renee simply kicked her shoes off and agreed.

When she returned with the drinks Sean had put on some music and was sitting on the couch. Renee had wanted to sit in the chair but Sean had been going through her CD's and had thrown them in the chair. She knew it would be awkward if she cleared the chair off to sit so instead she took a seat next to Sean, which seemed to please him. As they spoke Sean seemed to get closer and closer until his cologne was making Renee's head spin, she really loved that cologne. Renee knew herself and she wasn't crazy about Sean but at this moment with the music, the cologne and the neediness she was feeling since Kyle was gone, the closeness felt good. Sean brought his right hand up to Renee's neck and began to message it lightly. She simply closed her eyes and decided to let herself go for the moment. She could feel Sean's breath, as he got closer to taking what he had worked so hard for.

Chapter 44 LISTEN TO MY 9MM GO BOOM!

Present Day

Dion knew one thing for sure, once he put a cap in this ho's ass she wouldn't be able to come between him and his family no more. She needed to be reckoned with, and he was the one to put her in her place. She had fucked with his family and this was the pay back. Dion still had a copy of her key from way back when they first started messing around. He slipped it into the door as quietly as he could. He pushed the door open slowly not knowing where Sim would be in the apartment. He was happy to hear the music playing; this would allow him to creep up on her, without her hearing the floor creak. Dion slowly closed the door behind him and lifted up his mask. He saw a candle flickering in the bathroom, and heard Sim humming to the music. He tiptoed toward the bathroom, his heart beating faster with each step he took toward his revenge.

Joe locked his doors as he exited the Belt Parkway in Brooklyn and headed towards the housing projects Simone lived in. He had stopped to pick her up a dozen roses and her favorite bottle of wine. She was such a simple ho; anything material would shut her big mouth up. He did owe it to her this time, because he was supposed to take her to City Island over the weekend, but at the last minute his wife needed him to take her to her mother's house. Lorraine never drove in the dark.

Joe couldn't wait to see Simone; he couldn't wait to bang her. He was going to tear her up tonight, it seemed like ages since he'd had any pussy and she knew how to satisfy him. As much as Joe hated coming into the hood, at least when he went to her house he never had to worry about running into anyone he knew, or hiding credit card statements from fancy hotels – the only kind Simone would go to. Her favorite line was, "If I wanted to sleep in a dump Joe I would stay my ass at home." She killed him with her conceited self. Joe never parked his Jag inside the projects. He always parked it on a well-lit block across the street from the corner store. He armed his car and jumped out with the gifts he'd bought for Simmy.

He passed a group of young boys standing in front of the building on his way in. Some of them looked at him like they knew he wasn't from there, but Joe never showed any fear. He would have preferred taking the stairs but Simone lived on the 10th Floor and that was too much. Joe sometimes felt like the staircases in these buildings were more dangerous than the elevators because when the elevator had been broke, he'd seen a lot of drug dealing and prostituting going on in the stairway, and he always looked out of place running up with dress pants and loafers. Today he had worn the sneakers Simone bought him, he felt like it gave him a more urban look. The elevator finally arrived and Joe's dick was hard just thinking about Simone waiting for him in some sexy negligee.

Dion had a silencer on his piece so he knew once he shot her he would be out. He crept with his back against the wall. He could see her in the bathtub through the mirror in the bathroom. She had her eyes closed. In one fluid motion he turned off the lights in the bathroom knocking over the candle in the process and slapped Simone in the face with his pistol. "This is for fucking with my family Bitch! I never told you I loved you, and you still had to fuck with my wife!"

Simone mumbled, "Dion is that you?"

"Paybacks a Biiiiiitch," and with that he shot her at point blank range. When he turned around he noticed the flames from the candle starting to burn the sink. "You fucked with the wrong one baby" he said, as he looked at her with blood gushing from her body.

Dion quickly ran out the door and down the steps.

Joe stepped off the elevator. He jumped when he heard a door down the hall slam. The last thing he needed was any gunfights while he was creepin. As he walked towards 10C he noticed the door was ajar, and wondered why anyone living in the projects would ever leave their door open for any amount of time. He called out Simone's name as he walked through the door. She knew he was on his way over.

"Simmy why did you leave the door open? I see you're listening to the Jill Scott CD I bought you honey. It's nice isn't it?"

Simone didn't respond so Joe walked into the hall, and noticed a small fire starting in the bathroom. He screamed, "Simone what's going on? Are you trying to burn the place down!" He ran into the kitchen and picked up the mop bucket and quickly filled it with water. Then he ran back to the bathroom to douse out the flames.

"Jesus Christ!!!" He screamed when he saw Simone slouched in the tub, blood dripping from her shoulder. She appeared unconscious. Joe quickly took her pulse and breathed a sigh of relief when he felt a slight pulse. "We still got time baby, just hang in there." He pulled out his cell phone and called an ambulance, while he pulled Simone out of the tub. He ripped up some sheets and tied them around her shoulder to try and stop the bleeding. "Looks like the bastard was aiming for your heart and hit your shoulder instead. Who did this to you Simone, what kind of animal would do this??!!"

Simone lay with her eyes closed, with slight breaths coming out.

"Yes, this is Dr. Hooper out of Mt. Colonel Hospital. I need an ambulance at 1 Martin Luther King Drive, Apartment 10C immediately. The patient has a pulse so if we operate quickly enough there's a good chance we can save her life. Hurry this is a matter of life and death!" Joe immediately went to work trying to give her mouth-to-mouth resuscitation. He kept talking to Simone so she wouldn't give up. "Hang in there with me Simmy. You got a son that needs you don't give up, you're a fighter!" He felt a slight squeeze from her. "That's my girl, you're gonna be alright honey, I'm right here." At least that's what Joe was praying for.

Chapter 45   THE BLOW UP

Present Day

Brittany

Brittany looked over at Kyle and could feel his anger and anticipation. This guy was intense. She could see why things had happened so quickly between him and Renee; they were alike in many ways. She looked out the window and saw Sean's SUV approaching.

"Here they come," Kyle whispered as he ducked down a little and encouraged Brittany to do the same. Brittany could feel her stomach begin to tumble with nerves. She still wasn't sure what Kyle would do, and the look he had on his face was making Brittany regret agreeing to his terms. On the street Renee and Sean exited his Infinity, and as Sean came up beside Renee he attempted to grab her hand and hold it. At the same moment Brittany could actually hear a low growl coming from deep inside Kyle as he grabbed for the door handle.

But before he could jump out Brit took hold of his shoulder, "No Kyle! You promised remember, not out in public. It has to be in her apartment so you two are the only witnesses. Besides look she pulled away from him." Kyle looked out to see if Brittany was telling the truth and she was. She could feel his body relax a little. Thank God, she thought because Brittany hadn't told Kyle about the gun Renee kept in her apartment for protection. She worried that he would be too tempted to use it to kill Sean. Her plan was to get it from Renee once they were inside the apartment.

Brittany began speaking again, "We have a minute so let's go over this one last time. We go up and knock on the door."

Kyle cut her off, "I kick it in."

Brittany was getting frustrated, "I thought we agreed on…"

Kyle cut her off again, "It's better if we surprise him. I don't know if he has a weapon. This way even if he does he won't have time to use it.

This isn't TV, Brittany. I can't take the chance - I gotta go with street rules. And street rules are strike first. I don't want him to try and hurt Renee or use her as a shield."

Brittany was quiet as she contemplated his words. "OK OK you kick it in. Then you have your man to man with Sean and I grab Renee, pull her out into the hall and quickly explain. Remember Kyle as soon as we get to her floor I'm calling the cops." She looked over and Kyle had a far off look in his eyes. "Kyle," she said a bit louder. "Did you hear me?"

"Yeah I hear you," Kyle said as he began putting on a pair of heavy-duty canvas gloves that were in the back seat.

"What are those for?" Brittany asked.

"These are for the first part of my conversation with Sean. I'll take them off before we are done chatting." Brittany looked at Kyle speechless. "Don't worry Brittany. Don't you remember his little note - he's a real man he can take it."

Kyle

Finally Kyle thought. It felt to Kyle like he had been waiting months to get his hands on Sean. When he and Brittany reached Renee's floor he looked at her and nodded. She took out her cell phone and began dialing the precinct, not 911. This would give them more time to get the story right Brittany had explained. After she finished and hung up, they both went to Renee's door. "Ready?" Kyle whispered.

"Ready," Brittany responded. With one big kick of Kyle's right booted foot. Renee's door sprang open. There on the couch together was Renee and Sean. Sean had his hand around the back of her neck and their lips were almost touching.

"Stop," Brittany yelled in the nick of time. Renee and Sean had dazed looks on their faces. Before Sean could react Kyle had closed the distance from the door to the couch in one giant step. Something snapped in Kyle when he saw Renee and Sean in the intimate embrace. He jumped in the air to get more power, and hit Sean in the face so hard Kyle could hear a bone crack and blood from Sean's nose flew in the air and splattered Renee's blouse. Sean struggled to defend himself but he was in obvious pain and the blood was making it hard for him to breathe. Somewhere in the back of his mind Kyle could hear Renee cursing and Brittany screaming but he was too keyed up to care. He grabbed Sean's slouching body and pulled him up by the collar. Kyle delivered two hard quick blows to Sean's left kidney because he knew from experience that it hurt like hell. Sean fell to the floor grunting and gasping for breath. He was crawling away from Kyle like he could escape. But Kyle put a boot to his back, which served to pin Sean's chest and stomach to the floor while his arms and legs were spread eagle like superman trying to fly.

Kyle looked at him in disgust, "Where do you think you're going little bitch? Oh I forgot your sick ass lives in fantasyland. You probably think you can close your eyes and be beamed to a different planet. Well guess what mothafucka welcome back to earth! You're in my girl's apartment which means you're trespassing."

Kyle kicked Sean in the side twice hoping to break a couple of his ribs. Then he put a knee in Sean's back, leaned in close to his ear and whispered, "I got the picture with your little note to me. But the info is incorrect." As Kyle continued speaking he dug his knee deeper into Sean's back as he leaned over and grabbed his right hand. Kyle got closer to Sean's ear, "this is the hand you used to grab her ass right?" But Kyle didn't wait for an answer. In slow deliberate fashion he began to break Sean's fingers one by one. Kyle spoke steady, "Renee (the thumb breaks) is (pointer finger) my (middle finger) woman (ring finger)." At this point Sean really was screaming like a little bitch - sounds Kyle had never heard coming from a man before.

Renee
Renee had blood on her blouse and it sounded to her like Kyle had killed Sean with one blow.

"What the fuck?" She jumped up from the couch and was about to react when Brittany grabbed her forcefully and pulled her out into the hall.

Renee had a million questions, "Brit what the hell, why.." but before she could finish Brittany cupped her right hand fully over Renee's mouth.

Brittany was swift and practiced in her speech, "Renee, Kyle is good. Sean is bad. I don't have time to go into it. You need to get your gun and give it to me. The cops are on their way."

Renee ripped her hand away, "But why the hell is Kyle in there trying to kill Sean?"

Brittany began again, quick and with clipped words, "No time - Sean sick stalking you. Your gun is not registered. Get it and stop Kyle from killing Sean. I tried he promised but..." Before Brittany could finish they could hear awful sounds coming from her apartment.

"Jesus," Renee spat. "I don't care what he promised - he's killing him." Renee looked into Brittany's eyes with determination, "Wait here I don't want you seeing anything, if Kyle needs a lawyer you'll help him."

With that she shook Brittany slightly, "I'll help him," Brit agreed. She looked at Renee amazed. Renee was one of those rare humans that seemed to get calmer in extreme situations. Renee walked back in her apartment; it looked like a war zone. There was blood and broken furniture. Kyle was standing up taking off some gloves, and Sean was nowhere to be found.

"Kyle", she yelled which caused him to snap his head around. "Where's Sean?"

"The punk bitch went crying and crawling into your bedroom. I'm taking my time because that's a perfect place for the second half of our talk."

Renee was enraged, "Talk. Are you crazy Kyle – you're gonna kill him."

Kyle looked at her with fire in his eyes, "Why the fuck are you defending him? You like him Renee? Sorry dumb question it looked like you were about to tongue him down when we busted in."

Renee cut him off, "Damn it Kyle I don't even know what the hell is going on yet. Brit only had time to tell me pieces before I had to come in here and make sure you don't do something we can't fix."

Kyle just looked at her, his anger seemed to grow, "Fuck this shit I don't have time to talk. I'm in the middle of a man to man discussion with your new boyfriend."

Renee had to stop him. "Wait," she yelled as she jumped on Kyle's back but he just shucked her off like a coat. Then she remembered she kept her gun in her bedroom and fear shot through her like a knife. "Kyle please," she pleaded, and something in her voice made him stop. She ran in front of him and grabbed his neck and pulled him down into a hug. Then she whispered in his ear, "Kyle I have a gun in my bedroom.

I don't think Sean could possibly know where I hid it. But if he does..," Renee left the sentence like that and picked up on a new thought. "Please just let me go in first even if he has it I know my weapon better than him." She looked at Kyle with pleading eyes.

He looked back a bit calmer now, "You know I can't let you go in there Renee, I could never let you get hurt."

Renee grabbed his face on both sides and kissed him hard. When she pulled back she said, "Just give me three minutes. I couldn't live with myself if something happened to you. Besides it sounded like you injured him pretty bad. Do you really think he's that much of a threat? Remember he probably doesn't even know I own a gun."

Kyle was unconvinced, "Renee there's still a lot you don't know." Renee covered Kyle's mouth before he could finish.

She began, "there's a lot you don't know. Sean came up to my apartment I thought he was a friend but he tried to rape me. Lucky for me he didn't know my boyfriend and friend were coming by tonight. Sean and I were fighting. I couldn't get to the door, you heard me scream so you kicked it in. You saw us struggling on the couch and came over to save me." Renee still had her hands on his face tight. "You remember the story right." She was almost yelling, "You understand what I'm saying - you were defending me. There's no way I'm letting you go to jail." She kissed him hard one more time and searched his eyes. She finished in a softer voice, "because I want us to have a future." Kyle just shook his head in amazement. "Now I need to go into my bedroom and smack him a few times and break a few nails. If I need you or feel like I'm in danger I'll call for you I promise. Deal?" Renee finished.

When she said deal it reminded Kyle of the deal he had made with Brittany. He was going to break that promise and kill Sean, but Renee had talked him down. "I'm right here," Kyle said with clenched teeth. "One touch Renee let me know and I'll go in there and break his neck."

She looked at him and said, "I know baby." Renee looked away from Kyle at her bedroom door. The only thing on her mind was had he found the gun. She opened the door just a crack, looked in and saw Sean sitting on the floor with his back against the wall and the gun in his lap.

She looked back at Kyle and made the a-OK sign with her fingers as she slipped through the door and closed it back.

Sean looked up, saw it was her and lifted the gun in her direction with a shaky left hand. "I love you," he began in a weepy voice. "He'll never love you like I love you. The sick fuck! Look at my right hand Renee, he broke all my fingers. You want to be with a man like that."

Renee looked at him in confusion, "How can you love me Sean, we barely know each other?"

"Bullshit," he spat in anger. "I know everything about you - what you like to eat, the clothes you like, your favorite color, your favorite cologne. I watch you all the time. I know how you move. I know how you think." Renee was really starting to get freaked out by Sean's words. "I know you probably think I'm a punk now and I can't protect you. It's not true," he went on taking deep breaths to fight through the pain. "But you believe it - so now I can't have you. I know you want a strong man like your father." As he was speaking Renee was slowly creeping closer and closer to him.

"But guess what Renee?" She answered him slow, just a few more inches and she could tell.

"What Sean?" She crouched down as she replied.

"If I can't have you," Sean leveled the gun to her head and Renee felt a surge of adrenaline run through her, "No one will." With that Sean pulled the trigger but nothing happened. Renee quickly knocked the gun out of his hand and slapped him hard with her right hand. "What the.." he started to say but she smacked him again, then she took her fingernails and scraped the side of his face. She looked at her own hands and said under her breath - that should do it. Sean looked at her stunned, "I don't understand," he began.

Renee looked over at him in hatred, "You're sick! You love me, and you were gonna blow my brains out. By the way you forgot to take the safety off, or maybe you were just too dazed from my man kicking your ass." Renee took the gun and hid it under her blouse. She didn't want Kyle to know what kind of chance she just took. She bent down close to Sean's ear, "If I tell Kyle you put a gun to my head he'd kill you. But I won't you're not worth it." "Kyle," she yelled out, and he was through the door in an instant. "I'm fine," she assured him. "But did you hear the sirens?"

"Yes," Kyle confirmed. "Watch him and please don't do anything baby, I need to talk to Brit." Kyle nodded his agreement and Renee ran out to Brittany in the hall.

Brittany looked agitated and worried beyond belief. "I called 911," she yelled at Renee. "I got worried they weren't coming fast enough."

"It's alright," Renee assured as she pulled the gun from under her blouse and handed it to Brittany. Brittany looked at her relieved, "Is everyone alive in there?" she questioned.

"Barely," was Renee's answer. Brittany was looking at Renee's right hand, which was beginning to swell.

"What happened?" she asked.

"Nothing it's not important," Renee went on. "There's not much time, and I don't want Kyle to get in trouble." Renee looked in her friend's eyes. "Sean was trying to rape me. It was self-defense. Kyle was protecting me. Renee put up her right hand; "Look what I did to my hand when I was trying to fight him off."

Brittany just gave her a knowing smile and a nod. "Only for you Renee."

"Thank you," Renee said with relief.

Brittany then turned from friend back into lawyer. "Now go get those gloves from Kyle. I can probably fit those in my pocketbook too. And things would be a lot easier if there was only one side to the story, until they can search the van."

"What van Renee questioned?'"

"Long story," Brittany sighed. Renee thanked Brit again as she rushed back into the apartment. Kyle looked at her expectantly and they could both hear the sirens right under her window.

"You're so calm," he said perplexed. "I know it's how I am in crazy situations. I have a temper but I'm always able to think. I guess I've seen too much. Anyway don't worry, Brits gonna take care of things. Give me your gloves, and it would be better if he were unconscious for a few hours."

"My pleasure," Kyle smiled as he clenched his fists and happily exacted a little bit more revenge on Sean.

Chapter 46 YOU REAP WHAT YOU SOW

Present Day

Simone slowly opened her eyes. As soon as she opened them, she felt a terrible pain in her right shoulder. She looked and saw, her two best friends, Renee and Brittany talking to each other, discussing basketball as usual.

"Damn don't you two ever get enough of basketball" Simone said, happy to see them.

"She's awake" they screamed. Get the nurse Renee, I'll get Nanna and KJ."

KJ and his Nanna, Liz, came rushing into the hospital room from the hallway. "Mommy, Mommy, I thought you were going to die, I kept trying to talk to you and you never woke up."

Simone had never been so happy to see her little munchkin. "Come over here and give mommy a big hug."

The nurse entered the room. "Can you please clear the room, we need to take her vitals. Well Hello, Ms. Johnson, we have been waiting for you to wake up. The doctor will be in shortly to talk to you. How do you feel?"

"Like my right shoulder just got hit by a 24-wheeler." The nurse laughed, "well we were able to remove the bullet so that you would not suffer any internal bleeding. With some antibiotics and pain killers, you will be back on your feet in no time."

"That's a relief."

"Also if you are up to it, we have some police officers that will be coming by to see you. They would like to ask you a few questions while your memory is still fresh."

"Police officers." Simone didn't like cops. "What do they want from me?"

"They want to know if you have any information that will lead to the arrest of the person who shot you. Don't worry you probably have a good 30 minutes to get your wits about you. There were orders at the nurse's station to call the detectives as soon as you regained consciousness. In my experience it usually takes them 30 minutes to an hour to get here. "

Simone felt her head starting to hurt. She started having flashbacks of being in her bathtub. She could see Dion's face vividly, screaming at her and looking like a madman. She never planned for it to turn out this way. When she told his wife what was going on she thought he would be happy. She knew he loved his sons and all but she thought she had given him an easy out by telling Tammy about their affair. He always talked about how much of a bitch she was, and how he was only in it for the kids. It was now obvious to Simone that she was wrong.

"Can I talk to my friends for a minute please?"

"OK, but only for a few minutes. I don't want you to get too excited. The doctor will be in shortly to see you, and everyone will have to leave."

"Thank you."

Brittany and Renee came in as soon as the nurse walked out.

"Gurl you had us worried like a Mofo," Renee said excitedly. "You like to keep the drama going don't you girl."

Brittany reached out and grabbed Simone's hand, "I'm just happy your dramatic ass is back with us."

There moment was cut short by Renee's impatience, "Who did this shit to you girl? I mean, this was very personal!"

Simone's heart started to beat fast; she didn't really want to tell anyone. She was scared of Dion, she knew he was a prosecutor and had lots of connections, and quite frankly she was afraid of retaliation. It wasn't like he killed her, and Simone was starting to think she had it coming. She knew Renee, she would bug out if she knew and would not listen to anything Simone said. And Brittany, would want there to be a special investigation by Internal Affairs. Neither one of them would want to hear that maybe the best thing was to let it be.

"You know what yall, I was taking a relaxing bath after a long day, and I had started to dose off in the tub, next thing I knew I was bleeding and I heard someone running out the door. A few seconds later I guess Joe came in and started nursing my wound. I could here his voice in the back of my head but it was foggy and far away. It was crazy yall."

Brit and Renee were looking at Simone kind of strange as if they weren't sure if she was still groggy from the meds or straight up lying.

Renee stood up and looked at Simone she seemed agitated and began to pace the room. She was ringing her hands together as she began to speak," Your mind is probably still a bit hazy but it will come back to you and when it does I'll make sure it comes back to him."

Simone was getting nervous. She looked at Renee and could tell something was wrong her body posture and the look in her eyes was the old Renee. The quick tempered one that wanted to find Raysheeda and exact revenge for carjacking Brittany and Carmen. Later that same year Raysheeda had disappeared off the planet. Simone had been worried that maybe Renee had done something to her. But when Simone, Carmen and Brittany had asked Renee about it she simply said, "I never laid a finger on the bitch." They had all left it at that because Renee was a hothead not a liar.

Brittany's voice cut into the middle of Simone's thoughts," Renee come and sit back down and take it easy."

Simone smiled to herself Brittany was the only one that could get away with talking to Renee like she was a child.

Brit turned her attention back to Simone, "Don't worry Sim, Rae has been lashing out ever since her recent trauma."

Simone thought a minute, "Oh you mean finding out that Kyle abuses women." The sentence was barely out of Simone's mouth when

Renee jumped up in anger. "He doesn't abuse women." Simone was getting more confused by the minute.

All of a sudden Brittany got up too and grabbed Renee by the arm, "Damn it Rae if you can't control yourself go out in the waiting room didn't you just hear the nurse tell us Simone can't take too much excitement right now."

Renee's body relaxed as she looked over apologetically," I'm sorry Sim you've been out a couple days and we haven't been able to tell you everything that's going on. But, Renee spoke softer and lower this time, "Kyle doesn't abuse women." Simone was interested now. Some juicy info to keep her mind off her own troubles is just what the doctor ordered. "What happened? Simone said excitedly. She saw Brittany look over at Renee still a bit annoyed.

Brit piped up, "Look Simone I don't think this is the best time, you just woke up and this story is definitely on the censored list for gunshot victims that just woke up after extensive surgery. Simone smiled at Brit. Brittany smiled back and continued, "You know between the two of you divas competing for movie of the week. My wedding is getting lost in the shuffle."

Simone knew that Brittany was successfully changing the subject. At this Renee jumped back into the convo, "Are you crazy Brit that wedding and your relationship with Tyson is the only thing that still gives me hope. If it wasn't for you two I think I'd be convinced that the world has gotten to be so crazy that love was just a childhood fantasy, like Santa Claus and once you grow up you realize it was a fairytale for children but adults should know better. Simone looked at Renee she seemed a little down. She wondered again what had happened. Simone had to throw in her agreement, "Rae's right Brit you two are like this amazing couple. Getting shot can really put things in perspective."

"Tell me about it, "Brittany agreed.

Simone continued, "And I realize I've been jealous of you and Tyson the whole time. You've got this tall, handsome, rich basketball player boyfriend; excuse me fiancé now that loves you like crazy. I mean damn you about to be some top lawyer. You don't even need a man with money but bam you hit the lottery with that one girl." Brittany smiled at her two friends their love for her was showing.

"You know Simone, I don't love him for the money." Brittany explained.

"I know that girl that's why you get on my nerves. There's some poor chick out there probably dreamin about the dough your little honey buns has and miss successful Brittany sits here in my hospital room and truly doesn't care."

Renee laughed, "That gunshot to the shoulder didn't change you that much." Simone stuck her tongue out at Renee and Brittany laughed. Now things were getting back to normal.

Knock, Knock. "Excuse me Ms. Johnson, we are with the Newark police department. I'm officer Thomas and this is Officer Greenwood. We would like to ask you a few questions?"

"About what?" Brit interrupted.

"If you ladies don't mind, we would like this to be confidential right now. Please excuse us."

"Could you yall make sure KJ is ok, see if he's hungry or anything?" Simone closed her eyes trying to decide what she should tell them?

Chapter 47 ROOKIE OF THE YEAR

Present Day

On the way home from the hospital Brittany couldn't help thinking things had gotten really crazy in her world. Her best friends lives were in shambles. She hoped and prayed all this wasn't a bad omen for her, but then she smiled remembering how much she loved Tyson and how solid their relationship was. The more she thought about it, it wasn't that long ago that her and Renee went to the final game of the regular season. She smiled at the memory.

"Well Clyde the Slammers can secure the number 1 seed in the Eastern conference with this win. They are on their way to the playoffs, with home court advantage. This is the first time in 5 years that the Slammers have even made it into the playoffs."

"That's right Tim, and I think it has a lot to do with their star point guard, Tyson Myers. He has really elevated his game and taken his team to new levels."

Brittany sat in the front row with Renee at the final regular season home game for the Slammers. They were in their usual courtside seats, also known as celebrity row.

"Boy Simone would be beside herself if she was here," Renee commented to Brit. "All these rappers and professional athletes all in one section."

"I know, I know Brit laughed as she took a sip of her Corona. I'm excited to see my baby do his thing tonight. I'm hyped about the awards ceremony tonight, Ty has to get it."

"I know me too," Renee responded. "I've never been to anything like this. Can you believe not that long ago all three of us were in college, broke as a joke?" Renee giggled to herself and started singing the R Kelly song *Did you ever think*. Of course she had to change the verses to fit the situation "Did you think you would have all the riches and have to fight all these trifling little bitches." Brit laughed too as she hummed the beat for Renee and they swayed in their seats.

The sold out arena was really loud with excitement. Everyone was expecting the Slammers to beat the Runners in a good dogfight of a game because the Runners were the number 1 seed in the west, so this was a possible playoff preview.

As the players entered the arena for the shoot around the crowd went wild. "Tyson we love you!" a group of women screamed as they blew kisses. Renee was about to turn around and give them an evil look when Brittany grabbed her leg and said, "Don't sweat those groupies Renee. I'm sleeping with him tonight."

Renee smiled and gave Brit a high five. She knew what Brittany had been through with Tyson's first year in the NBA, but her friend had been able to put up a wall between her man and the rest of the world. "Aight homey, if you cool so am I." They both settled back to watch the game and carry on like men watching sports.

"Woo, good hustle," Brit screamed as Tyson scrambled for loose ball after loose ball. "My baby is on fire tonight Re!"

"Yeah my brother is breaking ankles out there!" Renee agreed, Tyson did a crossover move on the opposing point guard and took it inside for a dunk, the crowd went crazy. The Slammers went on to beat the Slammers.

After the game the big ceremony was to take place. Brittany was really excited for Tyson. This would be the first award of his professional career. He tried to downplay it to her, but he had already created a special section in his den for his awards.

The commissioner began to speak, "Ladies and Gentlemen, we are very excited about presenting this next award. Every year the league evaluates the performances of all its rookies and chooses one that has made outstanding progress throughout the year and brings his team a winning record.   The NBA would like to present . . . . Tyson Myers with the 2005 Eddie Gottlieb award for

Rookie of the Year." The crowd stood to their foot and cheered on their star player. Tyson stepped up with a huge smile on his face, as he shook his coach's hand and the commissioners. "Thank you Mr. Stein and Coach Harris. This is a great honor receiving this award. I would like to thank all of the fans and my teammates for their support throughout the year. This is definitely a huge honor. I would also like to thank God for giving me this talent to play at such a high level, but most importantly I would like to thank my mother, Francine who has been a mother and a father to me and my sisters all of our lives. Stand up ma, you deserve a standing ovation." The crowd applauded, as Tyson held the trophy over his head for the crowd.

Brittany sat next to Renee, both of them beaming and clapping. She still couldn't believe how quickly her baby was becoming a big star in the NBA, and up to this point he managed to remain humble. She prayed that he would stay this way.

Chapter 48 RENEE'S DIGNITY

Present Day

Kyle drove thru the streets of Newark and thought about how much it reminded him of his childhood on the streets of Paterson. A lot had happened since he beat the shit out of that pervert Sean. He couldn't believe how calculated the asshole had been. Brittany confirmed that he had set up microphones in Renee's apartment and tapped her phone. As soon as Brittany had discovered the intimate nature of most of the recordings Sean kept she had handed the case over to her most qualified peer. Brittany told Kyle she feared Renee would be embarrassed and feel more exposed than she already did if she thought Brit knew the intimate details of their lovemaking. Kyle didn't tell Brittany but he too was relieved that she would not hear the things that were only meant for Renee's ears.

This brought Kyle back to his current mission. Brittany had told Kyle when this all went to trial (which it would, Sean was pleading innocent) that a jury, and courtroom full of people would be listening to the tapes as evidence. There was no way Kyle would let this happen. But Sean was in jail without the possibility of parole because he was a suspect in the disappearance of Tamyka. Since Sean was safely behind bars Kyle had to reach out to people that didn't let bars stop them. Due to the intense circumstances of the situation Kyle had gotten to know Brittany much better.

It was obvious to Kyle that Brittany had decided he was a decent guy, because she began telling Kyle a lot of things about Renee, in truth the two were more like sisters than friends. Once it became clear to Kyle that Renee's background was more menace to society than the Cosby show he figured she might have some family members willing to help. Kyle had to bypass Renee's immediate family because according to Brittany, Renee's father, brother and even grandmother would encourage her to drop the charges. Kyle had asked her why and Brittany replied with a smirk, "They can't kill him in jail." He remembered he had gotten quiet and Brittany had been concerned, and hoped she hadn't said too much. After awhile he had laughed gently and she asked him what he was thinking. He responded that it was becoming clearer to him why he and Renee matched so well.

After this Kyle had began to tell Brittany his plan but she stopped him and put both hands up. Brittany looked him directly in the eye and said, "it's time for the family speech. You are a newcomer but something tells me you're going to be around for a while so here goes. I have three sides to my family my mom's side, my dad's side and the Renee side. No one in my family will be dumb enough to talk to the police or any other law enforcement official without their attorney present. Your attorney is a good friend of mine and once I pass the bar your attorney will be me. No one in my family will tell me ahead of time about any crime or criminal act they intend to commit. I will be an officer of the court and as such would be required to divulge any such knowledge to the proper authorities. I must have complete deniability. I have worked too hard to be derailed from my soon to be successful law career. That said I'm not here to judge you - only God can do that. So no matter how bad the charges are, or what they say, you did keep your mouth shut and call me." After the last statement Brittany handed Kyle one of her cards and a torn piece of paper with a name and phone number on it. Brittany got up, pointed to the paper and said, "This is a relative that would probably be happy to help with whatever you have in mind."

Kyle looked at the paper and recognized the name. This guy was big time in the game. "Renee's related to him?" Kyle questioned.

"She's his favorite cousin," Brittany said as she winked and walked away.

This conversation is what brought Kyle to these streets. He had called the number on the paper and C Money answered on the second ring. Once C figured out who Kyle was he simply said - "No phones," and gave Kyle an address in Newark.

Kyle said "thirty minutes", and C Money hung up. Kyle pulled up to the meeting place with his senses on high alert. After all, he didn't know C Money and the spot he picked was in the worst neighborhood possible. Kyle got out of the car and stood on the corner with his back against the wall. Across the street was a pack of homey's that was obviously working the spot. All of a sudden one of the bigger guys looked up and started to walk toward him fast – too fast, Kyle thought. This wasn't the right energy so Kyle quickly decided he was a threat. No time to get in his truck and abort this mission. So instead Kyle began walking, and turned the corner quick so that he was out of sight of his pursuer. When he was about thirty feet from the corner Kyle turned around and started at a dead run back to the corner. When the hood rounded the corner he had no time to react as Kyle rammed him. He picked him up like a football dummy and slammed him to the ground. Kyle heard all the air leave his body and knew the attacker was now at his mercy, but before Kyle could lay into him two more guys came out of nowhere and pulled him off. Kyle tensed all the muscles in his body in preparation for all the blows he was sure he would receive but they never came. Instead he was dragged into a doorway, which opened into a surprisingly luxurious apartment. The two men lead him to a chair, which sat across from a couch already occupied by a well-dressed young man. As Kyle was still struggling to get his breath back, the other man stood up extended his hand and said, "I'm C Money – you must be Kyle." Kyle stood up shook his hand and both men sat back down. C looked at the other two men and told them that everything was cool and they could leave. They were both silent for a moment sizing each other up.

Finally C Money said, "Not Bad, JD is one of my best and you put him down in five seconds."

"Sorry about your boy," Kyle explained. "But you shouldn't have had him coming at me like that. He felt like a threat – old instincts."

C Money sort of half laughed at the comment. "Make no mistake Kyle he was a threat. I was testing you. I don't want my cousin being with anyone that isn't man enough to protect her."

"So dude was just following orders?" Kyle seemed shocked.

"What?" C Money asked.

"It's just his energy felt like he had some genuine anger or fire toward me."

C Money looked pensive, "Damn son you are from the streets. You're right again. I picked JD because he's had it bad for Renee ever since we were all kids on the block together. So he was excited when I told him I wanted him to test your chin."

Kyle was a bit agitated, "So your boy's trying to holla at my girl?"

217

"No he knows he can't have her. Can't work in this business and have a woman like my cousin Renee. Don't worry about come back. I'm sure you just earned his respect." C promised.

"Well are you satisfied? Can we get down to business now?" Kyle asked impatiently.

"Absolutely," C Money assured. "We can talk here, I have this place swept for bugs everyday. I just had it checked before you got here, so speak freely."

Kyle began. He gave C Money the abbreviated version of all that had happened with Sean. Before Kyle could even finish, C Money said he heard enough and asked Kyle, which prison Sean, was in. C Money got up to signal that the meeting was over. This time he gave Kyle a more familiar hand pound and pulled him in for a half hug.

"What now?" Kyle said.

"Simple," C Money replied. "The problem goes away. My cousin has already suffered more than necessary. But that's all over now. You don't need to know anything else but this – take care of my cousin and if you ever need a job holla. I could use a man like you."

Kyle smiled, "Thanks anyway. I respect you but if we got into business together I couldn't be with Renee."

C Money just laughed and said, "You damn right you couldn't." Kyle walked safely back to his truck positive that the problem was solved.

Back in his apartment, C Money thought about how much he liked Kyle. In his business, C had to make quick judgments about people all the time.

He could tell this dude had it bad for Renee. But Kyle still had a few things to learn about his cousin, like the fact that she had already been to visit him, explaining how this lowlife Sean stalked her and tried to ruin her relationship with a real man, "Her man, Damn it" Quote unquote. Yeah his cousin still had some hood left in her and was more capable than most women of protecting herself. She had told C money to do what he does and not tell her shit. Renee could be hard when she wanted, but she had changed. She was a businesswoman now and had a different life. That's why he had tested Kyle; he didn't want Renee with some soft nigga that would hide behind her. Yeah, C Money reasoned, Kyle was old school from the street. He would protect Renee with every breath in his body and this made C Money very happy.

Chapter 49   AFTER THE BACHELORETTE PARTY

Present Day

"Oh my God she lives," Brittany giggled.

"What's up sleeping beauty?" Brittany questioned Simone.

"Sleeping Beauty," Renee huffed, "More like one-armed bandit."

All three were at Brittany's apartment, because both Simone and Renee's apartments were recent crime scenes, and neither felt comfortable there. Renee had taken up residency in Brits guest bedroom while Simone and KJ moved back in with her mom. The three were at Brittany's this morning after what seemed like the wildest bachlorette party ever.

"Could you both please shut up?" Simone said in a raspy voice.

"Did you lose your voice?" Brittany asked with concern.

But Renee just laughed. "If I was screaming 'Yeah sexy boy show me that ass' all night, I would have lost my voice too."

"Damn I said that?" Simone looked a little embarrassed.

Renee chuckled, "You said a lot worse than that. I was trying to be nice because you're injured. I think we're banned from that club now, but don't feel too bad. Brit's drunken lawyer friends were even wilder than you."

Brittany shrugged her shoulders and said, "Hey work hard - play hard. Besides Renee your little receptionist friend was really off the hook. She was telling all your business."

"What are you talking about?" Renee was surprised.

Brittany wanted to make Rae squirm a bit so she stalled by opening the oven to check on the biscuits. "The biscuits are just about done," Brit announced.

"How can you talk about food? No food, coffee I beg of you," Simone whimpered. Renee and Brittany disregarded her pathetic state.

"Brit," Renee said impatiently, "What did she say?"

"Oh yeah the crazy receptionist. Well in between humping one of the bouncers into submission, she went outside with a bunch of us on a smoke break and proceeded to tell all of us about how you and Kyle had sex in the parking lot one day." Renee had been cracking eggs and mixing in vegetables for omelets when she dropped the bowl on the counter.

"She said I did what?" Renee was mystified.

Brit calmly removed the biscuits from the oven and with a sly grin repeated; "She said you and Kyle had sex in the parking lot at work."

"Damn Rae," Simone said in her hung over slumber, "I always knew you were an undercover ho."

"Gimme a break Simone. I did not have sex in the parking lot at work." Renee assured.

Brit threw up her hands, "Hey I'm just telling you what she said." Brit paused for a minute then continued, "But she did give some detail that made it ring true."

"Yeah like what?" Renee said with apprehension in her voice.

"Like he was waiting with flowers. And we all know how often he gives you flowers. Then something about him snatching you up in a hard kiss and your knees buckling. Then, picking you up and throwing you in his truck, and grabbing at your chest. Or did she say he licked your chest." Brittany finished.

She looked over and Renee had her face hidden in her hands, "That little spy." She grumbled.

"Hah," Brittany said, "I knew it. Spill."

"Spill!   What - didn't you hear everything last night from the drunken gossip girl." Renee spat.

"Hell no I didn't hear everything. And don't blame the poor girl. That story is too juicy for any one to hold in especially at a bachelorette party. Plus why should I accept a second hand version of the story when we got one of the…" Brit was searching for the right word.

"Perverts right here," Simone finished Brits sentence.

Renee snapped, "You have a lot of nerve calling someone a pervert little girl. Do you know why I said you were a one armed bandit?" Renee didn't wait for a response, "because someone from our table spent the whole night grabbin the dancers asses, like a thief in the night. A couple of them complained, but they didn't have the heart to throw out a one armed woman." Simone looked a little sheepish.

But Brit piped up with a laugh, "Oh please! They all loved it Simone. You were the hit of the party. A pretty, one armed, drunken crazy girl was the answer to their dreams. As a matter of fact I think a couple of them signed their names and numbers on your sling." Simone's left arm and shoulder had been strapped to her body and supported with a sling. The whole arm had to be kept immobile for her shoulder to heal properly. Brittany moved Simone's good arm from in front of the sling, "I knew it. Look at all those numbers."

Renee couldn't help her curiosity and looked too, "Damn it's packed! Who had the felt tip pen?" Renee continued to stare at the sling; "Oh no Brit there's a couple of numbers for you on here too."

"What?" Brit gasped.

"Look," Renee giggled, "It says, 'Hey sexy almost married lawyer call me at 555-1212 before it's too late'. You better hope Sim can get a new sling before your wedding. Tyson will flip."

"No worries I'll pay for a new designer sling if I have to. But that thing will not be passing the church doors." Brittany assured.

"Now stop stalling and gives us the story Rae. Homegirl told us you were so excited you left your car unlocked. She locked it for you so you owe her." Brittany said.

"Her name is Dashawn, and I got her the job trying to help a sister out - and this is the thanks I get. She's probably blabbed to the whole office, and they think I'm some sort of hoochie now," Renee concluded.

But Brittany defended her. "She did not. I like her. She told us that she would never say a bad word about you to them. Because quote unquote 'Sisters got to protect each other'. She just thinks you're interesting. They're all boring according to her. You play softball in the summer, get together with your wild friends every other weekend, have a cute boyfriend that sends you flowers and tosses you around in the parking lot; and according to her you're the most profitable area coordinator they have."

"It's really true what they say about the receptionists knows all." Simone said proudly, "Because trust me no one knows my office the way I do."

"Well this time she's wrong. I didn't have sex in that parking lot and before you say anything Columbo," Renee said looking at Brit, "Yes the other stuff is true, but it was really just a kiss."

Simone looked at her suspiciously, "Bullshit you think you're slick. How far did you two get before you were getting busy?" Simone and Brittany both stared Renee down until she felt defeated.

"OK, OK, I'm busted," Renee blushed. "Probably about three streets away from the parking lot at work."

"We knew it." Brit and Simone said in unison while they gave each other a high five.

"The lovin must be right if you're ready to catch an indecent exposure charge," Brit giggled.

"The lovin is non-existent right now," Renee confessed.

"What do you mean?" Brittany was suddenly concerned.

"Don't worry Kyle's just punishing me for my lack of trust with the whole private investigator thing. He says we should slow everything down if I'm that apprehensive." Renee admitted.

Brit felt bad, "I was the apprehensive one. He knows I suggested it."

"Yeah but you're not his woman. You had no reason to trust him, but I did. Hopefully we'll get through this because I'm crazy about him," Rae finished.

Brittany went over and gave Renee a hug. "You know I like Kyle, he calls me every once and awhile and we talk. Trust me he's still mad sprung over you."

Renee smiled hopefully, "You sure?"

"Yeah I'm sure, "Brit said, "Now finish those omelettes so we can eat." Renee finished cooking the eggs, while Brittany put the rolls and sausage on a tray. The three friends ate and puttered around the kitchen until Simone's hangover was almost gone.

"OK," Renee announced, "Showers and then we're back in Brit's living room for a meeting."

"Meeting, I'm getting married in two days. I don't have time for meetings." Brit complained.

Simone chimed in, "Renee and I went over your wedding schedule and you do have time."

Brit was not giving in that easy. She went over to the giant schedule her mom had tacked up on the wall and looked at the time slot. It read, "Best friends give best advice." Brittany couldn't help but laugh. She looked at her two friends and said, "Don't tell me."

"Yep," Renee said.

And then all three said in unison, "Millie Martin strikes again."

In the shower Brit pondered her future with Tyson. She felt so blessed to be in such a solid relationship. She knew Renee was walking on eggshells with Kyle, and Simone's getting shot seemed to send Joe running for the hills. But through all this turmoil she and Tyson had held strong. It felt good to be an example of a positive black relationship. She knew it was probably just the stress of dealing with both friends going through some crazy stuff. But she had been feeling fragile and unsure lately. The bachelorette party that Renee and Simone set up had been just what she needed. Now the wedding jitters seemed to have left her and pure joy seemed to be taking its place. She really had to thank God. Great family, great friends, great job and the man of her dreams. Her life was full to overflowing, and Brittany knew it.

When she got to the living room Renee and Simone were waiting for her. They were actually whispering in each other's ears and laughing. "When did you two start getting along so well?" Brit questioned.

Simone sighed, "Well while you and your mom were busy doing wedding stuff, your girl over here started stopping by to grill me about who shot me. She doesn't seem to believe that I don't know. I told her if I knew, I obviously would have told the cops."

"You would have?" Brit interrupted and gave Simone a knowing look.

Both Simone and Renee hated cops. She understood they both had bad experiences with male family members being harassed. Tyson had told her how completely crooked and unfair cops had been with some of his teammates purely out of jealousy. To see a black man rich and successful drove some of them crazy.

"Of course," Simone said unconvincingly. "Anyway," she continued, "You know Rae can get a little crazy when someone hurts one of us. So it took awhile for me to convince her that it was random. Besides I'm more worried about that Sean character. That shit yall told

224

me was off the hook. I was telling Rae someone that obsessed don't give up." Simone reasoned.

Renee spoke up before she could finish, "I'm not worried about his sick ass."

Simone looked over at Renee and her eyes had gotten darker and had that distant look. This is why Simone would never tell Renee about what happened. Renee had a bad temper when it came to people messin with her or her friends. Sometimes it scared Simone.

"Let's forget all that. I've been stalked and you've been shot. Hey wait a minute." Renee huffed.

"What?" Both Brit and Simone said.

"I always thought I was the toughest but I'm the only one left that hasn't been shot." Renee realized.

"Well I'm not trying to brag on the shit like Fifty Cents. Most of my co-workers don't even know I've been shot." Brit admitted.

"Yeah the shit ain't fun Rae," Simone agreed.

"I know that. It's just ironic that's all. With my family and temper you would think…" Renee didn't finish the thought. "All I'm saying is life's unpredictable. Now back to my point. I've been stalked and you've been shot."

"We know," Simone said, "Stop reminding us."

Renee simply continued, "Pay attention because I'm about to get deep on you chicks."

Brit was smiling to herself, she always liked when Renee the activist showed up. When she was in the mood Renee could be Angela Davis like a mug.

"Do you two realize that in the black community getting shot has become more common than getting married? Getting shot or stalked is no accomplishment. But getting married, Wow that's what's up. I know you're gonna think it's corny. But couples like you and Tyson are the hope for the future." Renee was on a roll. "I mean how many young black men would have made better choices if they had a father like Tyson to help raise them - our young women too for that matter. Anyway Brit, Simone and I have been talking. I mean really talking about relationships and life. After a few arguments she reminded me that no one in her family is really married."

At this point Simone jumped in, "Yeah Brit, it's like my attitude was what's the big deal - boyfriend/girlfriend or husband/wife. In my world the only examples of this were your parents and Renee's parents. So in my life, big deal you're married and what's next. Most of the married men I know are wilder than the single ones. But after having Dion's wife attack me, and you two should have seen her, I mean she was mad but I could also see the hurt in her eyes. Then Renee explained that her mom always gets a different type of respect in her family because she's married and not just shacking up. I'm starting to understand it's deeper than just sex or sleeping in the same house."

Simone paused and Renee seized the opportunity to hop back into the convo, "So we both agreed that since you're the first one that's taking this incredible step, we need to put our pride aside and give you the best advice we can. Simone do you want to go first?" Renee asked sweetly.

"Yeah, I might as well get it over with." Simone looked right in Brittany's eyes with a sincerity that Brit had never seen before. "Alright homegirl here it is. You know I've done my share of shit and as a result I've slept with more than a couple married men. A woman like me knows how to play them. You need to know - men cheat for different reasons. Some cheat because they want to feel attractive and irresistible. Others cheat because they want to feel powerful and in control. And still others cheat because it's expected of them. They run in circles where the other men of power will think they're not as worthy an opponent if they don't have control over women. I know Tyson loves you and I don't think he would cheat. But the circles he runs in make it harder. The truth is if I were you I'd be worried. That said if you choose to keep your eyes open no one can play you like a fool. Look for change in patterns. If he calls asking where you're going to be at a certain time during the day be suspicious. All the best cheats I've been with always call their wives right before to make absolutely sure they're in the clear."

"They call right in front of you?" Brittany asked surprised.

Simone sighed and looked at Renee. Renee gave her a supportive head nod and Simone continued, "I'm ashamed to say they did. But you have to understand the mentality Brit. They were all cheating on their wives not me. I knew everything, which gave me power. I wasn't the dumb bitch being fooled. I'm sorry but that's how I looked at it. Anyway when you ask him where he's going to be, always get specifics, something you can check up on. I'm not telling you to be suspicious of your man, whoops husband all the time. Enjoy your marriage. Just beware. I guess the unfortunate truth is I'm more an expert of how to break a marriage up then keep it together. But Renee seemed to think that you would appreciate me sharing my experiences and advice. So I have." Simone finished. Brittany got up and gave Simone a big hug.

Before she let go she whispered in Simone's ear, "I know that was hard for you."

Simone smiled at her and said, "It was but it's making me face who I am." Brit went back to the couch and sat down.

She looked at Renee, "So I guess it's your turn."

Renee smiled at Brit with happiness in her eyes, "First of all I'm so happy for you. I've watched you and Tyson together from college to now. And you two are an amazing couple - the best one I know. I went to my mom and Gran to get the married perspective. I'm just going to touch on the cheating thing real quick. Mom said you need do at least two surprise visits a year. If things are as they should be it will be a pleasant surprise for him. Gran Gran is from the old school so her attitude is - even if he cheats he's still your husband forget that other Ho. And if we find out who it is the three of us should go whip her ass." Brittany and Simone bust out laughing at this comment.

"If nothing else, Gran is consistent. Beat their ass and they'll get the message," Brittany giggled.

"Hey," Renee began again, "It's been effective in her life. Her and poppa have been together 50 years now. And don't think I haven't heard stories. There was this woman that liked my grandpa. She worked with him on the assembly line. Anyway she used to carpool with all the guys and Gran had heard rumors about her trying to cozy up to papa. She didn't even know anything for sure but that didn't matter. One day she followed the carpool to see if she was going to sit beside him. Well sure enough when they picked her up she slid in real close to papa. Gran chased the car, cut it off in the middle of the rode and jumped out. She had one hand in her pocketbook and told the woman to get out of the car. The woman did because everyone knew Gran had a gun in her bag. She put her other hand in the woman's face and told her that papa was her husband and belonged to her. According to papa the woman and all the men were scared out of their wits because in his words 'your grandmamma is crazy'." Brittany and Simone were both mesmerized. Gran Gran stories were the greatest.

"What happened then?" Simone asked.

"According to papa the car pool kinda broke up after that and the woman stayed away from him and became interested in another one of the married workers. Papa claimed he never cheated with her. He said she was just a big flirt but that was enough for Gran."

"The way your grandmother totes that gun around I can't believe she's never done time." Simone commented.

Renee laughed, "Whose going to arrest her? The cops don't want any part of her. She knows everyone in the whole city. She helped raise some of them cops. Anyway I want to move on to my mom's advice because Gran Gran's justice is probably a little extreme for you Brit."

"Just a bit," Brittany laughed.

"Both Mom and Gran told me to tell you it won't be easy. Mom says even the best men have to be trained a little. She says even if you've been going out for a long time they change some once you get married. She said they get more possessive like this is my wife, my property. She said men are raised with this built in double standard that gives them more freedom in the marriage than a woman."

Brit interrupted, "That doesn't sound fair."

Renee continued, "Mom said it's not fair but you have to accept that things won't always be equal. She likes Tyson and said you are lucky to have such a good man, but he's a man and by nature is not the one that keeps the family together - it's the women that do that. She said a lot more, but the main gist was keep it fun, don't suffocate him, but don't let him get away with too much either. I don't know because I've never been married either, but I can tell you this Brit my dads a hard man and some how mom has tamed him. So I think her advice is good advice." Renee finished with a smile.

Brittany got up and gave Renee a hug, then she looked at Simone and said, "Get up damn it, get over here and lean in with your good shoulder so we can have a group hug. I love you crazy chicks," Brittany said with tears in her eyes.

Renee looked at her getting teary eyed herself, "We love you too. Don't forget about us just because you're getting married. We're still going to hang out right?" Renee asked looking a little nervous.

"Of course we are Rae, what are you talking about?" Simone said but sounded a little unsure herself.

"You know some people change when they get married they stop making time for their friends." Renee explained.

Brit looked at her friends and smiled, "Would you two please stop talking crazy. I'm marrying a basketball star that travels half the year. You two will probably get sick of seeing me."

"Never," Simone and Renee said together. As all three cried tears of joy knowing they were entering the next phase of life.

Chapter 50

FOR BETTER, FOR WORSE OR FOR NOTHING

Present Day

Brittany woke up with a smile on her face. This was her big day, the day that every woman dreamed of. All of the planning and organizing that went into a wedding, even a small one like hers, was finally over. This would be her day to shine and be the prettiest woman in the room – all eyes on her.

It was 6:00 a.m. and Brittany had a list of things to do. Her wedding was scheduled for 3:30 p.m. and it seemed like one hour away. Thank God for her mother and Maid of Honor, Renee. The night before, all of her bridesmaids had taken her out for drinks and gave her their words of wisdom, especially those who were already married. It took away some of her jitters and also gave her much needed comic relief. The stories her friends told her were unbelievable.

Her Mom, Millie, was the queen of organizing events. As a child Brittany always felt as though her mom should have been a wedding planner or an event planner, instead of her chosen profession – teaching. She got excited about the details of an event (something Brittany detested). She was extremely creative, and when she had an idea she ran with it like nobody else could. Mom took care of everything from the catering to the flowers at the church. The thought of organizing a wedding sickened Brittany. She was thankful that the only thing she had to be responsible for was picking out her wedding gown, which was enough work by itself. Brittany emphasized to her mom that this was a small, intimate wedding for family and very close friends. It was already enough hoopla surrounding the engagement, since she was marrying an up and coming NBA star – she didn't need any extra hype, it just wasn't her personality.

The first thing Brit had to do was meet Juanita, her hairdresser at the salon. She had agreed to open up early just for her. Brit had been going to Juanita for 15 years, and Nita told her, "If you let any other heifer do your hair for the wedding – I'll never speak to you again." Brittany laughed because she wouldn't dream of anyone experimenting on her hair for her big day.

After she left the hairdresser she would have to meet the girls at her moms house so that they could all get their makeup done together and take pictures. The limousine would be picking them up from there.

Were those butterflies she just felt in her stomach...wooooo time to get a move on....

Tyson heard his alarm go off and started cursing. Boy did he have the hangover from hell. Why did I do this to myself he thought??? His head felt like he had a ton of bricks in it every time he moved. He dragged himself to the bathroom to find some aspirin. He told his boys that a bachelor party the night before his wedding wasn't a good idea. 'They were like man; stop being a punk, if we give it to you any sooner you ass might not get married.'

After you see what we got planned, you gone' think twice about giving up the single life man! He knew he was going to be in for it, but nothing like what happened the night before.

His teammates and his friends had rented a penthouse at the Hilton for his party. He was expecting wild, but that shit was off the hook! They had a professional DJ set up in the suite for musical entertainment. First they all gave him a toast to his future, and they took turns telling jokes about the married life, and what he would have to give up. Since they were all drinking it turned into a cracking session among the boys.

Then came the cake. He knew he was in trouble when they rolled that cake in, because it was damn sure too big to eat. The DJ started playing, *I like the way you work it* by Backstreet one of his favorite tunes. He was definitely not prepared for what happened next. The first cake busted open and out came one of the sexiest women he ever laid eyes on. Boy his boys had really done some planning on this one.

'Mona Lisa', as she called herself was the first stripper. She began dancing very seductively around Tyson, shakin' it fast to the music, while she slowly unveiled her sexy costume. Tyson's boys made him sit in this big leather chair that was decorated with condoms. He smiled at the girl while she danced around him. He had made a vow to Brittany that he would look and not touch.

Then to his surprise another cake came in the room, while he was still admiring the first one. This one was 'Virgin Mary'. She barely looked 18 to him, but she sure did dance like a grown ass woman. Little girl was flexible as she displayed her talents with a series of splits and moves. The next thing that happened to Tyson he was not prepared for.

Tyson stared in disbelief as another stripper emerged from a big chocolate cake in the middle of the room. She wore a black mask over her face and her hair was wild and curly. But her eyes shown through the mask. She had on a cat suit that was cut up seductively, and Tyson thought for a second that he recognized those bedroom eyes. The last time he saw a chick that looked like this he remembered waking up in the VIP lounge of Pumps in the Bump, missing his curfew. He got rung out by his coach and was benched for a crucial game. He was really pissed because he couldn't remember what happened to him. It happened a long time ago, but he was still living it down with Coach Hill.

This woman caught more catcalls than any of the other woman because she had the body of a Playboy centerfold; and these guys didn't know how to act when they were drunk anyway. Jake had to keep some of the guys back from trying to get at her.

She did a very erotic number to *Your Body's Calling Me*, by R. Kelly.

Her body moved very gracefully and fluidly to the music. She was very enticing. The guys were throwing $50.00 and $100.00 bills in her crotch as she gyrated her way through the crowd. She finally made her way in front of Tyson.

Damn this woman was making him so nervous and uneasy. He reached for a napkin to wipe the sweat from his brow. Brittany's words kept going though his head – look but don't touch, look but don't touch... As the stripper got closer to him he leaned back in his chair – and the guys started roaring with laughter.

"Look at him man, it's too much for him to handle!!!!!!" They all cracked up. The dancer then leaned over him with her big *tetas* in his face. She smelled like sweet strawberries. When she turned her back to him and proceeded to give him what he thought was a lap dance, he

232

pushed her hard to the floor. It was probably harder than he had intended because he was drinking, but he did not care to be seduced by this professional whore.

Everyone stopped and the music halted.

"Yo man, what's your problem?" Jake questioned. "What you thought she was going to rape you?" They all hollered at that remark, falling over holding their stomachs and stuff.

The stripper just looked at him in shock. She had got pushed so hard that her face hit the floor first and her upper lip was bleeding. She just stared at him in dismay.

Tyson suddenly felt the room closing in on him. He didn't know what had come over him but he suddenly needed some air. He went out onto the terrace. Tyson didn't know why but that last stripper gave him a bad feeling.

Tyson dragged himself out of bed, shaking his head at the memory. Wow his boys had definitely given him a party to remember, but not in the way they had planned. That was creepy.

But today, he would marry the love of his life, Brittany Shanice Myers, he like how that sounded. Tyson got in the shower looking forward to his big day.

Chapter 51 THE CHAPEL

Present Day

Brittany heard the music begin...... This was the song she had chosen to play, Sade's, *"By Your Side."* She was so anxious, but she was ready as she would ever be. She looked at her Maid of Honor who was the picture of beauty and peace. Renee smiled at her and mouthed the words, "you look beautiful." Brittany smiled back, and prepared to enter the church.

Everyone in the church turned back and looked at her as she started her walk down the aisle. The first face she saw was her mothers, beaming at her with tears in her eyes. She kept telling herself - don't cry, don't cry, you'll smudge your makeup. Her bridesmaids looked beautiful in their champagne dresses, simple and elegant. They all had tears in their eyes.

Then there was her future husband, tall, dark and handsome as he wanted to be. Brittany couldn't wait to be Mrs. Tyson Myers. She kept taking slow steps down the aisle so that her Uncle Willie could get a nice video of her. This was definitely shaping up to be one of the best days of her life. In what seemed like an hour later, she was finally standing face to face with her fiancé. Tyson smiled at her, and when she saw a tear in his eye, she could no longer hold back. The tears just a flowed - tears of joy.

Tyson looked at his bride, and had a big wide grin on his face. She looked so beautiful with her blond locks pinned up to show her pretty smile and big brown eyes. When he looked at her he knew she was the only one for him. Mrs. Brittany Myers, you are the love of my life he thought.

The minister began his speech: "We are gathered here today"………..

Tyson and Renee began reciting their vows to each other. They had personally written their vows, because they had been through so much together in college and with their careers, that it was important to them that their vows sounded genuine; and not like a script. When they finished reciting their vows the pastor asked the proverbial, "Is there anyone here who objects to this union, speak now or forever hold your peace?" Brittany and Tyson were staring into each other's eyes when the doors of the church flew open.

"I do."

A gasp went across the congregation. Everyone turned around to face the back of the church. Standing in the door was Lola Diaz. "I'm carrying your child Tyson Myers, and I can't let you go through with this marriage to Brittany. I know how much you wanted this Tyson. I love you and I want us to be a family."

"What the fuck!"

The pastor looked at Tyson, and he said "sorry Rev, but this is the most important day of my life, and this skank is trying to ruin it. Gurl you better go head with that craziness, ain't nobody over here a father to your child."

Gran Gran who was sitting by the back door mumbled, "Somebody need to whip that heffer's azz."

Lamont Martin became enraged, "Boy I know I didn't spend 20 thousand dollars on this wedding for you to be messing around on my daughter boy!" Lamont's voice boomed throughout the church.

"Mr. Martin, I promise you I don't know this lady."

"Well what the hell is she doing in here protesting my daughters wedding for?"

"Oh my God, why is this happening to me," Brittany said tearfully.

Mrs. Martin ran over to console her daughter with tears in her eyes. "Carmen is that you?" Milly had been so busy consoling her daughter she hadn't really looked into the woman's face. But she could not mistake those eyes. "Carmen what are you doing here, bringing all this foolishness on Britty's wedding day?"

"You know her??" Tyson questioned. "Never mind that – you got some nerve….."

Just then Lamont Martin charged Tyson grabbing him by the ankles and pummeling him. The weight of Lamont caused Tyson to fall to the ground with Mr. Martin's hands around his ankles. "Boy I know you didn't humiliate Britty for a piece of tail, then you go and get her knocked up. I'm a kill you I swear!" Tyson was pinned down under Lamont's knee and was squirming to breathe. Jake, Tyson's best man scrambled to try and pry Mr. Martin off of Ty, but old man was angry and its hard to fight that kind of strength.

"CARMEN!!! What the hell are you doing at my wedding and how do you know Tyson? This can't be happening." Brit said, as she started to cry.

"You know her???!!!" Tyson yelled underneath Mr. Martin.

Brittany's father Lamont still had Tyson pinned down. "What you done did to my baby girl? You done got her up here in front of all these people to embarrass her with your hoing ways." Mr. Martin was not allowing Tyson to answer he kept pummeling him, while some of Brittany's uncles tried to get him off of Tyson. Then Brittany's cousin Tanisha came out of her pew and started cursing Carmen out. "How you gone try to play my cousin on her wedding day? You know you was always a ho and that baby probably ain't his, you low down dirty skank!" With that she slapped Carmen across the face, and the church gasped again. Carmen stumbled back from the blow and grabbed the pew to keep from falling. "You lucky you supposed to be pregnant, cause I would have given you a Brooklyn beat down if you wasn't Biotch!"

Tyson's mother dropped to her knees and started praying feverishly, "Oh Lawd, please bless this Union, the devil is up in here

237

trying to break up what you have already blessed Lord, please help us…….."

All of this was too much for Britt, she started feeling light headed and before you knew it, she had passed out in front of the alter, hitting her head on the lectern on her way down, causing even more of a raucous in the church. Suddenly it was pure pandemonium.

Mrs. Martin ran back over to see if her baby was ok – "my little Britty, oh poor baby she sobbed."

Meanwhile the pastor was trying to restore some kind of order to the church. "Let us Pray", said Reverend James.

PART II

Chapter 52 LIFE AFTER DEATH

Present Day

Brittany opened her eyes and looked around, wondering where she was. The first person she saw was Renee, sitting at the bedside holding her hand. On the other side of the bed was Simone looking sorrowful and sympathetic. Brit heard her mother Millie in the corner praying. When she heard Brittany's voice she got up.

"How you feeling baby? Don't worry; the Lord will help you get through this troubling time. Remember - God is not the author of confusion."

Renee chimed in, "Yeah Britty, remember what doesn't kill you, will make you stronger."

Simone nodded her head in agreement and said, "Also remember everything happens for a reason."

Brittany looked around at the women, and realized they were in Renee's apartment. She was trying to remember how she got here. She was trying to capture her last memory. Slowly the events of the day started coming back to her, and her heart began to beat rapidly. She screamed out, "That fucking Bitch! She ruined my life. After 7 years, she still has to be the center of fucking attention. How could she do this to me!! Where is Tyson? I need to talk to him right now!"

Millie jumped in, "Sweetie your father was ready to kill that boy after that jezebel showed her face in the House of the Lord. It took all of the groomsmen to hold Lamont back. He was about to break that boy in half. You know how much money your father put out for this wedding, and how proud he was of you - not to mention the humiliation Tyson put you through by having all his dirty laundry aired at your wedding of all places. Lord, please be with my baby during this difficult time. She didn't deserve this." She continued. She put her hand on Britt's face to soothe her. "Now don't go getting yourself all worked up Britty, its just going to raise your pressure. The devil is busy, but God will have the last word in this."

Simone snickered, "Brittany if you think your dad was about to kill Tyson, you should have seen Renee. Carmen brought out the g-h-e-t-t-o in her!! As soon as that heifer spoke, Renee kicked off her shoes and ran towards Carmen like a bull who just saw a red flag. It took all the ushers and about 5 relatives to hold Renee down. She was livid! If that child hadn't been pregnant, I think she would have got the royal beat down."

Brittany looked at Renee and smiled, "You had my back girl."

"Ya damn right! As soon as I saw you faint, I flipped. I was like how dare that bitch come back after all these years and try to ruin the most important day of your life. Britty, she was so scared when she saw me running up to her. Her eyes got real big and she started backing up. She kept saying, 'I'm pregnant, don't hit me, don't hit me.' I told her I didn't give a damn about her little bastard baby! I started having flashbacks of when she stole Tommy Jenkins from me in 10th grade, and how dare she come up here and embarrass you and Tyson in front of all your family and friends. She come talking bout 'I had no other choice, how could I let her marry a man whose child I was carrying.' Gurrrrl it wasn't nothing but the grace of God that kept me from pushing her down them steps."

"That's why you're my girl Renee, because you got my back when I'm weak."

"Let me tell you, that ho is lucky she was pregnant, because I would have hurt that girl. I know Carmen planned this whole thing! She always was a damn gold-digger. She was always competing with you from the time we were in high school. No one could have more than her skank ass!"

"So what happened after that?" Brittany didn't remember anything after Carmen entered the church.

"Tyson was trying to talk to you Brit but you blacked out on his ass," Renee said shaking her head. "I had to jump in front of him to keep you from taking his head off."

Renee's mother, who was a nurse, told her that they should give her a Tylenol and when she woke up they gave her a glass of wine to calm her down, because when she came to, she was hyperventilating. They told her she fell asleep and they carried her to Renee's house, since it wasn't far from the church.

"Can you believe that tramp? Last I heard her fast ass had gotten run out of town for stealing a couple hundred gees from a drug king in Brooklyn named Nino.

Simone chimed in, "Yeah word on the street was that he threatened to kill her whole family if he found her. So, she apparently left town to protect her family. According to Dion, Nino was a cold-blooded killer that the feds have been after for a while, but he never touches anything so the charges never stick." Apparently she has been going by the name Lola, she changed her whole identity.

"Yeah, she's a Lolita alright!" Renee said.

"I see, so things didn't work out with the drug dealer, so she decided to go for the NBA player. Next best thing huh? But he just happened to be my fiancé! I swear I could kill both of them!"

"Calm down honey," Millie interrupted. "Why don't you try and get some rest. We'll be in the living room if you need us." She gave Renee and Simone a stern 'mother knows best look' and the girls filed out of the bedroom.

Brittany looked up at the ceiling after she was alone and thought to herself, I'm supposed to be in St. Tropez right now, in a private villa chilling with my new husband. Why did Tyson have to humiliate me with Carmen, of all people? She didn't know if she could ever forgive him, because this hurt so bad.

Chapter 53 SLEEPLESS NIGHTS IN NEW JERSEY

Present Day

Tyson lay in his bed staring at the ceiling. Every time he opened his eyes he closed them again – willing the last 48 hours of his life to be a bad nightmare. He had been in his bed for 2 days. He'd taken the phone off the hook cause he couldn't talk to anyone about what happened, cause he didn't know his damn self what had happened. He just couldn't function, nor did he want to talk to anyone in the state he was in. What the hell had just happened to his life???!!!!

This chic Lola aka Carmen just appears at his wedding to tell all his family and friends that he was the father of her child. How the hell could that be possible??? He tried to explain to Brittany that he'd never seen this mad woman in his life. But that didn't go over well. Brittany just went into a tirade screaming and carrying on with him at her mother's house. He couldn't believe she tried to punch him in the face, but lucky for him Renee was there to intervene. When Renee told him she thought it would be better if he came back another time, he reluctantly left her mothers house. He never felt so dejected in his life. How could this be happening to them?

They were college sweethearts – he was a rising basketball star and she a budding lawyer. How could anyone or anything come between them – and on their wedding day of all days? Tyson left a message with Millie for Brit to call him when she was ready to hear his side of the story. Millie just nodded her head and led him to the door. Tyson had wanted to scream at the top of his lungs: I don't know that woman and she is NOT having my baby! But he figured then wasn't the time for it. After all, how many women show up to a man's wedding to disclose their lovechild to their whole family. Hell he didn't even understand how she knew so much about him and Brittany. And Brittany kept screaming, "You slept with Carmen!! You slept with Carmen! How could you do this to me? I wasn't enough for you Ty, you just had to fuck it all up before the wedding huh, had to sew your wild oats is that what it is. For the first time in his life Tyson had been crying in public and didn't even care. Why would someone want to do this to them and why would he do this to his fiancée.

Tyson popped a few more sleeping pills and pulled the blanket over his head, he did not want to be conscious through this living hell.

Tyson heard a banging noise in his dreams and put the pillow over his head. The banging continued but seemed to grow louder by the minute. He opened his eyes and realized he was not dreaming but Renee was banging on his bedroom window.

"Tyson, wake up, its me Renee I need to talk to you."

"Renee, is that you?" Tyson popped up from bed, If anyone could tell him what was going on with Brit, it was Renee.

"Hold on, I'm gonna open the door."

"When Renee walked in she had to step back for a minute. Wooo Ty – how long have you been in this house. I think you need to open up some windows and let some air in here. This place is a mess. "

Renee proceeded to open the blinds to let the sun in. "Let me fix you some tea or something Ty. You look like hell done over, and woooo, maybe you might want to take a shower while I'm getting the tea ready, cause you sure don't smell like roses bro!" Tyson chuckled for the first time in days.

"Well Renee if you had just lost the love of your life in front of all your family and friends, how would you feel?"

Renee's heart went out to Ty, because she knew if anything like that would have happened to her and Kyle she would be just as much of a basket case, especially if it had been Carmen who pranced through the door carrying Kyle's baby. Renee chuckled to herself knowing her grandmother would have probably cursed Carmen out before anyone had a chance to.

She turned her attention back to Tyson.

Well bro, that's what I came over here to talk to you about – the infamous Carmen. I figured you deserve to know the inside scoop."

The Video

Brittany found herself thinking about all the times in their childhood when Carmen had opened her legs to a man. She knew in heart that it would not have taken much for Tyson to fuck her...

Back In The Day

"*I'm telling yall, she made a video! I saw it!*"

"*Really Sincere, are you sure?*" *Julie asked incredulously as they all looked on. Julie was one of there girls from back in the day. Sincere was dating Julie at the time, but before he dated Julie he dated Carmen.*

"*She was in the video with 4 other dudes and it was crazy!*" *Renee,*

Brittany and Simone looked at each other like – wow we knew she was buck wild, but never that wild!!

"*Are you lying to us*"? *Julie asked.*

"*I'm telling you the truth, but yall can't see it – its too crazy.*" *When Brit thought about it, she knew Carmen's behavior was so promiscuous that if it was true about any body it had to be Carmen.*

Brittany thought back to the time when Julie had a get together in her house when they were in high school. Julie's mom was out of town. All of them were upstairs dancing and drinking coolers when suddenly Julie came into the room giggling – she motioned for them to follow her down to the basement.

They all crept down the stairs in the dark. Sure enough there was Carmen with her pants off laying on top of Devon, Julie's cousin, doin the nasty!! They all ran upstairs and bust out laughing.

When they got back upstairs Simone screamed, "Damn, I know he's cute and all, but did she have to do him!" Carmen had just met him that night. She always moved real fast.

Then there was the time the whole Bonified Homegirls Posse decided to go on a mission in Brooklyn/Manhattan and they all put their money together and checked in to a motel. They were planning to hang out in the city and party at their favorite club – "The Underground". There were 5 of them all chillin in the city.

One night while at the hotel there were these rough necks hangin out in their hotel lobby (probably local drug dealers) because the girls weren't exactly staying at the Ritz-Carlton. One of the guys started trying

245

to rap to Brittany. *She thought he was kind of cute, so she exchanged numbers and everything with him. Well, as the day progressed Carmen started to make her moves on him. This was her usual MO when she saw a man was interested in one of her friends. Carmen had always been very beautiful and voluptuous sort of Vanessa Williams meets Vanity so it didn't take her long long to get a man's attention.*

When it was time for them to leave the hotel and go back to NJ that Sunday, Carmen had decided that she was going to stay another night with her new thug lover, Justice. Julie had hooked up with his homeboy so she was staying too.

Everyone in the posse begged her to come, but she wouldn't budge – the girl was a ho at 15! Well this night would change the rest of their high school years and Carmen's reputation (what was left of it). When they caught on to her game, Brit flipped out on her in the hotel lobby. She told her girls, "she ain't going nowhere – the hotel is paid for and the dick is free! Leave her whoring ass right here!" After that scene they all jumped in the cab and left the hos there.

The next week in school Julie was showing everybody pictures of Carmen in bed with Justice, pictures that showed no innocence, nor kept any secrets. After that the whole school considered her a skank whore! She never lived it down and none of them spoke to Carmen for the rest of the school year.

Brittany laughed to herself thinking, a leopard doesn't change her stripes. And now that leopard is back and she's trying to steal my man!! Now that Brittany thought about it, anything could have happened with that conniving ho. She at least deserved to give Ty the benefit of the doubt, and hear his side of the story.

Chapter 54   HELL TO THE NO!

Present Day

Brittany saw Tyson's Rover parked outside his house. She did not want him to know she was coming, because she didn't not want him to think it was reconciliation. As she approached his house, she noticed a Ford Festiva in the driveway. Brittany thought to herself I never saw that car before – uhh maybe it was the maid service, since it was pretty early in the am. Brittany still had the key to Ty's house. He had never asked for it back, in hopes that they would get back together. She rang the buzzer as she entered the house. She didn't want to startle him. When she stepped into the doorway, and proceeded to call his name, she stopped in her tracks.

There she was sitting on the couch in Tyson's living room, Carmen Diaz!

"I'm sorry, am I interrupting something Tyson between you and your baby momma?" She didn't even look at the ho. "Yes you are", Carmen interjected

"You lucky you're a pregnant bitch, or right now me and you would be rolling on this living room floor!"

"Do not disrespect my wife like that in my house Carmen. You're lucky I let your sorry ass in. Brittany, it's not what you think. Carmen just came over here to explain to me how she figures I'm the father of her child. I don't believe the story she gave me, but we've decided that I will take a DNA test when the baby is born. It will show that she has the wrong guy. Baby I love you and I would never hurt you over a tramp like this."

Brittany couldn't help but smile, because she felt like she had won a small battle, even though her life was still in shambles.

"I think you need to go now Ms. Diaz. Me and my wife have a lot to talk about."

"Yeah you'll really have a lot to talk about when the paternity test shows that you're the father of my child."

With that comment Brittany slapped her clean across her face. God please forgive me but she had it coming.

"Get the fuck out!" Brittany screamed.

Tyson opened the door for her. "I have your card – I'll have my lawyer get in touch with you."

"Baby you'll see – you will always love your first born, especially since he's a boy."

"Get out now!" Tyson screamed. Carmen reluctantly left his house.

Brittany fell onto the couch and burst into tears. She had come over Tyson's house to get closure and all she felt right now was anger and resentment. Tyson came to sit next to her and put his arms around her. "Don't touch me! How could you sleep with that skank??? Do you know

how many men she's been with? You might want to get an AIDS test, Tyson."

"I already have babe. I'm negative. But forget that ho, when the DNA tests come back it will show that I'm not the father of her child. She's just looking for a rich man to take care of her."

"If she is not carrying your child, why did she bring her butt up all the way up here from Atlanta on our wedding day, to deliver her news?"

"I'm telling you these goldiggin tramps will do ANYTHING for money baby. You've got to believe me. I'll admit she's pretty and all but I would never jeopardize what we have for some new pussy. You know how many conversations we have had about this. Baby it's me your man you're talking to. Look at me. You have to believe me. And according to what Renee told me about homegirls past – this is right up her alley."

Brittany looked into his eyes. She wanted to kiss him and forget that this whole nightmare had ever happened. But she had to protect her heart. "Baby start from the beginning."

Chapter 55   NOT SICK ENOUGH

Present Day

Sean was working hard to get his strength back. He was lifting weights and jumping rope until the bit of pain still left over from his injuries made him stop. Johnjohn had been spotting him on the weights and saw him wince.

"Damn nigger Kyle really fucked you up. If you still feelin it like that," Johnjohn said with a little snicker in his voice.

"Nigga I had twelve broken bones. It takes a real man to come back from injuries like that as quick as I did. Besides, I told you before the nigga blind-sided me. If he was a real man he would have approached me face to face," Sean finished a bit annoyed.

"Whatever nigga. Let's go by the benches and plot. I love the way your sick ass mind works. You must have some real fucked up dreams at night the way you think." As Sean listened to Johnjohn ramble on he noticed that the whole crew had congregated around the benches. This was odd, usually some of the crew would be playin ball and some would be lifting weights. Sean didn't like changes in habits or patterns it gave him a bad feeling.

So he grabbed Johnjohn by the shoulder and asked, "Yo why all the boys huddled up at once like that? I ain't ever seen that shit before." Johnjohn shrugged his shoulder away from Sean.

"Damn nigga you scary like a mug. Don't bitch up on me now. It's just a meeting, gang business. We have them once a month. See that guard over there," Johnjohn pointed to the big guard with the baldhead.

"Yeah," Sean said.

"Well that's Big Tone's cousin. Course the warden and other guards don't know that but when he's on yard duty we have a little more freedom. So we have are meets. Now are you comin or are you trying to be a loner up in this piece. Cause if the other inmates don't see you with us. They'll know you're not with us. Get my meaning."

"I get the message and I am with yall. Damn nigga it was just a question and don't be calling me scary." Sean finished.

"Well come on then. We're missing it, besides maybe some of the other boys have some outside connections that could help us put the Kyle plan in action." Johnjohn began walking and Sean followed.

Once they got there all heads turned and Big Tone said, "There he is, the man we just been talking bout." Tone gave Sean a pound; half hug and then throw him in the middle. The rest of the crew surrounded him in a big circle so that Sean couldn't see out and no one else could see in. "What's going on?" Sean asked with alarm in his voice.

Big Tone walked up to him grabbed his arms and whispered in his ear, "We just want you to know you're joining a crew with some smarts. We ain't just a bunch of dumb niggas." While he was talking Johnjohn had put a piece of duct tape across Sean's mouth and now he was putting a piece of tape around his wrists. "Finally, I never thought he'd shut the fuck up. This nigga thinks he's a fuckin brain surgeon." It was Johnjohn that was talking, but his demeanor had changed completely. Sean noticed he was asserting himself. He seemed to be more in charge than Big Tone. "I know you like to know shit so I'm gonna do you a favor and break it all down real quick. Unfortunately for you we don't have a lot of time so while I'm talking a couple of the boys are gonna slice you up." After hearing this last sentence Sean started struggling and trying to scream but it came out muffled through the tape. Johnjohn was ready for this and yelled out, "Yo Tank, yo Pete you two start rappin and give em some that old Biggie shit so the guards like it."

The both started rappin' immediately like they had done this a thousand times before. Sean recognized the song it was a good one. He could hear it but it seemed to be way in the distance. In the rap someone was paging Biggie and he wanted to know who it was and why they were paging him so early.

In the front of his mind he could hear Johnjohn, "Back to business. Don't worry pussy boy. The slices won't kill you they're just for the pain it will help you listen to me better." All of a sudden two of the smaller men stepped into the middle with him. They both had homemade razors in their hands - both were fashioned from toothbrushes. Sean tried to jump around and dodge the swipes but the men were fast and when he would jump back from one razor the other would slice him quick and deep. When he got to the edges of the circle the men would push him back to the middle. The whole time this was going on Johnjohn continued to speak.

"So Sean you've probably figured out that I head this crew. But I know your dumb ass don't know the rest. The reason you're so confused is for once you're the one being played." Sean continued to be sliced and tortured and Johnjohn continued to speak. "I was just gonna kill your ass right off as soon as I found out who you are."

Who I am Sean thought, "Ah," he grunted another slice. What's he talking about who I am? In the back of his mind he could still hear the rapping. In the rap Biggie was being told that some nigga's was scheming on him and his loot, but B.I.G. couldn't believe it, they were his peeps and had love for him.

Love Sean thought. He still loved Renee. He wished the gun had worked. That would have been a better way to go out. Shoot Renee, then he would have placed his hand in hers and shot himself. Both of them lying peacefully in her bedroom hand in hand. If it wasn't for that damn safety, he should of remembered fucking automatic guns. That's why Sean always preferred revolvers, no safety just a strong pull of the finger. AH, AH, Two more slices and Sean was pulled back to reality.

"But then I got a visit from this dude Dwight. You know Dwight right Sean?"

"UM, UM," Sean grunted as he continued to get sliced.

"I'll take that as a yes," Johnjohn said. "Well anyway those slices you're getting right now are a present from him. He wanted us to get a cat to scratch your face up. But I told him this is the pen - where we're supposed to find a fuckin cat up in here? Then he came up with this idea. One of the wives had to sneak in the duct tape, works good don't you think."

"Ah, Ah," Sean continued his muffled screams but he was weakening and had fallen to his knees. He could still hear the rapping in the background. Like a twisted eulogy, the two dudes rappin were talkin about calling the corner, bringing flowers and people singing slow at a funeral. Sean was now a bloody mess with hundreds of little slices all over his torso. His shirt was almost completely ripped off.

"Alright yall stop slicing. I want the little bitch to hear it all before we say goodbye. So anyway Sean, Dwight says hi. He doesn't like you.

The only reason we kept up this little charade (yeah Sean I know words like that) is because Dwight wanted you to tell him where you stashed your cash. Remember he told you he needed money to pay for supplies. Now he knows. He agreed to split it with us. He told me at least $1000 but it doesn't matter. Even if he's cheating us I would have killed you for free." Johnjohn said as he bent down a little closer to Sean.

Why do you want to kill me? Sean was thinking. What did I do to you? He could still hear the song in the background: they were now rappin about bloodstains and guns with extra clips.

Johnjohn looked into Sean's eyes, "Damn nigga you still don't know do you. Probably just an insignificant part of one of your sick plans."

Johnjohn pulled a shank from under his shirt and stabbed Sean once in each arm hard. The pain was unbearable and Sean could feel himself getting nauseous.

Johnjohn put the shank right up to Sean's left eye; "Maybe I should stab your eyes out since you not using them to see." Sean panicked at this thought and began to shake his head from side to side vigorously.

"Calm down. Damn you really are a pussy. Big Tone come over here and hold this nigga still." Johnjohn ordered.

He turned his attention back to Sean, "I want you to know your gonna die, but I want you to know why and I want you to suffer more first. Big Tone stretch him out. Johnjohn put the shank back under his shirt. Bring the weights. Sean didn't like the sounds of this. He just wished his body would pass out. He wished he had one of those cyanide tablets the soldiers use to have, so he could bite down and end the pain. One of the stronger crewmembers carried a bunch of heavy looking weights in his arms and stood with them poised over Sean legs. Sean started writhing back and forth and tried to beg them through the gag to stop. But Johnjohn nodded his head and the thug dropped them with out a second thought.

Sean screamed as hot flashes of black and white blurred his vision. His legs were crushed and he was feeling a type of pain he never knew existed.

Johnjohn was looking at him unsympathetically, "Damn son that looked like it hurt. I hate to break it to you Sean but yard time is almost over."

He pulled the shank back out from beneath his shirt and stared Sean in the eyes, "I found out who you were from Cmoney. He sent someone to visit with the message. Didn't you know that Renee chick you were twisted up over is his cousin? If you didn't you should have because that is a serious brotha. He would have had you killed anyway but he knew I would do it for free."

Through the pain Sean was still trying to piece it together. Sean had an excellent memory for the people whose lives he touched. But for the life of him he couldn't figure out why this dude seemed to hate him so much.

"The simple bitch as you called her in the file. I had Dwight look that up too, was my sister. Did you hear me Sean?" Johnjohn slapped Sean to wake him out of his painful slumber, "I said Tamyka was my sister."

Oh shit, Sean thought. Tamyka.

"I know I wasn't there to protect her. But I'm here to make sure you get punished for it. You killed my little sister and now I'm gonna send your sick ass straight to hell." With these final words Johnjohn stabbed Sean five times in the heart.

Chapter 56 TEARS

Present Day

Brittany drove home from Ty's house feeling more confused than when she came. She thought visiting Ty would give her a sense of closure and confirm her feelings that her relationship with 'Mr. Rookie of the year', her college sweetheart was over. Brittany began sobbing uncontrollably at the prospect of a life without him. She had to pull onto the shoulder to regain her composure; she could barely see the road through all the tears on her face. Up until this point she had been angry and she'd felt too much betrayal to be upset. She hadn't seen or heard from Carmen in over 7 years, but she managed to get pregnant by her man!!!!!

She couldn't swallow that fact. Growing up, Carmen had always been very promiscuous, but not with just anyone. Carmen had always been a clever Bitch, conniving really, and she would stop at nothing to land herself a rich man.

The moment Brittany saw Tyson she wanted to jump into his arms, and smother him with kisses and forget this whole freakin' nightmare ever happened. She loved him so much and when she looked at him today, she was reminded of all the memories that they shared. Tyson seemed genuinely pissed and turned off by Carmen. That pregnant ho had the nerve to sit up in his living room like she was the woman of the house. As if she'd won the prize and that Brit was the sore, sorry loser! It made Brittany feel good when Tyson stood up for her, and made it clear that she was the one he loved – but that didn't take away from the fact that Carmen was carrying his child, or claimed to be. Ty admitted that he remembered seeing her in the strip club, but that's it. He said he only remembered waking up with his pants down. Brittany wondered how the hell someone could get to the point of having sex, but not remembering a damn thing. Either Tyson was lying, Carmen was lying or both of them were lying.

For the first time since the wedding she admitted to herself that she still loved Tyson, but the humiliation he put her through was too much to bear right now.

Tyson and Brit had agreed to wait for the results of the DNA test before making any decisions about the rest of their life. Even though Tyson was confident that it wasn't his, Brittany was still trying to figure out if it mattered.

Tyson lay in his bed watching DVDs. Ever since Brit had left him he couldn't sleep through the night. He kept thinking about how she was supposed to be in the bed with him. He wasn't used to this. He really wanted to kill that ho Lola, Carmen or whatever her name was.

Chapter 57   PILLOW TALK

Present Day

Renee opened her apartment door, stepped inside, closed the door and snapped the dead bolt tight. Then she pulled the gun from her purse. She dropped her coat and pocketbook on the floor, kicked her shoes off and began her new ritual. Room by room she turned the lights on and checked for intruders. Once she was satisfied that the coast was clear, she put the gun in her bedside table and headed to the kitchen for some water. She never told anybody - friends or family, but after she found out all the details of Sean's obsession she felt completely exposed. She couldn't stop thinking crazy thoughts. He had put microphones in her bathroom and bedroom. Renee knew she spent too much time obsessing over the extreme violation. The questions in her mind were a never-ending loop. What did I do or say to Kyle? Does my attorney think I'm a slut? Have both attorney's been listening to my phone conversations? Did I say anything on the phone about my cousin? Did I betray friends or family loyalties without even knowing it? Did I burp or fart - or do disgusting things thinking I was alone? The questions went on and on. There were key parts to Renee's life that were always private and guarded and now they were like public knowledge.

Renee still remembered how angry she was once she found out. She had torn into Kyle and Brittany. "What the hell were you two thinking? Leaving that van full of recorded personal stuff for some middle aged perverted cops to listen to?"

Brittany gave it right back, "Damn it Rae we needed the stuff in the van for evidence. I want Sean to go away for a long time."

But Renee was still angry, "I don't give a shit about the American justice system. The Jones family has it's own justice system. What I do give a shit about is a bunch of cops and attorneys knowing what sexual position I like best. And how loud I scream when my man and I are getting busy." She was staring at Kyle when she finished.

"I know Brit's on this whole letter of the law tip and all but what's your excuse Kyle. You're on those tapes too. Why didn't you torch the van? All the equipment you said was up in there you should have started some type of electrical fire, what were you thinking?

Kyle had a blank expression on his face and after a few seconds of silence answered, "I was thinking about killing Sean. I was thinking about keeping you safe. And so was Brittany. So stop taking your anger out on us."

He walked over to Renee and put his arms around her. She tried to struggle but Kyle wouldn't let her go. Finally she went limp in his arms. He whispered in her ear, "Renee he could have copies at home or an office we don't know. I'm sorry baby but you can't make this go away." The common sense and raw truth behind his words broke down Renee's last defense and she wept for a long time while Kyle held her. Every day those words played over and over in Renee's head.

You can't make this go away. You can't make this go away. She closed her eyes, "why can't I make it go away? Please God make it go away? I didn't do anything to deserve this." She said the last sentence aloud and then caught herself. She looked up at the ceiling wondering if someone was listening. Nothing was private anymore - her phone conversations, her moans of ecstasy, none of it. As she climbed into a hot bath after a long day, Renee prayed that she wouldn't spend the rest of her life paranoid and overly cautious.

Renee and Kyle were in his apartment on the bed with candles all around. He kissed her neck and behind her ear knowing what turned her on.

"Baby," he whispered in her ear "Please talk sexy to me, the way you used to. I want to hear that you want me."

She whispered back so low Kyle could barely hear her, "You know I want you." He licked each of her nipples once and then came back to her lips for a passionate kiss. "Come on sexy girl," he groaned. "It's just you and me here." Kyle's heart ached for the old Renee. This new Renee was guarded and careful.

"Are you sure no ones listening?" she said with a deadly serious look on her face. Kyle smiled at her. He grabbed her face and slowly kissed her forehead, then each closed eyelid, then her nose and finally her lips.

Then he just stared at her when she finally opened her eyes he said, "Stay here and don't move I have a surprise for you." When Kyle left the room Renee pulled the covers up to her chin, and felt bad that her paranoia was throwing cold water on a relationship that once had such passion. She knew it wasn't fair to Kyle and figured it was just a matter of time before he moved on. She signed aloud at the thought and felt her eyes begin to water. Kyle returned with a box full of goodies. He put the box down and went back to Renee on the bed. He sat down looped the fingers of each hand behind each of her ears and brought his thumbs under her eyelids to wipe the tears away.

"Now what's my baby in here thinking about that's got her all sad?"

Renee took a deep breath to calm her shaky nerves, "I'm sorry Kyle. I know I haven't been much fun lately. You probably think I'm some sort of paranoid psycho. I know it's not a turn on and I'm sure it's getting old by now."

Kyle began to kiss every part of her face again, "You turn me on, you're so sexy to me all the time, even when you're not trying to be. And I don't think you're a paranoid psycho. I think you're a beautiful woman that was violated and wants to protect her privacy. But I need you to know even if you were a paranoid psycho you'd be my paranoid psycho."

Renee leaned forward and kissed him fiercely. When she pulled back they were both breathless and completely turned on. She looked him dead in the eyes and said, "Kyle Terek Jackson I absolutely without a doubt love you."

He laughed out loud, "Well hallelujah woman, it's about time you told me that. Now sit back like a good little girl and listen to the events for the evening." Kyle began pulling items from the box. "First I'm going to put this vase full of flowers on the dresser across the room and you're going to look at them in the candle light and appreciate their beauty like you used to.

Then you're gonna drink this expensive glass of wine I'm pouring you, and when you're done you're going to pour yourself another glass." Next Kyle pulled out a bottle of oil. "Then while you're sipping your wine and looking at your flowers, you're going to think about how good my hands will feel on your body when I use this lavender massage oil to rub you everywhere for thirty minutes straight." He leaned down and blew hot air in Renee's ear and whispered, "I promise not to miss an inch of your body." Renee could feel goose bumps and butterflies in her stomach as he continued to speak. "And now for the grand finale, well a device that will let us have our grand finale. Walla." With a flourish Kyle pulled out a walkie-talkie looking device with a screen.

"What's that?" Renee asked.

"I'm glad you asked Sexy Momma." Renee giggled. She loved when Kyle was silly, plus the wine was getting to her and she was feeling much more relaxed. Kyle stood to speak obviously proud of his new toy, "This is the advanced pro bug detector, best anti surveillance equipment on the market. This is what the government uses, so you know it's the best."

Renee was beaming, "Damn it Kyle you're a genius. Why didn't I think of that?"

"Because it's my job to think of it. You're my girl; I'm the one that's supposed to protect you. And I will." Kyle said this with conviction and Renee knew he was making her a promise. "Now you're going to sit here and get tipsy on this wine while you watch me do my James Bond thing. Then I'm going to massage you into submission and we are going to make love like we used to. We will both know it's just the two of us. I'll be a possessive caveman asking you who that sexy ass belongs to and you'll be a wild cat and say all the nasty things I love to hear. Deal."

"Deal," Renee answered happily. Renee got semi drunk while Kyle swept for bugs. When he came back to bed he massaged and licked every part of Renee's body. When he was done she returned the favor. She climbed on top and rode Kyle the way she used to grunting and moaning and calling him big daddy the way she used to. Kyle was in heaven. He flipped her around in every position feeling her body respond and purr like it used to. He felt such joy he wanted it to last forever. So whenever he got close he would think of something else like his mean, ugly third grade teacher. Then he would feel her inner walls grip him and he was back on the bed with music, flowers, candles and Renee, his sweet Renee surrendering her body and soul to him. It felt so good. It felt so right. He was behind her now with her perfect ass in his hands. It was too incredible he just couldn't hold it any longer. He grabbed a hand full of hair and grunted, "Baby tell me you love me," She was panting hard reacting to his quickening pace.

Renee managed to respond in a raspy voice, "I, I love youuuuuuuu." "Oh God yes baby, yessss." They both collapsed on the bed exhausted and sublimely happy. Finally Renee caught her breath enough to speak, "Were you trying to kill me. I didn't think you were ever going to stop."

"I didn't want it to ever end, besides you seemed like you were keeping up just fine," Kyle said as he smacked her ass.

"Ow, watch it buddy. I did more than just keep up. You know you're whipped nigga." Renee bit his ear as she said it.

"Umm," Kyle reacted. "Be careful sexy girl don't start nothing you can't finish."

"Oh I can finish," she promised. "But first I have a question." Renee's voice had turned unsure. "I told you I love you twice tonight and I was just wondering, I mean you don't have to tell me if you don't want to."

Kyle put his hand completely over Renee's mouth before she could finish. He looked at her with a smug grin, "Renee would you please stop rambling on. I have loved you since you stopped me from saying it at our breakfast fiasco. God help me but as much as I tried the feeling would not go away. Even when you told me you heard I beat women, I still loved you. When I got the note saying you were engaged to someone else, I still loved you. When I found out you hired someone to check me out, I still loved you. I love you, I love you, I love you. Does that answer your question?" Kyle took his hand away and Renee was beaming from ear to ear. Kyle laughed at her. "I can't believe you look so surprised and happy. Did you really think I would spend $500 on an advanced pro bug detector for just anybody?"

Renee was laughing too.

"So listen," Kyle began "now that the silly questions are over let's talk about something real."

"Something real like what?" Renee giggled figuring Kyle was making a joke. But when she looked over he wasn't laughing. With a firm voice and a serious demeanor Kyle responded, "Like when are you moving in?"

Chapter 58   PAWN SHOP

Present Day

Simone stretched out her right hand and looked at the ring that had paid for her 'understanding' as Joe used to call it. Joe had saved Simone's life and for this she would always be grateful, but the bloody scene in her apartment seemed to be a real wake up call for Dr. Joe Hooper.   After the whole incident he had come to Simone's hospital room to visit, at which time he patiently explained to her that he was a respected physician and could not jeopardize his career by being involved with shootouts and police investigations. She remembered telling Joe that a shoot out usually involved more than one gun. He just shook his head and said, "you know what I mean."

This was after a short conversation that he ended with cold professionalism. She could still hear his words in her head - "they tell me your recovery should be quick and you'll be as good as new." Then he took her hand and said in a rehearsed fashion, "As far as we are concerned it's been fun but it's over. You're not the type of woman that should have any trouble moving on, so please Sim lose my number. I don't want to hear from you or see you again. My wife and I are going to try and make it work."

With that Joe was out the door and out of her life.

Of course Simone knew that it was all bullshit. Joe's little heartfelt speech about trying to make it work with his wife was all lies; she had already heard rumors that he was sleeping with a nurse two years her junior. What a simple fool. She thought to herself. Luckily for Simone her relationship with Joe was more of a mission than a love jones, which made it much easier to get over.

Now it was time to move on. Simone had gotten the ring appraised and knew she could get a pretty penny for it.   Renee and Brit had convinced Simone that it was time she went to nursing school. Whenever Simone felt jealous of Brit or Renee's accomplishments she would threaten to go to nursing school. She had been a medical clerk for years, filing charts and answering phones. Simone would talk about how much nurses made and how lucky they were to be able to choose between various shifts that suited their lifestyle. Until she was shot it was all talk. Her real plan was to work in the medical profession until she landed a doctor. So until now it had just been something to say.

Simone was never the best student and hated to admit her weaknesses, but in her last conversation with Renee she finally broke down and told her she was afraid of failing. Renee had been amazingly supportive telling Simone that her and Brit would help, which was a great comfort. Brittany was practically a genius and Renee had a determined intelligence that came from hard work and focus. Both her friends had an uncanny knack for reaching their goals.

Simone giggled thinking about the comment that finally convinced her. The three of them were together enjoying a glass of wine, when Renee said out of the blue, "You know I was talking to my mom the other day on my lunch break. She was home because you know she's working the 3 to 11pm shift now so she can sleep late. Anyway she told me that she saw six of the girls she went to nursing school with at a reunion that just passed, and 3 of them were married to doctors. It seems like nursing is the chosen profession for women that want to marry doctors."

Simone had laughed to herself because she knew what Renee was doing but it didn't matter, the point was still made, nursing is a good profession. A woman can make a very comfortable living, and if she gets lucky she might just marry herself a doctor. Simone was sold on this idea and decided to enroll in nursing school. The only problem was paying for tuition, but then she remembered all the jewelry Joe had bought her - especially the diamond ring. Simone had all the jewelry appraised and knew it would buy her at least one-year tuition in nursing school. She had even convinced her mother, Liz to provide her extra study time by keeping little KJ for an additional two hours in the evening.

Simone told her friends how she planned on financing at least the first year of nursing school and they both seemed to approve. Brittany had asked what she would do to pay for additional years. "Educations expensive" Brit had said, and then told Simone that paying for law school was kicking her ass. Brit explained that Simone could get a student loan like she did. True there would be one hell of a student loan to payoff when all was said and done, but she would have a nursing license. Simone knew it would not be as easy for her to get a student loan. She didn't have successful parents to cosign the way Brittany did.

Renee, always quick to pick up on a vibe had said, "and if you can't get a loan; I'll lend you the money. Don't worry", she had said. "I'll only charge you ten percent interest." Renee had tried to make a joke because she knew Simone would be uncomfortable borrowing money.

Simone had looked at her friends, smiled and said, "Look you two I was shot in the shoulder not the face. There are still plenty of men that want to holla at a sister. I know you two want me to turn over a new leaf but let's not get crazy. You really think I'm going to pay interest to a bank or worse you Renee when I can get a couple of men to gift me a few classes. Paleeeze!! I'm going to pawn the jewelry so I have a little time to hustle some moneymen. I did have a little crew of men but I let them go cause I was so focused on that asshole Joe. It shouldn't take more then a couple of months to get myself back out there."

Brit had looked at her in amazement "I thought you were trying to change and do things different."

"I am." Simone had answered. "No one married and no one abusive. But why should I go out with broke niggas. I mean if I'm back on the market I'm pricing myself as top sirloin."

Renee had looked at Brit and shrugged her shoulders. "I'm not surprised," Renee commented. "At least the little trick is going to nursing school so she doesn't have to depend on the Mack daddy losers she 's bound to find."

Simone just grinned and said, "Who you callin a trick, ho?"

Brittany jumped in before the two really started going at it. "Ok you two, chill out."

"We're cool." Renee assured, "but if you quit or flunk out of nursing school, Brit and I are gonna kick your ass."

Chapter 59   MOVING ON

Three Months Later

"You can't guard me man, my sister plays me closer than that, stay low stay low, I'm about to break an ankle," Tyson crossed over on Jim his teammate and went inside on him for an easy lay-up. Ty loved talking trash to anyone who was guarding him, it gave him incentive. Coach Harris blew the whistle at that moment.

"Defense, blue defense, you can't allow your guy to get an easy shot like that. If he's going to make that lay up he better work for it. Hassan, when you see Tyson setting up for his lay up, I want you to come over and help on the superstar so that he's forced to pass it out. Terrell Williams is their strongest scorer, so we have to make him work very hard on the offensive end, so that he's forced to give it up. No easy shots! Alright lets try this defensive set again." The team ran through a couple more drills before Coach Harris let them go.

Tyson was standing in the locker room about to take a shower when Jake approached him. "What up rookie good practice. Make sure you bring all that trash talking to the playoffs, we gonna need it."

Tyson chuckled, he was looking forward to his first playoffs as a professional. All of his teammates told him the playoffs were nothing like the regular season.

"So you know the Slammers have a tradition around here. All the fellas get together after the last game, and before the playoffs start and we go out, mingle with the honeys and get our swerve on. It's a tradition around here, seeing as we always go to the playoffs. Once the playoffs start the Slammers don't party or drink until it's over. So this our last chance to sort of hang loose and come together as a team, before its time to get serious and start annihilating niggas, you know what I'm sayin."

"Yeah I hear you."

"Cool, so plan to come by my crib tonight about 8:00, I'm hosting a little pre-cocktail party before we head out to 20/20."

"I don't know man, I have been staying away from the club scene and all since me and Britty broke up, it brings back to many memories."

Jake yelled at him saying, "Yo man, its been 3 months since you and Brit officially broke up dude – its time to let it go."

"I know how long its been man, but I'll go out when I'm good and ready. Jake man you don't get over this stuff right away."

"You sound like a woman man. The only way your ass is going to get over it, son, is by moving on, trust me. You need to check out some hot chicks, man, and you'd be surprised what it does to a brothers mood."

Tyson decided it wouldn't hurt him to go out for a drink with the fellas just to get his mind off Brit, and then he would come home. "Maybe you're right man, I'll do it for the team anyway."

"Aight son," Jake said as a big smile spread across his face, "my boy is coming back!"

"Later man."

Brittany lay on her couch watching her DVD's of *Sex in the City*. This had become one of her favorite pastimes during her post break up to Ty. She loved all the characters and they always made single life and New York City so sexy. It made her feel better. Just as the music started for the next episode of SITC to come on, Brittany heard her doorbell ring. Well it wasn't actually a ring but sounded like someone was laying on the bell. What the hell, Brittany thought to herself, she wasn't expecting anyone. When she looked through the peephole she noticed Simone and Renee outside the door giggling and acting silly, and sounding very tipsy.

"Yo Brittany open the door." She couldn't help but smile at the sound of her friend's chuckles.

"I see you two have started hitting the bottle pretty early tonight", Brit said as she opened the door.

"Yeah well you need to join us Brit, IT IS FRIDAY NIGHT." Simone teased.

"So what you doing tonight Brit?" Renee asked.

"Just chilling in the house, I'm starting to get used to chilling by myself you know."

Renee could see there was still a lot of hurt in Brittany's eyes behind her words, but she just shook her head in acknowledgement.

"Well Britty, my cousins from Detroit are in town and they want to hang out in the city. They don't' get out here too much so they want to go clubbin in the city while they're visiting. They asked me to take them out." Simone said.

"Oh so yall came over here because you want me to come out with you all? I don't know I was just going to….

Renee cut her off, "Come on Brit live a little, you could use a night on the town it's been 3 months since we all did anything fun together. And now that Simone is off all her pain medication she can drink," Renee added giggling to herself.

Simone jabbed Renee in the side playfully.

"Ok so it's decided. We'll give you about an hour to get ready and put on something sexy, and we'll be back to pick you up."

Brittany, realizing she was being bullied, relented. What harm could it do to go out for some drinks and dancing with the girls, it had been a while and she did miss them.

"Okaaaaay, why not."

"Don't come to the car dressed like no grandma either," Simone chimed in.

"Get out," Brittany said, laughing at her crazy friends as she opened the door. Brittany turned off her DVD – no Sex in the City tonight, I'm going out. She put in her Ritchie Spice CD and started looking for something to wear.

Jake didn't live too far from Tyson in Englewood, so it was only about a 20-minute drive to his house. As Tyson pulled into the circular driveway, he noticed several cars in the driveway. Tyson thought to himself, this guy is always entertaining in his crib. Tyson walked up the stairs and rung the bell at Jake's house. He heard Jay-Z blasting from inside so he hit the buzzer a few times so someone could hear him. After what seemed like 5 minutes Jake came to the door with a big Kool-Aid smile on his face. "Tyson Myers is in the hoooooooooooooouse!" He said it like it was an announcement. As Tyson entered the house he noticed there where some women in the place. I should have known Tyson thought to himself, Jake always had honeys at his house.

"So I guess its not just the fellas tonight huh J?"

"Well you know when they called they were in the neighborhood, so I told them to swing by. Since we were all hanging out and stuff I figured... hell the more the merrier dude."

"Of course you did dog," Tyson chuckled to himself. He made his way over to the bar seeing as he needed a drink at this moment. Jake always had a bartender on duty, his name was Hank and he was real cool. He minded his business and could make a hell of a drink!

"How you doing Hank? Let me get a gray goose on the rocks."

'You got it rookie". That was the name Hank affectionately referred to him as. As he took a seat at Jake's bar, a woman who looked familiar, sauntered her way over to Tyson.

"Hey Tyson, how you doing?" She said with the biggest smile.

"Chillin" he responded, not wanting to encourage her to keep talking.

"You know I really enjoy watching you play. You are like my favorite player in the NBA, and you deserved to get Rookie of the year. No one's stats compare to yours."

"Thanks for the support" he said dryly. She continued to sit there with the biggest smile on her face waiting for him to respond. "I'm Jordan Lee. I'm Linda's best friend. Linda was Jake's friend. She held her hand out for him to shake it. As he looked at her it dawned on him where he'd seen her before. She was on the latest cover of *Sports Illustrated* swimsuit issue. It was sitting on his coffee table right now.

"I thought you looked familiar, but I didn't know why. You're a model."

She kept up her Colgate smile, nodding her head.

Tyson thought to himself, honey did have a body on her.

At that moment Jake walked up to them, "Ahhh I see you two good looking people are getting acquainted. Yeah this is Linda's best friend from college, she just moved out here after she landed a modeling contract with Victoria Secrets," as he said that his eyebrow went up.

"Oh ok", Tyson said.

"Yo is yall ready to roll?????" Darren screamed, another one of Tyson's teammates. "Lets go listen to some good music and have ourselves a good time! I called the club and Rah has the VIP room ready for us at 20/20."

"Ty you two are going to ride with me and Jennifer. My driver is going to take us so we can all drink and not worry about driving, cool? The rest of the fellas will meet us there."

Linda was Jake's latest conquest. He loved dating strippers and models. Women who looked good and didn't talk much. Linda fit the bill.

When they got to the club, which was like a sports bar/club with lots of VIP rooms upstairs for the athletes and rappers who frequented the club, Ron, Jake's driver dropped them off in front. Jake slipped Ron a hundred and told him to have fun for a couple of hours, and he would call him when they were ready to leave.

"No problem boss."

Tyson felt strange going out as a single man. He had gone out lots of times with the fellas, but he always belonged to someone. Now he was going home to an empty bed. Jordan interrupted his thoughts.

Brittany heard a loud ruckus outside, and looked out her window down at the street. Of course it was Simone and Renee and what looked like Sim's cousins from Detroit. Brit screamed out the window – "I'll be down in 2 minutes." Brit found herself getting a little excited at the prospect of going out with her friends. It was long overdue, and she needed to have a good time. She was still young and life goes on right. Brittany took one last look in the mirror at herself. She had decided on a slinky black cocktail dress that still had the tags on it. She didn't usually dress super sexy, so this was a different look for her. She had pinned up her locks on her head and put on some long earrings, and her new Nine West strappy sandals with the 5 inch heals. They say if you look good you feel good, and when she looked in the mirror before turning out the lights - she looked great.

When Brit got downstairs she didn't realize that Simone's cousins were males – talk about rowdy! She thought Brooklyn cats were wild; these niggas were off the hook. Brit could hear the vibrations from

268

upstairs in her apartment, and when she got to the street it sounded like a block party coming from their car. As soon as she came down the steps, one of the guys in the back car shouted out, "I see a cutie tonight that should be having my baby baaaaby. Hey baby you want to ride with us?" Brittany waived at Simone's cousins and pointed at Renee's car as she climbed in.

"Whewwww Sim – dem yo cousins," she said in a real country accent, and Renee started cracking up.

"Didn't I meet some female cousins of yours from Detroit before Sim?"

"Yeah that's their sisters Denise and Yvette. They couldn't make it this time, cause their kids are still in school. So Chuck and them decided to drive down since they'd never been here before."

"But look at you Miss Thing, with your sexy cocktail dress and strappy sandals. We haven't seen you throw on the sex appeal in a while Britty, you look good. I can't blame Devon for calling you out."

Brittany smiled, "Yeah just a little something I threw on for girlz night."

"Little is right," Renee said as she turned around to eye Brittany's dress up close. "But God knows you got the body to wear it girl and you know what they say – if you got it – flaunt it!!!" They all said in unison as they high fived.

"So where we heading tonight ladies?"

"We were thinking about heading over to 20/20 because Devon and them said they heard about that club in Detroit, and they wanted to check it out."

"Ok."

When they got into the city they found a park a few blocks down from the club. As soon as Brittany put one leg out of the car she heard Simone's cousin hollering for her.

"Let me help you out the car pretty lady," he said as he reached for Brittany's hand. When she got out he said, "Allow me to introduce myself properly – my name is Devon Brown, born and raised in Detroit city – Detrooooooooooooooooooooooooooooit" he screamed out real loud on the sidewalk, causing a few people to turn and look.

Simone looked at him. "Leave that ghetto shit at home Devon, and don't be embarrassing me when we go in this party. I know the bodyguard at this club and he usually hooks me up with VIP treatment whenever I come, so please do not cause any scenes."

"Whatever cuz."

Simone introduced her other two cousins Malik and Chuck to Brit. When they got to the door, Simone threw on her sexy voice for her bodyguard friend. "Hey Jamil, how you doing? I got my family from Detroit here with me tonight."

"Long time no see Simone."

"I know I know."

"Do me a favor yall, come around the rope and I'll let you in." A line had started to gather in front of 20/20, but VIPs didn't have to wait in line.

Jamil told Simone – "make sure you speak to me before you leave tonight sexy."

Simone through her hair back and smiled, "you know it baby." Simone had calmed down a lot since the shooting with Dion. She had sworn off men for about 3 months, focusing strictly on her son and going back to school. But one thing that would never change is that she would always like attention from handsome men. Brittany giggled to herself thinking about it.

At that moment, Devon slid his arms through Brittany's.

"Don't think you're going to lose me in the party pretty lady. I sho nough want to get a dance with yo fiiiiiiine azz."

Brittany had to admit all this attention was great for her ego. Devon was hardly her type, but she was secretly enjoying his advances.

When they walked into the club Akon was pumping from the speakers. Chuck and Malik immediately started yelling the lyrics to the songs. The women in the club were giving them looks but they didn't care. They screamed out 'Detroooooooooooit' again. Brit and Renee started laughing, "Your cousins are too funny Simone." Renee said.

"They always act like that when they go out. Like they never seen women before."

"What would you ladies like to drink?" Devon asked them. After he took their drink orders, he went up to the bar.

"Looks like somebody has a little Jones for you girl," Renee teased.

"I guess" Brit said, as she swayed to the music. "It just feels good to be out and feel alive again."

"I hear that" Simone said, "BHG back in action." They all started dancing in a circle when their song *Be Happy* came on. Just then Devon came back with their drinks. "Thank you Devon," Brittany said as she smiled at him.

"You care to dance sexy?" Devon asked Brittany. Renee and Simone looked at her and smiled. Brit went because they were playing her song by Kevin Little, *Tempted to Touch*, and she couldn't keep still. Devon was a really good dancer which Brittany liked because she could dance for hours to good music, and it was always more fun when the man could keep up and look as good as her doing it. Brittany didn't realize how much she missed going out until that moment, when she didn't feel like she had a care in the world. The music had changed and Erykah Badu's *On & On* was playing and Devon being the ladies man he was, had pulled Brittany in a little closer and was kind of swaying with her. She had drunk 3 cosmopolitans at this point, so she was just going with the flow. Brittany put her arms around Devon's shoulder, and was enjoying *Baduism* when she looked over Devon's shoulder and thought her eyes were playing tricks on her. She looked again, then stood up straight. Tyson Myers was staring directly at her. He was staring so hard that Brit's heart started beating fast.

At that point Devon stopped dancing – "What's wrong Brittany you alright?" Brittany never took her eyes off Tyson and Tyson didn't take his eyes off Brittany. Then suddenly a tall slim chick came up next to Tyson and kissed him on the cheek. Brittany couldn't believe her eyes!!! Well dayam she thought to herself first Carmen and now this bimbo. He sure got around.

Brittany felt like the room was closing in on her and suddenly she was having trouble breathing. "I gotta get some air Devon" she said as she ran out the club.

Brittany ran out of the club so fast that she didn't see Tyson coming down the stairs to try and speak to her.

Brit reached the corner out of breath.

She had run like her life depended on it. She had felt that the faster she ran, the further she could get away from Tyson Myers and his bitches. She kept flashing back to how comfortable that tramp looked with her man. She shook her head; he was no longer her man. Brit found her cell and hit Renee's number on speed dial. As soon as Renee picked up Brit began speaking real fast. "Girl you and Sim gotta come out here fast. I just saw Tyson in the party with some tramp! I gotta get outta here."

"Oh my God! Simone just mentioned that she saw Tyson, but I thought she'd had too much to drink again. We're coming right out."

Brit stood on the sidewalk, leaning against Renee's car waiting for her girls. She couldn't wait to get home. As soon as Renee saw Brit she came up and hugged her. "I can't believe that SOB is tricking hos already! Don't let it get you down hon – men have to feed their egos."

The ride back to Brooklyn was quiet.

Simone finally broke the long silence. "I knew I seen that Bitch somewhere before. I think she's a fashion model because I've seen her in *Victoria Secrets*. I guess he's finally graduated to bimbos. I was wondering when he'd become like his teammates, especially that dog Jake."

"You know what," Brit interrupted Simone's tirade, "I don't even want to talk about it anymore. Tyson's my past and I have to start getting used to it."

Simone gave her sorry looks but didn't comment.

Brit then slouched down in the back of Renee's car and tried to hold back the tears that kept flowing.

After Tyson saw Renee and Simone jet from the club he knew something was up. He saw Brittany walk away from that chump she had been dancing with, but he thought she would be back. As soon as Tyson saw her cronies leaving in a hurry, he dashed out the door. Jordan called after him, asking him where he was going, but he ignored her. As far as he knew she was the reason for his Britty's dismay.

Tyson ran out the club and looked up both sides of the street. He decided to run east because it looked like there was more parking that way. He broke out into a full sprint because he knew he didn't have much time. This was Tyson's only chance. He tried so many times to call Brit but she had changed all her numbers, and wouldn't take his calls at work. He knew if he could just have a face to face with Brit he could get through to her. He had always been able to break her down, ever since they were in college. When Tyson grabbed her by the shoulders and looked her square in her eyes, and spoke from his heart - nothing rehearsed or pre-planned, straight from the heart no bullshit; he was always able to get Brit to see his side.

Tyson ran down Broadway looking for Simone or Renee's car. He knew they had picked her up, because he knew that Brit did not decide to come to 20/20 on her own. Tyson almost got hit by several yellow cabs when he ran across the street but he was blinded with passion. He stopped on the corner looking up and down the street. Neither car in sight.

"Fuck!" Tyson screamed. Then he started screaming Brits name. "Brittany Myers, Brittany Myers…" Tyson kicked the fire hydrant in frustration and dropped to the curb defeated. He must have run a mile looking for his baby. Tyson felt his heart beating real fast through his chest, but not from the run, but the adrenaline that was pumping through his veins. He had wanted so bad to share the good news with Britty face to face. His lawyer, Robert Blake had called him earlier that evening with the DNA results for Carmen's child, and they had come back negative. Tyson was not the biological father of Carmen's son.

"What's wrong baby?" That was the third time this broad had asked him that on the drive home to NJ.

"I'm just tired", Tyson said for what seemed like the 10th time.

Ever since Tyson saw Brit he couldn't get that look she had out of his mind. It had only been like 5 seconds, but she'd given him this look like – how could you do this to me again and so soon? He had wanted her to know so bad (when he ran after her) that Jordan was just one of Jake's groupies, and he'd much rather go home with her. Shit a brother had to deal with his loneliness somehow. Tyson had really wanted to settle the score with his woman. Besides it looked like she had some greasy nigga all up in her grill and Tyson didn't appreciate that at all!! Everyone knew Brittany Martin belonged to Tyson Myers! He slammed his fist on the seat not realizing it. Jordan jumped. Tyson made sure the driver dropped Jordan off at her house. He did not want to be around anybody right now. He promised her he would call her – but he knew he wouldn't.

Epilogue

Renee and Simone sat in a booth at Bennigans waiting for Brittany to arrive. They were both hoping and praying that today might be the day that Brit started acting like her old self again. Since her wedding disaster and break up with Tyson, Brit had become a different woman. She was always driven to succeed but lately it seemed like she was obsessed with perfection.

When Brit approached the table she looked tired and somewhat annoyed. She gave Renee and Simone a quick hug and sat down. She spoke immediately, "Who the hell chose this place?"

"This is one of our old spots. I picked it for convenience. You've been so busy lately I was scared if I picked somewhere out of the way you would cancel again." Renee said the word again with emphasis to make a point.

"I know, I know I've been hard to get in touch with lately but my studies and my internship have to take top priority. God I need a cigarette, couldn't you have picked some place with outside tables so I could smoke." Brittany complained.

In the past two months Brittany's casual weekend cigarette had turned into a full-blown habit and she would become annoyed and jumpy when unable to indulge.

"Damn girl, you smoke more than me now. You should slow down. Besides you were always the one that said anything in excess wasn't good for you," Simone observed.

Brittany looked at Simone unimpressed. "When did you become the bad habit police?"

"I'm not," Simone answered defensively "I'm just surprised that the few times we've gotten together lately I see you go through a half a pack of cigarettes."

"Don't worry I'll quit once I finish law school. It's just a crutch right now it helps me stay up to study. Anyway I have good news, it's paid off. I just found out today that I have risen to the top of the class," Brittany said proudly.

"That's great," Simone congratulated. "That means you're like within the top ten right?"

"Hell no!" Brittany said a little too loudly. "Fuck top ten, I mean I'm number one, numero uno baby."

Just as Renee was about to congratulate Brit the waiter came for their drink orders. Renee was sure Simone thought that Brittany's accomplishment was amazing but Renee knew better. She remembered a conversation they had once when Brit had said the people that graduate number one from law school are perfectionists with no life. She had joked with Renee, "If I ever get that obsessed give me a swift kick in the ass and tell me to get a life."

Well here we are Renee thought and you are that obsessed.

Unfortunately for Renee, Brit had been going out of her way not to hear anything Renee had to say lately. The waiter left and Renee chimed in, "I'm so proud of you Brit I know how much hard work and focus that takes."

Brittany raised an eyebrow. She and Renee were still best friends and she too remembered their conversation about number one law students. She decided Renee was being diplomatic around Simone but would probably confront her about it later. Brittany didn't want to have that conversation and decided to deal with it immediately.

"I know in the past I've said you have to be an obsessed law geek to get to number one, but I was being narrow minded. Let me tell you two what number one means. It means I can write my own ticket. I will get countless offers from firms and I can decide where I go and what I make. I know whereever I go they'll work the shit out of me but that's how all associates are treated. They know we all want to make partner cause once that happens the sky's the limit." Brittany finished.

Simone was looking at Brit confused. She didn't know anything about the process of becoming a lawyer because until now Brit never talked about it. When they got together Brit used to say it was her chance to take a break from all the pressure. Renee was in shock Brittany had never spoken like this before; associate, partner, money, sky's the limit. Brittany used to talk about making a difference. Brit had changed. But as much as Brit canceled their gym visits or didn't make time for their phone calls, she wasn't mad at her friend. Renee was mad at Carmen and

Tyson. That fucking bitch, Carmen, who ended up losing the baby that wasn't Tyson's in the first place.

While Renee was saddened by her friends new materialistic focus Simone was in awe. "Girl that's great. I bet you end up making more money than Tyson." As soon as she let it slip out Simone covered her mouth with her right hand while Renee gave her a harsh look. Renee had made Simone promise not to mention his name but it was hard. They had been a couple for so long it was natural for his name to come up in conversation.

Brit plastered a fake smile on her face and began, "Don't worry about it Simone. You can say his name, I'm not going to faint or cry. It's been awhile, and frankly he can kiss my ass. Anyway to answer your question I WILL make more than him. I've decided to go into sports and entertainment law, which means I will get a percentage of each client's salary. You would not believe how dumb some of these athletes can be. If it weren't for lawyers to negotiate their deals and manage their funds they wouldn't be living these lavish lifestyles."

Renee was more confused than ever. "Sports and entertainment law, do you think that's the best idea? I mean there's a good chance you could run into Tyson. Those circles are pretty tight."

"Yeah," Simone chimed in figuring this was a good time to spill her news. "I wasn't going to say anything but since we're on the subject, it's a pretty well known fact that Tyson's been with that supermodel we saw him with at the club that time. Apparently they're a regular item."

Renee wished Simone hadn't mentioned this and watched Brittany close for a reaction. Brit's eye's dimmed a bit and her shoulders slumped, but 10 seconds later she was sitting tall ready to make her point.

"I hate to keep repeating myself - but fuck him. I don't care if I run into him. He's one of the reasons I chose this type of law. Athletes are a predictable bunch that makes them easy to deal with, no surprises. I mean let's get real - what was I thinking to begin with being with Tyson. I thought he was going to be different, what a joke. He's turned into a boring cliché. Guy is great at sports, guy becomes basketball star, guy gets colleges to pay his education and kiss his ass, guy becomes NBA star, guy has groupies throwing their pussy at him everyday, guy sleeps around to prove he's a man, guy ends up with supermodel trying to impress the world, guy marries supermodel and has kids, supermodel divorces guy and takes all his money. Did I leave anything out?" Brittany questioned.

"I don't think there all like that," Renee said in a soft whisper. Renee still had a bit of a soft spot in her heart for Tyson. She knew Tyson, they were all close in college and she had no doubt that he had loved her friend.

"Are you serious?" Brittany was angry. "I hate when you try to defend them or him or whatever you're doing. The worse part is you know you're full of shit Renee. How many times did Tyson try and hook you up with one of his basketball buddies and you wouldn't. Why? Because you said you knew they were all egotistical assholes and you would not allow yourself to be treated badly. Well you know what -you were right, they are all egotistical assholes."

Renee was watching Brittany rant on and felt her eyes getting a bit moist. But Brittany continued mercilessly, "And you know what else Rae, you should thank your lucky stars that Kyle got hurt and stopped playing football. There's no way you two would be together. I like Kyle but even if he resisted and stayed loyal, it would be you not him that ended it. You know why because your temper and those aggressive groupies and hos don't mix." Brittany was starting to speak low now that she seemed exhausted from her emotional outburst.

"Sometimes I wish," she began in a whisper. Simone was silent. Renee grabbed Brit's hand and encouraged her to go on. "Sometimes I wish Tyson had been injured. I'm a Christian and it's not right to wish harm on someone but God help me I do. Not to get injured now as revenge, but back in college before the NBA ruined him. But he didn't get injured and now I don't know who he is. So it's time for me to move on, be successful, and let him and the whole world know that Tyson Meyers didn't break me. Do you both understand?"

Renee got up and gave Brit a hug and before they knew it Simone was there too and all three embraced. They sat back down and Brit put her fingers in her glass of water pulled them out and flicked the water droplets on Renee.

"Hey," Renee said in mock annoyance.

"Hey yourself," Brittany smiled. "Enough about me. What's your problem?"

"What do you mean?" Renee asked.

"I mean why won't you move in with Kyle?"

"Kyle asked her to move in? How come no one told me?" Simone sulked.

"Well," Brittany began "It wasn't my place to tell you, and Rae's been avoiding the subject even with me."

Renee bit her bottom lip and continued to remain silent.

"Oh Yeah," Brit piped up again, "While you're thinking about that, did you ever find the engagement ring? Because if you do, I want you to give it to Simone. She can pawn it and put the money towards nursing school."

Brittany was referring to the platinum engagement ring Tyson had given her. Brit had broken down in Renee's apartment after running into Carmen at Tyson house and threw the ring at a wall. It had bounced off and landed God knows where.

"Never found it," Renee answered a little too quickly.

"I don't really give a shit about it anyway," Brit said. "I just thought the extra money would be nice for Sim."

"Well," Simone said still a little hurt that she seemed to be the last one to know certain information.

"Well, what?" Renee stalled.

"Well are you going to move in with Kyle?" Simone finished.

Finally Renee said in the lowest voice possible, "No."

"No, why the hell not Rae?" Brittany was incredulous. "He's a great guy, he loves you. Give me a good reason not to."

"There are no good reasons Brit. I only have one reason and it has nothing to do with logic." Renee finished.

"What is it?" Simone asked.

Renee looked at her two friends. Brittany, the self-assured, over achiever who didn't realize it, but was oh so very vengeful in her own way. Tyson would be seeing Brittany alright; her poise and confidence might just make her the prize catch in that circle. Other men dating Brit would make Tyson crazy and she would have her revenge. Because a thousand supermodels still wouldn't add up to one Brittany Martin. Then there was Simone - the slender, seductive man-eater. Renee knew that intelligence didn't matter. She would hustle and scheme her way through nursing school and make a better life for her and her son KJ. These were her friend's – mature, strong women waiting to hear from her why she refused to move in with the man of her dreams.

When Renee finally spoke it wasn't the determined, quick-tempered woman it was the wide-eyed happy girl full of dreams that they met in the fifth grade.

"I won't move in with him because I still want the fairytale. You know happily ever after and all that jazz."

"After my wedding disaster," Brittany could help but laugh. "Girl you are a true optimist."

Simone giggled and added, "Brit let's forget that crazy wedding of yours and think about the bachelorette party. Now that was a night to remember!"

All three of them laughed at that.

"I think Renee's optimistic ass just wants us to throw her a bachelorette party," Simone was on a roll.

Renee laughed with her friends happy that Brit finally seemed to be her old self. She knew neither friend realized just how optimistic she was.

It was obvious Brit had given up on love, at least for a while. But Renee still held secret hopes and dreams for her friend. That's why Brittany Martin's platinum engagement ring sat hidden in a special compartment inside of Renee Jones' jewelry box.

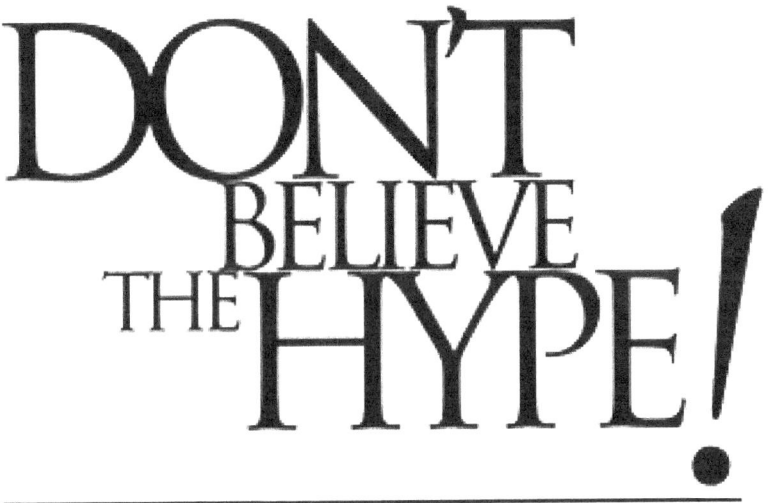

BY JACQUELINE FALL & NICOLE MICHAEL

For information on how to place orders, go to www.DBTHBOOK.com
to give feedback or speak with the authors please email at
jfall11218@gmail.com

www.ingramcontent.com/pod-product-compliance
Lightning Source LLC
Chambersburg PA
CBHW062140170626
46813CB00002B/768

* 9 7 8 0 6 1 5 4 2 2 4 5 9 *